DRAGON'S HEART

DRAGON'S HEART

Book IV of the
Pit Dragon Chronicles

JANE YOLEN

HARCOURT
HOUGHTON MIFFLIN HARCOURT
BOSTON   NEW YORK   2009

Harcourt is an imprint of
Houghton Mifflin Harcourt Publishing Company.

www.hmhbooks.com

Library of Congress Cataloging-in-Publication Data
Yolen, Jane.
Dragon's heart / Jane Yolen.
p. cm. — (Pit dragon chronicles ; bk. 4)
Sequel to: A sending of dragons.
Summary: Having been presumed dead, Jakkin and Akki finally return
to Austar IV with newfound skills, and the knowledge that what they
have learned could either transform their planet or destroy it.
ISBN 978-0-15-205919-4 (hardcover)
[1. Dragons—Fiction. 2. Fantasy.] I. Title.
PZ7.Y78Du 2009
[Fic]—dc22   2008025116

Illustration by Stephanie M. Cooper.

Text set in Fournier

Designed by Jennifer Kelly

Printed in the United States of America

[QUM 10 9 8 7 6 5 4 3 2 1]

For Michael Stearns, master of dragons and noodges.
For Jonathan Schmidt, master of the great blue pen.
For Adam Stemple, master of twisted plots.
For Deborah Turner Harris, first reader
and master of plot twists.

◆　◆　◆

In memory of David Stemple, who had
wanted this one from the beginning.

◆　◆　◆

And for all my fans who wrote demanding a fourth volume.
You are the ones who made this book happen.

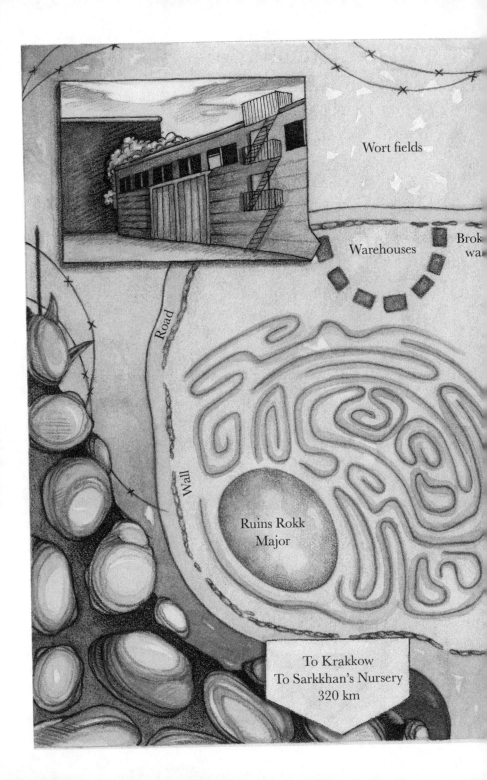

Wort fields

Warehouses

Brok
wa

Road

Wall

Ruins Rokk
Major

To Krakkow
To Sarkkhan's Nursery
320 km

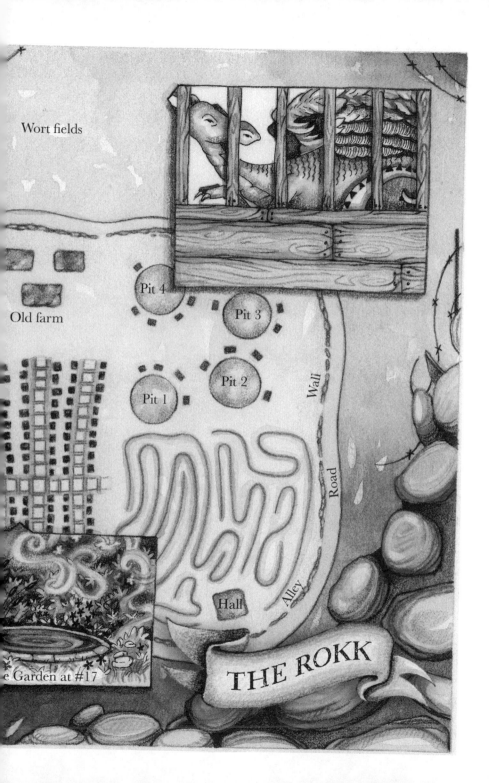

Wort fields

Old farm

Pit 4

Pit 3

Pit 2

Pit 1

Wall

Road

Alley

Hall

e Garden at #17

THE ROKK

☾ Introduction ☾

AUSTAR IV is the fourth planet of a seven-planet rim system in the Erato Galaxy. Once a Federation penal colony, marked KK29 on the convict map system, it is a semiarid metal-poor world with two moons.

Austar IV was originally chosen as a place to domicile convicts because of its difficult terrain and its daily cycle, which included a four-hour period during the night with cold so severe, humans could not remain outside without dying. The planet's lack of metal and the fact that its largest animals are huge dragons were considered additional reasons for making it a place to send sociopathic and dangerous convicts, those whose felonies were committed with violence (see holo map of the penal colonies, in the Criminal Activities section, vol. 10). Over the next two centuries, the progeny of the strongest and fittest convicts and wardens (the great-great-great-grandsons and -granddaughters of the original prison guards), now fairly stabilized at about a half million inhabitants, have managed to thrive through sheer grit. A caste/class system survived, long after the planet ceased being a penal colony, pitting the KKs — the prisoner class named after the brand on the prisoners' arms — against the master class. This caste system of masters and bonders was later institutionalized by Austarian law, with a bond price set as an entrance into the master class. Through the years, a small number of bonders rose by dint of hard work, talent, or careful savings into the master class, though most remained in bond (or fell back into bond) because of bad habits (doping, drinking, gambling), bad genetics, and bad luck.

Austar is covered by vast deserts, some of which are cut through by small, irregularly surfacing hot springs, several small sections of fenlands that have been drained in places to make arable farms, and zones of what were once thought to be impenetrable mountains. There are five major rivers: the Narrakka, Rokk, Brokk-bend, Kkar, and Left Forkk. There are also lesser rivers that run underground through the mountains.

Few plants grow in the desert; the combination of the heat of the day and the four hours of bone-chill cold known as Dark-After make only the hardiest plants viable. There are some fruit cacti and sparse, long-trunked palm trees known as spikka. The most populous plants on the planet are two wild-flowering bushes called burnwort and blister-weed (see color section) that grow in disturbed ground. The mountain vegetation, only recently studied, is varied and includes many edible fungi, berry bushes, and a low, oily grass called skagg, which, when boiled, produces a thin broth high in vitamin content. Skagg broth can also be frozen and sweetened with sweetroot for a dessert. Some of the farmers have made a good living cultivating offworld plants in hothouses, glass structures that are shut up at night with great wooden shutters to guard against the cold. The plants cultivated this way remain too expensive for all but the growing master class of Austarians. These plants include produce such as beans, squash, melons, rocket, mint, and hardy berries from Earth; picklers, stodgies, and sandwines from the Orion's Belt planets; bamboons, salt sawder, brown onions, and malt beans from the Mars Colony, and the like.

The planet hosts a variety of insect and pseudo-lizard life, the latter ranging from small rock-runners to elephant-sized "dragons" (see Animal Life holo sections, vol. 6). Unlike Earth reptilia, the Austarian dragon lizards are warm-blooded, with pneumaticized bones for reduction of weight and a keeled sternum where the flight muscles are attached. Membranous wings with jointed ribs fold back along the animals' bodies when the dragons are earth-bound. Stretched to their fullest, the wings of an adult dragon are twice its body size, enabling it to lift off the ground and fly above the mountains, where the prevailing winds aid it in soaring. The wings have "feathers," which are actually light scales that adjust to wind pressure. From claw to shoulder, some specimens of Austarian dragons have been measured at thirteen feet high. There is increasing evidence of a level 4+ intelligence and a color-coded telepathic communication among the largest beasts, though the recent embargo of the planet has effectively cut off all outside scientific study.

The Austarian dragons were almost extinct by the time the planet was first settled in 2303 by guards and convicts. The new population soon realized that dragons could be a rich source for both meat and leather, and so they began domesticating the few remaining creatures in dragon "nurseries." It soon became clear that there was another possibility for the dragons — being trained to fight one another in gaming arenas, which became known as "The Pits." And so an economic basis for Austar was laid down on the backs of these startling creatures. Quickly built were abattoirs for slaughtering the dragons culled for being too old or too timid for the fighting pits, meat shops for selling the dragon-based food, clothiers to create wear from the leather, jewelers working with the talons, bones, and scales. Veterinarians to keep the beasts healthy. Farms to grow food for them. The dragon nurseries needed cooks, trainers, barn boys, eventually becoming the greatest employer on the planet, as well as the biggest money maker. Within a generation, betting syndicates developed, and Federation starship crews on long rim-world voyages began to frequent the planet on gambling forays. Around the pits grew up bars, eateries, inns, as well as baggeries run by beautiful women. And of course a police force to oversee it all. Great fortunes were made by pit owners and nursery men alike. And some of the wardens.

Under pressure from the Federation, the Austarians then drafted a Protectorate constitution, spelling out the Federation's administrative role in the planet's economy, including laws guaranteeing humane treatment of the dragons, regulation of the gambling by offworlders, and the payment of taxes, which the Austarians call tithing, on gambling monies. In exchange, the Federation built, ran, and policed a series of starship landing bases on the planet, outside of the two cities, Krakkow and The Rokk. There the starship crews brought in money, barter goods, even banned items such as guns, offworld seeds and seedlings, and parts for trucks and cars. They transported visits by DDWPB — Doctors and Dentists Without Planetary Borders. Within the next several generations, a rich class of masters developed, far removed from their convict and warden ancestors.

In the mid 2500s, this cozy relationship with the Federation came to an abrupt halt. Disgruntled bonders became understandably angry at their continuing low place in Austarian society and the inequities visited upon their class. There was a huge and growing divide between the rich and the poor. Rebellious bonders began to foment a revolution, which culminated in a series of violent confrontations. They improvised exploding devices strong enough to bring down buildings. The worst of these was the bombing of Rokk Major, the greatest of the gaming pits on the planet. Thirty-seven people were killed outright; twenty-three died of their wounds in the months that followed. Hundreds of other people, both Austarians and offworlders, were seriously injured. With Austarian cooperation, the most violent of the offenders were caught and sent offplanet to other Federation penal colonies. The others were incorporated back into Austarian society.

After a year of further violent conflict, the Austarian

senate voted to free all bonders, which effectively stopped the rebellion. But the planet had already been embargoed, for a term of not more than fifty years, until the Federation judged Austar IV safe again for offworld travelers. This embargo keeps all official ships from landing, except for the occasional medical ships, which means that Austar IV is without sanctioned metal replacement parts or technical assistance for the foreseeable future. Infrequent pirate ships have managed to slip through the embargo lines. Intercepted coded transmissions to and from those ships and eyewitness accounts by the doctors have indicated there had been a further power struggle between the classes. Frequent references to "dragonmen," "trogs," and "sendings" remain unclear. The complete story of Austar IV will probably not be understood until the embargo is lifted and a petition from the planet for a reversal is successful in Federation courts. Only then will the Austarians be able to speak for themselves.

— excerpt from *The Encyclopedia Galaxia,*
thirty-third edition, vol. 1: Aaabarker–Austar

☾ Preface ☾

At the end of book 3, *A Sending of Dragons*, Senator Golden has located Jakkin and Akki in a meadow near a high waterfall. Led to them by Heart's Blood's now full-grown hatchlings, Golden has set his copter down and confronted the two runaway teens. He seems not entirely surprised that they are still alive. They'd been accused of being part of a rebel cell and helping in the appalling bombing of the Rokk Major pit, but had in fact been infiltrating the rebels on Golden's orders. Trying to escape, they were helped, surprisingly, by the old bonder Likkarn. After being left for dead in a mountain shoot-out, the two had managed to live in mountain caves for a year. There they discovered new powers, dragon powers — the ability to stay out in the cold of Dark-After, and a telepathic bond with dragons and each other. Near the end of that year, they'd been captured by *trogs* — cave people. Beaten, threatened, they finally escaped through an underground river to the waterfall and meadow, along with two of the trog dragons: a hatchling and a full-grown female they have named Auricle.

Book 3 ended this way:

"Why are you here?" Jakkin asked Golden. "Why now?"

"To find you, obviously, and bring you back."

Akki smiled but Jakkin's eyes narrowed. "Bring us back how? As friends? As prisoners? As criminals? As runaways?"

"Not exactly as prisoners, otherwise I'd be home and the wardens would be here. But not exactly free, either, though all bonders are now technically free. Let's say you are wards of the state."

At their puzzled glances, Golden added, "You see, I ran the investigation of your case from my hospital bed — when Dr. Henkky allowed me! — and cleared you two of the charges of planting the bomb at Rokk Major."

"I don't understand," Akki said. "If you've cleared us of the pit bombing and all bonders are free, why aren't we?"

"Because, my dear Akki," said Golden, putting his hands on her shoulders, "I cleared the names of a romantic young *dead* couple. Once you return alive — well, there are bound to be some difficult questions, which as my wards and prisoners, you won't be obliged to answer."

"Then what comes next?" Jakkin asked.

"I'll take you back to the nursery farm now," said Golden. "If you're ready to come."

"We're ready," Jakkin said.

Akki nodded her agreement and reached down to pick up the hatchling who had been lying against her ankles. The hatchling snuggled into her arms, its tail looped around her wrist.

Jakkin watched as Golden and Akki climbed into the copter. He walked over to Auricle and placed his hands on either side of her broad head.

"Thou beauty," he sent. *"Try thy wings once more and, if thee will, follow the other dragons to the place where we live, the nursery. It will be a safe place for thee and thy eggs."*

He didn't wait for an answer. Whether she came to the farm or stayed in the world, she was free of the tyranny of the trogs in the mountain caves. That was all that mattered now.

Climbing into the copter, Jakkin sat behind Akki in a seat that seemed much too soft for comfort. Golden turned and showed him how to buckle his seat belt across his lap. Then Golden turned back to the copter console. As the great machine engine started up, the noise was deafening.

Golden shouted, his voice barely rising above the churring of the rotors. "We won't be able to talk much until we're down again. Too loud." He pointed to the ceiling, then bent to fiddle with the controls, a panel of winking, blinking lights that reminded Jakkin of dragons' eyes.

Jakkin put his hand on Akki's shoulder and their minds touched, a clear, clean, silent meeting. Then he looked out the window as the copter rose into the air. Austar stretched out below him in great swatches of color. He could see the dark mountain with its sharp, jagged peaks and the massive gray cliff faces pocked with caves. He could see tan patches of desert where five ribbons of blue water fanned out from the darker blue of a pool, and the white froth of the waterfall. Running into the waterfall was a blue-black river that gushed from the mountainside like blood from a wound.

He sent a message to Akki full of wonder and light.
"This . . . this is true dragon sight, Akki. We're like dragons in flight above our world."

Mind-to-mind they talked of it all the way back to the nursery and home.

HOME

☽ 1 ☾

THE COPTER set down in the front yard of the dragon nursery under a burning sun. The whirling blades raised such a dust storm, Jakkin had to squint to see through the windows, and still the world outside seemed filled with sand and grit.

"*Home . . .*" Akki sent Jakkin the single word as they landed, her mind decorating the sending with a picture of the nursery: gray stone surrounded by red sky, which lay beyond the sand and grit. She pushed a strand of dark hair back from her forehead and pressed her face against the window.

"*Home,*" Jakkin answered, his sending the blue of the five rivers twisting through tan sands. A cooler reaction, almost as if he were afraid. Only he wasn't afraid, just being cautious. It was an old habit, but a good one.

As Golden's slim hands danced across the console of lights, the blades slowed, then stilled. "Good landing," Golden said. Then he turned and grinned at them. "Even if you two don't know the difference."

Soon the dust settled. A minute more and Jakkin could

see through the grit that the landscape was neither as red and gray — or as tan and blue — as their sendings.

Akki laughed — a soft, delightful sound — and Jakkin was reminded of other times she'd sounded like that. Not many recently; hardly any when they were on the run in the mountains, and none at all in the caves of the trogs. But he remembered them all.

Overhead, Heart's Blood's five — Sssargon, Sssasha, Trisss, Trisssha, and Trissskkette — wheeled away, disappearing behind a cluster of trees. In his mind, Jakkin heard them bidding a good-bye, their sendings as bright and fluffy as clouds.

"*Sssargon goesss. Sssargon fliesss high,*" sent the largest, and only male. As ever, his sendings were full of himself. And full of what he was doing now. Dragon time was always now. They could remember a trainer, their hatchlings, their nest. They could be taught enough movements to fight warily in a pit. They could recall where a particularly fine patch of wort existed. But otherwise they lived in the now. Still, they'd been able to hold on to enough to bring Golden to the rescue, to guide him to where Jakkin and Akki had been on the run from the trogs who slaughtered dragons in their caves.

"*Thanks, my friends.*" Jakkin's sending to the dragons was open-ended, brightly colored. Those dragons were the one constant in Jakkin's life besides Akki. He hoped they weren't going far. They linked his past and present, sky and earth, nursery and the wilds. "*Good flying, my friends.*" They were behind the trees, so he couldn't see them anymore. Couldn't hear them, either. But just in case, he called out again with his mind, *"Fair wind."*

A sunny image flittered back to him, actually more like a brain tickle. *So at least one of them heard. Probably Sssasha, always the sunny one.*

"Here we are," Golden said, flicking the last switches on the console. Turning his head, he nodded at Jakkin and Akki, his river-colored eyes glinting at them. "Home. The nursery. Back where your life begins."

It was unclear if he was making a joke or a simple statement. Jakkin had never been able to read Golden easily, and unlike the dragons' minds, Golden's was closed. Of course Jakkin knew that humans had closed minds, but it was something he would have to get used to, now that they were back.

Back home.

Unbuckling his seat belt, Golden stood and stretched. Walking to the copter door, he pushed it open, then flicked a switch that unfolded a set of stairs. Descending the steps backward, he signaled Jakkin and Akki to follow the same way.

As Jakkin climbed down from the copter, he looked over his shoulder. The shock of it all — gates, wood-and-stone walls, dusty yard, and the blue water in the weir — seemed overwhelmingly like a dream. So self-contained, so comfortable, so . . . familiar.

He and Akki had been living for a year as outlaws, exiles. Running, hiding, afraid all the time. Well, maybe not *all* of the time, but a lot of the time. Living in caves, without real beds. Worrying about where their next meal would come from. How often he'd dreamed about coming home to the nursery, but he'd never really believed it could ever happen. Too many people with too many grievances were still looking for them. Like the Austar wardens who wanted to put them in jail; the rebels who wanted to kill them outright.

Yet according to Golden, all that was no longer true. At least the rebels were satisfied, the wardens, too. Jakkin set his lips together. Not that he mistrusted Golden, but it seemed too good to be . . .

Now, of course, they had another problem — the trogs in the caves probably wanted Jakkin and Akki dead, because they didn't want the secret of their caves to come out. And they probably wanted their two dragons back as well.

I regret none of that, Jakkin thought. *None.*

And none of the past year, either. Oh, it had been a hard year. But, though hard, life in the mountains had given both Jakkin and Akki a taste for freedom. He mulled that over. *A taste for freedom.*

He hadn't realized he'd sent it till Akki answered him. *"And a hunger for home."*

Jakkin nodded. Many times he'd been sure they would die up in the mountains, with only Heart's Blood's hatchlings to mourn them.

"And Sssargon to comment on it all." This time there was a bubbling laugh in Akki's sending.

But home? He'd never really believed they could return.

Reaching solid ground, Jakkin turned, then stared at the dragon nursery. Without realizing what he was doing, he rubbed the thin bracelet of scar tissue on his wrist. The whole of that year in the mountains, he'd tried to keep his deepest longings for the nursery shielded so that Akki couldn't read his heartache and add it to her own. Now that they were actually back, he felt he should be elated. What he actually felt was . . .

"*Scared?*" Akki's sending was tentative, wavery, like the water at the bottom of the falls.

"*Stay out of my mind!*" he answered, with black and gold arrow points. Sharper than he meant. To soften it, he turned back and reached a hand up to help her down, for she was facing forward as she came down the steps, carefully cradling the young dragon hatchling. Its back and belly were still patchworked with the last of its gray eggskin, and it looped its tail securely around her wrist.

"Thanks," she whispered to Jakkin, and smiled — a tremulous, tentative smile. It said even more than her sending.

"*Scared.*"

This time the sending was not Akki's. Anxiously, Jakkin looked around. Finally he spotted the sender — Auricle, the pale red adult dragon they'd brought out of the caves before she could be sacrificed by the trogs. She was crouched on the far side of the nursery yard, tail twitching. Not one of Heart's Blood's brood, she was possibly a cousin, for her color and sendings were reminiscent of the red dragon's. He and Akki had gotten her out of the caves just in time. Into the air. Showed her that she could fly, that she could be free.

Auricle's neck arched downward and her neck scales fluttered, which meant that any moment she might bolt. *It's astonishing that she's landed here and not actually flown off with the others*, Jakkin thought. In *her* mind, men were not safe. Not even her rescuers. *Not Akki. Not me.*

"*Here?*" Jakkin hadn't meant to send the question, blue, stuttering, but Auricle caught a glimpse of it anyway.

"*Here,*" she answered in the same color, but even more faded. The membranes on her eyes closed, effectively shuttering them.

Jakkin's thoughts followed one another in quick succession: Auricle was probably *here* because she wasn't used to flying, having been kept in that underground prison the whole of her life except for the one time when she was bred. Or perhaps she was *here* because Akki had the dragonling. Or because she was exhausted. Or because she was . . .

"*Scared.*"

"*Gentle Auricle.*" This time Jakkin's blue sending was edged about with soft beige billows. "*Do not be afraid. We are with thee. Soon thee will be altogether safe.*" Dragon masters in the nursery always spoke that way to their charges, "thee" and "thou." Jakkin didn't know why. It was just how things were done. And it certainly calmed them down.

Auricle lifted her head slightly. Her eyes were dark but without the fire of a fighting dragon. Even if she hadn't sent her fear to him, he would have known it by her posture: the crouch, the lashing tail, the shuttered eyes. She was afraid of the copter, of the nursery, of the memory of the trogs. Well, she had a right to be afraid of the trogs. *I'm afraid of them, too.*

"Jakkin!" Akki's voice gave a warning.

He thought she meant he was broadcasting his own fear to the terrified Auricle, but Akki was pointing in a different direction. He turned, caught something out of the corner of his eye, and startled, before realizing that the door of the bondhouse had flown open.

Out ran the fat cook, Kkarina, though it was more like a fast waddle. Her haste was understandable. Any copter was a rare sight at the nursery. Usually the appearance of one meant bad news. Wiping her hands nervously on her long apron, Kkarina stared at Golden, who was standing several steps away from the copter's blades. Her hands left dark red stains on the white cloth of her apron, stains that could have been either takk or blood.

Jakkin licked his lips, just thinking about a cup of takk, the taste a sudden vivid recollection in his mouth. After a year of drinking boil — that thin soup made from greasy skagg grass — he was more than ready for takk. A whole pot of it. Two whole pots of it! And then he remembered what it was made of — dragon's blood. *"It's back to boil,"* he sent Akki, at the same time including a picture of him bathing in a pot of the gray-green stuff. Akki broke into sudden, nervous laughter.

Hearing Akki's laugh, Kkarina gasped, her face an alarming crimson. She turned and finally registered who Golden's passengers were. Without warning, she burst into tears and threw her apron up over her head.

"Kkarina," Akki said with a sweetness Jakkin hadn't heard from her in a while, "Kay — it's me." That set the old woman to crying even harder.

Still sobbing, the cook lowered her apron, waddled up to them, and gathered up Akki and Jakkin in her massive arms, which threatened to break bones and bring bruises. Kkarina smelled of fresh bread and sharp takk, and something burnt.

She smells of home. His knees suddenly buckled. *Home.*

"Oh, oh, oh . . ." Kkarina said over and over. "Oh, oh, oh," without letting go of either of them.

At last Akki cried out, "Kkarina, you're crushing me — *and* the dragonling." It was true. The old cook had enfolded all three of them in her hard embrace.

Jakkin was incapable of speech.

"Oh, oh, oh," Kkarina said one more time, then let them go.

Again, out of the corner of his eye, Jakkin saw movement, this time on his right. He stepped in front of Akki, to shield her, before realizing it was only old Balakk, the plowman, coming in from the fields. Next to him was Trikko and someone else, a moonfaced boy with stringy blond hair whom Jakkin didn't recognize.

Balakk had spotted the copter, then Jakkin and Akki, and began complaining even before he was close. They had to strain to hear him. "All those days of mourning," he started. "And me hardly able to work, thinking about you two dead out there in the mountains in the cold. Little Jakkin, little Akki." Though of course neither of them had been little — then or now. Indeed, they hadn't been little for quite some time. And of course neither of them had been dead, though how was poor Balakk to have known?

Jakkin stared at Balakk's moonfaced companion, wondering who he was, how he'd gotten to the nursery. Of course, a year was a long time to be away. People could die, move to the city, be sent offworld. People could grow old, forgetful, take on new apprentices. People could change.

"We apologize for being both alive and well," Akki said, but with a smile to take away the sting of it.

The dragonling resettled itself, curling up so tightly in Akki's arms, it was almost a dragon ball. At this point, it seemed to regard Akki as its mother.

That would be funny, Jakkin thought, *if it weren't so . . . so inconvenient.* The hatchling had imprinted on Akki early and refused to be parted from her.

Trikko winked at Jakkin as if to say the year away had simply been a ploy to be alone with Akki, but then Trikko's mind always worked that way, from the slightly off-color to the positively filthy. *He couldn't,* Jakkin thought, *understand real love.*

But looking confused, Balakk turned to Golden, spread his hands, palms to the sky. His new helper touched his arm, as if in comfort. At the same time, a roar from the stud barn made them all turn around. A male dragon, sensing roiling emotion nearby, was simply trying to bring the attention to himself. It was an old dragon trick, and as usual, it worked.

"Typical male," Akki said with an exaggerated eye roll, which broke the tension, and they all laughed — even Jakkin.

Only Auricle still seemed perturbed; her sending to Jakkin was laced with red spots that looked a great deal like blood.

"Danger?"

"No danger," he answered soothingly.

"How?" asked Kkarina, meaning how were they still alive?

"When . . . where?" Balakk added, waving a hand.

Trikko's knowing smile spread slowly across his face.

The answers to any of those questions had to be given carefully. Guardedly. Because there *was* danger, great danger, even if he'd just assured Auricle there was none. He and Akki had to be certain that they said the same things, that their versions of the past year's adventures matched exactly. If not, the future of all the dragons on Austar IV could be a bloody one indeed.

"If the secret gets out — our secret..." he thought, adding, *"Akki, take care."*

"I'm not stupid," she shot back, the red lightning bolt accompanying it lancing through his mind with such force, he almost winced. *"But there's no way it can get out unless you tell. Me — I'm silent as the grave."* Facing him directly, so that no one else could see, she lifted her hand to her mouth, then surreptitiously drew her finger across her throat. *"See — dead, grave, got it?"* Afterward, she smiled broadly at Kkarina, at Balakk and his helper, at Golden, even at Trikko. "First, showers, food, rest. Then we'll tell you all."

"All?" The picture Jakkin sent was a frantic, dark red, roiling cloud.

"We'll only tell them what we want to, silly," she soothed, her sending shot through with a golden light. *"But we'll tell them that it's all."*

And he *was* soothed. They would find their way through this difficult place together. Keeping secret how they'd sheltered in Heart's Blood's birth cavity as she lay dying. Keeping secret that they'd emerged with dragon ears and eyes, and a dragon's brave heart as well. Keeping secret their astonishing ability to speak mind-to-mind. They'd keep all the secrets safe, and that way keep all the dragons safe, too. *Because if the people of Austar find all this out, they won't stop to think that it's only hens who'd recently given birth who can give them the dragon gifts. Most Austarians don't know a female dragon from a male. They'd probably slaughter all the dragons just in case.* Jakkin shivered. He couldn't let that happen.

"What's this? What's this babble?" An old man pushed through the knot of nursery folk. His sharp, ravaged face fell when he saw Jakkin, his one good eye staring, though whether it was shock or disappointment, Jakkin couldn't tell because the man's eyes immediately seemed to shutter, like a dragon's.

"Hallo," Golden said, "look what I've found!" His voice bright, as if he were enjoying a vast joke.

"It's little Akki, little Jakkin," Balakk explained.

"Of course it's them," the old man retorted. "Any piece of worm spit can see that."

At that, any good memories of Likkarn helping them escape a year ago into the mountains left Jakkin, and he felt a returning rush of dislike for the man.

Kkarina collapsed in sobs again.

"Well, here's a welcome home," Likkarn said, "though you'll find us all changed. You can tell us why you're alive later. We've still got a day's work to finish."

It was more a slap in the face than a welcome home, and Jakkin almost said something, but Akki sent him a picture of his head going under a cold tap. *"Just stay cool."*

She's right, of course. No need to fight with old Lik-and-

Spittle now. After all, he *did* owe the old man something for helping them escape from the wardens. So, instead, he said, in what he hoped was a cozening voice, "We found a new dragon, Likkarn. Maybe related to our dragons. Her color is interesting, at any rate. Could she have been sired by one of our escaped males?"

Likkarn said nothing.

"We thought we could —" Jakkin stopped, thinking that he'd be damned if he would beg.

"We?" Likkarn was not going to help one bit.

"Akki and me. You remember Akki, Master Sarkkhan's only child?" Jakkin was losing his temper again, and even a sending from Akki showering him with a waterfall of cold water didn't slow him down. "She probably owns the nursery now that her father's dead."

Balakk said, "No, no, no."

And Kkarina added, "We *all* own it."

Likkarn smiled slowly. "I was the only one mentioned in Sarkkhan's will, boy. He knew Akki didn't want the place, and I was the only one to run it. And I now own half. The rest I've given to the nursery folk. Time served. You know."

But he *didn't* know, and Jakkin's face showed it. He touched the dimple on his cheek, a sure sign that he was upset. *If I'd been a young dragon in the pit, I'd have been down on my knees in front of the older, slyer dragon by now, the two ritual slashes across my throat.*

"So, will you let us board her here?" It was Akki, the little dragon carried in the crook of her arm. "And this little one as well?"

Likkarn laughed, and though it didn't have a particularly

happy sound, it was clear he'd given in. "You've always been able to get around me, young lady. Welcome home."

Noticing no welcome home for him, Jakkin thought about getting another mental dunking from Akki if he said anything. He didn't want that so he let his anger go.

"Akki can shower first," Jakkin told Likkarn, Kkarina, Balakk, the boy. He ignored Trikko. "I need to get Auricle settled in." It was only then that the others even seemed to notice the pale dragon crouched by the side of the wall.

"Back stall. Keep her away from the rest of the nursery dragons for now," Likkarn said.

As if I didn't know that.

"Take the hatchling, too." Akki handed the ball of dragon over to him. The minute he touched it, the hatchling uncurled in his hand, its tail now anchored firmly around his wrist, and looked longingly back at Akki.

"*Or,*" Jakkin thought, "*as longingly as a dragon can look.*"

Akki sent a bright orange warning. "*No more sendings, not when we're close enough to speak. We might make people suspicious.*" The color was flame-shaped. "*You look different when you're sending to me. Your eyes get all squinty and you stare at me with great concentration. I bet I do the same.*"

Jakkin nodded. He tried not to stare, hoping that it looked as if he were simply agreeing to take the hatchling, which he was. But he was also nodding to Akki about the sendings. Not that Golden, Kkarina, Likkarn, and the rest of them could know that. After all, they couldn't hear the sendings or see the colors. "Yes," Jakkin said aloud. "*No more sendings,*" he added in a sending, looking away so he didn't stare at Akki. "*Not this close.*"

Golden took Jakkin and Akki by the arms and pulled them aside, giving them a hug. "Better to say too little than too much until I've figured out the ramifications of your rescue."

"Ramifications?" Jakkin asked.

"To us or to you?" Akki added.

"To Austar, of course," Golden said. Then he stepped back from them and waved his hands vaguely, as if he were campaigning for something.

Kkarina turned to Golden. "You'll be staying to dinner, of course?" She twinkled at him.

He smiled regretfully. "You're my favorite cook, Kay, but I've too much work back in the city. There's a senate race going on in The Rokk. I've got competition this time." He turned and ran back up the steps to the copter.

"Flatterer," Kkarina called back, and then Golden was gone, through the copter door, and moments later, the rotors started up. Kkarina turned to Akki and enveloped her again, as if determined to shelter Akki from the sand and grit the copter was throwing around, as if she could shelter her from the world.

Over Akki's head, Kkarina said to Jakkin, "Tell us what you want. What you need. You must be exhausted. A year! A year! And now you're home, where you belong. Who would believe it?" She began to sniffle loudly, as she led Akki away into the bondhouse.

The door snicked shut behind them.

☾ 2 ☾

AKKI FOLLOWED the chattering Kkarina as if she didn't know the way. Kkarina was a gossip, though there was nothing mean about her. She just liked to talk. And talk. And talk. Akki was too tired to talk back, tired from the last weeks in the trog caves, from their escape through the cold underground river, the copter ride. And from the arrival home. After a year with just Jakkin — and a few weeks with the brutal, silent trogs — so much talking overwhelmed her.

"Let me get you something to eat," Kkarina said, turning to Akki. "You must be starving. What can there be out there in the wild? Leaves? Mushrooms?"

Akki *had* to answer. "Yes, and berries, boil, teas, flikka soups."

Kkarina looked positively ill. "*Flikka* soup? No, really — it's a wonder you didn't starve." She always thought people were starving.

"Shower first, Kkarina," Akki said, almost pleading. "Then we can have food talk after."

"I can bring something into the shower room for you." Kkarina's little eyes were like berries in a huge white pudding. "A good cup of hot takk at least? It's always been your favorite."

Akki couldn't help herself; she shuddered, and her stomach turned over. "No thanks, I need that shower right now. I can't begin to explain how dirty I am. After that, bread and cheese. And a small glass of chikkar."

"You remember where the shower room is?"

Akki put her hands on Kkarina's. "I've only been gone a year, Kay. Unless you've moved the shower."

Kkarina laughed. "Not since this morning."

"I'll need a towel, and soap."

"Soap in the shower dish. I'll find you towels. You'll need one for your hair, too. Your poor hair. It used to be so lovely. How well I remember brushing it when you were a child, and braiding it, and . . ." She wandered off, still adrift in reminiscences.

Akki walked down the hall to the shower room, thinking, *That went all right. At least she didn't ask any real questions. Like why I shuddered at the mention of takk. And how did we last through the cold.*

Turning on the hot water, Akki stepped into the stall. As the water pounded down from the metal showerhead — one of her father's early offworld barters — she instantly felt the entire horrible year disappear, like dirt down the water hole. *Oh, there'd been some good points,* she thought as she soaped up her hair, her poor hair that used to be so lovely. *Being alone with Jakkin was the best.* She'd gotten to know him in a way she'd never have been able to living at the nursery. Time to talk away from any teasing. Time to learn one another's rhythms, hungers, fears. And she'd also learned to speak mind-to-mind with the brood. Taught herself to cook and to make pots and . . .

But hot water . . . There's nothing like hot water. For several minutes she simply gave herself up to it, without thought, without worry. However, once the water ran clear, the soap all washed off, she began to think about what had to be done next.

She had to figure how to get to The Rokk, the larger of the two cities on Austar, and look up her old teacher Dr. Henkky. Only there, at a real lab, could she finish her training as a doctor and figure out how to make or synthesize or re-create whatever had happened to them when they sheltered in Heart's Blood's egg chamber. How they'd emerged being able to hear what was in a dragon's mind, could mind send to one another, and could stay outside even during the ice-cold bone-killing four hours of Dark-After. And she had to figure this out without telling anyone — especially Henkky — what she was doing.

Thinking about Henkky and the city, she began to wonder if it was safe to go there, if anyone would recognize her — besides Golden and Henkky. Anyone who might question why she was alive, who might wonder if she'd had a hand in the Rokk Major disaster. After all, though The Rokk was the larger of the two cities on Austar, there were only about a half million people spread between it and Krakkow, and slightly less on the farms, the nurseries, in the countryside. She could hide out here at her father's nursery forever and be protected by the folks who'd known her since she was a child. But could she do the same in The Rokk?

Maybe I should *just stay here, make a lab, and try to figure out about the egg chamber and* . . . But that was no good. Though there was a small hospice here in the nursery, stocked with bandages and salves and medicines bought from off-worlders, there were no microscopes, no slides and pipettes and other stuff. She didn't even know the actual names of all the equipment she needed or how to get it. She hadn't learned enough yet to use all of them. But in The Rokk, Henkky would have everything she needed, of that she was sure.

But what do *I need?* She didn't even know what she was looking for. Had the blood of the dying dragon's egg chamber somehow gone through them into their own bloodstreams? Had their DNA been changed? Their brain chemistry? Was the thing that gave them their new gifts a virus, a bacterium, a disease? Or just a miracle?

Finally, she put her head in her hands and had to admit to herself that she'd done only a little bit of hands-on medicine with Henkky and some vet work, here at the nursery, on dragons. She was no researcher, even if Jakkin thought she was.

It's impossible. How can I figure out what I need to know when I know so little to begin with? She felt herself starting to cry, the tears mixing with the hot water. Jakkin believed in her, was counting on her. The dragons needed her. Everything was on her shoulders.

And I know nothing.

She had never felt so useless in her life.

"Chikkar?" A hand with a glass half full of the golden liquid seemed to float into the shower, interrupting her misery.

Taking the glass, she let some of the shower drizzle into it, watering it down, before taking a sip. She hadn't eaten anything that day, and the chikkar did what it always did — hit her in the back of her throat, sending a lightning strike down to her toes. One sip. She didn't dare take more yet.

She handed the glass back. "Whoa, Kkarina, I'm definitely not ready for that. Even watered down, it's too much for me." Turning off the shower, she stepped out and let Kkarina wrap her in a large, heavy towel. It felt almost as good as the shower. There hadn't been any towels out in the wild.

Her misery momentarily forgotten, Akki dressed in the new set of leathers that Kkarina had brought to her. They fit perfectly. Then she had a sudden shudder, remembering that the leathers came from the body of a dead dragon. But there was literally nothing else here at the nursery for her to wear except, maybe, one of Kkarina's old aprons. She giggled, picturing herself wrapped in such a garment.

"Good, girl, that you can still laugh. Must have been awful out in that worm waste they call mountains. Lots of weeping and wailing, I would guess."

No good telling Kkarina what she was laughing about. Or anything good about being out in the mountains. Nothing about how beautiful the stark landscape could be, especially at night during Dark-After, because then they knew they were safe. "How did you guess what size I needed?"

"And didn't I raise you from the time your father brought you back from the city?" Kkarina's face was bright red from the heat in the shower room.

Akki knew that Kkarina was talking about the baggeries, where her mother had died. Akki thought, *Kkarina is my real mother, in action if not blood.* One part of her wanted to tell the old cook everything, then nestle in her fat arms, head against her plump breast. Drink in the familiar smells, part yeast and takk, part clean sweat. *But that's impossible.* Impossible until they figured out how the solution could be shared. *Until I figure it out.* She wanted to cry again.

"Why are you looking so strange, girl?" Kkarina asked.

"I'm thinking I have to get to The Rokk and learn to be a doctor for real this time," she said, only lying a little. "Another year of my apprenticeship should do it."

"But you just got home." Kkarina's eyes filled. "Surely you can stay here a bit. There's no hurry. Or is there?"

"I wanted to see you, Kay-Ma," Akki said, her old special word for Kkarina, which always worked for her when she wanted something. Though she felt guilty using it now. Still, she had to get Kkarina off the scent.

Kkarina used the bottom of her apron to wipe her streaming eyes. "I never thought to hear that name from you again."

Taking Kkarina's hands, Akki said, "Can you help me get to the city?"

"If you promise to return."

"Of course," Akki said, and meant it. "Whenever I can. After all, the nursery is my home." This time she wasn't lying at all. Threading her arm though Kkarina's, she added, "Now tell me about all that happened this past year."

And Kkarina told her about: the rebels being caught — "Thank goodness!" The Federation embargoing the planet — "As it should till we sort ourselves! All those nice young offworld star pilots killed, and your dear father." And the senate voting to free all the bonders — "Not that they asked me, but you should see what that's done to our poor world: roaming workers, bond pairs severed, life as we know it over —"

"And me home," Akki said, laying her head against Kkarina's huge shoulder.

"Ah well, there's naught ended that can't be mended," Kkarina told her with a happy sigh. She patted Akki's head, ignoring the fact that Akki's hair was wet.

I shall remember that, Akki told herself, as they made their way to the kitchen, where bread and cheese awaited her. And maybe another sip or two of chikkar. *"There's naught ended that can't be mended."*

☾ 3 ☾

THE COPTER BLADES sent up a new dust storm, shutting Jakkin and Auricle away from the sight of the others. The hatchling, once more curled into a ball, lay in Jakkin's right hand. His left hand tugged at Auricle's ear and he gently but firmly guided her toward the incubarn.

The instant they passed through the great arched door, Auricle started to tremble, like a mountain shuddering.

"Aaaah," Jakkin crooned, and sent her a still, blue pool.

That helped a little, and once she recognized the familiar scent of other females and their broods, she quieted entirely, sending little rivers of pale color rippling through Jakkin's mind. Female dragons liked to give birth within easy calling distance to one another. Probably something they did in the wild. *As much for safety's sake as for comfort,* he thought.

"Safe?" Auricle sent him, picking up on his thought. *"Comfort?"*

He assured her with gentle rainbows but kept leading her on. At least she trusted him enough to go in without a fight.

They went along the wide hallway, heading to a back stall. Jakkin sensed snatches of sendings from the dragons they passed. Soft pastel rainbows, querulous bubbles that expanded and popped, even a rough, dark snort that chased them down the hall. Each time he sent back a calm, watery blue picture — *"Gentle, fire-tongues, gentle"* — as he used to, unthinkingly, back when the nursery was truly his home.

Jakkin knew that Auricle would like to be with the other hen dragons. But at the same time, she'd be happier as far from the nursery workers as possible. How could she possibly know that they would be kind to her, not rough like her former masters, the trogs.

"Trust me," he whispered to her, then sent it as well, his sending decorated with gold.

Auricle grunted but betrayed no hint of being mollified.

Jakkin led her farther back into the barn and Auricle turned her head inquisitively, the great neck swiveling like a giant flower on a giant stalk. If anything, Jakkin sensed her fear begin to grow. She'd become quiet, and a ripple erupted under the neck of her skin — a waterfall of fear.

They were past the other females now, way past, deep into the darker recesses of the incubarn. Since nursery rules dictated that any incoming dragons remain quarantined for seventeen days, her placement was not Jakkin's decision to make. Diseases like Warp and Slobbers could wipe out an entire herd, so nursery folk were extremely careful about such things. She would have to stay away from the others that whole time. Jakkin had no way of explaining the rule to her. He worried that she might equate it with being in the caves, isolated, ready to be killed.

"Thou beauty," he whispered to her, though she was not really pretty at all, but a rather mousy creature, her pinkish color showing no sign of a fighter's spirit, none of the brightness that made a dragon great. Not like Heart's Blood, who'd been a deep and gorgeous red. In fact, if Auricle had been born in the nursery, she'd have been an early cull. *She would have been used for her meat and skin,* he thought, then shuddered. Perhaps the nursery folk and the trogs were not so different after all.

"*Danger?*" questioned Auricle again. Her sending was a tremulous yellow wave, matching Jakkin's shudder.

Steeling himself, he forced his voice to calm. "Thou strong heart," he said aloud, so that she might gentle under the sound, but softly, so as not to wake the hatchling, now sleeping in the crook of his right elbow. The hatchling never stirred.

And then he thought, *Auricle truly has a strong heart.* Hadn't she survived the trogs, the underwater swim, the waterfall, the long flight here? Wouldn't she make a great breeder? "*Thou strong heart,*" he sent her, and this time meant it entirely.

Finally, they were at the last stall. Jakkin opened the door gently with his left hand, which was a bit awkward, but he managed. Then he stood back, holding the door ajar, and told Auricle to go in.

She lifted her head and sniffed, tugging herself free of his hand. "*Danger?*" He was leading her back into a place not unlike the birthing stall where the trogs had kept her. Her sending was alive with small red flames.

"*No danger,*" he repeated, damping the flames. "*I will let no one harm thee. Trust me?*"

At last, she relaxed, her great head dipping up and down, and after a moment, she moved into the stall. Putting her back to the far wall, she dropped to her knees, then rolled onto her side. Never having flown before, being far from all she knew, she was exhausted. Jakkin thought, *Fear is exhausting, too.* But she trusted him. *And one day she'll trust the rest of the nursery folk.* She would have to.

"Guard the hatchling," Jakkin told her. He settled the little dragon between her front legs. *"Guard it well."* It would give her something to do, take her mind off her own fears. And it would help the hatchling, too.

Auricle pulled the hatchling close and began thrumming, a sound that was part hum, part snore. It reverberated in her chest and the hatchling snuggled even closer.

As Jakkin left, she was licking off the last of the hatchling's gray eggskin. Underneath it was a pink already darker than she. Auricle worked on the dragonling, sending a lullaby of soft colors into its sleeping mind. It didn't respond, its mind a blank fuzz.

Jakkin blanked his own mind as he passed the other hen dragons, careful not to roil them. Careful not to get too friendly with them, either. If they were suddenly too comfortable with him, the other nursery workers would notice and might wonder why. It was important that neither he nor Akki raise any sort of questions in the minds of the nursery folk. Questions would lead inevitably to answers. False answers. Made-up stories. Lies.

And anyone, he warned himself, *no matter how careful, can trip himself up over a lie.*

ONCE JAKKIN was at the bondhouse, he was overcome by the warmth and the smell of sweat and bread and takk. *Familiar smells.* Surrendering himself to them, he closed his eyes. When he opened them again, he saw several men he recognized, and several he did not. One, Jo-Janekk, who ran the nursery store, grabbed him by the arm.

"After your shower, son, come see me. We'll outfit you. For free." He grinned at Jakkin.

Jakkin wasn't surprised Jo-Janekk knew he was off to the shower. The nursery was always a hive of gossip, innuendo, guesswork, and talk. But he was stunned at such generosity — bonders usually had to pay for everything.

"I will," he whispered to Jo-Janekk, wondering if home had changed so much in just a year.

THE SHOWER he took was long and hot. He'd all but forgotten what they were like, then remembered with a fierce attention to every part of his body. Having recently swum through an underground river, he thought that he could hardly be all that dirty. But it was as though this one long hot shower was able to wash away a full year of dirt. He luxuriated in the heat, the force of the water pounding on his shoulders, his head, his back. He let more than just the dirt wash away. He let go of suspicion, terror, longing, doubt.

Wrapped in a towel, he made his way to the bondhouse store, where fresh clothing was piled on marked shelves, sandals hung by their straps, sturdy gloves, knives, anything a bonder might want and be willing to pay for.

Jo-Janekk saw him and said, "Size?"

"I was 14s," Jakkin said.

Jo-Janekk whipped around to the 14s shelf and took down a shirt. He held it out to Jakkin. "Not any longer." Another grin.

Jakkin took the shirt and held it up against himself. In the year he'd been gone, he'd grown several hands more, put on muscle.

Head cocked to one side, Jo-Janekk sized up Jakkin. He took a shirt and leather vest and pants from the 18s shelf. "This should be right."

Jakkin went behind the changing wall, stripped off the towel, and got dressed. The 18s were a perfect fit.

"As I said, no charge. Not that you have any coins yet," Jo-Janekk told him. "Sandals — well, that's a different matter. When you're ready for new ones, come with a pocketful of coins and we'll see." He brushed a bit of graying hair back from his face.

"What do I do with my old clothes?" Jakkin asked.

"Put 'em in the burn barrel," Jo-Janekk said, then laughed.

Jakkin laughed as well. *Maybe that's where my past should go, too — into the burn barrel.* He sent out a loud crackling red-hot picture, as if everything in the past year was afire. *Everything except for Akki, and the dragons.* He sent out the fire picture again, but Akki didn't respond. She may have ignored him by choice, or been asleep, or out of range. And of course no one in the nursery responded, either.

☾ 4 ☾

AKKI CONSIDERED taking a quick nap. She even allowed Kkarina to walk her down the hall to the room at the end of the corridor, a room she was to share with two other girls, both newcomers to the nursery. Vonikka was a redhead with a crooked grin. The other, a mousy blond whose looks were at odds with her rather outsized personality, was called Larkki. Kkarina had arranged it all while Akki had been showering.

"But my old room . . ." Akki began. The idea of sharing with two girls who were more than likely to be chatterers suddenly made her feel slightly sick. *All that talking . . .*

"Everyone's been resettled in different rooms," Kkarina told her. "Voted on it. Consequences of being free, so they tell me. Though I'm too old to change, and I told them so. 'If you want me up and cooking every day, I need my own place.' And they gave it to me. As for the rest . . . well, rooms assigned by age and by pair-bonding. Even Likkarn shares. Though I suppose, just for now, you could bunk in with me. It would be like old times, when you were a little girl and had nightmares and would run into my room for a snuggle and to fall asleep in Kay-Ma's arms."

Kkarina will ask more questions than a dozen strangers, Akki thought. "I'm too old for nightmares," she said, sweetening it a bit by adding, "though if I have any, I'll know where to go."

"Here we are," Kkarina said, pointing to a large sunny room with two double bunk beds, standing against opposite walls. She added, without actually needing to, "You've the choice of two beds."

They were both lower bunks, and she chose the one on the north wall. There were sheets, pillows, pillowcases, and blankets folded on top of the mattresses.

A mattress! It had been a year since she'd slept on a real mattress. Even an old, lumpy nursery mattress seemed like her idea of heaven.

"I'll help you make the bed," Kkarina began, but Akki pushed her out of the room.

"Just send someone for me when it's time to eat." She closed the door.

"I could bring you . . ." Kkarina's voice came through the door.

But Akki didn't answer, having already gone back to the bed and flopped down on the unmade lower bunk. Curling around the stack of bedclothes, she snagged the pillow and stuffed it under her head. Without giving any more thought to what she was doing, she fell fast asleep.

Akki dreamed of caves and beatings and holding her breath beneath a pool of blood-red water. She woke sweating, still holding her breath.

"Jakkin!" She sent him a reprise of her dream. But wherever he was, he was too far away to hear her. Or

else — and here she made a brilliant guess — he was in the shower. Water blocked sendings, as they'd discovered in the cave pool.

She got up with no idea of how long she'd slept. It hadn't been an easy or comforting sleep, anyway, so she had no regrets about leaving the bed. In fact, she felt even more exhausted than she had before lying down.

There was a small mirror tacked to the wall over a shared dresser. She stared at herself for a moment. No wonder Kkarina had been pressing food on her. Though she'd always been slim, now she was thinner than was healthy. *I could cut someone with these cheekbones.* She wondered why Jakkin had never said anything.

"Jakkin!" She tried again, though they'd talked about not sending to one another, at least not when they were close. Surely they were far apart now. But she stopped herself from calling again.

Something teased into her brain. Not a sending, but . . . an odor. It was sharp and sweet at the same time. She could smell cooking. Her stomach began to growl. Looking at herself once again in the mirror, she shook her finger at her image. "Time to eat, skinny girl."

She patted her hair down. It was still damp. So, she hadn't slept all that much after all.

Leaving the room, she turned right and headed down the hall. She made her way quickly to the dining room. A low, quick chatter from the diners came through the closed door.

Standing outside, she knew she couldn't go in alone. Of all the things she'd overcome in the last year, facing all the nursery workers — her old friends — in the dining hall now suddenly seemed the most overwhelming of all.

~

BY THE TIME Jakkin got to the dining hall, the place was packed with nursery folk. He was surprised to find Akki waiting outside the door.

"Forget how to open it?" he asked.

"I couldn't face them without you." She sent him a tremulous small waterfall. "Just dealing with Kkarina was hard enough. I'd forgotten how much she likes to talk."

He nodded in understanding, then peeked in through the door at the diners. Most of them he recognized, but he was surprised by the number of new faces. Normally, nursery workers didn't move about a whole lot, even in a year. He was about to send Akki an answering waterfall to show how he was nervous, too, when a tap on his shoulder made him turn.

Slakk — less a friend than a hatchmate — grabbed his hand to shake it, and in his curiously flat voice, peppered Jakkin with questions. "I heard you were here. I heard! Are you okay? You've lost weight. Are you glad to be home?"

Then, without waiting for any answers, Slakk pulled them both into the dining hall, where Jakkin's hand was shaken not once, but many times, by his old companions. Akki was enveloped in broad hugs. It was as if by touching him, by hugging Akki, the nursery folk could be sure that the two of them were really alive after all and not just a rumor.

"Awfully solid for ghosts," Akki whispered to Jakkin, before she was whirled away from his side by more hugs.

And the questions came at them like a rattle of rocks against a wall. "Were you hurt? Seen any feral dragons? What did you eat? How did you sleep? Did you learn to make fire? What about . . ."

It was overwhelming and they both ended up silenced by the onslaught.

Once they managed to sit down at a table, seated across from each other at the long dinner table, Jakkin realized that Akki was in new clothes, too. Bonder pants, a leather vest laced up the front, her hair still wet from the shower and tied back with a leather string. She sat upright, as if ready to flee, her mouth stretched thin, taut.

Jakkin sent her a compliment, flowers in a green field. Her answer was a nod and a tentative smile, but she said nothing. She sent nothing back, either.

His closest nursery bondmates — Slakk and Errikkin — sat on either side of him, and soon Akki was enclosed by two new girls. *But,* Jakkin thought, *Akki is right.* He'd forgotten how much people in the nursery liked to talk. *Aloud!* In the mountains he and Akki had spoken mostly with pictures. Sometimes they went days without speaking aloud. And the trogs didn't speak aloud at all. This cascade of spoken words was beginning to be a problem.

Attending to the food seemed the easiest thing to do, so Jakkin dug in and for long minutes paid no attention to the conversation which flowed around him.

The only one besides Jakkin and Akki who remained silent was Errikkin. He seemed a bit in awe of Jakkin, or possibly still embarrassed about his role in Jakkin's near-arrest a year earlier. He held back, eyeing Jakkin with more curiosity than relief.

But Slakk was irrepressible. Once he'd gotten through several slabs of lizard meat and a cup of takk, he started up a conversation. Perhaps *conversation* was not the right description, as he simply started peppering Jakkin with questions again.

"Where were you?" he asked. "How come you didn't die? Why did you stay away so long? What did you find for food? Did you sleep on the ground? Did you know that we thought you were dead? Did you think about us? Did you try to get back home? Did you care?" All this rushed out like a river in full flood.

Jakkin continued to eat slowly, gesturing to his full mouth, which worked at first.

But the questions were taken up by the rest of the table.

"Were you frightened?" This from one of the girls near Akki, a redhead with cropped hair.

"Did you find an old barn or house to stay in?" asked Trikko, with that sly, knowing smile still plastered on his face.

While they asked, Jakkin ate four boiled lizard eggs, using it as an excuse to offer nothing in return.

Akki was equally silent, though she actually ate very little, mostly just pushing the food around her plate.

Slakk went on. "Were you really in the mountains or did you get to Krakkow or The Rokk? Did you hide on purpose or by chance?" There was an inquisitive line running down between his eyes.

Still Jakkin continued to stuff food in his mouth, holding up a finger as if to forestall any more questions. If he answered all their questions truthfully, the secret of the dragon's blood could come out. He had to sort through which questions to answer, which to sidestep.

"Danger . . ." Akki sent. Red and black and orange. Doom colors.

Jakkin concentrated on not squinting. *"We agreed no sendings when we're this close."*

"Don't be a pile of fewmets!" Her sending was bright red, steaming.

Jakkin looked at Slakk, then at the others, choosing his words with care. "We lived in caves. Boulders pushed against cave openings seal in the heat. Especially with a dragon or two inside to add to the warmth." That was both true and not true. True that there'd been caves with boulders for doors, but not true that they had found those caves right away. Or the dragons.

"What dragons?" asked Trikko. "Not ferals?"

"No, of course not ferals. We'd never have been able to coax ferals into a cave. Never could have trusted them."

Everyone at the table nodded.

"Your father . . ." Slakk said, his voice trailing off.

It wasn't a secret. Jakkin's father had been killed by a feral dragon. He'd been trying to train it. But ferals were dangerous. Unpredictable. None of the bonders would ever have believed that he and Akki had been befriended by ferals. Besides, it wasn't true. Jakkin took a careful sip of water.

One of the girls leaned toward Akki. "What did you say?"

Whatever it had been, Akki had spoken too quietly for even those next to her to hear. So she repeated it. "Heart's Blood's hatchlings."

Jakkin suddenly realized that the girl who had asked was Terakkina, who only a year ago had been a small bubbly blond child, the pet of the nursery. Now she was quite grown up.

"Heart's Blood's hatchlings," Akki said dramatically. "They found us. They saved us."

Terakkina said, "Really?" She clapped her hands. "How wonderful!"

Not so grown up, then. Jakkin added, out loud, "Heart's Blood's five. A male, a singleton female, and a triplet of three females." He spoke with a kind of tamped-down passion, but he didn't have to make it up. It was a safe comment, and all true.

"Triplets? That's amazing," Trikko said. "I've only ever seen twins from one egg."

"Always lucky," Slakk put in, in that jealous way he had.

A year hasn't changed anything for him, Jakkin thought. Slakk acted as if living apart for a year in constant fear and danger was somehow luckier than living in the familiar safety and comfort of the nursery.

"Luck, if you count it so," Jakkin said, and then had to define his terms and explain some more about caves and boulders and dragons and boil, and all the while being careful not to say too much. Or too little. Not to seem to be hiding anything, yet not telling the whole truth. It was truly exhausting.

At last, Akki stood. "Kkarina needs help," she said. "In the kitchen."

Bounding to her feet, Terakkina said, "I'll help, too."

Jakkin glared at Akki, willed her to stay, begged in a sending, but she left, anyway, Terakkina at her heels. He was angered by Akki's preferring Kkarina, who she'd already admitted was overwhelmingly talkative, to helping him here at the table, bombarded with questions.

"*Runaway!*" he snapped at her in a sending, forgetting their promise. "*Coward!*" The sending was bright yellow, puslike.

She didn't turn around, but her return sending — a long black lance — pierced the yellow pus-bubble, which suddenly looked surprisingly like his head.

Errikkin had been sitting silently for some time with his tongue between his teeth, the sign that he was thinking deeply. Suddenly he burst out with, "Surely you had more to eat than boil." His face reddened as he spoke. "In a year. In an entire fewmetty year." Those were the first words he'd uttered to Jakkin since he'd come home.

Jakkin smiled. "Some eggs. Some cave mushrooms, some berries, some —"

"Have *you* ever eaten boil?" Balakk's helper, the moon-faced boy, asked.

"Aye, Arakk. It's awful," L'Erikk, another of the boys, answered, making a face. "Thin, bland."

"It's not bad. And awful only if you're not hungry," Jakkin pointed out. He was gratified to see some of the new folk nodding at that. Especially Arakk.

"No one goes hungry anymore," Trikko said. "'With work comes food.'" It was an old nursery saying.

Slakk laughed, though there was little mirth in it. "And there's plenty of work." He gestured grandly around them with his hand. "We're expanding."

"Expanding?" Jakkin asked. That certainly explained the new faces.

"They're building up Rokk Major again," L'Erikk told him. "Never mind the embargo. Because there won't always be one. And we have to be ready." He said that as if quoting authority and not speaking on his own.

"Embargo?" Golden hadn't said anything about an embargo. Jakkin turned on the bench and stared at Slakk. "What embargo?" He didn't actually say he hadn't any idea what was meant by the word.

"For up to fifty years," Slakk said flatly. "No Feder ships in . . ." His arm made a swooping movement.

"Until we prove ourselves," Errikkin interrupted, his handsome face now darkening with some sort of anger. "Always *proving* ourselves."

"Or *im*proving ourselves," Slakk shot back, and a ripple of laughter ran around the table. It was clearly an old argument between them.

"As bonders we didn't need any improving," Errikkin said.

The table now erupted in laughter.

Arakk said, "*Im*proving, *dis*proving, *un*proving."

"*Re*proving," added Trikko.

"That's not a word," Arakk said.

"Is too."

"Is not."

Arguing like little boys, Jakkin thought, suddenly feeling old. "I don't understand," he began. "If no Feder ships can fly in, how does rebuilding the Rokk Major pit make any sense? Who will go to the pit to bet on dragon fights? Who will bring in money? How do we fill our bags?" Though he'd already filled his and was a master himself. *Some master, with no money and no great dragon.*

Arakk's face registered surprise. "There aren't any."

One of the girls said, "No bond bags."

"Aren't any *bonders* anymore," said Slakk. "While you were off in the mountains playing with dragons, we were all set free." He pulled up his leather shirt to show Jakkin his bare chest. It was pasty white, hairless, and a bit flabby. He slapped himself with the flat of his palm. "No bond bag." He laughed. "No more trying to fill that fewmetty bag and failing. No more feeling guilty when I use a coin for pleasure."

"You never felt guilty," Trikko said.

"And you rarely have any pleasure," added Arakk.

Everyone laughed, Jakkin loudest of all.

And then Jakkin remembered Golden telling them about freeing the bonders, when he'd first picked them up in the copter. But Jakkin had been so exhausted and exhilarated at the same time, he hadn't paid much attention. Getting back to the nursery, settling Auricle, dealing with the questions from the nursery folk, had taken all his concentration. But of course now he recalled what Golden said. *No more bond.*

"Slakk, that's great," Jakkin said.

"Not just me, Jakkin. *All of us,*" Slakk said. His hands gestured to the entire room, even as his whiny voice made it sound like a complaint.

"I get it," Jakkin said. "Golden told us."

But they wouldn't let it go. "A charter from the government, filling all our bags," Arakk added.

Both Arakk and Slakk were smiling broadly, and Trikko's face was all grin, but Errikkin was unaccountably grim and his normally blue eyes seemed to have gone the gray of stone.

Slakk put a comforting hand on Jakkin's. "Don't mind Errikkin. Old Mope Face always did prefer being a slave. Remember how proud he was to have you as his master?"

For a moment Jakkin remembered. Errikkin *had* been proud. At first. But all Jakkin had felt was how embarrassing it had turned out, with Errikkin even trying to take a cloth and wash his face for him. And after, they'd had a horrible fight. Funny how he could hardly remember what the fight had been about. Later, believing Jakkin had actually blown up Rokk Major, Errikkin had led the wardens right to him. *But I've forgiven him that.* Jakkin bit his lip. *In a way, Errikkin was right. But how strange, that my best friend — my bonder, Errikkin, who loved me — turned me in to the wardens. And Likkarn, who hated me, lost an eye giving Akki and me a chance to escape.*

"Now," Slakk continued, "we work for wages, for our food and our housing. And we share in the nursery profits as well. But no work — no pay. Errikkin hates *that* part!"

"Don't put words into my mouth," Errikkin said loudly.

Equally loudly, Slakk said, "If I had my way, we wouldn't put any *food* there, either. Not when you haven't earned it."

Errikkin swung his legs over the bench and stood in one graceful, sure movement. He didn't say a word more but walked off, holding his shoulders squared and never looking back, his sandals making a *snick*ety sound as he strode away across the dining hall.

Jakkin was reminded of a dragon hackling.

In the sudden silence, Jakkin called Errikkin's name. At the same time he searched his friend's mind. Of course it remained absolutely closed. Errikkin didn't show that he'd heard anything, just flung open the dining hall door and walked through.

Pulling his hand out from under Slakk's, Jakkin slammed it against his own chest, a gesture left over from the time he'd worn a bond bag. *Everyone free!* Maybe true, but hard to believe. He thought, *There's always been bonders and masters, from the very beginning. Austar was settled by jailers and prisoners.* Then he bit his lower lip. *Surely this is a good thing, being free.*

But something about the news bothered him. Not Errikkin's anger. Not even Errikkin's hackled response. Errikkin had always ducked out of work when he could, and that was an old argument between them. However, Jakkin wondered if his own unease had more to do with the fact that he'd had to win his own freedom with hard work.

Bonders used to say, "I fill my bag myself." Did they anymore? Why would they, if somehow the hard work of filling a bag no longer mattered? He shook his head. He'd never thought about such things before. Of course freedom for everyone was more important than how hard he'd worked in the past. He was suddenly ashamed of having thought otherwise.

"Anything else I should know?" he asked at last.

Trikko said, "The rebels."

"Senator Golden told us something about them."

"Rounded up," Trikko said.

"The rebels," L'Errikk added, then wiped his mouth on his sleeve. "They were all rounded up. And rounded upon." It was a stupid joke, but that was L'Errikk. *He*, at least, hadn't changed in the year.

"Of course they no longer have anything much to rebel against," Slakk said, smiling. "No bonders, no rebels. What do you think of that?"

Jakkin returned the smile, but then remembered that Golden had added that the *worst* of the rebels — the ones who'd set off bombs and planned other disasters — had been sent offplanet to penal colonies maintained by the Federation.

"I think," he said, "that I have lots to learn about the last year."

Slakk banged his fist on the long table. "Lots to learn!" he said in rhythm to the bangs. "Lots to learn!" And soon everyone at the table except Jakkin was banging away. The takk pot bounced up and down precariously. Kkarina stomped out of the kitchen, charging toward their table and brandishing a large wooden spoon.

"Fair warning," she cried, slapping the spoon down on the table by Slakk's fist. "Next time it's your head, Master Slakk. And that fat bawbie will split open like an old mello."

Mellos grew in the back kitchen glasshouse, yellow and round. If not picked in time, they cracked open and spilled out their bright red contents.

Everyone in the room applauded and laughed and the game was over.

"Some of the old rebels are even working in nurseries now." Arakk spoke quietly, looking down at his plate, which had been scraped clean as if he — and not Jakkin — had spent a year eating poorly. "The ones who are left on planet are to be considered *led astray*."

Jakkin remembered the meeting with the rebel cell. None of them seemed to have been led astray. "Except for us, of course," he said under his breath. The real rebels had all appeared horribly committed to what they were doing, especially those angry acts of random — or not so random — violence. "Are there any here?"

Just then, Kkitakk, a large, plain-faced man, sat down at the table, his plate piled with slabs of lizard meat. "Not here, boys. We won't have them rebels here." Jakkin recalled that Kkitakk had been Balakk's helper. Before. And hardly so large then. "Not since those lizard drools killed our Master that was, Sarkkhan."

There was nodding agreement all around.

Jakkin let out a huge sigh. "Then who are all the new faces?" Jakkin gestured with a hand that took in the entire dining room.

Looking at his full plate, Kkitakk said, "Workers from other nurseries, dragon handlers who'd worked Rokk Major. Folk who had nowhere to go after the explosion."

Jakkin nodded and filled his cup with some cooling tea.

He said quietly, "So — *our* nursery took them in. That's good. It honors Master Sarkkhan's name. "

"The odd thing is," Kkitakk added, "only a handful of nurseries are still open. Bond kept 'em together. Freedom's torn 'em apart."

"More Errikkins around than we knew!" Slakk said.

"What do you mean by that?" Jakkin asked.

Slakk shrugged, but the girl with hair as red as a fighting dragon answered in his stead. "My nursery mates took a vote and most decided to go work in The Rokk. In groceries, feed stores, restaurants, bars. A couple joined the wardens. One took nurse training. 'No more fewmets' was what they all said. But I think they expected to work less now that they were out of bond. Hah! What slackers. 'Freedom takes *more* work, not less,' I told them. No one listened to me. But when our old master sold up and moved to his other home to live off his winnings, I came here, because it's the best nursery that's still running."

"It's *always* been the best nursery!" Kkarina said curtly.

"That, too," the girl agreed, "but as a *bonder* I couldn't very well choose *where* to work, could I? And now I can. Still, I'm a country girl and dragons is what I know. So, here I am!" She grinned after delivering this speech, and several of the men gave her a flat-hand salute to their chest, which she returned.

"And Austar now embargoed for up to fifty years." Slakk said this with a satisfied look. "We should be well settled before then." He nodded at Jakkin, clearly expecting him to agree that such an exile was good for the planet.

"But we'll all be as old as Likkarn then," Jakkin said,

which made everyone laugh. Slakk slapped him on the back, hooting.

Still standing over them, Kkarina nodded. "We *need* the Federation. We need their metals and supplies."

"Nah, nah," Slakk said.

Jakkin had a sudden memory of the trogs and how they worked metal. He could tell the nursery folk where to go to find metal; he could tell Golden. But then the secret about the dragons would be out as well. And the killing of all the dragons would begin. He couldn't hazard that, not till Akki solved the problem with science.

Kkitakk said, "What have the Feders ever done for us but stop in for a quick bet at the pits and off again. We've never been anything to them but the back end of the world. It's the dragons they like, not us. Dumped our great-grands here and forgot about us."

"Time to forget about them," agreed the redheaded girl.

Trikko added, "And if you think being part of the Feders will mean anything good, well, we'd have to use *their* laws, and a Feder governor instead of the senators. We should stay a Protectory."

"Protectorate," Jakkin corrected.

"At least the senators know us," Balakk said.

"And their hands always out for something," put in Kkarina.

"Like that Golden you love so much, old woman?" Balakk said.

"Hmmmph!" Kkarina slammed her spoon down again on the table, as if it were an enormous gavel, reminding them that *she* was for the Federation. "Golden and I go further back than senator. *I'll say no more.*"

"Small chance of that, Kay," Trikko said.

She tapped the spoon on the top of his head, spun around, and stomped back to the kitchen.

The young nursery workers were aroar with laughter, only some of it *with* Kkarina but most of them laughing *at* her. They all knew she'd been a bag girl once, but really, it was hard to see a slim alluring girl in that huge shapeless form.

"That's all very well," Jakkin said, "but what about the Feders bringing in medicines and truck parts and such? What about news of the latest scientific developments? Couldn't we just use what we want and . . . and . . ." Without some of those things, Akki would be seriously handicapped in figuring out how to give the dragon gifts to everyone on Austar.

But there was another side of the Federation. Jakkin remembered a book of Golden's that he'd worked hard at reading. It said that the Feders — having outlawed violence in their home worlds — encouraged blood sports on non-Feder worlds so that those who still needed a shot of blood-spilling came to Protectorates like Austar IV.

All of a sudden he knew what to say. "Think of the Federation as a super-big dragon. Dangerous and unpredictable. And didn't Master Sarkkhan always tell us, 'A man should learn from his dragon, just as a dragon should learn from the man.'"

"Not a dragon," Kkitakk put in. "Saying Feders are like dragons maligns dragons."

"Well, I have a different question. With all of us free, whose going to deal with the fewmets!" Slakk asked.

Kkitakk and Balakk laughed and Kkitakk said, "That's easy. You boys will do it!"

"What about us girls?" asked the redhead. "I'm as strong as all of you boys. Stronger than some." Pointedly, she named no names.

And then the arguments really began, quickly jumping over to the other tables. Soon the dining room was aboil in loud talk.

It was suddenly all too much. Weary of the intensity of the talk, battered by the noise, Jakkin stood.

"Where are *you* going?" Slakk asked. "Start an argument and then duck out? You think you're Errikkin?"

"I need sleep." In fact, Jakkin's face was gray and he was swaying.

Slakk and L'Erikk nodded together. "Exhausted."

Suddenly, it was true. Jakkin needed to lie down, to be alone, and after, to talk with Akki, mind-to-mind.

Slakk stood, too, slapping Jakkin enthusiastically on the back and nearly knocking him over. "You're bunking in the old room, with me and Errikkin and —"

"And me!" said Arakk. He seemed genuinely pleased at the idea.

"So all being masters now doesn't even give us our own rooms?" He'd had one before. That rankled a bit.

"The older men get the singles now. Seemed fair. We voted on it," Kkitakk said, not adding what everyone knew: that there were more older men than boys voting. "And Kkarina has one, too."

"What about Sarkkhan's house?"

Kkitakk appeared peeved. "What about it?" He sounded oddly defensive.

"Who lives there now?"

"We've turned it into a guesthouse for visitors who want to spend a few days at a dragon farm."

Maybe I should declare myself a visitor so I can stay in that quiet house. Not that anyone would let me get away with that. Suddenly light-headed, he still made it to the door with his head held high. Behind him the babble of voices continued, like the *pick-buzz* in a field full of insects. He paid them no more notice.

On his way to the bunkroom, Jakkin forgot about the argument over Federation status and thought instead about the way Errikkin had angrily fled the dining hall. It was puzzling. A year ago he and Errikkin had been close. *Best friends.* He'd bought Errikkin's bond with the money he made when Heart's Blood became a champion. Even offered to free Errikkin — had forgiven him.

But now Errikkin seemed changed.

In truth, everything was changed: Jakkin's friends, the nursery, the world. Some for the better, some for the worse. And he and Akki — especially — had changed. More than anyone at the nursery could imagine.

Shivering suddenly, as if the earth beneath his feet trembled, Jakkin sighed. *We're going to be more alone here, surrounded by everyone and everything we know, than we were out in the mountains.* There was no comfort in that thought.

☾ 5 ☾

NIGHT.

Dark.

Jakkin woke and stared at the ceiling of his shared room for a long while before deciding to get up. The mattress felt uncomfortably soft beneath him and he was no longer sleepy. And even if he were, the snores of the boys around him guaranteed that falling back to sleep would be impossible.

Careful not to make any noise, he got dressed in his bonder pants and shirt. Though he supposed they weren't called bonder pants anymore. *Maybe freedom pants?*

Carrying his old sandals, he tiptoed along the corridor until he got to the front door of the bondhouse. He eased it open, careful not to let it squeal, and stepped out into the black night.

Once outside, he put on his sandals, then stared up at the twin moons. Soon it would be Dark-After and its death-bringing cold. "Dark-After, nothing after," bonders said. Everyone knew that only crazy people, no-hopers, or weeders went out once the bone-chill settled in. And if they went out, they died.

Of course, he was neither crazy nor suicidal, and once away from the bondhouse, walking quietly along the path, Jakkin would be safe. No one else could follow him into the night — except Akki, of course. Most of the windows would be shuttered against the cold and everyone was asleep. No one would see him. He felt an iciness on his cheeks, on his hands, but it was more of a tingle than a searing cold.

Above him, in their red phase, the twin moons sailed across the sky, leaving a trail of crimson. The path was outlined in their red light. He shivered. Not with cold, but with a chill of premonition. He felt the moons were scribbling a warning. A warning written in blood.

The blood of the egg chamber?

He shivered again. Maybe it was a premonition of spilled blood. The blood of all the dragons on the planet, slaughtered so humans could have the gift of mind-sendings, the ability to withstand the cold of Dark-After. This time when he shivered, he couldn't stop.

Reaching the round incubarn, Jakkin hauled on the door. As before, it squalled in protest. He heaved again and at last got it open. Inside, the heat was so intense, he felt as if he were walking into a stone wall. The barn was kept at a constant thirty-four degrees centigrade, partly by electrics and partly by dragon body heat.

In the cozy stalls where hen dragons bedded down with their dragonlings, something squawked. He figured it was one of the little dragons, for they often peeped and piped their distress at being awakened before they were ready. In separate quarters, half-grown dragons huddling together for company and warmth houghed as Jakkin went past. Only the full-grown males were separated in the stud barn.

Jakkin kept his thoughts mute. No need to disturb the dragons any more than he had already with the noisy door. He didn't want the hens standing and stomping their huge feet, challenging him, and perhaps inadvertently stepping on some of their broods. Or the half-year hatchlings might get into squabbles brought on by lack of sleep, injuring one another or themselves. There were hundreds of ways dragons in nurseries could be hurt, mostly by the carelessness of their human caretakers. He didn't want to harm any dragon, by intention or inattention, and certainly not on his first day back.

Jakkin let a bit of the dragons' thoughts leak into his mind. They were puzzled but not alarmed. Their sendings were pale blues and greens, not the sharp reds and blacks of fear.

As he kept on down the hall, the barn behind him finally quieted. The hens and their broods settled back into sleep so quickly, his mind was soon filled with their low, hazy dreams. As he neared Auricle's back stall, he hoped he would find her asleep with her great jointed wings folded up against her sides.

Lifting her head, Auricle sent him a tentative rainbow in shades of gray. He picked up her sending, shot soft color through it, and sent it back. *"Thou art fine, little mother."*

He and Akki had let everyone think Auricle was a wild

dragon. That wasn't strictly true. She'd been *rescued,* from the trogs, the same cave dwellers who'd made Akki and Jakkin slaves — another secret to be kept. Until he and Akki had returned to the nursery, Jakkin hadn't realized how many secrets they'd been burdened with in a single year.

"Thou art fine, little mother," he repeated, this time aloud. Though she wasn't fine. Not yet. She was gravid — pregnant — but with all she'd been through, there was a good chance her eggs wouldn't hatch. They might have already broken apart inside the egg chamber. Though she'd had no viscous bleeding, which at least was a good sign. Or the eggs could emerge cracked, the dragonlings dead inside. But Akki had assured him that if the worst happened, Auricle would still be able to breed again, have eggs again, raise a brood.

The hatchling nestled, wide-eyed, between Auricle's front legs. Some of Jakkin's thoughts must have leaked to her, or maybe his voice had awakened her. She looked up, pipped for a moment, sent him a picture that looked remarkably like Akki, then settled down again. She fell asleep almost instantly, her mind fuzzy, the colors softened by sleep.

Jakkin smiled and — only when he was sure the hatchling was deeply asleep — opened the stall door. It was well oiled, not like the front door, and swung open without a sound. He went in.

Kneeling by Auricle's side, he scratched behind her ears. She thrummed her pleasure, the throbbing pulse going through her and right up his arm and into his body. The hatchling neither noticed, nor stirred.

"*I will stay with thee awhile,*" he sent her, keeping his own colors muted. Then he sat down, his back against the dragon's broad shoulder, and began recalling in strong colors how the copter had rescued them from the mountains and the silent, murderous trogs.

"*Thou art safe here,*" he finished, "*in my home.*"

If he'd meant to calm her he was wrong, because she started to stir uneasily as soon as he mentioned the trogs.

Fewmets! I've gone about it the wrong way.

Auricle stretched out one pale wing, then snapped it shut again, as if closing a door. At the sound, the hatchling opened its eyes and began a frantic pipping. To soothe the little dragon, Auricle lapped its head with her rough tongue. Finally the dragonling calmed down and fell back to sleep.

Worm waste! Jakkin cursed himself. *She doesn't need any reminders of where she's come from.* Closing his eyes determinedly, he put all thoughts of the rescue out of his mind. But his determination itself communicated to Auricle, and she suddenly moved behind him, sending back a stuttering bit of color.

"*Danger?*" she asked in a shower of gray and red. Little shivers, like tremors on a hillside, ran down her back.

"*No danger,*" Jakkin assured her, his sending a cooling, watery blue. "*No danger.*" Because at the moment there was none. His sending must have convinced her at last, for Auricle drifted back to sleep.

But Jakkin couldn't fall asleep as easily. Instead, he forced himself to sit quietly for a bit longer, an hour or more, hardly daring to breathe.

Everything is changed, Jakkin thought as he had earlier in the evening. He wondered what Golden might be thinking, whether he agreed Austar would be better off fixing its own problems than relying on the Federation. Wondered whether Golden would now have to run against KKers for the senate. Wondered if he could win.

Maybe, Jakkin told himself, *maybe the embargo's meant to be.* Since he and Akki needed to solve the problem of the dragon's blood without help from anyone else, why shouldn't the planet do the same with *its* problems? Some of those problems were already solved, anyway. With the bond system dismantled, no one could rebel against it, could they? His mind was racing now; he felt like a child spinning around and around, getting dizzy by its own exertions.

Why can't I just lie down here with Auricle, shut down my mind, and go back to sleep like the dragonling?

He sighed deeply, and some of the sigh went out as a sending. In reaction, the soft skin of Auricle's underleg trembled, like ripples skimming over the surface of a pond. Luckily, she didn't wake.

Jakkin wondered if Akki was sleeping soundly, or if she wanted to talk. "Akki," he whispered, sending out a tentative pale pink tentacle, but her mind seemed firmly shut against him, as it often was when she slept.

"Fewmets!" He hated being so cut off. Which was odd, seeing that they'd only had the ability to send for a year. But that year had made all the difference.

He wondered if he should go back into the bunkhouse and wake her. Or just stay put. He'd never been this indecisive in the wild, on the mountain. Only here at home, where he'd been a boy and a bonder. And now he wondered if that was why — his own history being held against him.

Time to sleep, he insisted to himself. *At the very least it will stop the questions.*

But he wasn't in the least bit sleepy. So, standing, he glanced around the stall, checking everything one last time. Auricle's water tub was half full, her straw bedding clean. There were burnweed and wort in the feed stanchions. He couldn't put off the inevitable any longer. It was past time to go back to the bondhouse. Perhaps there he would go to sleep.

Walking quickly down the central aisle, Jakkin passed about a dozen empty stalls till he came to the ones where dragonlings lay sleeping by their dozing mothers. He stopped, checked the stalls, saw one dragon awake, and whispered the opening of the lullaby he used to croon to Heart's Blood when she was small.

> *Little flame mouths*
> *Cool your tongues,*
> *Dreaming starts soon*
> *Furnace lungs . . .*

At least none of the babies woke, used as they were to their human caretakers. Only that one hen opened an eye, quickly shuttering it again when he sent her a calming blue pond with hardly a riffle disturbing the surface.

He was relieved that things had been so easy. In. Out.

Pushing against the heavy, squalling incubarn door, he stumbled out into the cold. In the morning, he'd get some grease from the kitchen and oil the hinges.

It was fully Dark-After now and Jakkin could just about feel the icy stream of night spilling down his body. Moving his shoulders a bit to loosen them up, he ran his fingers through his hair.

He glanced up at the sky. Whatever warnings the twin moons had written earlier had long since been erased by night. The sky was dark, clouds hiding the stars. Behind him, though he didn't see it, something darker than the clouds sailed across the sky. It flew north to south, silently passing a spikka tree well past its blooming, and then the dark flier was gone.

☾ 6 ☾

IN THE DARKENED hallway of the bondhouse, someone grabbed Jakkin by the arm. The grip was tight as a claw. A low voice said in a sharp whisper, "All right, worm brain, explain."

Jakkin stared into Likkarn's face without blinking. The old man's cheeks were furrowed like plowed fields. He was older, grayer, thinner, angrier. And of course there was the dead eye, a bit like a boiled egg. Once Likkarn had towered over Jakkin. Now they were the same height and Jakkin's shoulders were broader, his reach longer.

"Explain what?"

"Explain where you've been so late at night, out in Dark-After." Likkarn glared at him, but there was something more in his good eye than anger, something Jakkin couldn't read.

Jakkin took a deep breath, spoke slowly, not exactly taunting Likkarn, but close. "I was in the incubarn, tending my dragon and her hatchling." He pulled his arm away. "And it's only just now gotten too cold to be outside. I ran as fast as I could. It's not that far. I've run farther in the mountains in the cold."

Likkarn laughed, and that's when Jakkin realized what he'd seen in that washed-out eye hadn't been anger at all, but a shared joke. Likkarn knew something, only Jakkin wasn't sure what it was.

"Just cold enough for *you*, boy," Likkarn said. "And Akki. And — sometimes — me." Likkarn had closed his eyes and Jakkin suddenly felt a tentative sending, a probing, into his mind. The sending was unfocused, unformed, more like a pulse than a picture. But it was definitely there.

Jakkin didn't know what to think. He gasped and Likkarn opened his eyes, the good one and the boiled-egg one as well. Drawing back, both in mind and body, Jakkin gave an exaggerated shrug and turned the gasp into a cough. "Cold," he whispered. "Got into my lungs a bit." He coughed again, though even to him it sounded fake.

"So what do you think?" Likkarn asked.

"I don't know, what you mean, old man."

"Oh, you know, all right," Likkarn said. There was a bit of spittle in the left corner of his mouth.

"You're weed-crazed." Jakkin spoke with more fear than anger. Mostly, he was afraid of giving anything away.

Likkarn folded his arms as if waiting for Jakkin to acknowledge the tentative sending, then smiled annoyingly. "Weed? Haven't touched the stuff since you and the girl disappeared. The pain of a broken leg and arms shocked me out of it. The arms and leg I broke," he reminded Jakkin, "helping you get away. And this . . ." He pointed to the bad eye.

Jakkin nodded. Likkarn had fought with the wardens who were trying to capture them. It was the one good thing the old man had ever done for him.

"Go into my mind, boy. See if you find any weed there. *If* you dare." All this was said in whispers. Likkarn suddenly looked feral, haunted.

Jakkin shook his head. He, too, whispered. The last thing he needed was to wake the sleepers in the bondhouse.

"I don't understand you." But he did, because he suddenly remembered something Golden had said in the copter, about Likkarn living in the mountains with dragons long ago. So Jakkin couldn't help darting into the old man's mind and out again. Then, of course, he had to keep his face from showing his surprise. Likkarn was telling the truth. The *absolute* truth this time. There was no sign of weed. Not a bit.

"See?" Likkarn was grinning now. "So now you know. And I know you know."

Jakkin was suddenly tired of the whole whispered conversation. "Know all you like, old man," he said sharply, because whatever else was going on, the secret had to be kept. He suspected that if he gave Likkarn any room at all, he would move right in. "Or guess whatever you want. But I'm cold, exhausted, and going off to bed."

"Right. Best not speak of it out loud," Likkarn whispered, putting a finger to the side of his nose. "We'll keep it our little secret."

Not your secret, and not so little, either. Turning away, Jakkin started down the long hall toward the bunkroom and never looked back. But in his head he could hear the old man's whisper: *"Our little secret . . . secret . . . secret."*

He had to tell Akki as soon as possible. But how could he sneak down to the women's wing of the bondhouse and have them all guessing wrongly why he was there. They'd giggle about it. He couldn't stand that.

But Akki had to be told.

~

AKKI HAD awakened three times already, each time from another bad dream. She'd had to pee each time, as well, though after the first — when she banged her head on the top bunk — she'd moved carefully until out in the hall.

This fourth time, she sat up carefully, slipped out of the bed, and bumped into Jakkin in the hall.

"What are you doing here?" she whispered.

He put a silencing finger to his mouth and sent her a danger sign, a blood-red picture of an old man.

"Likkarn?" she mouthed.

He nodded, holding out his hand.

Soon they sat crouched together near a window in the dining hall.

"What about Likkarn?" she asked in a whisper.

"He can send . . . sort of."

She seized his left hand and squeezed it hard. "What do you mean?" Not being able to read his face in the dark, she ducked into his mind. It was in turmoil. She sent a cooling shower. *"What do you mean?"*

"Some trainers — not many," he sent, *"have a bit of a mind connection with their dragons. Like I did with Heart's Blood. And the trogs do, of course. And some of the stewmen link a bit with the dragons they kill in the stews."* He pictured each in turn — trainers, dragons, trogs, and the stews.

Akki shivered.

"But only you and I — and the trogs — really communicate."

"And Likkarn?"

"More than most." He sent her the conversation he and Likkarn had just had.

"That's it then," Akki told him. "We don't dare send to one another here in the bondhouse or outside when Likkarn is anywhere around. Because if he can read us —"

"Agreed."

"Jakkin . . ."

"Akki . . ."

"I have to go to The Rokk soon. I have to get started on the lab work. I'm not . . ." She was going to tell him how little she knew. How long it would take to learn enough to do any good.

He pulled away. *"What's that?"*

She listened hard, heard footsteps in the hall. Making a quick decision, she threw herself into Jakkin's arms, put her hands on either side of his face, and kissed him hard.

"What are you doing?"

"Just enjoy it."

"I am enjoying it," he began, before surrendering to the kiss. The lights suddenly went on in the dining hall and Likkarn's laughter spilled out.

Akki drew away from Jakkin, turned, and stared at Likkarn as if surprised to see him. "Well," she said, "enjoying the sight?" Then without waiting for an answer and pretending fury, she stood and marched off through the door.

Jakkin hurried after her, saying aloud, "Akki, Akki, don't go." But he was acting as much as she was.

"I'll see you tomorrow, Jakkin Stewart," she whispered. "And no more sendings."

He nodded, and she went quickly back to her room.

This time she slept without dreams.

~

JAKKIN FOUND his way through the dark to his own bunkroom and didn't even bother getting out of his clothes, though he did kick off the sandals.

Around him in their own beds, the three other boys snorted, snored, blew out small bubbling sighs. They dreamed the comforting dreams of the innocent, without secrets to trouble them. But Jakkin fell onto the bottom bunk and into a deep sleep, his fear of exposure, fear of damaging the dragons, keeping him from dreaming anything.

In the morning Jakkin barely saw Akki, for she was off, first, in the kitchen helping Kkarina, then away in the truck with Jo-Janekk to pick up supplies at a farmers' market an hour up the road.

In fact, for the rest of the day — and for four days after that — she seemed too busy to talk to him, and since they both kept to their promise of not sending to one another, he hardly spoke to her at all.

(7 (

MORNING LIGHT slanted in through the window, falling heavily across the foot of Jakkin's blanket. He woke and kicked the blanket off, then lay still for a moment, trying to enjoy the feel of mattress and pillow. *A year is a long time to go without mattress or pillow.* They had done what they could in the wild to stay alive, to make themselves comfortable. And comfort aside, it had been wonderful.

What am I thinking? There'd been the loss of his beloved dragon, real fear, scrabbling from meal to meal, the need to always keep out of sight. In the mountains, all he'd cared about was staying alive — and getting home — yet not quite a week home in the nursery and here he was suddenly wishing he could go back. Now that time shone in some sort of golden light, like a miracle. And miracles, by their very nature, only happen once — and are gone.

"Wake up, lazy legs." It was Akki, her sending snaking into his head. *"I'm already up and eating breakfast."* The sending bubbled with the dark, popping red of a cup of takk, though neither of them drank the dragon-blood-based drink anymore.

"Akki!" His sending was nearly a shout. It had been too many days without her constantly in his head. That was what he missed more than anything, what had made the year in the mountains wonderful. But still he had to ask. *"Why are we sending?"*

"Likkarn's already safely away in the barn. Kkarina says he's been there all night. Must be a hatching. He won't be able to hear us. And no one else can."

"I'm there," he said, getting out of the bed.

"What?" Errikkin sat straight up in the top bunk next to Jakkin's.

"Breakfast," Jakkin said, a finger to the side of his nose. "Smell it? I'm there. You coming?"

Errikkin shook his head, then turned over, showing only his rounded back.

Jakkin shrugged. Five days of Errikkin's back was enough. If Errikkin wanted no part of him, then he'd let the friendship go, though he did wonder what had happened in the year he'd been away to change the always pleasant boy he'd known into this sullen, angry stranger. *It can't just be the bond thing — can it?*

Putting on his sandals, Jakkin stood. He had enough problems without making Errikkin another one.

Arakk was already up and pulling on his shorts. "I'm with you."

Jakkin grinned at him. At least Arakk had a sunny disposition, unlike sullen Slakk and my-back-to-you Errikkin.

"Breakfast. That's the answer. It's always the answer!" Jakkin said.

"To what question?" Arakk asked.

Jakkin laughed. "To every one of them." At the same time, he unleashed a sending toward the common room, where Akki was waiting. *Get some lizard eggs ready for me!* He sent a bright red bubbling landscape to her. He wanted to say more, but he'd leave that for later.

A rushing, gushing river of color came back from her, burbling away. *Why is she so happy?*

Arakk laughed. For a moment Jakkin was confused, having forgotten he'd been speaking aloud to the moonfaced boy. Then he slapped Arakk on the back. "Any more questions?"

"Breakfast to every one of them," Arakk said. It had hardly been funny the first time, but the two boys laughed all the way to the breakfast room, leaving their sullen, snoring bunkmates behind.

As far as Jakkin could tell, everyone but Errikkin and Slakk — and Likkarn, still out in the barn — was already in the dining room when the clanging breakfast bell rang out. It didn't interrupt the noisy commentaries at the twelve tables. Breakfast was hardly a quiet affair, and Jakkin was only just getting used to it again.

Each table was ruled by a large ceramic takk pot in which the rich red drink brewed. The older men tended to sit together. That left the younger nursery workers at their own tables. One table had been set aside for the solitaires, who preferred not speaking at breakfast. There were three of them and they ate as far from one another as possible. Jakkin had considered it on his first morning back, but Akki had convinced him it would raise more questions than they wanted to answer, as he had not been a solitaire before.

Jakkin sat down next to Akki, who passed him a plate of

eggs without a word or a sending. But she smiled, flicking her long dark braid over her right shoulder as a kind of welcome. She was wearing a gold band around the bottom of the braid, and a matching gold band on her wrist. It had been a year since she'd had such things to wear, except for twists of wildflowers. Jakkin remembered the wildflowers with a sudden sweet longing. Ruefully, he smiled back at her, saying nothing.

Akki sent a tickling, colorful sequence of rainbows into his mind.

"I thought we said . . ." he whispered, and when she glared at him, he looked down at his plate.

"I'm sorry, I'm sorry," she whispered back, though she hardly seemed sorry. The exchange was so quick and so hushed, no one else noticed.

Jakkin took some eggs, a slice of mello, and a cup of minty tea. When Trikko passed the platter of meats along, Jakkin shook his head, almost shuddering. "Not that hungry," he said.

"You used to be hungry all the time," Trikko said. "It must be looooove." He drew the word out, to the delight of the rest of the table.

But it had nothing to do with love — or hunger. Of course, Jakkin couldn't tell them the real reason. He just couldn't eat lizard meat anymore. Lizards might not send with the power of their larger brothers, the dragons, but their minds were full of whispery, shadowy, pale sendings that flitted in and out of Jakkin's mind whenever he passed one by. Eating lizard meat would be like eating a relative. *A silly, slightly addled relative.* Though Jakkin was fine with the unfertilized eggs. Or with kkrystals, the translucent insects, dipped in egg and batter. He wondered if he could teach Kkarina that one.

After his first sip of tea, Jakkin looked up and forced a smile. "Sleep well?" He said it to the entire table, but he meant it for Akki.

She sent him a rude bit of color, full of snags and sparkles. Like a mind belch.

The sending made him laugh, and that was so inappropriate, he immediately covered it up with a cough, as if he were choking on the eggs.

Looking down at the table demurely, Akki said loudly, "I don't know about anyone else, but I slept like a baby. Easier on a mattress and bed than the stone floor of a cave. And you?"

He sent a mind belch back at her, and steadfastly refused to apologize.

At that point, Slakk came into the dining hall and joined them, sitting at the far end of the table, which was then awash in complaints about snoring roommates, pillows that needed new feathers, slats missing in beds — the usual.

"And you," Slakk said suggestively, pointing at Jakkin. "You came to bed awfully late last night."

"Ooooooo!" The comment ran around the table, and suddenly everyone stared and grinned at Akki. Reddening, she set her lips together so tightly, they looked like a thin scar. Her actual embarrassment served as great camouflage.

Jakkin swallowed quickly. He'd been out late again in the incubarn and run back to the bondhouse just before Dark-

After. He hadn't seen Likkarn that time, but if Akki was right, the old man must have been couched down with an about-to-lay hen. He reminded himself to be more careful.

Still, he had to deal with Slakk's accusation. "Stomach problems," Jakkin said, making a sour face and pointing to his belly. "Not used to all this rich food." He rubbed his palm over the offending stomach, but no one seemed convinced. *And really, how bad could it be if they think Akki and I are to-gether at night. It would give us more chance to move about.*

Just then Kkarina came out of the kitchen and over-heard him. She stood in the doorway, hands on her hips, glaring, though her face gave her away as she tried to hide a smile. Jakkin saw her and gulped.

"Rich, *good* food," Jakkin amended loudly.

She came over and clouted him on the head with her open hand.

"Nice save," Akki sent, with a picture of a drowning man being lifted from a river by a very large red dragon. It set the man down on a beach, then clouted him gently with a paw.

He grinned at her. *"Nothing,"* he sent to her, *"is as im-portant as breakfast."* His sending was bright and full of oval balloons, like giant eggs.

Akki laughed out loud, and the others — thinking she was laughing belatedly at Kkarina's blow to Jakkin's head — laughed with her.

~

AFTER BREAKFAST, and after checking the chores list, Akki called Jakkin to the side door.

"We really have to stop our sendings," she warned quietly. "Or we're going to make them all suspicious."

"They're *already* suspicious," he whispered back.

"They're suspicious that we've pair-bonded. Likkarn probably told someone about that kiss. Wouldn't you be suspicious of two people off together for a year, keeping 'warm' in caves?"

He shrugged, smiling at the memory.

"And one of them going walkabout at night. Where *were* you? We can't afford to let them suspect that we . . ."

". . . communicate without words or can go outside during Dark-After?"

She turned away from him, sending, *"You really are exasperating."*

"Wait a minute." His hand was on her shoulder. "You're the one who keeps sending. Not me."

"I know, I know. I said *'We.'* It's just so easy." She shrugged off his hand. *"See,"* she sent, *"we can both shrug,"* and opened the door, looking out into the glaring light. "I think Slakk is already guessing."

"Not Slakk. He's not that smart. He's just jealous of me, that's all. Errikkin's too angry about something else to be guessing anything. The rest don't know either of us well enough. Except . . ."

She spun around. "Except?"

"Old Likkarn, of course."

She glared daggers at him. "*I* can handle him. You're the one who has problems dealing with him. I wish I knew why. He's really all hough and no harm." That was something nursery folk said about male dragons.

Jakkin's face scrunched up, the way it did when he was going to say something hurtful. "Maybe he never harmed *you*," he began, "but there's not a boy in the nursery who hasn't felt his heavy hand. He thinks a bang on the head or arm or back is a good teaching tool."

"He's only treating you the way dragon studs treat the young males," Akki said. "That's all."

"And me worse than all the others combined."

"Sometimes," Akki told him, "boys whine too much." She turned and walked out the door.

He raced after her. "Where are you going?"

"To the incubarn, to check on Auricle and the hatchling." She kept walking, a fast, long stride.

"She was fine last night. And if there's a change, we'd know because Auricle would have sent to me. Or you."

Akki stopped suddenly, looked at him over her shoulder, glaring. "Auricle is a dragon, not a doctor." She resumed walking.

"You're not a doctor either, Akki," he shot back cuttingly. "Not a *real* one."

That was too close to the bone. Too close to what she feared the most. Akki rounded on him angrily. It was easier getting mad at him than getting mad at the world. "I'm the nearest *almost real* doctor this place has. That's why visiting the quarantined dragons is on *my* list of chores, not yours." She felt taut, like stretched wire. "Likkarn and the men know that I'm the one they have to go to for medical knowledge — especially now, with the embargo. Likkarn says that though medical ships are allowed through, few have actually come."

"I didn't mean —"

She suspected *that* at least was true, but couldn't stop herself from saying, "You never do."

He put his hand out beseechingly, as if he wanted to touch her. Instead he said, "We never fought out there." He gestured vaguely toward the mountains.

Her anger ebbed, her face softened. She took a deep breath. "We fought all the time out there, Jakkin."

He shook his head. "Not really. Not fought — we argued. But we always agreed on the important things. The life-or-death matters. And there were a lot of those." A soft breeze touched Jakkin's face, lifting the hair on his forehead, then letting it fall again, almost obscuring his eyes. Watching him, Akki suddenly felt terribly young and vulnerable. But she couldn't let herself feel that way. Too much was resting on her shoulders, and it frightened her. She wanted him to understand.

"Jakkin . . ." She was ready to tell him about The Rokk and the lab and how she'd gotten Kkarina to find a way to get her there and that only this morning Kkarina said there was a truck coming to take her off. Today. "Jakkin, about the nursery —"

"We're safe here, Akki, safe from the wardens and the rebels and the trogs. We're home. It's where we belong. I've finally just this minute figured it out. We don't really have to do *anything* about the dragons, you know. Just keep the secret safe. If it's safe, so are we. And so are the dragons. So why are we still arguing?"

And then the moment to confide in him, the moment to

tell him how all on her own she'd made plans to go to the city, to work on the most important problem Austar had — that moment was gone. Her fear and her anger flooded back. "Because . . . because after a year of freedom, we're not just back home, we're back in bond." She turned away and walked off.

"There *is* no more bond on Austar IV," he called after her. "Haven't you been listening?"

She sent back a loud and very clear hot, pink landscape, with streaks of red.

"Oh, I've been listening, but that's not what I *heard!*" she called over her shoulder. Then, using two hands, she pulled the squalling door of the incubarn open and clumped inside. "We are more in bond than ever," she said, before slamming the door in his face.

☾ 8 ☾

JAKKIN DIDN'T understand her.

He guessed he'd never understand her.

He let her go without a response.

Desolate, he walked to the stud barn to start his own chores. He and Akki had been given less than a week's grace to get over the oddness of being back at the nursery before they had to start working. But he hadn't complained. All his life he'd taken work for granted, and now that there was no more bond system, he knew they would have to work even harder. *Still, the rewards should be greater.* And his chores were familiar ones.

Today he had to lead three big male dragons to the mud baths. They would keep his mind off of Akki.

Sometimes, before a male dragon mated, its skin got flaky, the scales discoloring. "Scales like mud, little stud" was not just a nursery rhyme. It was true. In the wild, dragons usually soaked themselves in the muddy rivers, lying down on the river bottoms until only their eyes showed above water. The mud and the river flow scoured their scales clean.

The cleaner the scales, the more likely that the male dragon could impress a female. So it was up to the nursery folk to make sure their male dragons had scales that shone like small suns. No use keeping the unpredictable males around unless they could sire more dragons. Or win big in the pits.

The mud pools in the stud barn were part of a great triple-forked water system. One fork sent drinking water into individual stalls, one funneled away wastewater when the stalls were cleaned. The third fork led into the mud baths, and that was where Jakkin went to shepherd the dragons under his care.

But leading a dragon is dangerous work. Just because once in, a dragon enjoyed the mud didn't mean that a worm always cooperated. Many a nursery boy had been nipped or stepped upon while moving a testy male toward the baths. But danger was what Jakkin needed now to stop him thinking about Akki.

Jakkin let himself into the stud barn, and the familiar power of the musk that greeted him almost made him smile. There was simply nothing like it. A hen's smell was softer, cozier, but the smell of a male dragon simply took one's breath away. Going down the long left-hand corridor, Jakkin came to the stall of the first of his assigned dragons, old Blood Bath, who was lying down on his straw and looking gray, dingy, worn. He was the grandsire of Heart's Blood, the great-grandsire of her brood, so Jakkin had a lot of affection for the old worm.

"Not good, not good, old boy," Jakkin whispered, but his sending to the dragon was much sunnier. The orange-colored dragon looked at him with shuttered eyes, the membranes having grown thick with age, leaving him almost blind. Suddenly the membranes lifted, and he stared at Jakkin with dark, unreadable eyes. Those eyes held not even the slightest flicker to signal that he'd once been a fighter and, for a long time, the best stud in the nursery.

"Let's get thee into the bath right away. Thou will feel much better in the mud." He sent the dragon an image of the warm, bubbling bath. "And thou will be a better stud for it."

Startled by the sending, Blood Bath lumbered to his feet, his great head starting to weave back and forth. Standing up, he was huge, even for a dragon, but his underskin beneath the orange scales was horribly faded.

He really is ancient. Probably not able to mate anymore. But he'd been one of Sarkkhan's first fighting dragons, a mighty winner in his day, who sired many other winners. Yet here he was, still in the stud barn, eating his head off. Jakkin wondered if Likkarn kept him in the nursery in honor of his past glory, instead of selling him to the stews.

If so, good for Likkarn, he thought begrudgingly.

"Come, thou brave fighter." Jakkin let the dragon sniff his left hand, which brought the great head way down. Then, with his right hand, Jakkin hooked his finger around Blood Bath's ear. Ears were one of the few sensitive areas on a dragon's body and a tug was one way — possibly the best way — of urging a beast out of his stall.

Slakk was suddenly in the corridor ahead of them.

"Bell!" Jakkin called to him, and Slakk ran up to the nearest pull and yanked at it, sending a warning to anyone else in the barn that a stud dragon was unstalled. Then Slakk pressed into the closest safety niche in order to let them go by. Always best to be out of the way when a stud — even an ancient one — was being led to the baths. Though a niche wasn't entirely safe, especially if the dragon hackled and rampaged down the corridor, which sometimes happened during the rutting season. Many of the older nursery men sported blood scores and claw marks that made their arms and legs look as pitted as a desert landscape after an infrequent rain.

But this day Blood Bath was quiet, almost sleepwalking, as they moved toward the bath. Jakkin called back to Slakk, "Clean his stall for me, and I'll second on *your* dragon."

Slakk much preferred raking out the old fewmets and settling new straw for bedding than leading any of the dragons to the bath. In fact, Slakk hated dragons. He'd often threatened to run away from the nursery, and Jakkin was actually surprised — since there was no more bond — that Slakk was still here.

"Done," Slakk called back.

If necessary, Jakkin could trade all his dragon work with Slakk. Unlike Slakk, he loved the beasts. Loved their power, their beauty of movement, their single-mindedness in feeding, in fighting, and in the rut. And now that he could speak to them mind-to-mind, Jakkin loved them even more. As for the fewmets — well, he'd take a blood score any day. *Let Slakk stay up to his knees in the steaming stuff.* Jakkin chuckled at the thought.

When he opened the door to the sunken mud room and

let go of the dragon's ear, Blood Bath happily waded in, moving faster than he'd done before. Behind him, Jakkin rode the doorstep platform over the bath.

"Good for thee, old man," he called to the dragon, as he picked up the wire brush from a hook on the door. "Looks like you're not done for yet!" He sent the dragon a bright sparkle of colorful stars. At least he could do that with the dragons though not right now with Akki.

Blood Bath lifted his head, as if astonished, as if he'd already forgotten the earlier sending that had startled him out of his stall. Then he sank down gratefully in the mud. When he was ready, he'd come over for a good scrubbing. And after that, the cleansing shower.

It's a wonderful life. Why have I forgotten just how wonderful? It was also predictable. And, if a nursery boy was careful and knew what he was doing, it was safe. *Safer than joining a rebel cell or being in a cave full of murderous trogs,* he reminded himself. *Safer than loving an unpredictable girl.*

And then he had another thought: *How could Akki say we're still in bond?* That she should do so rankled. He felt like a hackling dragon. His shoulders went up and his mouth set in a thin line. *She's wrong, so wrong. And in so many ways.* He'd tell her as soon as he saw her again. Or maybe he'd just send her his feelings. Of course, that might charge up the dragons, if they heard him. *And words . . . words are so much more precise than sendings.*

He must have leaked some of his feelings to the dragon, for Blood Bath looked up and sent a comforting spray of bubbling colors into his mind.

"Okay, okay, I will attend *thee*, old man," Jakkin said at once, feeling stupid to have forgotten that dragons were safe where a bonder took care and paid attention only to them. And then he remembered there weren't any bonders anymore. He forced himself to stop thinking about Akki, about their fight, about home, wherever it might be — and gave himself over to the musk, the moisture, the dragons, and the heat of the mud.

AFTER OVERSEEING mud baths for his own three dragons, and then two of Slakk's, Jakkin took the rest of the afternoon off. Yes, he loved the work, but he hadn't been given any other jobs, and he'd suddenly realized that there was something else he wanted to do. Not something to do with the nursery dragons and definitely not something to do with Akki.

So he wandered over to the stone weir at the northernmost corner of the stud barn. Here, water channeled from the Narrakka River was a bright blue, reflecting the clear sky. For a moment he looked across to the sand dunes, remembering how often he'd sneaked away to the hidden oasis where he'd raised Heart's Blood, a stolen dragon, from a miscounted clutch. The best fighting dragon in all of Austar.

Running a hand through his hair, he wondered, *Is it still there?* Meaning the oasis, meaning the wellspring, meaning the reed shelter. *Or has it changed, too?*

He plunged into the weir, knee-deep in the blue water, and waded across. At the third join, he climbed out and, by habit, kept low, though it mattered little now if anyone saw him. Heart's Blood was long dead; there were no young, uncounted hatchlings to raise away from the nursery. Since all the nursery folk now owned the dragons together, there was no need to steal one, to raise it secretly in the hopes of training a winning dragon and buying oneself out of bond. He wasn't scheduled for night duty in the incubarn for several days. And since there was no more bond, there was no need for secrecy anymore.

Except for the giant secret he and Akki shared.

The desert air quickly dried his legs and sandals. The water hadn't come anywhere close to his thigh-length pants. Some of the sand from the dunes clung stubbornly to his legs, but he quickly brushed it off. For a moment, he wondered if there was even any reason for visiting the oasis now. And then he simply went on.

Memories were reason enough.

~

JAKKIN WALKED for nearly an hour before he found the place. The steady Austarian winds had blown away any semblance of a path, had recontoured the dunes just enough to confuse him. He hadn't actually gotten lost, but he was bothered for a while.

His first sight of the spring, rising as if from nowhere, was a bright ribbon of blue water threading through the golden sand. It made him sigh in recognition, made him remember Heart's Blood as a hatchling, eager, ready to learn, and waiting for him.

He had to bite his lip not to cry. *Think only of the oasis,* he reminded himself as he looked around. The pool he'd made when he widened the western edge of the stream was smaller than before. Now a rim of kkhan reeds ran around it entirely instead of only on one side.

But everything's still here! He gazed at it all with both wonder and relief. Running his fingers once more through his hair, he spoke the words out loud: "It's still here." He tried sending the thought back to Akki, though of course she was much too far away to get it. Or to answer. *Even if she wanted to.*

Looking a second time around the oasis, he realized not *everything* was there. The little reed shelter was gone. He'd no idea if it had been taken down by human hands or blown away by the wind dervishes that frequented the dunes. Something in his chest hurt. Just for a moment, then it was gone.

He started toward the spot where the shelter had stood, when a sudden sending, like a lightning strike, crashed through his mind, so loud and boisterous, he flinched.

"Sssargon waits," came the intrusion. *"Sssargon hungers."*

"Thou great beauty!" Jakkin cried, spinning around to look for the source of the sending.

About a hundred yards away, Sssargon stood up to his shoulders in a patch of burnwort. The red stalks were fully leafed out and long past their smoldering stage, and tall enough to have hidden the dragon almost completely until now. Sssargon was grazing, his long tongue reaching out to snag the top of a wort plant, then his jaws grinding and crushing the leaves as he walked on to the next.

Sssargon would spit out the burnwort seeds before swallowing. Any that he swallowed by accident would emerge later in his steaming fewmets, to drop into the patch and grow a new crop of wort. Nature on Austar was very conservative. "Waste not, want never" went nursery wisdom. But people had to be taught that wisdom. Dragons lived it without thinking.

"Sssargon full. Sssargon lies down." Just as Sssargon sent his thoughts to Jakkin, the big worm swept his pinioned wings close to his sides, the scaly feathers pushing the sand away from his body. Then, with surprising delicacy, he lay down. Surprising because up till now he'd been much more graceful in the air than on the ground.

Growing up. Jakkin smiled. *My babies!* And then he laughed at himself. *Big babies!*

Sssargon fidgeted for a moment before settling into his sandy hammock and making a humming sound.

Are the dragons really all in danger? Jakkin wondered again. *Only if the secret gets out. Only if we tell.* He really had to talk to Akki about it. Make her see. If there was no real immediate danger, then she had no reason to hurry to finish her training as a doctor. All they really needed was to keep quiet about it. *A secret kept secret can harm no one.*

Just then, Jakkin's head was filled with a barrage of red bubbles and sounds like *SPLAT! SPLAT! SPLAT!* that overwhelmed all thought. Jakkin glanced around the oasis for the rest of the brood, but the only dragon he could see was Sssargon, now fast asleep on the sand.

SPLAT! SPLAT! SPLAT!

He looked up. Far above him were four dots, circling the oasis. Having finally gotten his attention, they sang out to him in color as they came in for a well-timed landing. They touched ground together with hardly a tremor. For all their bulk, the brood was incredibly dainty.

"Home. Home. Jakkin is home." Their voices twined in his head, their phosphorescent sendings welcoming him. The triplets' high-pitched twitterings were still mostly incomprehensible, but Sssasha made up for them with her clarity and warmth.

Gazing around the oasis, at the five dragons, at the bubbling spring, the tall reeds, the bowl of blue sky, Jakkin flung out his arms. They were right, of course. The nursery wasn't home. The oasis was.

⸱ 9 ⸱

AKKI HAD FIRST checked the hens in the incubarn and especially the one Likkarn felt was ready to lay. The dragon was calm — no hackles, no shuttered eyes, her tail lying flat against the stall floor. In fact, she was a lot calmer than Likkarn.

"It's Heart O'Mine and she's never had a successful clutch," he told Akki. His eyes were reddened, and the bad eye's lid was drooping. Clearly he'd had little sleep. "She's just about at the end of her laying days. Another few years and her nursery time will be over."

"Do you want me to check her again?" Akki asked, wondering if she should forget about her ride to The Rokk.

"Please," he said.

Akki wasn't sure she'd ever heard him say that word before, and she wondered if Likkarn, too, wasn't nearing the end of his time in the nursery.

"She was the first hen your father gave me and I thought she'd make my fortune," he explained as she knelt down to examine Heart O'Mine's protruding belly.

The dragon's belly was tight as it should be, and when

she put her ear down, she could hear a kind of gurgle, very light and yet constant. "Burble means babies," she recited. It was one of the earliest things she'd ever learned about gravid females.

Likkarn laughed mirthlessly. "Oh, she burbles all right. She goes into heat, freshens, accepts the male, then eggs form and they burble away. She lays them just fine. But the eggs never open up on hatchlings. I don't know why." He turned to the dragon. "Nor do thou, my lovely, my darling."

"She's three or four days away, I'd say."

"Two."

"We'll see."

He stood. "Will *we?*" he asked. "The truck's coming to take you to The Rokk."

She was stunned. Her mouth opened, closed.

"The master of a nursery has to know what's going on at all times," Likkarn said. "Your father taught me that. And if you think you can get Kkarina to do anything without telling me, well, think again."

"Well, perhaps when I think again, I'll change my mind and *not* go." She stood, too. "That's what my father taught *me.*"

"We need a good doctor and a better vet, especially with the embargo. A lot of the old vets and doctors were here on rotation from other Feder worlds and have gone back home. So, if you're set on finishing your apprenticeship, we want you off to The Rokk as soon as possible." His sharp face took on a crafty look. "Your father would have wanted that, too. Now go and check those two ferals."

He meant Auricle and the hatchling. It was his hand that

had written the visit with them on the chore list, all the while knowing it might be her last day with them for a while. The master of the nursery. *Yes, I suppose he's that. Now.* For the first time in almost a year, she thought of her father with real regret. He'd been a difficult father, but a great master.

As she left the stall and headed to the rear of the barn, she considered how well Auricle had settled in. Not so the hatchling. *The poor thing has so imprinted on me, she's pining for me as if for a mother.* Akki sighed. *But what can I do?*

Henkky's house in The Rokk was no place for a growing dragon, but Akki feared the hatchling would die before she was able to get back for a visit. For all their size and power, dragons could go down fast for any number of reasons, and imprinting on the wrong mother was one of them. In only another month, the hatchling would be ready to fledge. *What if it doesn't last that long without me? Either I wait a month before going or . . .* That way she could see Likkarn's dragon through this laying, fledge the hatchling, get Jakkin used to the idea of their being apart. But there was always going to be one crisis after another. That's how nurseries worked. As her father always said, "We lurch from bad to worse." If she stayed this time, it would be even easier to stay through the next crisis. And all that time given was time lost. The planet's dragons might all be consigned to death because of her. She felt time weighing heavily on her. The sooner she began working on the problem facing all the dragons, the better. Taking the hatchling along seemed to be her only option.

I have to go to The Rokk now. I have to set up a laboratory now, learn all I can now. Likkarn already knows some of the se-

cret. The trogs know the rest. And if the trogs came boiling out of their caves, it would be a real disaster: the secret out, people killed, and more dragons — maybe *all* the dragons — killed.

But I can't go without telling Jakkin! She sent a tentative gray sending, trying to find him. But then she realized she was too close to Likkarn and stopped herself. Jakkin was no doubt still in the stud barn, working with the big male dragons. She'd just go and tell him.

Stilling her traitor mind, she went on to Auricle's stall, patted her and sang to her, and settled her down. Then, collecting the hatchling, who'd all but attached herself to Akki's side, she left the barn. There was a truck waiting by the kitchen door.

"Oh, fewmets!" she said aloud. There was no time to see Jakkin and say good-bye. She'd have to send. Something short, definitive. As soon as she was ready to go.

But first she needed to pack. Not that she had anything to pack. At least, nothing for the city. She decided to start with the nursery store.

~

THE STORE was unattended. It didn't matter. She picked out a change of leathers, a second pair of sandals, and a soft carry bag, then left a note that she'd borrowed them.

Back in her room, with the hatchling perched on her bed, she packed the bag with the new clothes and several of her old hair ties that Kkarina had been keeping. A hairbrush, comb, toothbrush, and that was all she needed.

No, she thought, *not quite all.* There was a pair of shears on top of the chest of drawers. It gave her an idea. Just in case there were any rebels still roaming The Rokk, she'd make herself unrecognizable. Picking up the shears, she cut off her long hair in three large, dark clumps, and shoved the clumps into the burn sack in the hall.

Back in the bedroom, she took a quick look in the mirror. With that short cap of hair, she barely knew herself. That made her smile. "Good-bye, Akki," she whispered to her reflection.

She picked up the carry bag, but when she tried to gather up the hatchling, it hissed at her.

"Hey, I'm still me," she whispered to it, holding out her hand. The hatchling sniffed at the proffered hand finger by finger before deciding that she smelled all right. But it took a minute more before it was willing to settle into the crook of her arm.

Carrying bag and hatchling, she went to say good-bye to Kkarina in the kitchen. The smells of hard soap and pots soaking in hot water filled the place.

Errikkin was sitting at the kitchen table having a late breakfast or an early lunch. He dimpled at her. She didn't take it personally. He dimpled at everyone.

"Going somewhere, stranger?" he asked.

The hatchling hissed at him. *It must be his tone,* Akki thought. *I want to hiss at him, too.*

"She's off to The Rokk to do some studying," Kkarina said. Her hands were in the water, scrubbing the pots. "To be a doctor." She banged the clean pot down on the wooden rack. "And a vet."

Surely Errikkin should be cleaning the pots. Of course, he always used charm to get out of work.

"She'll be home again soon," Kkarina said, lifting a third pot up and shaking the water out. "And her hair will be all grown out again." It was all she said about Akki's shearing.

"I will indeed." Akki smiled and shifted the hatchling from her left arm to her right.

Errikkin had a funny look on his face. "Does Jakkin know?" It almost seemed that he hoped it would come as a surprise. Though whether he wondered if Jakkin knew she was leaving or that she had cut off all her hair, Akki couldn't tell.

"Of course he knows," said Akki, which was only partially a lie. "He was the first." And that ambiguity was what she left Errikkin with, walking out the door to the truck, holding the bag in one hand, the hatchling in the other and not looking back.

☾ 10 ☾

THE RIDE to The Rokk was less comfortable than the one she'd had on her last trip, over a year ago. The truck bounced along the road as if the cab were sitting directly on the axle with nothing to cushion it.

Akki didn't complain. After all, the black-haired driver had a face that didn't invite complaints. Especially, she guessed, from girls. She feared that he would just put her out on the road, with her satchel of clothes in one hand and the hatchling curled up in the other. And while she could last through the night if she had to, it would just make things even more difficult to explain should he ever go back to the nursery and talk to Kkarina. Or Likkarn.

Besides, now that I'm actually on the road, I want to get to the city as soon as possible. And as anonymously as possible.

The hatchling stirred, and she gentled it with a finger-tickle under the chin.

"Never did like those things," the man said, his face patchy with moles. His eyes were a cloudy color, neither gray nor blue nor green. And his nose looked as if he'd been in one too many fights.

"Things?"

"Dragons. Don't trust them lizards." There was a short, deep scar on his face — *possibly a blood score* — that moved when he spoke, and not in a pleasant way. When he grinned, she saw that one of his front teeth was predictably black.

"They're not exactly lizards," she said.

"Close enough."

"Same family, though."

He wiped a gloved finger under his nose. "You some kind of scientist?"

"Close enough."

"Boomer," he said.

"What . . ." She turned toward him, making sure that the hatchling was kept slightly behind her.

"My name."

"No double *k*s?" She wondered if his parents had been masters. Or wardens. Or had bought themselves out of bond. And if so, why was he driving a truck? Why wasn't he a senator or a store director or owner of a large farm?

He laughed. It was a low rumble, not actually unpleasant, but more animal than human. "After the dumb-bumbling senators set us all free from bond, who wants to be a double *k* anymore?" He put his hand out to shake hers.

She got a stubborn look on her face, which Jakkin would have recognized in an instant, and refused to put out her own hand. "Akkinata," she lied. Her true given name was Akkhina. She pronounced all the syllables for the maximum effect, almost spitting out the *k*s.

"Ah well, you're only a girl. No need for you to change

now, is there? You'll change soon enough when you get paired. Pretty girl like you, got to have a man."

Furious, she considered telling him how much she'd already changed. Not only the dragon sight and dragon speech, but how, just before getting into his truck, she'd cut off her hair.

He laughed at her silence and said, "Is there one?"

This time she thought about snarling. About screaming. Thought about how she'd even prefer walking to keeping quiet in the cab of Boomer's bumpy truck. But she needed the ride more than he needed to give it to her. She couldn't carry her bag and the hatchling and get to The Rokk with any ease. So she bit her lip, swallowed her anger, and shook his gloved hand, imagining — by the spongy feel of it — what it was disguising: the swollen, hairy knuckles, filthy nails bitten down to the quick. One shake was all she could manage before turning to look out the window, which was way better than staring at his ugly face. The hatchling thrummed in the crook of her right arm.

~

IT FELT LIKE half a day, but only an hour by the sun, when Boomer suddenly pulled onto the grassy verge and stopped the truck.

Akki was instantly on guard. Her sudden nervousness communicated to the hatchling, who in turn scratched her on her little finger, a long, thin red line.

"Ow!"

Repentant, the little dragon licked the blood with its forked tongue, which felt cool on her skin.

"Danger?" The hatchling sent a huge red arrow coursing toward her.

Akki sent back a cooling spray of blue-white rain that enveloped the red arrow, turning it pink, then erasing it altogether. *"No danger."* She was delighted that the hatchling was sending to her. And such a strong image. The trogbred dragons tended to be muted, their sendings beaten to grays. Clearly she and Jakkin had gotten the little hatchling out in time.

"I told you them lizards aren't to be trusted, *Akkinata.*" He spoke her made-up name with the same staccato accent. "Want me to dump it?"

"NO!" she said, louder than she meant to, though not as loud as she might have wanted.

"Danger?" The hatchling's baby hackles rose just a bit.

Her finger throbbing in response, Akki soothed the hatchling with a stroking motion. *"No, silly. None. Just silly humans playing silly human games."*

"Silly 'uman," came the dragonling's sending, and she began thrumming again.

"S'alright," Boomer said. "I know how you girls get attached to those things."

Akki suddenly understood. He believed the hatchling was a Beauty, a miniaturized dragon taken as an early cull and purposely stunted. City girls loved such things. Akki thought them an abomination. The Beauties, not the girls.

"Yes," she said carefully. "Very attached."

"Okay. As for me — gotta go. Use the . . . well, find a bush . . . well, a tree, anyway." Obviously talking about bodily functions to a girl was enough to make him babble incoherently. He opened the door and leaped down from the cab of the truck. Then he walked briskly out past some small bushes, more gracefully than she would have thought, his black hair under the bandana swinging from side to side.

Akki looked away toward a straggly copse of trees on her side of the road. The last thing she wanted to watch was Boomer peeing.

She considered driving away in the truck on her own. After all, she knew how to drive. Her father had taught her on the nursery roads years ago. She wouldn't have to worry about Boomer getting caught out in Dark-After. They weren't that far from Krakkow, after all, and there were always the small roadside houses dotted around the landscape for any bonders left outside at night. He'd be fine. *Furious, of course, but fine.*

However, when she leaned over for the keys, they were not in the ignition. Suddenly, *she* was the furious one. *He doesn't trust me!* He'd taken the keys with him.

Just as well. She laughed at herself. She needed to stay focused on getting to The Rokk, not stealing a truck and running from the wardens once she got there. Her work — finding a substitute for the blood in a dragon's egg chamber — was more important than taking a thug's truck. In fact, it was the most important thing in the whole of Austar right now, though only she and Jakkin knew it.

Jakkin! She bit her lip. She'd tried, *really* tried, to communicate with him about Kkarina and the truck and driver. And after, in the incubarn, she'd tried again. She sent and sent and never heard back. *He's probably off sulking some-where.* And then she thought, *Boys!*

Shifting the hatchling to her left arm for a bit while Boomer was out of the cab, Akki sighed with relief. She shook her right arm, trying to get back some of the feeling. It might have been a mistake bringing the hatchling along. She could see — could feel, actually — how much the dragonling was growing daily. Pretty soon, unlike any of the Beauty dragons, the hatchling would be too heavy to haul around. And how was she going to take care of the lit-tle dragon in a city house? *But really, what choice did I have. I couldn't let the poor thing mourn itself to death.*

As for Jakkin — she was angry with him for not an-swering her sending. And sad, too. The last things they'd said to one another had been so hurtful. She'd only wanted to shake him out of his notion that being back at the nurs-ery meant that everything was fine again.

"Stupid . . . fewmetty . . . worm drizzle," she said aloud, just as Boomer climbed back up in the cab.

"I hope you're not aiming that mouth at me, girl," he said, his tone light but the pit on his face now a deep red color, as if it alone were blushing.

"No," she said, "I'm just mad at myself for something I said to . . . to my boyfriend before we left."

"Should have known a pretty girl like you would treat the boys badly," he said, and began to laugh, pounding one meaty hand on the wheel. Then, putting the key in the lock, he started up the truck and steered it back out onto the road.

Smiling prettily at him, or at least she hoped so, Akki

then turned away again, to stare straight ahead at the long road. Often wild east winds swept across the road, burying parts of it in sand. But there'd been winds from the north recently, and so the raised paving was clear. She hoped that was a good omen for the rest of the trip.

☾ 11 ☾

THEY RODE for quite some time in silence and Akki was glad of it. Glancing out her window, she glimpsed the Narrakka River, dark and swift and threatening. Toward the north were the brooding mountains. She shivered just looking at them.

Half an hour later they passed the convict city of Krakkow, on the one rim road around it. Soon they'd be heading through the heart of the desert toward The Rokk. Her excitement communicated to the little dragon curled against her, and it thrummed loudly.

"What's that noise?" demanded Boomer.

"Nothing worrying," she replied. "Just the hatchling."

"I don't trust them lizards," he repeated, his lips pushed out, which made his face strangely alien.

Neither spoke much for the rest of the trip, which was just fine with her.

The road between Krakkow and The Rokk had a numbing sameness to it. On both sides, the desert was a light-colored sandscape, hardly relieved by any greenery. It could have been soporific, but Akki was too keyed up to nap along the way. Besides, she didn't trust Boomer. He might stop at one of the roadside houses, pleading tiredness, then make her get inside. He might try to take the hatchling away. Or hurt it somehow. He might . . . she couldn't begin to imagine all of the things Boomer might be capable of doing if she didn't stay awake.

Boomer. What a stupid, troglike name. She shifted uneasily on the seat, resettling the hatchling next to her, curling her arm around its back, enjoying its dozy thrum. She sent it a gold-colored chuckle that looked a great deal like reeds waving in a soft wind.

"Comfy, girl?" Boomer asked, scratching up under his bandana.

"Mmmm."

"You can nod off if you want."

"No thanks." Her answer didn't encourage any more questions, and for a long time he didn't ask any.

All the way, in fact, to The Rokk.

∼

WHEN THEY CAME at last to the outskirts of the city, Akki sat up straight. As always, the sight of the great walls struck her with awe. In her heart. Or her stomach. She wasn't sure which.

Stone towers, like dragon wings, stretched out on either side of the main structure. Her usual response to spotting The Rokk had been to laugh. This time she just sighed.

"Quite a thing," Boomer ventured. "Never seen it afore, I bet."

She turned and said sharply, "Oh, I've seen it often enough. Even worked here for a while."

He nodded, as if understanding. "Bag girl!"

"*Not.*" Her voice held contempt that she hadn't meant. After all, her own mother had been a bag girl. Had died in a baggerie. And Kkarina, too, had started in a baggerie before turning to cooking. Being a bag girl was an honest profession. She rephrased and softened her answer. "Not a bag girl. A student doctor."

Boomer laughed. "Of course." He obviously didn't believe it. "And that's a waste."

Now that they were in sight of the city, Akki suddenly felt a need to set him straight. If he threw her out here, she could walk — even carrying both the satchel and the hatchling — and be there inside of an hour.

"*Of course,* you pig. Nothing wasted about me. I was an apprentice doctor and working with one of the finest research doctors on the planet. Her name is Dr. Henkky. Maybe you've heard of her?"

He shrugged noncommittally.

Akki continued. "I'm not one of your pretty girls, Boomer whatever-your-real-name-is. And my father, Master Sarkkhan, owned the nursery where you picked me up."

So much for remaining anonymous.

Immediately she regretted having said anything at all. He could sell that information, could pass it on to . . . to . . . She had no idea who might want to know, but suddenly sure she should have remained nameless. In his own way, Golden had told them both that before he'd left them at the nursery.

To her astonishment, Boomer began to laugh, full-throated, head back. For a moment she was afraid they'd go off the road. But it would only mean getting stuck in sand, nothing dangerous.

When he finally stopped laughing, he slashed the back of his arm across his eyes as if to wipe away tears. "Oh my, it's lucky you didn't have a stinger with you, Akki. I'd be a dead man already. Deader than a drakk shot out of a tree."

The voice was suddenly sweeter, the pronunciation more precise, more familiar, less . . . less Boomer. And he'd called her Akki, not Akkinata. That was when she remembered how he loved disguises. Fake mustaches. Fake scars.

"Golden?"

He grinned. She realized that the black tooth was beginning to shred.

"Golden!"

He tore off the bandana and the fake hair. Stripped the padded gloves from his hands. Took out the strange lenses from his eyes, which were now the calculating river blue she remembered. "Akki, you need to control your urge to give answers where no questions are asked," he said, his face now serious. "What happened to the girl who managed to infiltrate a rebel cell in disguise?"

"She killed her father and dozens of other people and dragons, lived in a cave for a year with a sweet friend, and barely made it home. That's what happened to her."

"Well," he drawled, "that could change a person, I suppose."

She exhaled in exasperation. "I almost drove off with the truck, you know. When you leaped out to —"

"I was ready for that maneuver and wasn't a bit worried. Unless you knew how to turn on the engine without the key." He grinned at her, and despite the black and peeling front tooth, she knew him now. His hands were sweaty from their long stay in the bulky gloves, but they were hardly the meaty, hairy, nail-bitten, filthy things she'd imagined.

Golden seemed to think a minute, then added, "Though it's a fine skill, hot-wiring a car, and I'll teach it to you someday."

She slammed her left fist into his arm. "Golden! But why?"

"To see if you were ready for this."

"For '*this*'?"

"This *adventure,* for lack of a better word. This plan of mine."

"*Your* plan? It's *my* plan!"

He laughed, then suddenly looked serious. "What plan?"

"To . . . to . . . to —" She couldn't tell him, not about the trogs, not about her new abilities. She took a deep breath. "To study to be a doctor and a vet."

He didn't look entirely convinced.

To get him off the scent, she said, "But what plan of *yours* brought you to the nursery?"

"Well, I was going to come to get you and Jakkin to help me save the senate. Hadn't actually planned when to do it. Any day now. Then Kay sent me a note with one of the food truckers saying that you wanted a ride into The Rokk. Well, it was a sign and much too good to pass up. I didn't want her or Likkarn to know it was me, though. Too many questions, too many people knowing my business. Though now I'll have to come back another time to get Jakkin."

She was totally confused. "Save the senate from — who exactly?"

"From the new ragtag voters, ex-bonders and ex-rebels who haven't a clue as to how the country *can* be run or *should* be run, who will vote for the one who promises them free chikkar or a new job or brings on the bag girls. They want entertainment, not governance."

She understood now. "You want us to help save your senate seat."

He nodded, grinning.

"And what do you have in mind for Jakkin and me to do?"

He pulled over to the side of the road, stopped the truck, turned to her, and said with great earnestness, "You're to tell them about what the rebels did, their plans, how they fooled you, how they —"

She was stunned. "How about how *you* put me in danger, how you set in motion the events that made Jakkin and me carry a bomb into Rokk Major, which killed my father and —"

He put his hand toward her but when the dragon hissed, he drew it back. "You were our only hope to infiltrate that cell, Akki. They sussed out all our other operatives, were killing them off one by one. We never thought they'd trust you that soon with a bomb. *Fewmets*, girl, we didn't even know that they actually *had* bombs. We just wanted to learn their plans."

"We?"

"Your father, several of the senators, me."

"Ah — the plot sickens, as my father used to say."

He laughed. "Thicken or sicken, the plot still needs your help."

Suddenly she was as furious with him as she'd been with Jakkin. Maybe more so. *Boys and their games!* "Couldn't you have just flown to the nursery in the copter and asked if Jakkin and I wanted to be your mouthpieces? Given us the choice? Though who in her right mind would have thought you'd be good at being straightforward and honest?"

He bristled. "I'm a senator. And . . ."

"Not to be trusted."

He laughed. "That too, I suppose." Turning his head toward her, he said, "*Think,* Akki."

She said slowly, "Last time you asked for my help, I was almost killed. And my father *was.* Part of your *peaceful* revolution, was it?"

"Think some more, Akki." Now he was looking straight ahead.

"Damn you, Golden. 'No more masters, no more slaves,' you said, and we believed you."

"And haven't I delivered?"

"With how many deaths tacked to your door?"

"What's done is over." She could tell he didn't say it lightly. His jawline, even padded by something in his mouth, stiffened as he spoke.

But she wouldn't let him off that easily. Putting a hand on the wheel, she said, "You always did prefer making a game of things. Well, I am done with helping you. Dead and dying people and dragons are no game. Next time ask me in a straightforward manner. No lying, no deceit. Maybe I'll join you, maybe I won't. But you have to promise it will be done in the light, not in the dark."

He was no longer smiling. Sticking the bandana back on, rearranging the long black wig, he put the lenses back in his eyes and drove into the city without stopping. And *without* promising anything.

☾ 12 ☾

JAKKIN SPENT the rest of the sun-drenched day with the Heart's Blood's five. Never a quiet place when dragons were around, the oasis also hummed with the *pick-buzz* of insects. Jakkin swatted at them occasionally when they came close, but they were not biters. They preferred the clusters of burnwort to the sheen of perspiration on his skin.

However, the dragons, already full of wort, were ready for play. Forgetting the insects, Jakkin gave the brood his complete attention. He began by romping with them in the water and letting them churn up the bottom of the spring with their strong feet. Then they lay down contentedly, bubbling in the mud. Their sendings were predictably golden with pops of color.

When they were done with their baths, he played catch-me-catch-you, though of course the dragons always caught him. The triplets — Trisss, Trisssha, and Trissskkette — were especially good at this game, figuring out where he was by some sort of mental trisection. They conversed through a series of high-pitched twitterings, so different from the full-throated roars of other dragons, and their sendings were the same: sputters and spatters of colors almost impossible to read. They were always gentle with Jakkin, though accidents did happen. Trisss, especially, bumped into him more than once. His right arm would be black-and-blue in the morning, but as all dragon masters knew: *No bruise, no love.*

Now was the time to test their fires. Dragons grew into their ability to flame and they were surely old enough now.

He called to Sssargon in a sending filled with red shafts of light. *"Give me fire!"*

Sssargon had lain down after the game and now stood reluctantly. Smoke billowed in two thin lines from his nose slits as if he couldn't be bothered to flame.

"Fire!" Jakkin sent again.

The thin lines of smoke fattened a bit, then thinned out again. Sssargon shook his head and lay down.

Jakkin just laughed. Sssargon was rarely one to do anything on command.

He turned to Sssasha, and even before he asked for it, she shot a polite little flame across the narrowest end of the pool. When she abruptly stopped, tiny pieces of ash floated down, looking as if there were bugs congregating on the water.

"Brilliant!" he sent to her, with red skyrockets bursting, though her flame had been just a small controlled burst, nothing brilliant about it at all.

The triplets didn't even bother to answer him, but continued their high twitterings, as if telling a private joke about him.

Jakkin shrugged. Now that he'd made up his mind about the secret, there'd be plenty of time for real training. In fact, all the time in the world.

Finally the dragons all lay down, and Jakkin lay next to them. Because he had no wire brush to clean them with, he burnished their feathery scales with sand. As he worked the sand across the individual scales, he crooned to the dragons one at a time. Then, taking off his shirt, he polished each dragon from tail to nostril slits. First Sssargon, of course, because he demanded it. His running commentary made Jakkin laugh. Then Sssasha, because she never would have asked to be next. And finally, the triplets, until each one thrummed contentedly. The thrumming slipped and slid through their sendings — blue and green ribbons that perfectly reflected the oasis stream.

At last, night came creeping in across the sandy dunes, casting shadows under the water like silent, dark fish. Jakkin put his shirt back on, not caring that it stank of dragon, that it was filthy with mud and sand, that it had been shredded in places by dragon scales. He bedded the dragons down around him and sang them to sleep with an old nursery lullaby.

> *Hush and sleep,*
> *Your fires keep,*
> *Your dreams are deep,*
> *So hush.*

Night is here,
Dark-After near,
But never fear,
So hush.

Sssargon fell asleep almost at once, the membranous second eyelid shuttering across his black eyes. His rest was punctuated with great *hough*ing snores that gusted sand up and around his body. Even asleep, his mind was noisy.

Sssasha settled much more quietly, her body slowing, ears fluttering back and forth, back and forth, the only sign that she was deeply asleep. The sound of her breathing was steady, gentle. Unlike her brother's mind, hers was a silent landscape of rolling hills.

The triplets curled around one another and their breaths made little syncopated popping noises, rather like a strange musical band. It was astonishing that they didn't wake one another. Perhaps it was because they had always slept together, breathed together, even — as far as Jakkin could tell — held the same thoughts, though those thoughts were often unreadable.

He gazed at them all with great affection. Offspring of his beloved red dragon, he couldn't look at them without thinking of her. And of her death — though he pushed that thought away the moment it came to him.

Despite all the noise they made, the sleeping dragons barely stirred. But watching them, Jakkin realized that he was tired, too. In fact, he was exhausted. His right arm ached. Even more, he had to return to the nursery before

Dark-After's cold settled in. Just in case Likkarn was watching for him again.

Standing up quietly, he stretched and yawned. Then he turned and tiptoed away from the oasis so as not to wake the sleeping dragons. *Though probably it would take an explosion to do that!* he told himself.

When he was far enough away so he couldn't possibly disturb them, he headed off over the dunes at a run. *Wait till I tell Akki about today. And about the secret.* He was sure it would lift her spirits, as it had lifted his. At the least it would be an apology between them, without getting into whose fault the argument had been.

As Jakkin waded back through the weir, the cold water turning his thighs to ice, he saw that Akka — the second moon — was all but caught up with her older brother, Akkhan. When they came to the horizon side by side, Dark-After would spill its four-hour bone-chill everywhere.

He had only a little time left to get to the nursery. Shaking his head, he whispered the old bonder prayer, "Slow, Akka, slow, give me time to go."

As Akka's front rim touched her brother's back, a shadow crossed her. It was a dark, sinuous shape flying in a straight trajectory and heading for Sukker's Marsh. There was no mistaking the creature's long snakelike head.

"Drakk!" Shuddering, Jakkin spit out the name. It left a sour taste in his mouth. "Damned dead-eyed egg sucker."

Like any nursery worker, he hated drakks. One alone could destroy a complete nest of dragon's eggs. And there was never just *one* drakk. They lived in colonies high up in the spikka trees. The only thing they were good at was destruction. An adult male drakk could rip off a dragon hatchling's leg with a single swift movement of its razored talons, or eviscerate the hatchling, eating the poor thing from the inside out as it lay dying. Even the youngest drakk could puncture the tough shell of a dragon's egg, sucking out the contents in less than a minute.

Austar would be well rid of them. But they were hard to find, harder to kill.

"Drakk." He spat the word out again.

He wasn't worried about Heart's Blood's brood asleep in the oasis. They were yearlings, and even the smallest of the triplets was three or four times the size of an adult drakk, more than a match for it. Especially since they now had flames.

But for a nurseryman, there was nothing good to be said about drakks. They were a disaster from start to finish. There were hatchlings in the incubarn. And hens ready to lay their eggs. And drakks meant danger for all of them. He would have to let the other nursery folk know. He'd have to tell Likkarn. Tomorrow they'd be hunting drakks for sure. Jakkin shuddered. Hunting drakks was a deadly, dangerous business. *And worm's drool — the smell!*

Passing the incubarn, Jakkin barely heard the pipping sounds of dragonlings inside, sounds that would certainly draw in the drakk. He tested the doors, making sure they were all shut tight. Windows, too. After that, he had no other thought than to spread the word.

When he opened the door of the bondhouse, the angry buzz inside told him that the nursery was already on the alert. A huddle of men in the dining room were hunched over a large map. Likkarn was pointing at a spot on it, jabbing his finger angrily, while the men nodded and talked at the same time.

Slakk came toward Jakkin, a bundle of bedclothes over his arms and a stinger slung across his back. He was dressed in boots and hunting leathers.

"I'm off to the incubarn," he informed Jakkin dourly. "Want to come?" He held the door open. "Errikkin's in bed pretending to sleep. He can't stand the buggers. As if the rest of us loved them. Everyone else will be there, though."

"The incubarn stall windows and doors seem tight," Jakkin told him. "I already checked."

"Can't be too careful. Drakk can slip through a fewmetty bunghole."

Jakkin agreed. "Drakk can slip through anything larger than their heads." He touched the blood score on his cheek. "I want to talk to Akki first, then I'll meet you there." He went past Slakk to the door into the women's corridor.

"Akki? But she's gone." Slakk's tone made it sound as if this were somehow Jakkin's fault.

Jakkin turned back. "*Gone?* What do you mean, she's gone? We've only just got here. We haven't been home a week. Gone where?" Though he could guess. His heart seemed to take an extra, stuttering beat in his chest. He was sure Slakk wasn't lying. Slakk's eyes got round and big when he told a lie.

Slakk shrugged. "She grabbed a ride with a big truck going to The Rokk. Driver was tough-looking. Had stayed here overnight. In the big house. Like a visitor. Shaggy black hair. Deep scar." His hand described a hole like a well. "Kay supposedly knew him, or had asked him to come. Or something like that. But *I* wouldn't have gone anywhere with him. And I'm not a girl."

"Thanks for explaining that to me," Jakkin said. He rubbed the scar on his wrist, thinking. *That* description could fit a dozen different men. Slakk wasn't the most observant person.

"When did she go?" he asked.

"This morning, right after we were in the stud barn." Slakk put his head to one side and stared at Jakkin. "At least that's what Errikkin said."

"Why didn't you tell me then?" Jakkin's voice trembled. "I could have stopped her." Though he wondered if she would have listened.

"I didn't know *then*, Jakkin." Slakk turned away toward the door. "Errikkin told me later, as if it was a huge joke. Which I thought it was, at first." He said over his shoulder, "And after, when I knew it *wasn't* a joke, I couldn't find you." He stopped, his brow furrowing like the sands by the oasis after a rush of wind. "Where *were* you?"

Jakkin didn't bother answering, because his head was filled with Akki's name. He cried silently, the sending going farther than any he'd ever tried. Out the door, past the incubarns where several sleeping dragons answered him back with a wail of color. Past the weir, over the sands.

He couldn't believe she'd leave without telling him, without discussing it, without asking him to go along.

Akki . . . Maybe it was a last-minute decision, because the truck was here. Maybe she tried to find him. Maybe it was because he'd said they didn't need to do anything, just keep the secret, which he'd only said at the time because he was angry with her. *Well, not angry, exactly, but hurt.* And now he truly believed it was the right thing to do: say nothing, do nothing. But she'd gone, anyway, without a word. And all the time, he'd been playing with Heart's Blood's brood while Akki was leaving in a truck. He cursed himself for being away then, out of sight, out of hearing, out of sending range.

Akki . . . Maybe she left because he'd gone off into the oasis without telling her. Or maybe she resented the fact that he loved being back at the nursery, working with the dragons, while she had the more important and harder job of finding out how to save them all. Well, he could tell her now she didn't have to worry, didn't have to go. Could come home.

Akki . . . The sending was a red arrow, bound about with gold ribbons, a burst of red fire as bright as dragon's gout, a spray of hot dragon's blood bleeding out of his brain. It traveled along the roadway, north to Krakkow and on past to the great city of The Rokk, which was probably where she was going. *Akkiiiiiiiiiiii.*

Anyone with dragon's ears could have heard it, the pain of it so sharp and true. But wherever Akki was, she was too far away to hear. Too far away to know how hurt he felt.

And how betrayed.

☾ 13 ☾

AKKI'S ROOM, which she had shared with Vonikka and Larkki, was at the rear of the bondhouse. The others who inhabited the women's area of the bondhouse were Nakkie and Lakkina, who tended the nursery gardens, and of course little Terakkina, who had her own small room. Kkarina's own suite of rooms was nestled near the kitchen. The rest of the women were paired with men and stayed in other corridors.

When Jakkin got to Akki's room, its door was ajar. He ducked in, looking around for some sign that Slakk had been mistaken. Or had lied. It was not beyond Slakk to lie for effect, or to elaborate on something he'd only half seen or heard. He'd even played a cruel joke or two in his time.

Though the room was a mess of girl stuff — brushes, flower sachets, baubles, rings — it was empty of anything he could identify as Akki's. Hair comb, color bands she put around her braid, even the brush — all were gone. Jakkin remembered that she'd been wearing a gold band at breakfast. And gold was her happy color.

Happy because she was already planning to go? He felt a sudden heaviness in his belly, as if a stone lodged there. But when could she have made plans? *We've been back less than a week. She said nothing to me about plans to leave.*

Jakkin left the room and went down the corridor, slipped through the door and into the men's wing of the bondhouse. He headed directly to the room he shared with the boys.

As Slakk had said, Errikkin was in his bunk, face to the wall, under a blanket, pretending to sleep. But Jakkin could tell that his breathing was irregular, not slow and even, every third breath held, as if expecting a blow.

"So you're not going to help out on the drakk hunt?" Jakkin tried to keep his voice calm, but failed.

Errikkin didn't stir, though his breathing began to speed up.

Still furious about Akki's betrayal, Jakkin grabbed the blanket and ripped it off Errikkin. "What's wrong with you? Why are you acting this way? I thought we were friends." The stone in his belly seemed to jump, and he felt a sharp pain in his chest as if the stone now lodged in his heart.

With slow reluctance, Errikkin turned over. His usually handsome face was blanched and ugly with rage. He said with slow deliberation, "We were friends a year ago. *A year.* I thought you were dead. We had a funeral for you. I mourned. I missed you. I got over it."

"You led the wardens right to us, Errikkin. You mourned because you felt guilty. That's hardly my fault. I forgave you long ago. I got over *that!*"

But Errikkin refused to hear him, saying instead in a low, steady voice, "You chose Akki over me."

"That's not fair . . ." Jakkin began. *But true,* he thought. *And why would I ever have chosen you?*

Errikkin turned back, saying in a voice so low Jakkin almost missed it, "Besides, they don't need me for hunting drakks. Not right now, anyway. The hunt can't start till tomorrow."

All right — act that way. Jakkin threw the bunched blanket back onto the bed at Errikkin's feet. *We'll never speak of that old, dead friendship again.* He kept his voice equally low and deliberate. "Some of us will be in the incubarn tonight. Keeping watch. Why not come out there?"

Errikkin didn't move. He'd already turned his back on Jakkin, on the room, on the conversation. "I hope you get a good night's sleep out there among the fewmetty dragons and their stink. I'll make do with a real bed."

Stunned by Errikkin's tone, Jakkin gathered up his own bedclothes in one great swoop and hung them around his neck. As he left the room, Errikkin's final words kept resounding in his head. What had he meant? Did he so hate dragons? Or the nursery folk?

Or just me?

～

THE DINING HALL was empty, so Jakkin grabbed a set of leathers and a stinger from the table. He walked quickly out the bondhouse door, and raced through the growing Dark-After. The night was already black, and the cold ran across his body in rivers. Though that didn't bother him, Jakkin didn't dare take his time getting to the incubarn. He had to act as if the cold were brutal and likely fatal if he didn't move fast enough.

The door of the barn had stiffened in the cold, but at last he managed to open it a crack, and while it squalled its protest, he slipped inside. Once again, the heat of the place hit him like a fist.

"Lucky you didn't freeze out there," young Arakk commented, closing the door after Jakkin with a shove of his shoulder.

"Dark-After's only just starting," Jakkin pointed out. "And I had enough blankets and stuff around me to keep me warm for that short dash."

"Yeah — that much cold would make me run fast, too," Arakk said, laughing.

His sunny response made Jakkin smile. Then he walked down to the end of the incubarn, where he peered into Auricle's stall.

"Hello, thou pretty girl," he whispered once he was inside, sending her a shower of gold circles. But halfway down, the shower turned blue, looking more like teardrops. The dragon looked up with her unreadable black eyes.

Glancing around quickly, Jakkin noticed that something was wrong. It took him a moment to realize that the hatchling was gone. He dumped his bedding in the stall. Going over to Auricle, he put a hand on either side of her great head and looked into the black shrouds of her eyes.

"Where is thy hatchling?" he asked, though the hatchling was only hers by adoption.

She sent him a picture of a hand cradling the hatchling. A hand with a gold band around the wrist.

Akki.

"Akki has the hatchling?"

Auricle crowded him, licking his cheek. Her rough tongue nearly took the skin off. She sent him the same picture: hand, gold band, hatchling.

Why would she take the hatchling?

Once again he felt cold. Not the cold of outside, but a different, duller, aching cold. As if the place that had been home was suddenly something else. And the person he'd loved more than anyone had turned into a stranger. *She'd only take the hatchling if she's not planning to come back.*

"I'll stay here with thee tonight, girl," Jakkin told the dragon. "After I find out the men's plans. When I return, you and I will talk."

As he left the stall, Auricle's sending answered him. It was a soft picture of Akki's face, her long dark hair wrapping her like a shawl. *"Girl safe. Boy safe. Dragon safe."*

Safe? He didn't answer. He didn't know what to say.

~

THE OTHERS were in the main room of the barn, where buyers were taken while awaiting a tour of the latest hatchlings. The visitors' room was the one comfortable place in the incubarn, with soft chairs and a three-person sofa covered in multicolored eggskin.

A window overlooked the courtyard and Jakkin saw in one quick glance that Dark-After had settled in for the night, spreading itself into every niche and nook and cavity, like old Kkarina in a chair. Balakk was just closing the heavy wooden shutters to help keep out the cold.

In front of the window, arms on his hips, staring out with anger at the blackness, stood Likkarn. Around him, sprawled on the chairs, sofas, floor, the boys and men of Sarkkhan's Nursery seemed uneasy as they awaited their instructions. No women — not even Vonikka and Larkki — had been allowed in the hunt. *Too dangerous,* Jakkin supposed, *though no more dangerous than all that Akki has been through.*

Jakkin's entrance into the room stirred them all into action. Some got up, some simply stretched. Balakk began to speak to Arakk, who listened with quiet intensity.

But Likkarn stopped them all simply by turning around and holding up his right hand. Sudden silence filled the overheated room.

"How many have gone on a drakk hunt before?" Likkarn asked.

Jakkin understood that Likkarn asked the question simply to focus everyone's attention on him. He already knew the answer, as they all did.

Several hands went up. Jakkin slowly raised his own. He remembered that one drakk hunt all too well. How frightened he'd been, sweating out his fear into his leathers. But that fright was long over and what was left to him was an instinctive hatred of drakks.

"Good," Likkarn said. "We will need you on the actual hunt. But tonight . . ."

Tonight we have to guard the barn, with its new crop of hatchlings. All of the men would be needed for tonight. Jakkin thought angrily of Errikkin tucked up comfortably in his bed. Looking around, Jakkin realized that every other man and boy from the nursery was here. Surely Likkarn would note Errikkin's absence and say something in the morning. But tonight — tonight they were one guard short and that might make all the difference.

Balakk gave out the masks first. "Snap these on to your jerkins. The smell of a drakk — especially a dead drakk — can be overpowering. Don't be embarrassed to use the masks. Trust me. Strong men have passed out from the stink, especially in an enclosed space."

A small ripple of laughter ran around the room, and Kkitakk said, "You weren't all that strong, my friend."

"I am now," Balakk answered.

Laughter once again rippled around the room, only this time the men looked pointedly at Balakk, who began to blush.

"I was a boy! *A boy!*" he protested.

Likkarn raised his hand again. "Take the masks." It was the end of the laughter.

Having already had a run-in with the stench of a dead drakk outdoors, Jakkin was not eager to be in a closed room with one, so he took the proffered mask eagerly.

Then Balakk handed them each a long knife with a straight blade and bone handle. "We don't dare

use extinguishers — that's sting-guns for you new boys —
within the barn for fear of setting the straw bedding on fire.

"Or hitting a hatchling — or a dragon," Balakk added.

"Or each other," Kkitakk remarked.

Frankkalin laughed. "There speaks the worst shot in
the nursery."

"Not any worse than you!"

"How many times did you hit the tree instead of the
drakk?"

They were referring to drakk hunts long past, so Jakkin
snuggled down on the floor, his back against the sofa.

"More importantly," Balakk added, "we have to save
the power packs as much as we can. With this fewmetty embargo, it may be years before we get any new ones." He
paused. "If ever." His face was no longer blushing and almost seemed to light up with the thought. Like Slakk, he
reveled in bad news.

Nodding, Likkarn told them, "We're working on finding new ways to recharge the packs, as is every nursery
crew on the planet. There is a building in The Rokk
dedicated to the work. What scientists we still have get
shipped there."

Akki . . . Jakkin felt cold. *So he's sent Akki there. Without asking me. Without telling me. Without* . . . But if true, it
meant she hadn't gone on her own. It was all Likkarn's
fault. He should have guessed.

"But for now, we use the knives," Likkarn finished.

Balakk added, "In small spaces they're best, anyway."

Everyone agreed.

But Jakkin was thinking, *Extinguishers. Stingers.* It would be a hardship indeed when they could no longer use them against the drakks. *Maybe Likkarn was right to send Akki to The Rokk.* Knives meant close work. With a stinger, a man would be outside the reach of a drakk's sharp talons. *And if Akki is with other scientists, maybe it will be easier to . . .* He wiped the thought from his head. *Without Akki, nothing is easier.*

Slakk raised a hand. "Do we work in pairs?"

"We do." Likkarn took a roster from his vest and showed it around. Though few of them could actually read, Jakkin could. He found his own name even before Likkarn said, "Slakk — you and Jakkin are in the back stalls, with the new dragon, Auricle, and her hatchling. Be especially watchful there. Things aren't as tight in the rear of the building. There might be some holes. Jakkin did well on our last drakk hunt. Slakk, follow his lead."

Jakkin could hardly believe his ears. A compliment from Likkarn! And then he realized that Likkarn thought the hatchling was still in Auricle's stall. *But if he sent Akki to The Rokk, he would know about the little dragon.* Confused, he put it down to forgetfulness on Likkarn's part. After all, the old man was surely in his fifties already.

He glanced over at Slakk who was steadily gazing at the floor. He wondered if Slakk considered being on guard with him a good thing, or a bad one. Slakk always managed to get out of the hard jobs, and his partners always had to do twice the work. Not like Akki, who always did more than her share.

Not like Akki . . .

He turned back. Likkarn was still speaking.

". . . do some work several months ago," Likkarn was saying, "where a dragon — it was that scamp, Bloody Mess — who had scraped away a hole, going after some wort growing outside. There may be areas we've missed." He handed out small leather bags to everyone. Jakkin recognized them — they were old bond bags. His hand went automatically to his chest.

"Use the nails in these bags if you find any loose boards," Likkarn said. "Hammer them in with the handle of your knife.

"Balakk," Likkarn continued, his voice tightly controlled, "you take Arakk and Frankkalin and Kkitakk, here, and the four of you patrol the new hatchling area, sleeping two on and two off."

They nodded.

"Atkkin, Tolekk, Trikko, you stay here with me. The rest of you will be with the broodless hens. In pairs." He read them off by twos.

Likkarn probably ordered Akki into the truck with that same sharp tone. Jakkin gritted his teeth. *Even though she wanted to find me to say good-bye.* He stopped, ran his hand through his hair, thought again. *But then he would have seen the hatchling in her arms.* No, that didn't make any sense. Maybe he was wrong. Or partially wrong.

Still, Akki could have sent him a farewell, with roses and blue skies and balloons and . . . She could have sent something and she hadn't. *Why?*

His heart was thudding again. *Why?*

Everyone stood, and Arakk was already at the door into the corridor when Likkarn growled, "Wait!"

Everyone waited.

"Remember to come at drakks from behind." He paused. "*Never* assume a drakk is dead." He put a finger to the side of his nose, his face grim.

Balakk interrupted. "Knew a man once, who . . ."

Laughing, Arakk finished for him, in a fair imitation of his drawl, ". . . had his leg nearly took off by a drakk he thought a goner." His hand smacked his leg above the knee. His moon face seemed to split in two as he grinned at everyone.

They all laughed then, even Balakk, whose normally dour face was almost handsome when he smiled.

Angry as he was at Likkarn, at Akki, at himself, Jakkin laughed, too. The laughter went a long way toward breaking the tension in the room. Then each man and boy trotted off to his appointed place.

~

AURICLE WAS SNORING, a deep frothy sound, when Jakkin and Slakk reached her.

"Maybe we should check the empty stalls first," Jakkin said.

"There are five," Slakk pointed out.

"Two for you, three for me." Jakkin spoke before Slakk could complain. "And I'll do Auricle's as well." Anything to keep his mind off Akki's desertion with the hatchling.

And Likkarn's complicity in sending her off. And Errikkin's dismissal of their friendship. And the difficulty of working with Slakk. And most of all, the possibility of finding a drakk. "Then I'll take first watch. Of course, if Errikkin were here . . ."

Without a change of expression, Slakk said, "We'd have had to babysit him. Best he stays away." Then he nodded at Jakkin and set off toward the two left-hand stalls.

"Of course," Jakkin muttered to himself, "Slakk *would* take the smallest ones." He turned into the stall closest to Auricle's and started his search.

Crawling along the base of the stall and looking especially at the outside wall, he tapped the boards with the handle of his big knife. The boards seemed solid and snugged right down into the ground. There was not even a whisper of air coming through them, nor the cold of Dark-After sneaking in.

"Tight." He nodded with satisfaction.

The second stall seemed just as solid.

In the third stall, he found a single loose board and hammered it shut with three well-placed nails. Then he packed extra dirt around the bottom of the board, stomping it down with his sandal. He promised himself to check it often.

Finally, he went into Auricle's stall. She'd slept through the hammering and the whispered conversations with Slakk and all the to-ing and fro-ing. He guessed she could probably sleep through the end of the world. When he slid into her mind, it was all muzzy, a kind of purposeful gray landscape.

Checking around her stall, Jakkin found the boards tight, though her tail lay against part of the back wall and he couldn't get her to wake in order to check behind. Any drakk willing to chance a full-grown dragon was a dead drakk, anyway. However, there was always the possibility that a dragon's fiery breath could set the whole incubarn aflame.

Always something else to worry about, he thought. But he let Auricle sleep.

And soon after, he let Slakk sleep as well. As promised, Jakkin took the first watch himself.

☾ 14 ☾

THE FIRST COUPLE of hours were quiet with only a few hammering sounds coming from down the corridor and the occasional pipping of hatchlings. Jakkin walked through the stalls, checking and rechecking the walls and floors. When he found himself beginning to yawn, he woke Slakk.

"Your watch."

"Already?" Slakk said without much conviction and a whine in his voice. With Slakk, every conversation started with a complaint, and Jakkin knew better than to argue. *But why is Slakk still around?*

"You used to say," Jakkin began, his voice pitched low, "that when you bought yourself out of bond, you'd never work with dragons again. Yet here you are, a free man and still at the dragon nursery."

Slakk shrugged but didn't answer. It seemed as if he was not yet awake enough to talk.

However, that shrug told Jakkin everything. Slakk's complaints were simply part of his personality. And after all, what else did Slakk know but dragons? At the nursery he had three meals a day and a warm place to sleep. If he got sick, there was the hospice. If he got old, he could help in the kitchen. If he pair-bonded — though Jakkin could hardly believe anyone would put up with his constant complaining — there was special housing for couples. Jakkin shrugged back, keeping his own silence.

They changed places, Slakk standing, stretching, scratching behind his shoulder, making soft grunting noises, occasionally wandering into the various stalls assigned to them.

Jakkin took the blanket and went into Auricle's stall, where he lay down close to her for warmth, though the barn was certainly warm enough already. But the familiarity of lying close to a dragon was comforting. Shutting his eyes, he was fast asleep within moments, snoring lightly.

He dreamed of Akki, not as she'd been in the caves or in the great city of The Rokk, nor as she'd looked out in the oasis back when he'd first trained Heart's Blood. The dream took place where he first met her, in the hospice, her black hair hanging straight down her back, her generous mouth laughing at him, as she nursed him back to health.

Why did you leave? he asked her in the dream.

To save the dragons, she answered, holding up the hatchling by its tail.

Why did you leave? he asked a second time.

To save the dragons, she answered, holding up a full bond bag. She shook it and it rang with the sound of coins.

Why did you leave? he asked a third time.

She began to scream.

Jakkin woke, startled, his heart beating wildly. Oddly, the screaming continued even though he was wide awake, staring into the dark. The screaming wasn't just out loud, but in his head, too, accompanied by a series of horrible images: blood-red rivers, bones piercing through skin.

Suddenly he realized that Akki wasn't doing the screaming. Slakk was. And there was an awful smell in the barn.

Drakk! Jakkin reached for the mask that was still attached to his vest. The smell was everywhere and the mask did little to filter it out. The stench was overpowering. He wanted to vomit. *But not in the mask!* he warned himself. *Not in the mask.*

Leaping to his feet, Jakkin grabbed his knife and stumbled toward the stall door, but his feet tangled in the blanket and he nearly fell forward, cursing loudly. "Fewmets! Worm waste!"

Now Auricle was standing behind him and screaming as well, rocking back and forth, her voice high-pitched, her sendings frantic, huge, streaking lightning bolts plowing through a muddy sea.

Righting himself, Jakkin stepped out of the tangle of blanket, and turned. *"Lie down, thou beauty."* He meant it to be calming, encouraging, but it came out as an order.

Auricle was used to orders. She lay down.

Turning back, Jakkin rushed through the door, looking around till he found Slakk in one of the two smaller stalls he'd claimed as his own sleeping room. He was on his knees, shaking, covered with blood.

"Slakk!" Jakkin cried, his voice filtered oddly through the mask.

Slakk looked up, screaming silently, his eyes wide open, haunted. His mouth gaped. He kept sending gouts of blood and flame into Jakkin's brain.

A sending? Jakkin was sure of it. *But how?*

In front of Slakk was a female drakk, rather small, but deadly nonetheless. Even a tiny drakk could open a man up, spilling out blood, bone, intestines.

This drakk, however, was dying. Jakkin could hear her pain, her anger, her astonishment. She had a gaping hole in her belly and a slash ringing her neck, so wide that her oily green snake head lay half off. But still she kept moving, gashing the air with her vicious talons. Each time she lifted those talons, her wings lifted as well, disclosing scabrous sensor organs that pulsed like a beating heart. In her opened belly lay a clutch of white eggs.

A female. A young breeding female. Jakkin shuddered. Likkarn wouldn't like that.

Slakk's hand clutching the knife slashed down again, this time smashing the eggs. He screamed as his fingers touched the hot blood that pooled in the drakk's wounds. Then, as if waking from a nightmare, he looked down at the horror in front of him and tried to scrabble back from it. Whimpering, he held his knife hand against his chest. The drakk's hot blood must have scorched his hand. Suddenly he began crawling backward, all the while continuing to howl.

"Slakk!" Jakkin called, but Slakk didn't seem to understand him. So Jakkin walked carefully around the dying drakk and bent down, trying to take the knife away from

Slakk before he hurt himself with it. Slakk wouldn't loosen his hold on the bone handle. He was weeping loudly now and babbling, though Jakkin could make no sense of what he was saying.

There was a sudden movement in the stall behind them. Turning swiftly, Jakkin brought up his own knife and looked around frantically, his entire arm trembling.

"There, lads." It was Balakk, with Likkarn next to him, their masks securely fastened over their noses. They'd come to check on the noise.

Likkarn stepped around the drakk and, with a swift purposeful slice, cut the drakk's head off. Then, with his boot, he kicked the back of the creature's body, which sent it sailing over to the side of the stall.

The stench was now overpowering. Jakkin gagged, then fought down the impulse to throw up. *Not in the mask! Not in . . .* Grabbing off the mask, he vomited so hard into the straw, bits actually came out of his nose as well. Wiping his mouth and nose with his sleeve, he replaced his mask. His stomach was no longer roiling, but now he was having trouble breathing and his mouth felt as if he'd been eating fewmets.

Balakk and Likkarn ignored him. Instead they searched around the stall, rechecking every bit of it carefully — walls, floor, and joins.

Once his nausea had passed, Jakkin helped them in their hunt, though Slakk remained sitting on the straw-covered floor, rocking back and forth, his damaged hand cradled against his body.

Eventually Balakk found a small loose floorboard through which the drakk must have crawled. Slakk had missed that on his inspection, and for a brief moment, Jakkin thought he deserved what he'd got. But only for a moment. Slakk looked so miserable and hurt crouching there, not far from the drakk's awful head, that without thinking, Jakkin sent him a comforting ribbon of light.

Slakk never noticed.

I must have been mistaken about that sending. But it had been so loud, so definite.

Balakk hammered seven nails into the board. He would have kept going, but Likkarn bent over and laid a hand on his shoulder.

"It's almost all iron and no wood now," he told Balakk in a soft voice.

"That will do," Balakk said at last. "That will do." And he stood.

They made another round of the stall but found no more loose boards, no holes in the floor. All the while, the smell continued to get worse. Even Auricle, three stalls away, complained, sending Jakkin pictures of bilious gray-green mud, popping and splattering.

Only after the men were sure of the stall did they check Slakk, who was now just whimpering. Balakk placed the mask over his face and patted his shoulder, though Slakk responded to that no more than he had to Jakkin's sending.

"I should have put the mask on him," Jakkin said.

"You had other things to think about, boy, as did we," Balakk told him, though Jakkin wasn't sure if he was referring to his getting sick or his looking about for the hole the drakk had come through.

"We can't get him to the hospice until Dark-After is done," Likkarn said. "Another few hours." He looked at Jakkin carefully. "But at least we can take him out of here. The smell alone will kill him."

"Or me," Jakkin said. The nausea had returned and he fought it down. He didn't want to throw up again, though he doubted there was anything much left in his stomach.

"Or any of us," Balakk added.

"Will you watch him, keep him warm?" Likkarn asked.

Jakkin had never heard the old bonder speak in such soft tones. "It's already warm," he said. He was sweating in his leathers.

"He'll be in shock, chilling. Keep a blanket around him. Bed him down near your Auricle, if she'll have him with that smell. Otherwise, you lie down by his side. He'll need it."

Jakkin shrugged.

"Only get that fewmetty knife away from him first."

"I'll send Arakk back here to take turns with you," Balakk said.

Jakkin nodded. He looked over his shoulder at the drakk's body. Even without a head it was still moving sluggishly.

Likkarn said gruffly, "That piece of worm waste must have been desperate for food."

"She had eggs in her belly," Jakkin told him.

"Ah. That explains it."

"Slakk smashed them."

Likkarn nodded. "Good boy."

They got Slakk to his feet, though he wouldn't let go of

the knife, and led him as far from the little stall as possible. The stench followed them. Slakk had been drenched in the drakk's blood.

Auricle screamed when they came near, reacting to both the smell and the blood. *And possibly the knife, too.* She hackled as well, the back scales of her neck rising up like a small fan. No amount of sendings could quiet her, so they moved Slakk into a different stall, an empty one, halfway back down the corridor.

"When you can," Balakk whispered to Jakkin, "get the knife and wash it off with sand." There were boxes of sand along the corridors. Sand was always available to help clean out stalls. "Otherwise the blade will be eaten away by the blood."

"I will." Jakkin was actually more worried about Slakk suddenly using the knife on him than he was about blood eroding the blade. "I will," he repeated.

"And as soon as it's light, you can get him back to the bondhouse, and a bath for both of you." Balakk talked about them as he would a dragon.

"I wish it could be now," Jakkin said, his skin already itching for hot water and yellow soap. He could do it alone, could get back to the nursery house through the cold of Dark-After, but that would give away the secret. And it wouldn't help Slakk at all.

WHEN THE MEN finally left him alone with Slakk, Jakkin stared at his friend as if he'd never seen him before. The boy's face, gray and sunken, had only begun to soften, though that somehow made him look worse than ever. His hand clutching the knife, though, had not relaxed at all and was still tight around the handle.

"It's all right, Slakk," Jakkin said to him in the same soft tone he'd used with the hackling worm. "You're a hero. You can sleep now. Give me the knife."

Slakk said nothing, but held on to the knife till his knuckles turned white. He kept shuddering like a young dragon.

Jakkin remembered how Slakk had managed a sending — the blood-red rivers, the bones, that scream. *Or did I only dream it?* Jakkin wondered.

No, he may have been asleep at first, but he'd been wide awake when Slakk sent the blood and flames. And if Slakk could send and Likkarn could receive sendings . . . *I need to find Akki as soon as possible, to tell her. It may be important.* He put a hand on Slakk's shoulder. "There, there," he said, trying to find his way back into Slakk's mind. He sent a calm river, a long meadow of green grass, then waited.

Nothing.

He tried again, this time sending a rainbow, all bright and cheery and easily picked up. But Slakk's mind was closed to him, and no amount of nudging and pushing could get it to open again.

"Never mind," Jakkin said, still speaking in soft tones. He led Slakk to a corner of the stall, where he might feel protected on three sides. Putting a blanket over Slakk's shoulders, Jakkin knelt and tucked it around Slakk's knees.

All the while he crooned, "There, there, there," as if talking to a hatchling instead of a seventeen-year-old boy.

Just then Jakkin heard a strange sound and looked up. Slakk was weeping and the knife had fallen to one side.

"I'll hold on to this," Jakkin said, grabbing up the knife. Slakk made no protest. "You sleep. I'll stand guard the rest of the night."

Without any nod of agreement, or word to show that he'd understood, or even an acknowledging grunt, Slakk closed his eyes.

Jakkin couldn't tell if Slakk was actually asleep or only pretending. But true to his word, he stood over Slakk until Dark-After was done and the bell for morning rang through the incubarn, signaling day.

☾ 15 ☾

THE BATH took almost an hour and — hot water followed
by cold — Jakkin still didn't feel clean. The drakk stench
lingered on his hands and in his hair. He could taste it each
time he swallowed.

And if he was bad, Slakk was worse, coughing frothily
as Jakkin scrubbed his wrists where the drakk blood had
soaked through the gap between leather and shirt. Then the
cough turned deep, sounding like a death rattle. Of course
it was really only his lungs trying to clear themselves of the
drakk smell. Or so Balakk explained afterward.

Between them, Balakk and Jakkin got Slakk out of the
bath and to the hospice, though it was clear that he hadn't
been badly injured. A bit of burn on one hand was the worst
of it. But he hadn't said a word to any of them since the
drakk attack. Every now and then he whimpered piteously.
And kept on coughing.

They left him at the hospice, with a visiting doctor from
the nearest dragon nursery in attendance. Evidently Likkarn
himself had been up at first light to drive off to fetch him.

"Don't worry," said the doctor, a man with a series of blood scores on his right cheek and neck. "A bit of rest, a bit of feeding-up should do him."

"That doctor knows more about dragons than men," Balakk said as they walked out into the sunshine. "It's the same thing he says when he looks at failing studs. 'A bit of feeding-up should do him.' He's an old fraud." He spit to one side, raising dust by the walk.

Jakkin laughed, a short sharp hough of a laugh, but remembered how it had taken days for him to adjust after his drakk hunt. And he'd never had his hands deep inside a drakk like Slakk had. "Will Slakk be all right?"

"Slakk his name and slack his mind. His body will be fine, though he'll have scars," Balakk said, which was not what Jakkin wanted to hear.

～

AS SOON AS they'd grabbed some breakfast they joined the drakk hunters.

"We don't go hunting on an empty stomach," Likkarn warned. "No food, no form." It was what was usually said about fighting dragons before they were taken to fight in the pits. It was the same thing for this drakk hunt.

For once the dining room was quiet. Jakkin was glad of that. His mind was abuzz with everything that had happened. He couldn't have stood being further burdened by talk.

The hunters sat to one side, guzzling their takk and mint tea, and no one else in the room asked questions. It was as if the seriousness of the hunt ahead silenced them all.

Kkarina came into the room a half dozen times, on tiptoe, which — given her bulk — was pretty amazing. It was a kind of rolling walk, yet graceful. *Like Sssasha,* Jakkin thought. She never spilled a drop of the takk — or the tea — as she refilled cups. The slabs of lizard meat were eaten without a word said. Jakkin had three eggs, which he pushed around the plate, finally eating one because he had to. Even though it wasn't true, everything smelled of drakk to him.

At last the hunters were done eating and rose as a group, taking turns going to the johnnyloo. Then they met outside, where they formed two lines behind Likkarn and Balakk.

"Check your equipment now," Likkarn warned them. "There'll be no time to do it once we spot a drakk."

They each took a moment to look over their leathers, their masks, their knives and stingers. Jakkin put his right hand to his knife, checked the mask with his left. Thankfully it was a new mask and didn't stink. There weren't enough stingers to go around, and he — like Arakk and Tanekk, both about his own age — went without, having to rely only on his knife. *Well, Slakk did fine with just a knife.* But no matter how strongly he thought it, Jakkin couldn't convince himself. He felt vulnerable without a stinger, though he'd never actually used one and had no time to learn.

"We need to be well prepared, lads," Likkarn told them. "You all know what happened in the incubarn last night. If there are other females ready to lay eggs, we won't just have a drakk problem, we'll have a drakk *invasion.*"

There was muttered agreement from all of them. Jakkin bit his lip, imagining dozens of drakks swarming up through loose boards in the incubarn.

"That means we must be prepared up here as well," Likkarn added, touching a finger to his temple. His scarred face was fierce, the dead eye like an immovable white light, and he looked as if he were ready to take on the drakks all by himself.

How do we do that? Jakkin wondered. *How do we prepare ourselves mentally?* He thought about Slakk in the hospice, about Auricle screaming her distress, about the beheaded drakk still moving sluggishly in the sand of the stall. *Stop thinking so much!* He wasn't preparing himself mentally, he was *un*-preparing.

But how was he to stop thinking so much when he kept flashing back to the one drakk hunt he'd been part of, more than a year earlier? Just remembering made his stomach churn again. He wondered if the other hunters felt this way, for many of them had been on that same hunt. In fact, many of them had been on more than one such hunt. When he glanced around, all he saw on *their* faces was a kind of grim determination. Likkarn with his eyes narrowed, Balakk moving his jaw left to right over and over again, Kkitakk rubbing a gloved hand across his face. Even Frankkalin seemed grimly ready, hawking a great glob of spit onto the sand and rubbing it in with the toe of his sandal. The other men were equally stolid.

However, the boys did not look so sure. Rather, they were wide-eyed, clearly fearful. Arakk, normally the sunniest of the group, was breathing too fast, his round face white, like the foam on the top of waves. There were only two spots of color on his cheeks, as if he had a fever. Then suddenly he looked up at the sky and screamed, "Drakk! Drakk! Drakk!" while jerking his fist up at the red sun, to give himself courage. To give *all* of them courage.

Likkarn watched him for a minute, eyes narrowing even further. At last, he said quietly, "Let's go."

They started down the road, heading toward the nearest stand of spikka trees, which was where drakk normally roosted. This copse was not more than two kilometers from the nursery.

"We should have cut those trees down last year," Likkarn said to Balakk, but loud enough for all of them to hear, "when we found that family of drakk nesting there."

Balakk shook his head. "Trees hold water," he said, reminding Likkarn what they all knew: in a desert area, trees are vital to keep a place alive.

Likkarn grunted an answer. But Jakkin understood that the old nurseryman was actually agreeing with Balakk. As did they all. Without water, there could be no dragon nursery. What was having to hunt drakks now and again compared to living in a desert empty of life?

They walked on in silence, though the sound of their boots crunching on the sandy road was a comment all its own.

Jakkin listened carefully to the *pick-buzz* of insects whose tiny minds hardly registered in his brain. He received hasty flitting sendings from the many little mottled brown lizards as they skittered away from the marching men. But he heard nothing from any drakks. Either they were nesting elsewhere, farther away, or they were mindless — which he didn't believe for a moment, remembering the female drakk's pain, anger, astonishment.

Or perhaps they have a way of shielding their thoughts. Like the trogs did in their caves. As Akki and he had learned to do when they had been prisoners of the trogs. Building a thought wall, slowly, with care, not only a good idea for a prisoner, but a good idea for a predator, as well.

Belatedly, he realized that he hadn't had any warning in the incubarn before the drakk had come through the loose board. Not a peep in his head, not a single sending. If only Akki were still around, he'd have discussed that with her. For a moment he considered asking Likkarn, but that would have given away part of the secret. He would have to puzzle this out on his own.

Just as he was thinking, a tenuous band of color threaded through his mind.

"Sssargon help. Sssargon come."

Sssargon . . .

"No!" Jakkin sent back a wave of color, a wall of it. *"Sssargon, stay where you are. You'll scare them away."* He pictured the drakk, their snaky heads hissing.

An answer, almost like a snore, was returned to him. *"Sssargon listens. Sssargon stays."* He sounded almost relieved. Like a winged Slakk.

Jakkin grinned. *Sssargon and Slakk — what a combination!* He was careful to guard his thoughts. *The last thing I need is to have to deal with Sssargon's idea of helping. He'd set the entire copse of trees ablaze, and then expect applause.*

~

THEY ARRIVED at the spikka trees quickly, downwind of the copse, and with a minimum of fuss. They'd all been warned: drakk had bad ears and eyes but were excellent scent predators. It was important to keep them from smelling their human hunters.

The copse was large, even by Austar standards, about forty tall spikka trees, fed by an underground stream flowing from Sukker's Marsh. The spongy ground made walking difficult, and noisy — for each time they lifted a foot to move on, there was a loud sucking sound.

Making a cutting motion across his neck, Likkarn pointed to the treetops. Everyone understood: no mercy to any drakks, whatever age.

The male drakks usually squatted on the tops of trees during their rut season and were therefore fairly easy to spot. Jakkin had seen none on their march to the woods, and Likkarn and Balakk had pointed out nothing, so he assumed there were no males around. If rut was over and nesting had begun, the males would have flown off to the mountains. They never stayed around the nesting sites. The females wouldn't let them. Male drakks would just as happily suck the contents of their own eggs as dragon eggs. *Not great fathers!*

But just because there were no males around, the hunters couldn't relax. After all, the females were trickier, hiding in their nests, hard to see. They'd have to be shaken down, and the drakklings — if there were any — tipped out of the nests and killed on the ground. That was in some ways the most dangerous job of all.

Jakkin hoped there were no hatchlings yet. Females on a nest of babies were merciless. The female killed in the incubarn had been full of unlaid eggs. *Maybe that's a good sign. Maybe all the females are off their nests and no eggs yet to be sat upon.* But he didn't dare believe it. The female killed by Slakk had been young. And hungry. If drakks were anything like dragons, the young females, first-timers, always laid their eggs late. It was the older females who went early. And that could mean there were already drakklings in the treetop nests.

Likkarn pointed at three hunters. They were to go left with him, four to remain, four more to move to the right. There was a boy in each group. They would be the climbers. The men and larger boys were simply too heavy to scramble up the spikka trunks, for the trees narrowed drastically at the top. Since every single tree in the copse had to be climbed and searched for a nest, it was up to the lighter boys to do that job.

This meant that he and Arakk and Tanekk would be doing the climbing, though Jakkin was almost too big to take on the job. In fact, pound for pound, he was probably bigger than old Likkarn. There were only five boys at the nursery light enough for the job, anyway. With Slakk in the hospice and Errikkin sulking in his bed, that left the three of them to do the climbing.

Jakkin bit his lower lip, shook his head. He had a bad feeling about this hunt. A *dreadful* feeling.

But then he had a bad feeling about drakks in general.

◖ 16 ◗

JAKKIN KNEW what to expect next. On his other hunt, Likkarn had made a peeping noise like a dragon hatchling, to tempt a drakk to come out in daylight. But this time Likkarn didn't even try calling.

"Just up and get them. We know they're about," he said grimly, pointing to the trees.

Jakkin's team stood before a spikka that was as high as a two-story building but quite slim. He looked up at it, his heart stammering. Then he checked around his feet, where there was a scattering of blisterweed in the spongy ground, all too small and leafless to worry about.

The three men with Jakkin scanned the tree as well, shaking their heads, indicating that they could see nothing in the high leaves. Then together they pushed and pulled on the tree trunk, shaking it till the top swayed precariously. All the while they listened carefully for a warning hiss from above.

Silence greeted them, and Balakk cut a deep slash in the tree trunk, indicating that the tree had been searched. There were half a dozen such trees, too slim for climbing, supple enough for shaking. If any nests had been in those trees, they would have come loose and tumbled to the ground.

However, each of the really thick-trunked trees in the copse had to be climbed — and there were many of them. Jakkin paid little attention to the instructions that Likkarn gave them. He had done this before and knew what to do. Tying the piton clamps to his sandals, and putting on the leather gloves with their own set of climbing clamps, he started up the first of the thick trees. No reason to hesitate. If he hesitated, he would begin to think. *Thinking* would only make things worse. The more he thought, the more he would become frightened. And he was already scared enough. The smell of the dead drakk in the incubarn was too recent a memory to erase.

Jakkin looked to his left. Arakk was having a bit of trouble with the sandal ties, his hands shaking. Further on, Tanekk was all ready, and he had a hand on a spikka trunk, but he wasn't moving just yet. Instead he stared up, looking quite pale. Jakkin could see the fear stamped on both their faces. He wanted to say something, to warn them about the fear.

"A frightened climber is a careless climber."

Jakkin wondered — had he said it aloud? Then realized it was Likkarn who spoke.

Jakkin added, "We've enough to worry about without carelessness." He smiled at the other two boys. Whether that helped them, Jakkin didn't know. But suddenly he felt easier himself. He'd done this before. It was dangerous but doable.

Now he remembered the instructions he'd been given over a year ago at his first drakk hunt, as if that other hunt had been just an hour before. "Don't be a hero," he'd been told. "Just find the drakk. Find the nest and drop straight down. Show by fingers how many drakk are in the nest. We'll do the rest with the stingers." He hadn't paid enough attention then. He was determined to do better this time.

Nodding at Arakk and Tanekk, he started up just as Likkarn was giving them all instructions. The slippery gray bark of the tree was no match for the sharp piton blades. He kept his breathing slow, quiet. It wasn't a race, anyway. Just get to the top, peer into any nests, and if there are any drakklings, count them, and drop.

Simple.

Straightforward.

Easy.

As long as there weren't any of the creatures waiting at the top. Then things could get seriously scary. But he didn't allow himself to dwell on that.

Glancing quickly again to his left, he saw that Arakk was now already more than halfway up the tree. *In a hurry. Wanting to get up and get it over with.* Jakkin shook his head. He knew that moving too fast could make you sloppy, could make a dangerous situation worse. He hoped someone would caution Arakk to slow down.

Giving another furtive glance, this time to his right, he saw that Tanekk was still standing on the ground, his face closed in on itself. Frankkalin had gathered what looked like an army around him, talking earnestly into his ear.

L'Erikk was there. *Probably telling him a joke. That should get him up the tree fast enough!*

Then he thought, *I was like that.* Though it had been Likkarn pointing a stinger at him that had gotten him up his first tree. He remembered thinking at the time that the drakks were probably not half as dangerous as Likkarn, though he'd been wrong about that. Very wrong.

Inching up the spikka, he neared the top leaves, checked again on the other boys, and saw that Tanekk was now a few feet up his tree. Jakkin let out his breath. He hadn't even realized until then that he'd been holding it.

Under his right hand was a deep slash in the bark, black against gray, clearly from a long-ago drakk hunt. This copse was notorious for drakk nests. Maybe Likkarn was right. The big trees could be felled, but the smaller ones left. There were always more spikka. They grew quickly.

And then he thought about how even more quickly the desert reclaimed the land on Austar. Thought how much more desert there was at his oasis than there'd been a year ago, the sand taking back what the water once owned. Balakk had it right: Leave the trees.

Another few inches, and this time when he looked down, the three men below his tree seemed oddly squat, like badly shaped boys: Balakk almost bald, the other two with thick heads of hair, but they all belled out at the bottom. Their stingers were up and ready. The barrels were a comforting sight.

Now Jakkin had but inches to go. *The hard inches.* His heart had begun thumping so loudly, even a deaf drakk could surely hear it, could find it with one quick slash of its talons.

Stop thinking, he warned himself again.

He climbed a bit more and his head was now level with the top leaves, so he took a deep breath, balanced himself. Using his teeth to take the glove off his right hand, he reached down to detach the knife from his belt. Then he pushed the knife carefully through the nearest pair of leaves to get a look inside.

He let out his breath, a huge gusty exhalation. *No nest! No drakks!* He had to contain himself from letting out a victorious whoop. Putting the knife into its loop on his belt, he took the glove from between his teeth, and then scaled back down the tree twice as fast as he'd gone up. The spongy ground greeted him, feeling much more solid than it had before.

He made a circle with his fingers and mouthed to Balakk, "No drakks."

Balakk nodded, crossed the slash he'd made minutes earlier with another to make an X, then pointed to the next tree.

At that, L'Erikk came over and whispered in his ear, "Have you heard the story of Fewmets Firkkin and the drakks?" L'Erikk knew more Fewmets Firkkin jokes than anyone at the nursery.

Jakkin shook his head.

"I'll tell it to you when you get down safely."

Jakkin shook his head. "No jokes," he whispered back. "Until we're all home." He was pleased when L'Erikk backed away, hands raised in surrender.

Glancing up at the tree, Jakkin suddenly realized that he

felt little fear about climbing the second spikka. Or even the third.

He was right to be so fearless. There were no drakk nests in any of them. And when he looked over at Arakk, who was racing ahead, and Tanekk, who was just starting down his first tree, Jakkin knew that he could tackle anything now — drakk or dragon — with equal ease.

~

IN FACT, there were no drakks in the entire copse, and after a morning of futile searching, the hunters sat down for a lunch that had been packed — even overpacked — by Kkarina.

As they ate their egg sandwiches and drank the cold takk and warm tea she'd sent along in pottery flasks, Balakk said, "Tell us again, young Jakkin, which way that drakk was flying."

He pointed. "Straight toward Sukker's Marsh."

Likkarn shook his head. "Not many spikka there."

"Enough, though," Balakk said. "Maybe they've learned from previous hunts not to nest here."

"Hah!" Frankkalin sounded more like a dragon than a man. As he spoke, pieces of egg sputtered from his mouth. "Don't be a fool. Drakk don't learn. They're dumb beasts. The only thing that learns on Austar is us." He slapped his right hand against his chest for emphasis.

"Well, maybe not you, Frankkalin," Balakk said, and the others laughed.

Putting a finger beside his nose, his usual gesture,

Likkarn added, "They don't hear or see well, Frankk, but neither do I anymore."

Frankkalin laughed. "But you smell plenty, old man!"

Ignoring him, Likkarn continued. "Nothing we know about them says they can't learn."

"And nothing says they can," Frankkalin retorted. He wiped his sleeve across his mouth.

Jakkin kept quiet, but he was thinking that if drakk could learn, maybe they could also learn how to fight off hunters. He shivered at the thought, and fear, like an old argument, began to gnaw in his belly again.

But it was Arakk who interrupted the men's talk. "Are there closer trees?"

Likkarn and Balakk shook their heads and Frankkalin said, "None."

"Then why are we arguing?" Arakk asked.

"Not arguing, discussing," Balakk told him.

"Not arguing, figuring," Frankkalin added.

"What's the difference?" The boy looked truly puzzled, all joy wiped from his face.

"*You* argue, *I* explain," L'Erikk said, and the men laughed. All except Likkarn, who put up a hand to stop the talk.

"And *I* tell you what to do," Likkarn said.

"Why *you?*" The words were out of Jakkin's mouth before he could stop them.

Likkarn smiled. It was not a comforting smile. "Because I have been here the longest, gone on more drakk hunts than anyone, and Sarkkhan left the nursery to me.

Which makes me master of it," Likkarn said, thumb jabbing at his own chest.

"Except there are no masters anymore. Or so I thought," Jakkin said.

Likkarn smiled at him a bit crookedly. "No masters, no bond, except as we feel it here." He touched a finger to Jakkin's chest.

Jakkin shivered, remembering what Akki had said about that.

Akki! Without thinking, he pushed out a sending that was like a wail, orange streamers flying. He got no answer, of course, but Likkarn looked at him sharply. Jakkin closed his mind at once and tried to look innocent, which made him look guilty instead.

Likkarn ignored him after that one quick look, and raised his hand. "Now, listen. We need to concentrate on the drakks. And most importantly, we don't rush into dangerous things without finding out all we can."

Kkitakk huffed. "And that's how you broke all those bones, old man? By not rushing in?"

They all laughed again, and this time Likkarn deigned to join them.

Even Jakkin smiled, his mouth twisting around, suddenly remembering Likkarn a year earlier, helping to distract everyone when Akki and he had to get away. Maybe Golden was right and he'd mistaken Likkarn all along. Except . . . except he was sure it was Likkarn who'd pushed Akki out, sent her to The Rokk. Away from Jakkin. He shook his head. None of it made sense.

"The marsh, then," said Likkarn, speaking to them all, avoiding Jakkin's eyes. He rose and brushed the crumbs from his jerkin.

That got them all to their feet and moving toward the marsh, while behind them a dozen or so small lizards browsed on what was left of their lunch, before it soaked into the spongy earth.

☾ 17 ☾

SUKKER'S MARSH had been well named. Most things that landed there — animal, vegetable, mineral — were eventually sucked down below its boggy surface. A person had to be very careful around the marsh. Some years when there was an overflow of rain and it couldn't handle the extra water, Sukker's resembled a shallow lake. This disguised the sinkholes all too well. Even feral dragons were known to be pulled down into the mud and drowned there. Occasionally whole skeletons were spit out again, the arch of bone describing the calamity that had befallen them. Yes, Sukker's Marsh was well named.

But such a lake was a rare sight. Jakkin had only been warned about it. In the ten years he'd lived at Sarkkhan's Nursery — brought there by his grieving mother after his father had been killed by a feral dragon — Jakkin had never seen the marsh at flood. It was simply a dangerous, boggy place, where a variety of gray-green grasses and occasional spikka trees grew. But the sinkholes were easy to spot. They were gray and black circles where nothing grew — not moss, not fern, not weeds.

A strange variety of blisterweed and burnwort popped up in the marsh, though never at the sinkholes. They were not red like the weed and wort grown in the desert, but a greener color, and rarely smoked out. These were the ones weeders preferred because the plants were stronger and darker and lasted far longer than the weeds grown in the arid desert. The older men often discussed such things at the dinner table. But hardly anyone smoked blisterweed these days, at least no one who was an Austarian, though there'd always been a brisk trade in the drug with off-worlders, *another thing affected by the embargo.*

In the marsh lived an immense variety of creatures, most of them insects, winged biters, or, as the nursery folk liked to call them, tiny suckers. Some were no-see-ums, so small and translucent, they were all but invisible — until they filled up with their hosts' blood. Others flew about on incandescent wings, making a humming that was warning enough. But here were also slugs and slogs, doughy gray and slimy mud dwellers that attached themselves to the legs of unwary walkers, feasting on the blood and infecting it at the same time with a low-grade fever that took months to fully shake off.

No one wandered around the marsh for fun. And no one ever went in alone. It was too dangerous and too un-healthy for anything but fliers. Being on the marshy ground was not healthy for men — or other beasts.

Jakkin agreed with Balakk — if the drakks were capa-ble of learning anything at all, they'd probably learned that Sukker's Marsh was the one place their human hunters would avoid. At least until there was no other choice.

Within a kilometer, the marsh began to smell, the stink being dank, murky, and slightly rotten, as if a whole army had died there. And recently.

Not as bad as the drakk, Jakkin thought. *Nothing smells as bad as that.* But still the stink from Sukker's Marsh was certainly unpleasant. And uninviting. Definitely unnerving.

"Perfect for drakk," Arakk said. He was on Jakkin's left and nudged him with his elbow, his moon face aglow.

On Jakkin's other side, Tanekk walked, head down, staring at his feet. His pointed chin was practically buried in his chest.

"Are you all right?" Jakkin asked him.

Tanekk didn't answer.

"He's praying," Arakk said. "He's *always* praying."

"I'm praying, too," Jakkin said to Arakk. "Praying that *you* find the drakk, not me."

Arakk's head went up. He laughed silently, but way longer than Jakkin's stupid quip deserved. It was laughter brought on by nerves.

Ahead of them Likkarn raised his hand for silence and they gathered around him. Without a word, he pointed out the trees. There were nine in all, hardy and thick-bodied, their gray bark unslashed by knife but still pocked with black marks. *Possibly from animals sharpening their claws there,* Jakkin thought. *Dragons? Or drakk?* He realized suddenly that he didn't know enough about drakk to be sure that they sharpened their claws.

Likkarn formed the hunters into the same groups of four. There would be three trees apiece, none of them shakable, especially as the men had to stand under them on the boggy ground. They tested the ground around each tree with care. Only one tree was set close to a sinkhole.

The boys were sent to their first trees, pitons tied to their sandals, and gloves on.

Thinking that climbing with a mask was preferable to smelling the marsh gasses firsthand, Jakkin put the mask over his nose and mouth before starting up the tree. Neither Arakk nor Tanekk followed his lead.

Let them retch, then. Neither of them has ever been up close to a drakk, so what do they know! The mask was a pretty good filter for the gasses, though the stench of drakk could get through anything. And linger for an awfully long time.

Arakk had already scooted up his spikka, and Jakkin was not far behind on his own tree. However, Tanekk remained standing with his hand on the trunk for a long, silent moment. This time Jakkin understood why.

"Pray for me, too," Jakkin whispered as he hitched himself up. He hugged the tree as he went, and tried to clear his mind of fear, almost succeeding.

There were no drakks at the top, and he all but fell back down the trunk in gratitude, then turned to give the all clear to Balakk.

At this point Tanekk was halfway up his tree and Arakk was already to the top of his second spikka. *Hurrying.* Jakkin thought of calling out a warning, but didn't, knowing it could alert any drakk in the trees.

Instead, Jakkin set his hand to the gray bark of his next climb and was about to start up when he heard a huge hissing from above him. Then a shout. A scream. He stepped away from the tree and stared straight up. The hissing wasn't coming from his tree, but somewhere else.

Looking around, he saw that Tanekk was still halfway up his spikka, clinging to the trunk, not moving. But in the other tree, Arakk was windmilling his arms against a dark blur. Then he began falling backward, followed down by a very large, very angry female drakk, her talons outstretched, reaching for his face.

Jakkin drew his knife and raced toward the base of the tree, forgetting about the boggy sinkholes and the pitons on his shoes, forgetting about the possibility of slogs and slugs. He ran past two of the men, and his feet got sucked into the bog as he ran, almost toppling him.

Just then Arakk hit the ground, on his back, and the drakk was on him. Waving his knife at the beast, Jakkin beat it off for a second, but it circled and returned, this time heading straight for Jakkin.

"Down, Jakkin, down," Likkarn cried. "Stinger!"

For once Jakkin listened. He threw himself over Arakk's body, then heard the sound of several stingers striking home. He smelled the death of the drakk. Even with his face close to the dirt, even with the mask on, he could smell it.

Good! It's over. Then he sat up, knelt by Arakk's body, knees sinking into the spongy earth.

Arakk had not moved.

The dead drakk was not far from them, its feathery scales burned black. Its front legs reached out sluggishly, as if still seeking a target.

Standing, Jakkin went over to look at the drakk, and saw that it was very dead. "Good!" he said aloud but no one was listening. Balakk, Frankkalin, and Likkarn paid the creature no attention. Instead, they'd formed a tight circle around Arakk.

Jakkin walked back and pushed between Frankkalin and Balakk, looking down nervously. Arakk was still on his back, staring up at the gray sky, unseeing. He, too, was dead and there was *nothing* good about that. Nothing at all.

"I didn't mean it," Jakkin whispered, tears suddenly running down his cheeks. "I didn't mean it, Arakk, when I said I was praying that you find the drakk, not me." Only deep inside, he *had* meant it. The whole ugly thought.

Balakk took off his leather vest, and after closing the boy's staring eyes, placed the vest reverently over Arakk's face. Then he began to weep huge, blobby tears. Oddly he made no sound.

Jakkin had never seen a man cry like that. In fact, he couldn't remember ever seeing a nurseryman cry at all.

☾ 18 ☾

THEY STOOD for a long time just staring down at Arakk's body. Finally, Likkarn spoke. "There's no helping the boy. He's gone. And we honor him by making sure there are no more of these beasts in the trees."

Jakkin wasn't sure what kind of honor that was, but he knew Likkarn was right about one thing. They didn't dare leave any more drakk alive near the nursery. He drew in a deep breath, ready to climb. Unlike Arakk, though, he would be deliberate and keep his long knife at the ready.

Using their knives, the men girdled the drakk's spikka, and the tree bled black blood that ran down the gray trunk. When the bottom of the tree was entirely black, the men rocked the trunk back and forth until it broke and tumbled to the ground, spilling out the nest that had been hidden in the spiky upper leaves.

Four nestlings crouched inside, beaks open, eyes still blind. They croaked piteously, and for a moment, Jakkin felt sorry for them. But only a moment. He forced himself to look over at Arakk's body and all pity fled.

The nestlings were killed with a single blast from Balakk's stinger. "Ahhh, ahhhh," the old plowman cried, drinking in the awful smell.

No one else said a word.

Though they looked, they found no more drakks. However, Jakkin discovered an empty nest and, with his knife, sent it tumbling to the ground. Likkarn destroyed it with the stinger, saying, "No need to leave that for another mother to find. Makes it too easy for them."

"Maybe," Jakkin said, "maybe it was the nest of the drakk that Slakk killed in the barn. Since they all live in groups."

The men and boys looked hopeful at that guess, but Likkarn, ever ready to bring them back to reality, shook his head. "We have no way of knowing that and we dare not make guesses based on hope."

They agreed, then went on to tackle the rest of the trees in the marsh, working until the sun was just beginning its downward descent. There was no time to waste discussing things, and barely time to eat. They gobbled food as they girdled the trees. Everyone knew that they would have to move quickly to finish checking all the trees and get back to the nursery before Dark-After.

When they were done, Balakk picked up Arakk's body as if the boy had been a small child and not a hefty sixteen-year-old. Then they hurried home without another word spoken.

There were no more tears.

After all, nurserymen don't cry.

KKARINA SAW them through the kitchen window and ran out with her hand to her ample breast, calling, "Who? Who?"

When they showed her Arakk, she showered his face with her tears, enough for all of them. Then they laid him out on one of the dining room tables and left her to wash him thoroughly and put oil on the back of his hands and on his feet. It was an old Austar custom, honoring the dead. Jakkin had been sent to bring fresh clothes to bury him in.

As he walked back to the room, Jakkin remembered how his mother had spoken about burying his father without any oil to consecrate him and to ease his passage into eternity. It was something she'd never gotten over. Then he remembered the feel of his father's cold shoulders and hands. He'd helped bury him in the desert. A boy of five and a small, delicate woman burying a big man. He remembered how his own hands had ached and felt cold for months, as if his father's death had chilled them.

Then he remembered the other dead man, the one he'd found in The Rokk, who'd sought him out in an alley and died before they'd exchanged but a few words.

In some ways, touching Arakk had been the worst of all, a boy his own age, doing the same job Jakkin had been doing. It was only luck that Arakk had gotten that tree. Bad luck.

It could just as easily have been me!

He looked up at the ceiling, willing himself to be calm. Trying not to see Arakk falling, falling, falling. Always falling.

Jakkin found Arakk's good clothes in the third drawer of the dresser, a shirt of linen and his best leathers. He brought them to Kkarina, pointedly not looking at Arakk's now naked body lying stiffly on the table. Kkarina took the clothes, then waved him away, and he was enormously relieved not to have to stay.

Returning to the bedroom, Jakkin tried to talk to Errikkin about what had happened out in the spikka copse, but once again Errikkin gave Jakkin his back and stared at the wall.

"You can talk to that wall all you like," Jakkin said, "but that doesn't change anything. Things would have been different if you'd been there."

"How?" Errikkin's voice was hollow, even ghostly, with grief. After all, he'd known Arakk much longer than Jakkin had. "How would it have been different?"

How indeed? Jakkin suddenly realized he'd no idea at all.

∽

LATER THAT EVENING, everyone in the nursery gathered in the dining room. They weren't there to eat — that they'd done in Kkarina's kitchen — but to sit by Arakk's body, laid out on one of the tables. They were supposed to say what they best remembered about him, but it took a while for anyone to speak.

Jakkin glanced quickly at the body, and as quickly away. *He looks both like and not-like Arakk,* he thought. Though having known Arakk for only a few days, he couldn't quite put his finger on what he meant by that. Maybe it was that the glow was gone from his moon face. Maybe it was Arakk's utter stillness, a stillness so complete, he might have been carved of stone.

There were copper coins resting on Arakk's closed eyes. "For the Dark Angel," Austarians liked to say, meaning the Angel of Death. Jakkin wondered if Kkarina had supplied the coins. Whether she had a collection of them just waiting for dead nursery folk, for they were not the kind of coins used for money in Austar. He looked again, as if pulled back by an invisible thread.

It — a body. Not Arakk — a person. That's the real difference. He felt tears prickling behind his eyes but wouldn't let them fall.

Finally, the men began to talk about Arakk. Balakk had the most to say. It was he who'd first come upon Arakk during a trip to The Rokk last year, after the explosion that brought Rokk Major down. Arakk had been living on the streets of the city. A food seller, he'd been orphaned and without work since the bomb blast. He wanted to come to the country and "learn dragons," he said.

"He'd not been good with the big beasts," Balakk told them. "Almost like they was poison to him. Old vet called it an allergy. Broke out in hives when he touched one, he did, though dragon meat and takk never phased him." He wiped an arm across his eyes. "Not scared, mind. He tried his turn with them. 'Twas the hives defeated him. He was happier to be out with me in the fields."

"He always had a smile," said Frankkalin.

Everyone nodded. The word *smile* seemed to run around the room.

"He never failed in the field, whatever the season," Balakk said.

Jakkin thought that a good epitaph.

Then Likkarn stood slowly as if his bones ached. He spoke to the men but he was addressing Arakk, really, staring at the boy's body with an intensity that was palpable. Jakkin felt a cold chill go down his spine as the old man talked.

"We don't always know a hero when we see him," Likkarn said. "And sometimes, too late to tell him, we recognize what splendid things he's done." He paused, wiped a finger under his nose, then continued. "Arakk gave his life for the rest of us. For us and for the dragons he was no good with but still loved. He went eagerly up the tree to meet his doom. That makes him a hero, in every sense of the word."

Not eagerly, but he went quickly. I think that makes him more of a hero. Jakkin didn't say that aloud.

Kkarina brought out a bottle of brew then, and the sweet strong liquor was passed around, with everyone having a small taste. It was too expensive and precious for more than a tiny sip apiece. Jakkin hardly wanted any more, anyway, for it made his head swim. He passed the bottle to Errikkin, who took it without thanks, his sip more like a slurp, which he swirled around in his mouth before swallowing.

Errikkin did an odd thing then. He glared at Jakkin, stood, put a hand on Arakk's cold hand, lifted it to his lips as if kissing it, and then went out of the room.

His head whirling from just a sip of the strong drink, Jakkin left, too, but he went outside, where the twin moons were once again writing their blood-red warning. This time Jakkin understood what they were saying, but the warning had come too late. Arakk was already dead. Slakk was injured. Jakkin was very aware that in both cases it could just as easily have been himself.

He strode swiftly to the incubarn and, once there, headed directly to Auricle's stall. As he walked along he barely listened to any of the hen dragons or their mewling hatchlings. All he could hear was Auricle, who was still shaken over the drakk and the drakk-death smell that sat like a noxious cloud over the back stalls. Besides, she was still grieving over the loss of the hatchling, gone off with Akki.

At last Jakkin got to her stall, opened the door, and went in. Auricle looked up at him, a small orange light flickering in her black eyes. It was the first time he'd seen any sign of a fighting spirit.

He put a hand to her head and sat down suddenly, almost as if his legs had collapsed. She scooted up next to him and he was grateful for the warmth. It occurred to him that he'd felt cold ever since Arakk's death.

"Thanks, thou beauty," Jakkin sent, along with a soft, gray river winding endlessly toward a far horizon.

What she sent back to him was equally gray, as if mist had descended on the river, cloaking it on all sides.

They sat that way for a long time, without sound, without further sendings.

"Well," Jakkin said at last, "we certainly aren't going to

be much help to one another tonight." The lingering smell from the dead drakk was still potent. He had to leave or be sick.

Patting the dragon's head once, Jakkin stood and left the incubarn quickly. He got back to the bondhouse just as Dark-After began.

~

IN THE MORNING, they put Arakk in a box made of spikka wood. Balakk had carved Arakk's name at the head of the box, with an etched spray of wheat drooping on its stalk. *He must have been up all night working.* Jakkin hadn't known the old plowman had any ability with a carving knife.

In fact, I know nothing about any of them, he told himself. *Not Balakk or Likkarn or . . .* Even though he'd lived most of his life among them, they were strangers. He knew the dragons better.

What he did know, however, was that there were always three or four burial boxes kept in a back room of the stud barn. It was an open secret within the nursery, and no one spoke of it for fear of bringing down disaster. "Do not call the Dark Angel, for he will come" was a nursery saying.

But disaster has come, anyway. Jakkin was beginning to think that *he* was a curse set among them. How could he have considered this place home?

Look at all that had happened because of his presence at the nursery — his mother dead, Sarkkhan dead, Heart's Blood dead, Likkarn partially blinded — old news. And now Arakk dead, Slakk hurt, Errikkin crazy, Akki gone.

All somehow my fault.

Put that bluntly, it sounded stupid. Crazy. Clearly he hadn't killed anybody, but all those things had happened in part or in whole because of him.

All somehow my fault?

He couldn't shake the feeling that there was some truth in that. He tried to sort it out as he walked behind the six men carrying the box to the burial ground. They set the box under the gray-green weeping wilkkin trees.

All somehow my fault?

Jakkin stared down at the deep hole where the box would soon be lowered. He could find no answers there.

He remembered how after his mother had been buried, he'd spent long hours sitting by her grave, calling to her, thinking that if he could just say the right words, she'd return. Kkarina had found him there, a stunned five-year-old. She told him that his parents were in a long, unbroken sleep, and worked with him to make a stone for his mother's grave. It had Mummy on the top, but below it her name, Mairi. Her free name. She'd been known in the nursery as Makki, because even though she'd been born free, she'd put herself and her young son in bond in order that they might live.

Live. He snorted like a young dragon. She hadn't lived, but died of a broken heart soon after bringing them both to safety, leaving him at the nursery alone and in bond.

After a time, of course, he'd stopped visiting the grave. Except on feast days, or days he and Kkarina picnicked in the graveyard. Or when, as now, he trailed after a new burial. He'd all but forgotten what his mother looked like, how soft her voice was.

There's still a part of me that thinks I can call the dead back with the right words. He hadn't known the right words for his father or mother, or for Sarkkhan, or for Heart's Blood.

If I don't have the right words for those I love the most, how can I possibly know the right words for Arakk, who I hardly knew?

Suddenly everyone around him broke into song, a hymn that Jakkin had learned from his mother, or maybe Kkarina. He sang along with them, which made him feel a little better, as if borrowing words from the old song could serve when he had none.

> *Oh, God, who sends the double moons,*
> *Who spreads the singing sand,*
> *Take pity on your children here*
> *Upon the bonded land.*
>
> *For we have been but late in jail,*
> *Our lives not ours to give,*
> *Still with your grace we will arise*
> *And learn once more to live.*

He looked down at the red earth, thinking how much it looked like blood. How so much of Austar was blood beneath his feet: human blood and dragon's blood and drakk blood combined. His eyes filled with tears and he breathed slowly, deeply. But he was a man now, so of course he didn't cry.

☾ 19 ☾

THAT NIGHT, long after everyone was asleep, but well before Dark-After, Jakkin crept back out to the incubarn once more. He had a leather bag filled with sweet wikki fruit, and a drinking pouch tied to his belt. Opening the creaky door, he went in, standing for a moment to drink in the musky smell. Now the sharp, awful drakk odor was gone and it was all dragon stink again, a familiar smell, and one he loved.

Dragons were so simple. He understood them. And now that he could speak to them mind-to-mind, he could know all their secrets as well.

But humans . . . well, they were much too complicated. He hardly understood his own feelings. Of course he didn't really believe he was a curse, the cause of all that had gone wrong at the nursery. But for the moment, watching Arakk's coffin being lowered into its grave, he'd been sure of it.

And then there was Akki. His smile was crooked as he thought of her. Everything came back to Akki. From the first moment he'd really been aware of her, him lying in the hospice bed and she his nurse, till their last quarrel, over . . . He couldn't even remember what the quarrel had been about. It didn't matter. Without Akki, he had no reason to stay at the nursery. He would go to The Rokk and try to convince her that they only needed to keep the secret. If Akki was determined to solve the problem of the dragons' gift, then they'd do it together.

After I get some sleep. He was exhausted from the drakk hunt, the burial, the roil of emotions. The few hours he'd slept in his bed, while Errikkin snored in the bunk above, hadn't helped. A few more hours of sleep, this time surrounded by dragons, and he'd be all right again.

Walking slowly into the incubarn, Jakkin listened in on the dreams of all the dragons. The hens' minds were full of slow, pink clouds; the hatchlings all atwitter with bouncy blobs of color. He dipped in and out of their night thoughts.

Auricle, being neither mother nor hatchling, had a clearer mind: cool and somehow soothing. Jakkin went into her stall and plopped down by her side. He adjusted his back against her great pale flank and was asleep within minutes.

—

WHEN HE AWOKE, it was fully Dark-After. He could sense it, the tendrils of cold finding ways into the barn, through small pores in the stone and wood. But the heating system worked well enough, and the dragons added their own warmth.

Jakkin got up, careful not to wake Auricle or any of the

others, and left the barn. Predictably, the door squalled, both opening and closing. He should have oiled it when he'd had the chance.

No lights went on in the bondhouse, and Jakkin moved swiftly around the side of the barn.

Once there, he dashed to the weir, then splashed across and headed to the oasis. There was hardly a sound; not even the insects were awake. Overhead the sky was a deep blue shot through with ribbons of purple. It could be read as dangerous, or exhilarating. Jakkin sighed. The rest of the nursery folk would see only the danger, not the beauty. They didn't have dragon eyes.

"Sssargon!" he called aloud when he was finally close to the oasis. "Sssasha! We're going to find Akki. Now." He hoped they were still there, sending a tentacle of color in red, the color of their shared blood. *"Come. Come."*

For a long moment he heard nothing. Cold crawled across his shoulders. The brilliant sky was still.

And then suddenly he heard the flexing of great wings. A mumble of color crowded into his head. The dragons were beginning to wake: Sssasha first, next her brother, and finally the triplets. They stood, stretched, looked around with eyes that could pierce the dark. They crowded around him, pushing at him with their great keeled chests. Poking into his mind, they sent him rainbows.

"Akki . . . Akki . . . Akki," they called, picking up his conviction, until his head was a riot of color — first greens and blues like rivers crossing the Austar sands, and then their signature colors of red and rose.

"Yes, Akki," Jakkin crooned to them, caressing their heads, the scales cool under his probing fingers.

The dragons all knew, as he did, that they had but four hours of Dark-After to make a good start without the interruptions of men. Four hours before the nursery folk realized that Jakkin — like Akki — was gone. Four hours till they began to wonder how and where Jakkin was going, till Likkarn figured it out, sent someone after him.

It was suddenly, brilliantly clear that Likkarn wanted Jakkin and Akki separated. He didn't know why Likkarn felt this way — but he knew *absolutely* it was so.

The five dragons leaped into the air, their wings fanning whirlwinds in the sand, deviling winds that erased some of Jakkin's tracks.

"Good, good," he sang to them.

"Sssargon goesss, Sssargon sailsss, Sssargon soarsss," came the big dragon's voice in Jakkin's head, as if Sssargon were the only one in flight. *Typical!*

The other dragons said nothing, sent nothing, but Jakkin could hear the flapping of their heavy wings while they searched for a current. Then one by one they each found a road in the sky where they could finally soar silently above the dunes.

Hunching his shoulders, he began to walk. Not back toward the nursery, not toward the road, but across the great sweeping dunes, heading first north and then east. To the city. To The Rokk, some 300 kilometers away. Above him the twin moons showed the way, chasing one another across the night sky.

"Be my eyes and ears," he told the five dragons, and one by one they called out their assent in colorful sendings.

Sssargon circled back, his wings stirring up even more cold. Jakkin could feel it like a wind against his ears, his neck, his spine, but it was not so cold that he had to find shelter.

Four hours. That would give him a good start on Akki's trail. He needed to get away from the oasis, from the nursery. Then he could catch a truck somewhere along the road once Dark-After was done and the sun shone down full force.

Jakkin watched as the five dragons spread out against the deep blue, looking like moving mountains.

"Thou beauties!" he called, his sending a conflagration of fireworks: sparks of red, blue, and blinding white. As his sending blasted toward them, Jakkin wished as never before that he, too, could fly. Wished he could sit on Sssargon's back, wrap his legs around that mighty body, and soar. But anyone who tried any such foolishness would have the inside of his thighs slashed to ribbons by the dragon's sharp scales, scales that moved whenever the dragon moved, sliding across one another in sharp precision. Besides, any dragon, its flight muscles cramped by a rider, would likely tumble down into the pitiless sand.

"I fly with the wings of my mind!" he cried aloud. "My brother, my sisters, I am with you." Even to himself he sounded crazed. But he wasn't mad. He was determined . . . determined to find Akki, talk sense into her, and bring her home.

This time the five dragons answered him with comforting sendings: clouds and streams and — from Sssasha — a small sunburst. Then they banked and were gone from sight, winging away toward the horizon.

It was time to put his head down and simply trudge along the sand. Jakkin counted on the dragons to warn him of any problems ahead or behind, but he would need to keep his own ears sharp as well.

There was little on Austar that could hurt a human at night besides the cold. Drakks never attacked men, unless the men were climbing trees or poking at their nests. Most feral dragons would be asleep at this time, or so he hoped. Dragons were mostly creatures of the daylight, not nocturnal, not like drakks. And ferals attacked only when provoked. He understood that now. His father had died trying to train a feral in the sands. The feral had not been amused. An angry feral, an unarmed man . . . Jakkin shook his head. What *had* his father been thinking? Why not just live at a nursery and work with the dragons there?

Stopping for a moment, Jakkin realized that all he could hear was the hearty growling voice of Sssargon in his head. *"Sssargon sailsss. Sssargon looksss. Sssargon staysss awake."*

"Thank you, Sssargon," he called back, knowing that the dragon would take such thanks as his rightful due. He even sent a spray of fireworks. Sssargon liked fireworks, the louder and brighter, the better.

Of course all five of the dragons would stay awake this night, the other four needing neither his thanks nor his permission. But he sent them each a lovely picture of a boy in the dark, surrounded by his own red aura, the exact color of their mother, Heart's Blood. They would understand and be pleased that he took the time to send it.

He himself wouldn't sleep until the early dawn, and then only for about an hour. Walking would keep him warm enough in the cold of Dark-After. He sang one of the old nursery marching tunes, to keep himself awake and moving.

Wings abeating, cold arising,
Time is fleeting, dark disguising,
Onward flying on the course,
Death-defying dragon-saurs.

Wings aflapping, moons are setting,
No more napping, time forgetting,
Set for landing with great force
Together banding dragon-saurs.

Wing-to-wing with scale and feather,
Fire-breathing, all together
Heading toward the common source,
Sun and moon and dragon-saurs.

And it worked. For a while.

☾ 20 ☾

NOW JAKKIN could feel a slightly warmer river of wind across his back. It was time for a quick nap. He found a tree — not tall and spindly like the spikkas, but something less grand. He didn't know what it was called. It had an outline that reminded him of Kkarina, being as round as it was tall. The leaves each had four broad fingers, fanned out like an open hand. There was a hollow in the dark trunk, and he curled into it to sleep.

While he slept, the brood landed on the sand near him and crept close. The triplets fell asleep instantly, wrapped around one another like scaly spoons. Sssargon slept standing, on watch. But Sssasha moved as near to Jakkin's tree as she could, slipping under the lowest branches and creating a radiating warmth with her body, a warmth that covered him like a blanket. He wasn't awake enough to realize why he was warm, but he smiled in his sleep.

When the sun climbed above the horizon, Sssargon shook himself all over and sent a message to his siblings and Jakkin. *"Sssargon wakesss. Sssargon readiesss. Sssargon fliesss.*" Pumping his mighty wings, which caused the sand to eddy all around him, he leaped into the air.

The triplets woke at his sending, but slowly, twittering to one another.

Stepping back from the tree with a lightness that was extraordinary given her bulk, Sssasha bent her great neck to check what was behind her. Satisfied, she stepped back, then nudged the sleeping boy before blasting him with a cascade of yellow bubbles.

"Come," she sent. *"Come."*

Jakkin woke with a start, popped the bubbles. Sat up. Hit his head on the inside of the tree's hollow, and cried out, "Fewmets! Fewmets! Fewmets!" His sending was large, dark, and stinking, just like fewmets. He'd been dreaming about a cave and a sending, a dark vine, a pillar of light. And dreaming about something else.

"Fewmets!" he said again, remembering.

Sssasha and the triplets laughed.

Rubbing his head ruefully, Jakkin emerged from his sleeping quarters. *"Couldn't one of you have reminded me I was in a tree?"* He looked up at the sky, saying aloud, "How long did I sleep? Is it late?"

Sssasha sent him a dark horizon line with a red sun hovering a tiny space above.

Standing, Jakkin looked around. It was barely day. His eyes were full of grit, his mouth felt as if he'd been eating dirty sandals, his head ached as much from the awful dream as from the bang on his temple. "But at least I haven't overslept." He laughed a bit ruefully, the chuckle turning into dancing dust motes that he sent to the dragons, who chuckled in return, though they were laughing because he was laughing, not because they understood the joke.

Humor is tough enough among humans and almost impossible across species, he thought.

He checked where the sun was rising, over the long low outline of the dunes with rolling hills beyond. It would be another hour yet before full daylight. He turned and pointed toward the northwest.

That way. It was not as flat as the sand to the east. In fact, farther along there were hills, rolling and stubbled with a kind of green fuzz, like a short bad haircut. And behind the fuzzy hills, the winding Narrakka River, contained within vertical cliffs. And then — the mountains.

Mountains! Brooding shadows that reminded him of drakk hunched in the nest, ready to kill anything that came near. Jakkin shivered thinking of the mountains and the foothills honeycombed with caves where the wild trogs lived, where danger waited at every turning. But even while he shivered, another part of him ached with longing for the places where he and Akki had lived together happily, peacefully, for a year.

Sssargon sent a loud, blood-red waterfall that washed over them both. *"No mountainsss! No!"*

"Of course not," Jakkin said, all the while smoothing the red waterfall away until it was a cool blue and white. "We have no need to go back into the mountains."

And they didn't. All they needed to do was to find a truck barreling along the road, a road that should be just past the sands and right before the rise of the cliffs that contained the river. Then Jakkin could ride to The Rokk and the dragons could follow the snaking road from above. *"Find me a truck, my beauties. Fly up. Fair wind."*

Obeying him, Sssasha pumped her wings and rose, slowly, stately, till she was even with her brother. The triplets fairly leaped into the air, almost crashing against one another, their twittering voices cascading through Jakkin's mind.

Once again Jakkin wished that he, too, could fly. But it was feet not wings for him. Another few miles and they should be at a crossroads. That's where he'd have his best chance of finding a ride.

As Jakkin suspected, the road lay ahead with the hills on one side, the flat desert on the other. The flying dragons kept sending him colorful maps that frequently overlapped and were often contradictory. So Jakkin climbed a hillock, then hunkered down to gaze at the snaking gray road far below.

"We can wait here until a truck comes," he said aloud, sending a picture of a boy on a hilltop, resting. *"Wake me for the truck."* Then he curled beside a gray-green bush that had small spikes of new growth, and began to drift off.

The world was quiet around him. No sound on the road yet. The birds strangely still. Sleep came quickly, grabbed him by the neck and wouldn't let him go.

~

HE DREAMED of flying over the hills, over the mountains, touching down before a cave. A cave he recognized, with a knot of intertwining branches of caught-ums making a screen over the entrance. He put his hand out carefully, to open the door and —

The dragons intruded loudly, sending black bomb blasts, yellow and orange fire shooting into his brain. He heard Sssargon shouting: *"Wake! Wake! Wake!"* There was smoke, coughing, anger.

Fear.

Jakkin woke, to find himself bound like an animal, his arms tied to a stick behind him, almost yanking his shoulders out of their sockets. He was pulled roughly to his feet. His head ached where something must have struck him.

"Who?" he said aloud. But he already knew.

Above, the dragons screamed, but they didn't dare flash fire down at his captors. They might burn Jakkin by mistake.

"Watch," Jakkin sent to them. *"Warn . . ."*

He was suddenly clipped on the back of his head, and at the same time, a brutal sending — black and hard as iron — filled his mind. Then everything went dark. Not sleep. Just blackness.

When Jakkin woke again, the dark was everywhere, not the blackness of night with the twin moons lighting the way, but a darkness unrelieved by any light in the sky. He remembered this darkness, but couldn't imagine why he was in it again. Nothing made sense. Besides, his skull ached, his teeth seemed to be loose and clattering together, and his knees hurt from kneeling on a stone floor.

I'm in a cave. He tried to move, but his arms were still bound behind him. *How did I get into a cave?* But of course he knew.

He sent out a tentative tentacle of color and it was immediately severed, replaced by a crackling that blocked out almost everything else in his mind.

Trogs! But how they had found him and where they had taken him were beyond his ability to understand. His fingers were pins and needles. His arms felt yanked from their sockets. The crackling in his brain, added to the pain of the blow, made his head hurt so horribly, he began to cry. It was a silent crying, just tears crawling down his cheeks. Then he took a deep breath.

Someone swatted him. *"Do not krriah like a youngling!"* The words came into his head; they weren't spoken aloud. Oddly, it was the very first thing a trog had said to him before. In the cave.

His tears stopped at once and he thought angrily at his captor, *"You folk aren't much on conversation."*

That earned him another swat, and more crackling, but he was glad of it. Anger would serve him much better than self-pity or fear.

"Fewmet head!" he sent, along with an image of a great pile of stinking worm waste. That got him another blow.

He smiled. Even if they couldn't see it, they would sense it. Sense it and know that he wasn't going to be cowed by them again. No more tears, no matter how much he hurt.

First, he told himself, guarding that thought behind a quickly constructed wall of thought bricks, *I have to figure out how many trogs there are.*

Second, I must get out of my bonds.

And third . . .

He didn't know if there was a third.

Suddenly he was pulled upright from behind.

"GO!" The sending was a dark shout in his head, leaping over the thought wall. There was lightning along with it, which made his head hurt even more than before.

He ignored it. "Whatever happened to *please?*" he asked out loud, expecting another blow to the head, bracing himself for it. But it never happened. So he repeated the question in a sending. And suddenly, there was a group chuckle in his head. Frantically he tried to sort them out, to count the voices. Maybe three of them? Maybe four?

Someone behind him put a hand on his shoulder and Jakkin worked hard not to flinch.

"Strong," came the voice in his head. *"Good."*

And the echoing of three others agreeing.

"Got you!" Jakkin whispered. *Four of them. Maybe that's not so bad. I can handle four. With the dragon brood's help.*

Then his mouth twisted. Who was he kidding? These guys were all muscle. He remembered the first time he'd seen a trog, how astonished he was at how stocky they were, how broad-shouldered, how they could see easily in the dark caves.

Well, he'd wanted to know how many of them there were. And now, for better or for worse, he knew.

He suspected it was for worse.

☾ 21 ☾

THE TROGS started a fire in the cave, squatting in front of it. In the firelight, Jakkin recognized them. They were wearing eggskin loincloths and leather sandals. Hairy-chested, shaven-headed, they gabbled at one another mind-to-mind for what seemed like hours, the fire shining on their metal bracelets, their "bands." As they mind-spoke, their hands designed images in the air. It was as mesmerizing as it had been back in their own cavern.

Jakkin dozed, woke, dozed again.

It was the second or third time he woke that he realized what was going on. They were waiting for dark. They weren't going to move — or move him — until night, when they'd have little chance of being seen.

Of course.

He sent a little mind fire at them, red and orange, upbeat, even perky. *"I need help standing. Help going outside to relieve myself. Something to eat."*

They ignored him.

"How about my arms unbound for a minute. Someone to

talk to. Maybe a joke? A song?" Anything to remind them he existed.

They ignored him.

He tried to listen in on their mind conversations. They seemed to be using some kind of code. Or dialect. He heard *"Bonds"* and *"Dark-After."* They repeated *"Great Mother"* a good many times. The rest was beyond him.

It was then that he remembered Makk, the leader of the trogs, saying, "One day go to place of Bonds and throw them over." Meaning one day the trogs would rise up and attack the civilized humans, like the nursery folk and the folk in the cities. Not that the trogs could win such a war. Nursery folk had stingers and knives and fighting dragons they'd trained who could breathe fire at will. City folk had trucks, copters, stingers, and guns. The rebels had explosives, or at least they'd had such things a year earlier. But all the trogs had were sticks and some forged metal weapons. Any battles would be bloody but awfully one-sided. Still — if the trogs burned buildings at night, many of the civs would die in the cold of Dark-After. He closed that image out of his mind lest he help the trogs make a plan.

He tried again. *"Make water? Eat? Unbind my arms?"*

Still they ignored him.

So he began to think about why the trogs were here, now. Why they'd tracked him. *Certainly, finding me hasn't been any simple chance encounter.* And once he started thinking . . .

"Great Mother," they'd said not once but many times. That was their name for any female dragon who gave

birth. The dragons they worshipped and then killed in order to nestle their own babies in the dragon's egg chamber. Auricle had been one of their Great Mothers, gravid but not yet ready to lay her eggs. *And we saved her from that bloody worship.* He supposed the trogs had tracked him by his sendings out in the oasis and wanted him to take them to Auricle.

Fewmets! How could they think he'd ever do such a thing?

Except — he could hardly feel his arms now.

He had to pee so badly that he was afraid he'd ruin his leather pants.

Hunger stabbed at his belly and he wondered where his bag of fruit had gotten to. And the tea.

But he could still be strong. *If* he had to. And, he reminded himself, he had to. Trogs respected strength.

What if I tell them that I understand their anger? That I know they're upset that Akki and I rescued — er, stole — one of their Great Mothers. And probably not too happy that we were able to get away from them by swimming the underground river. They probably fear we'll expose where they live. I could explain . . .

But no sooner had he thought this than one of the trogs left the fire, came to him, yanked him up, took him to a corner, undid his bonds.

"Make water. Have food. Sleep more. Soon we move."

So, they'd been listening to him. *That's not good.* He quickly constructed a wall of thought stones higher and thicker than the bricks, with one loose stone he could remove when he had to speak to them or listen. It was imperative that he keep them out of his mind the rest of the time. He and Akki had worked hard at such walls when they'd been captive in the caves.

Then, as if he'd not taken any time at all to make the wall, he did as he'd been told. After all, there were four of them and only one of him. Explanations, excuses would have to wait.

~

AFTERWARD HE SLEPT again, dozing fitfully, always waking with a start, his hands bound behind him once more. By the time the trogs were ready to leave the shelter of the cave, Jakkin figured he'd slept away an entire day.

Well, at least I'm all caught up on my missed sleep!

The last time that he woke, it was to find that his hands had been unbound without his noticing.

He sat up, rubbing his wrists. He removed the loose stone in his thought wall and sent, *"Thanks,"* on a small gray cloud. There was no response from any of the trogs, so he slammed the loose rock back into the wall.

Stupid, he told himself. *Saying thanks to my captors marks me as weak.* He wouldn't make that mistake again.

The trogs were busy stamping out the fire. Jakkin watched as they scattered the ashes throughout the cave. It would do no good trying to run. He didn't know the cave turnings, and they could see better in the dark than he could. They also knew which way they'd come in. He'd just get lost and make them so mad that when they found him, they'd probably give him a beating. Better to let them lead him outside. He loosened the stone again.

"Out." The sending was short, curt, followed by a black lance winging toward him by way of punctuation. *"Now."*

He wondered how long they'd been ordering him out. He'd have to remain ready, leave the little stone out more often. But Jakkin at least had had enough sleep. The trogs would have had to remain on guard. Perhaps he could wear them down.

He let them lead him out into the night. With his mind wall up, and the trogs on the alert, he didn't dare try to send to the dragons. Four of them were female and the trogs might consider them a trade. No, he couldn't chance that. And, besides, the dragons no longer seemed to be anywhere around.

THE ROKK

⸨ 22 ⸩

THE MAZE of streets in The Rokk were easier to walk through than drive, for many were signposted ONE WAY. Other streets — which she'd walked along on her own the last time she was here — were much too small to be driven through.

On the narrowest streets, the sand-brick houses leaned precariously across the road, so close to their counterparts that the householders could watch their neighbors eating, and — it was said — could even count the number of lizard eggs going down a gullet.

It was not yet sundown, hours before the Dark-After chill would cover the city. Still, the bars and stew houses were already open for business, light spilling out of their windows and open doors. Men staggered along the road-way or propped themselves up against a convenient wall to drink some more. Backlit, women in baggerie windows signaled to their lovers. It was said in The Rokk: "Only the cold stops the drinking and bagging, though only the drinkers pass out cold."

Golden drove the streets with an easy expertise, hardly ever looking straight ahead. As a passenger, Akki only had to close her mouth and remember. And remember she did: the streets, the avenues, the alleyways, the wynds, the dead ends.

Suddenly the twists and turns evened out. Now the truck was on the broad avenue that led directly to and around Rokk Major Pit.

Or what was left of it.

Akki held her breath. She hadn't seen the Pit since the explosion that had killed so many. Once it had been a proud, domed arena, towering over the city. It had looked, as Jakkin had said, like an enormous dragon's egg. But what would it be like now?

The car went around one final slow bend in the avenue.

"Aaaah." Akki breathed in, then out, unable to say anything. At the very least, she'd been expecting a giant hole, a great nothingness. But the Pit was a jumble of rocks and bricks, and twisted planks that pointed accusing fingers at the sky. "I thought it was being rebuilt."

"No," Golden said. "Nothing has been done to the site yet. That will happen as soon as the election is over."

She got her breath back. "Why the wait?"

His smile was not comforting. "After the bodies were pulled out, identified, buried — and as a senator representing The Rokk, I went to more burials than I can count — then the arguments began. The rebels were rounded up. The worst were sent offplanet, to penal colonies run by the Federation. Those considered re-educable, we kept in prison here or, if we felt they'd benefit by freedom, we set them free. Then the Federation declared its embargo. More arguments. About whether building the Pit again made sense with no visitors allowed."

His face had turned sour during this recitation, but he didn't stop talking. "An election was called. And then no one wanted to start something that a pack of new senators might immediately turn their backs on." Now his voice was low, without inflection. It was impossible to guess his real feelings about the restoration of the Pit. "So far, it's just been a waiting game. But we've been collecting donations, funding building plans in secret. There *will* be a new Major Pit. It will help convince the Federation to cancel the embargo. I'm just not sure when we will start."

The wreckage seemed to burn itself into Akki's eyes; she couldn't look away.

"But now . . ." Golden stopped, took a breath, then went on. "As the bonders like to put it, 'Dragon time is now!'" He gave a quick wrench of the wheel, and suddenly they headed away from the site, into the heart of the city, into the maze of streets.

Akki didn't look back. She didn't have to. She could still see the broken site in her mind. She was pretty sure that they hadn't needed to come that way to get to Dr. Henkky's house, and she wondered why Golden had brought her there.

I could ask, but could I trust his answer? As always, Golden's motives seemed unclear. To everyone. *Maybe even to himself.* Dr. Henkky had told her — warned her —

of that often enough a year ago. Obviously she hadn't listened. *So,* Akki thought angrily, *I'm listening now.*

And then they drove past streets Akki knew well.

Now the sun was starting to set, though it was still high enough to reflect crazily on the mirrored windows of the city. The windows made the mazed roads even harder for anyone to keep straight. That mirroring had all been done on purpose, back when the city was built. The Rokk was *meant* to be a labyrinth, the only maps in the possession of the wardens and masters. Any convict trying to escape was soon lost in the maze. And if not found by Dark-After, the escapee would be a dead man. Or woman.

"I'm taking you to my house," Golden said. "Number seventeen."

"That's not where I'm planning to go," Akki told him.

"That's where you're meant to be. Henkky has moved into it. There's an entire basement I never used that she's turned into a hospice. Treats patients there as well as at the baggeries."

"So she's in on this, too?"

"She knows you're coming, and that's all. I told her we have to call you by a different name in the beginning. To keep the real you anonymous, in case there are still people out there after you."

"Like Colonel Kkalkkav?"

"Oh, not Kkalkkav anymore. Like a lot of people ashamed of bonder names, he's taken a new one. Calls himself Calli now."

She laughed. "Of course he does."

"And what will we call you?"

"Whatever you like. Though there's no guarantee I'll answer to it." She made a face at him.

~

THEY DROVE on in silence.

After about fifteen minutes on a long street, Golden pulled the truck up in front of the place where his house squatted. It was one of several gaudy three-story buildings set about by paving and dirt squares in which spindly spikka trees fought for life. The trees were visibly losing that fight, their leaves brown and curling.

"I'll leave you here, *Aurea*. That's a Feder name, by the way. It means 'golden.' Do you like it?"

She figured he'd picked out the name even before he'd rescued them in the mountains. Had it all ready, just in case. So she ignored him until she got the cab door open.

Looking back over her shoulder, she said, "Aurea. Nice touch." Then she hopped down, her satchel in her left hand, the hatchling in her right. She left the door open, which meant Golden would have to lean far over to close it.

That, too, is a nice touch.

He called out, "Number seventeen. You can't miss it. Senator Golden sends his regards."

She didn't turn around but called back, "I'm sure he does."

As she walked on, she heard the cab door slam, the wheels squeal on the roadway, and then Golden was gone.

☾ 23 ☾

FOR THE FIRST time in hours, Akki was breathing easily. She hadn't realized how tightly she'd been holding herself in. Now her step developed a swing. She almost felt like singing. Sending the little dragon a rainbow of colors, she received a rainbow back.

She thought about going elsewhere, finding another place to stay. But who else did she know in The Rokk, really, and if Henkky had a hospice in the house, she might have other supplies as well. Or at least could tell Akki where to find what she needed.

If only I knew.

The number seventeen had been splashed like dragon's blood across the gaudy yellow door of the fifth house. The number reminded her of her father: *Big and red-faced, bigger than life, and bigger than death, as well.* They'd not always gotten along, more like two hatchlings in a stall fighting for dominance. But in the end, before he died, she'd grown to like him, to understand him, even to love him.

There were sudden tears prickling in the corners of her eyes, and she stood still for a moment in order to fight them back. She was *not* going to greet Dr. Henkky weeping.

When at last she had control of herself, she set the dragon on her shoulder, its tail curled around her upper arm. Then she banged her knuckle on the door, right above the seven. The reverberation was loud enough for everyone on the street to hear.

Be anonymous, she reminded herself.

Just then, the door was flung open and she walked in.

The person at the door was no one she'd seen before, a girl about her own age but about a foot taller. She got the impression of dark hair, brown skin, slim, muscular arms, a solemn closed-down face. The girl sketched a quick curtsy.

So much for freedom. Akki supposed certain rules became habit after a while. Maybe freedom had to be learned, slowly and with great effort.

"I'm here to see Dr. Henkky. She's expecting me."

Without saying a word, the girl did her quick curtsy again and disappeared through a door, shutting it quietly behind her.

Akki looked around. Before she could react to the wild colors of the inside of the house — overwhelming orange and pink, purple and red wallpaper — the hatchling unwound its tail from her arm, chittering loudly. Pumping its little wings, it stretched its neck out toward the sound of splashing water.

As Akki watched, the dragonling flew to a fountain, where transparent pipes in the center of the room carried water in and out. The hatchling dove in and began splashing delightedly until water flooded out onto the tiled floor. Akki gasped. She was not used to such lavish use of water. It had been over a year since she'd lived for a short time in The Rokk. In the desert, every bit of water had to be conserved.

Hurrying over to the fountain, she tried to get the hatchling out of the pool. Suddenly she blushed as she realized the water pipes were shaped like a man and woman embracing. And then she noticed that the pictures on the wall were all filled with couples in compromising positions.

"Oh, a pig indeed, Senator Golden. And what appalling taste you have."

She hadn't heard a door open, but a familiar voice answered her. "That's not the *real* Golden, but the public face. The sexy party thrower, epicene and charming. Come into the hall and I'll show you what I mean."

Turning, Akki saw Dr. Henkky in the doorway, her deeply tanned face full of amusement.

"Oh," Akki said, startled. "But the dragon . . . let me clean up . . ."

Henkky laughed some more. "It's only water. The poor little thing must be absolutely parched after the journey. Senekka can mop it up later. And you, too, must need a drink. Come on."

Senekka must be the curtsying girl. Leaving the hatchling to play in the water, Akki followed the doctor toward the hall, where Golden's house began to take on a more settled air. Though the walls were still brightly painted, orange on the right, yellow on the left, the pictures were more subdued —

landscapes with dragons. One picture in particular, of the two moons chasing across a night sky, made Akki stop to look more closely. The painting was so realistic she could almost feel the cold of Dark-After coming next.

"Lovely, isn't it," Henkky said. "And so restful after the Great Hall."

Akki nodded.

"Here," Dr. Henkky said, opening a door in the orange wall.

When Akki stepped through, it was as if she were in an entirely different house. The room was extremely comfortable-looking, with three whitewashed walls and the fourth supporting a floor-to-ceiling bookcase packed full of books. There were books on history, geography, folklore, betting systems, a book on furniture, and several atlases — of Austar, the Protectorate planets, a sky atlas, and one labeled simply FEDERATION. There were dictionaries, a shelf of medical books, a shelf and a half dedicated to natural science, and a shelf of slim volumes of poetry. She recognized a few titles: *Red Flight*, *The Sullen Green*, and *Dry, Engaging Bones*. Books even spilled onto the carpeted floor. Akki had simply never seen so many books in one room before. She bent and picked one up. *On the Raising of Dragons*, by Master Arland. She recognized that one. It was on her father's bookshelves back at the nursery.

Overhead was a spinning sky globe. A small fire burned in the hearth, just embers, really. In the center of the room a large sofa and two easy chairs shared space with a low table between them.

"Sit," Henkky said, pointing to one of the chairs. "We have takk on the boil, springwater, or a cooler flavored with a bit of grape."

"Grape, please," Akki said, sinking into the chair.

Henkky turned to a wooden desk by the bookcase. Rolling up the top, she disclosed a serving bar chockablock with mugs and glasses, a stack of dishes, a small sink that Kkarina would envy, and about a dozen different bottles filled with liquids. She chose one and poured out a light green drink into two glasses.

"After our drink, I'll find a cage for your Beauty somewhere. Can't have her dropping fewmets all over Golden's house. Senekka is fine with cleaning up water on the floor, but she absolutely draws the line at fewmets. She used to work in a nursery and hated every minute of it."

Akki gulped half the contents of the glass, before saying, "Not a Beauty, a hatchling."

"Oh, my," said Henkky. "We'll have to make a dragon pen for her then, out in the back garden."

"You have a garden?"

"Golden's pride. There are only a few of them in the city. We have a greenhouse, too. I think it's why Senekka remains, actually, the lure of all those exotic fruits and veg."

Akki looked down at her hands. "I'm not actually staying that long," Akki said quickly. "Just long enough to . . ."

Henkky looked confused. "But the run-up to the election begins tomorrow and the election itself is not for a month from now. Golden has planned for you to be here the entire time. We're expecting your Jakkin as well. Golden told me so only a few days ago. Or have I gotten that wrong? Sometimes, I admit, I only half listen to him. He does run on."

Putting the glass down with great care on the table next to the chair, Akki said, "Well, *I* have no plans to be a part of Golden's election. And frankly, I'm surprised that you are. I remember how often you warned me against him. As for me, I'm here for two reasons and two reasons only. And neither of them has to do with any election."

Henkky sat down heavily on another chair and stared at her. "Damn that man. This time I actually believed him. Perhaps because I wanted you to stay. I could use the help. He said you'd agreed."

"I haven't agreed to anything. In fact, I didn't know till this morning that he was bringing me here."

Henkky shook her head. "That man breathes cabals, conspiracies, and intrigues for fun." Her mouth twisted. "I'm so sorry, Akki. But you're here now. And obviously I can't get you back any earlier than tomorrow afternoon. I'll have to find a driver. We have the first of three debates in the evening, so we can't possibly drive you there ourselves."

Akki nodded. "But if you can help me, I'll stay. Not for him, though."

"And you say that you have two reasons?"

Leaning forward, Akki told her, "Number one: I need to finish my apprenticeship as doctor and vet. I owe that to the nursery."

"Yes," Henkky said, "of course. I already guessed that.

Sarkkhan wasn't only Golden's friend, you know, he was mine as well. And that nursery is still such an important part of our future. The future of Austar IV. Those owners who've closed their doors because of the embargo are shortsighted. The embargo won't be forever."

"Fifty years, he said."

"Hardly that. We . . . Golden has plans. They will take years off the embargo."

Akki leaned in. "He said something about rebuilding the Pit. And what else?"

But Henkky held up a hand. "Not for me to say." This time it was Henkky who leaned in. "Ah, yes — and the second reason?"

Akki closed her eyes for a moment, trying to think of the best way to frame the request. Finally, having made up her mind, she opened her eyes and stared right at Henkky. "This has to remain between us. No one else can know. Especially not Golden."

"I don't understand —"

"There's a problem with the dragons," Akki said. "Something I have discovered with . . ." She hesitated. "With their blood." Not entirely true, but not entirely false either. "I have to sort it out. It may be the only way to save all of them."

"*Save* them!" Henkky gasped. "Are they in danger? Without them, Austar will wither away."

"Terrible danger," Akki said. "So I need to be able to use your resources. Will you help me?"

"Tell me what the problem is and you can have the run of the laboratory I have downstairs," Henkky said.

"You have a laboratory? Golden said it was a hospice." Akki sat back in the chair, unbelievably relieved.

"Then, what's the danger?"

Akki's face closed down. "I *can't* tell you. Not yet. I need to do some experiments first. Trust me, if the secret gets out before I have a solution, *all* our dragons are at risk." Just as she spoke, something stirred by the hearth.

"Danger?" The sending was ringed with a soft violet halo.

She turned, expecting to see the hatchling, though how it had gotten into the room without her noticing was a puzzle. Suddenly, coming out from behind the other chair, stiff-legged and stretching, was a thigh-high Beauty, yellow with a spattering of red freckles on its nose and a smattering of red around its neck, like a jeweled collar.

"Down, Lib," Henkky said to the dragon, making a swift cutting motion with her hand.

The dragon dropped, quivering, onto the rug. *"Danger?"*

"No danger," Akki sent, sorry to lie like that. *"Not to thee, little one."* That much was true. No Beauty could breed. No breeding, no bloody egg chamber.

Lib stopped quivering, and lay quietly.

"Sorry for that," Henkky said. "Actually, she's a good girl and will leave us to our talk. Afterward, we can let the two of them, Lib and your dragon, out into the back garden for a romp. What's her name?"

Akki suddenly realized she had no idea. She'd just been calling it the hatchling. Then a snarky thought came to her, the perfect name. "Aurea," she said at last.

Dr. Henkky's head went back and she laughed so loud and so long, little Lib stood and quickly went behind the chair and didn't come out again. "That's the name Golden was going to give you, the female equivalent of an old Earth word for 'golden.' His little joke."

"I know," Akki said. "We girls can play games as well as the boys!"

"Then let's give you another name. Let's give you something to show you're free."

"But your name still has double *k*s."

Henkky's lips drew down into a thin line. "I'm spelling it with one *k* now. But for you — how about . . . *Argent.* Another word from Earth."

"What does it mean?"

"Silver."

Akki smiled. "I like that. And it sounds stronger than Aurea."

"It is, though not worth as much to the Feders."

"What do they know?" Akki said. "Except to spend money and rule with a heavy hand."

"What do they know indeed, Argent."

Akki put her hand out, then gave Henkky's small, strong hand two long shakes. She felt the first bit of real hope for the dragons that she'd had since coming home.

"Now," Henkky added, "let's do something just for us. Something with your hair. It looks as if it has been cut with garden clippers by a drunk."

"Close," Akki said, and laughed. "Very close."

ᴄ 24 ᴄ

AKKI SAT on the double bed in the bedroom Dr. Henkky shared with Golden. Henkky drew a pair of surgical scissors from her pocket and proceeded to even out Akki's cap of black hair, though the fringe over her eyes was left jagged.

"There," Henkky said, picking up a hand mirror from a bedside table. "Now it looks like a real haircut, not something chopped off with a knife."

"It was a pair of shears," Akki said.

As the two of them were close enough in size, Henkky gave Akki two dresses — one green and one blue — and a pair of elegant heeled sandals.

"You can try these on later," Henkky said. "I was going to give them to Senekka. She likes my old clothes. And these are *quite* old — from my childhood! But you'll need to look presentable at the debates tomorrow."

"Tomorrow?" Akki was stunned. "But . . . but I'm not going . . ."

Henkky frowned, picked up the scissors, made one more snip on Akki's hair. "You'll be introduced as Golden's niece."

"Argent. But I'm not —"

"Well, that's a story that will need to be firmed up before we get there, don't you think?"

"So I *am* going?"

Henkky nodded and then they laughed.

When Henkky held up the hand mirror, Akki stared at herself. "It *does* look good."

"And it changes your face, emphasizing the planes. You've lost weight, and now with this haircut, you look younger and more innocent."

"How do you know this sort of stuff?" Akki touched the fringe. "You're a doctor."

"You'd be surprised what someone can learn hanging around with the baggerie girls." Henkky set the scissors and hand mirror down on her dresser.

Akki thought for a moment. "Is that a good thing?"

Henkky shrugged. "It's *useful*. Like right now. And I can promise you that no one who has known you before will know you now."

"No one but the two of you know me here."

"How about the girls in the baggeries you helped treat last year? The members of the rebel cell you joined? Your father's old friends?"

Akki shrugged. "The girls paid no attention to me. The rebels have all been rounded up and sent offworld. And my father's old friends looked on me as an annoying little girl."

"Don't be so sure," Henkky told her.

Akki picked up the mirror and looked again. *Maybe she's right — but* I *don't recognize me.* Still, she wanted nothing to do with Golden's senate race. "Do I *have* to go to the debate?"

Dr. Henkky put her hands on Akki's shoulders. "We must do everything we can to get Golden reelected. His election's necessary — for Austar, for the dragons, for Sarkkhan's Nursery, for everything we hold dear."

"Good haircuts, fine dresses . . ." Akki couldn't disguise the bitterness in her voice.

"Now, my girl, there's dear — and dearly bought. You have to learn the difference. I know I have, though it's taken this last year for me to see it. Golden can help us — master and bonder, freemen and freewomen all." Henkky's face was unreadable, but there was a slight twitch under her left eye.

Akki hesitated, before saying, "I believed that once. Entirely. When Golden came to my father's nursery as Ardru. When he helped Jakkin give his dragon a fighting chance in the pits. When he was my father's friend. When he helped us escape from the mountains. But now . . . How can I trust him now? He's lied to me. He's manipulated me."

"And me," Henkky said. "It's his nature." She turned away, almost as if she didn't want her face to deny what her mouth said. "Whatever you think of him, he stands between us and total chaos. If I'm to keep working as a doctor, if you're to save the dragons, if we're to keep the rebels from our throats . . ."

Akki stared at Henkky's back. "I thought the rebels were gone, the worst ones sent offplanet, the innocents transformed into model citizens — *freed* model citizens."

Henkky whipped around. "Who told you that?"

"Golden did. In the truck. Today. Though I'd already heard it in the nursery from . . . well, from everyone. I mean, it's common knowledge. All the men in the nursery have been talking about it." Looking at Henkky's furious face, Akki took a deep breath. "I guess they're not to be trusted, either? Boys and their games and all that. Like Golden."

Henkky smiled slowly. It didn't change the anger in her eyes. "The men were repeating what they'd been told. But not all the worst rebels have been caught yet. Or sent away. And believe me, Golden's *not* to be trusted. He'll charm you out of your last copper. Or into another of his lizard-drool schemes. But even eyes-open and knowing he's not to be trusted, you go along with him. You have to."

"Why?"

Henkky looked down and said nothing.

"Because *you* love him?"

The doctor's answer spread across her cheeks in a red glow.

"You *love* him," Akki repeated, suddenly thinking of Jakkin. Even when she was angriest at him, she loved him. Sighing, she sent out a fall of soft gray rain with his name running through it in dark blue. Just in case. Just in case he'd managed to follow her to The Rokk.

Immediately, she received two sendings.

"Danger?" It was a soft violet aura, instantly recogniz-able. *Golden's Lib.*

"Danger?" It was brighter, more pointed, not an aura but a zigzag pattern of light reds and pale blues. The hatch-ling. *Aurea.*

Akki took another deep breath and sent back reassurances in the shape of a rainbow that incorporated both Lib's violets and Aurea's reds and blues. But though she listened with all her might, opened herself to the faintest of sendings, there was nothing from Jakkin. Not a signal, not a sending, not a sign.

"Fewmets! Where are you?"

She didn't trust Golden. She could not now entirely trust Henkky. She guessed that she was really on her own.

———

THEY ROUNDED UP the two little dragons and led them out of the back door into the garden.

Akki had never seen anything like it. It reminded her a bit of Jakkin's oasis, where she'd helped him train Heart's Blood. There was a miniature pool, rimmed with reeds, and some high tufted grass in the background, as tan as the reeds. Patches of leafed-out burnwort were wreathed in smoke near the tufted grass.

To one side of the pool stood a wooden structure with various flowers twining over its poles. She didn't recognize any of the flowers. *Offworlders. Like Golden.* A one-and-a-half-story greenhouse, with glass panels and wooden shutters, sat against the far wall, the sun flooding into it. It was filled with gourds and beans and other things she couldn't name.

A swath of cut grass, green as the eyes of little stinging insects, lay like a rug under a wooden table and chairs. The grass was all so perfect — and so perfectly astonishing — Akki was afraid to step off the walkway for fear of leaving crushing footprints.

The two dragons had no such fear. They galloped onto the green, Aurea banging into and overturning one of the chairs. Then they dove together into the pool, emerging to shake themselves dry. The water drops sailed across the grass to puddle near Akki's feet. The dragons then began to munch happily on the wort. Lib ate daintily, one leaf at a time. But the hatchling grabbed up an entire cluster of leaves all at once. She looked so silly, with several smoking leaves hanging out of the sides of her mouth, that first Akki and then Henkky laughed aloud.

The noise startled the dragons, and they bounded away, back to the pool, where they started the whole performance all over again.

"What have we here?" It was Golden. He'd come into the garden silently. Of course, the dragons had been making so much noise, it wasn't a surprise that they hadn't heard him until he spoke.

They turned as one to greet him, Henkky giving him an embrace and Akki glaring.

"What, my darling goddaughter isn't pleased to see me?" The exaggerated drawl, the slight mocking smile, the tight-waisted suit that was the color of the grass, all this made him as different from the Golden she'd known in the copter, as the Boomer she'd met in the truck.

Akki was at a loss for words.

"*Niece*, you old faker," Henkky said. "We'd better get that story down pat at dinner." She held out her hand to him and sat him down at the little table.

"And dinner will be soon, I hope."

"Senekka is at it now."

"How can I be bonded to a woman who can't cook? I should take Senekka to be my bondmate instead."

"She's not your type," Henkky said smugly. "And you love me because my work is more important to you than food."

He put his arm around her waist and drew her close, winking at Akki as he did so. "Nothing, my darling, is more important than food. As our young friend/niece/goddaughter there found out in the mountains. Food and shelter. And she will tell you all about it, once she finds her tongue." Laughing, he stood and led the doctor back into the house, where Akki, half reluctantly, half eagerly, followed.

～

AKKI DIDN'T expect it, but the dinner was astonishingly good. It wasn't the mash-and-bash dinners that Kkarina served up at the nursery — hearty, to be sure, but numbingly familiar. This dinner consisted of small portions of freshly picked and nicely steamed vegetables from the greenhouse. When bitten into, they released exotic herbs and spices. There was some sort of rice-and-egg dish that was entirely filling. And large crusty rolls with an empty center that could be filled with a sweet berry jam or a salty nut spread. She'd never had such a wonderful meal in her life, and said so to Senekka as she rose to help bring the dirty dishes into the kitchen.

"Sit down, goddaughter." Golden spoke in a drawling, haughty voice that was as much an act as Boomer's graceless sentences.

"Niece," Henkky reminded him.

Akki smiled at him. "If all Austarians are now equal — master and bonder — then shouldn't we do equal work?"

He leaned back in his chair, his hands clasped over his chest, and laughed. "When you can cook as well as Senekka, you will command her price. And it's not a small price, either, especially since all my friends have been trying to tempt her to leave me and go cook for them. She'd leave, too, if she weren't so enamored of me. Isn't that right, sweet-meatling?"

Senekka made a face at him.

He shook his forefinger at Akki. "So, till your skills are equal to hers, sit down and let her work at her own pace."

Senekka took the plates from Akki's hands. "He's right, you know. The kitchen is my domain. Not his. Not hers. And definitely not yours. I don't like anyone else banging around in it." It was more than she'd said so far, and she disappeared immediately through the kitchen door after making the pronouncement.

"And now," Golden said, the drawl gone for good, "let me tell you what tomorrow promises."

As if I'd go. But Akki was curious, and so she listened.

Tomorrow, it seemed, would pit the four men running for Golden's senate seat against one another in a debate at the senate hall. In the actual debate, they would be allowed to speak on any subjects they wanted to for twenty minutes. In the free-for-all that followed, they would challenge one another's assumptions, proffer their own in exchange, and none of it done politely.

Henkky added that in the free-for-all, they might also call an opponent names, mock his suit, his ideas, his physical attributes, or his ancestry. "In fact," she added, "everything is allowed then but violence."

"Well, at least the candidates have to be above the 'violence of the hand,'" Golden said. He seemed to be quoting actual rules, and only half seriously at that. Standing, he went over to a side table on which takk was bubbling away in a glass pot.

"Though not 'the violence of the mouth,'" Henkky added. She held up her cup for a refill, which he quickly poured for her. "Wit and wisdom combined with a wicked tongue are what wins the day."

"Is that *truly* how a senator is elected?" asked Akki, who'd never voted, having up to this time been too young, too female, too rural, and a proclaimed bonder. "It's . . . barbaric."

"Truly," Golden said charmingly, his hand on his heart. "You must trust me in this." But as Henkky had indicated earlier, there was very little to trust about Golden at all.

ᴄ 25 ᴄ

AFTER DINNER, Akki didn't stay up long. At Akki's third yawn, Henkky thrust her out of the dining room, where she and Golden were on their fourth cups of takk, topped up with chikkar, "the liquor of the gods," as Golden called it, though which gods he declined to explain.

"Down the hall, second bedroom," Henkky said. "You'll find your satchel on the bed. There's a shower room attached. See you in the morning." She held up her cup in a mock salute.

Akki left them gladly. As welcoming as they'd been, they seemed much happier in their own company and not eager for her to stay on with them. Besides, she was furious with them both, and disappointed, too. She disliked being manipulated, and hated even more being told what she had to do. Anger had raged inside her like dragon fire since the beginning of dinner. She thought she would burst apart with it if she had to remain a minute longer. She was surprised it took Henkky three yawns before dismissing her.

She found the room easily, unpacked, and took a quick shower. As a nursery-bred girl she was always careful about using too much water. Then she scrambled into a nightshirt, which was scrunched by its long day in the satchel, and hung up the two leather outfits.

There was a scratching at the door, and when she opened it, the hatchling raced into the room, sniffing in all the corners before settling itself on the rug.

Yawning for real this time, Akki fell onto the bed, an Austarian double, which was one and a half times the size of her bed at the nursery. Although she meant to stay awake and sort through her feelings — as well as her options — sleep grabbed her by the throat and wouldn't let her go until morning.

IT WAS the sound of the city rousing that finally woke her up — trucks starting, loud voices laughing, the slapping of boots on the paving. She'd forgotten how different those sounds were from what she was used to at the nursery or in the mountains. There, the first signs of morning were natural sounds — birds, insects, the pippings from the incubarn. For a moment she was unsure of where she was, but then quickly remembered: Golden's house, her own room, this big bed.

As she lay there stretching, she considered how the day might unroll. She knew the end of it, of course — the debate. But there were many hours to fill till then.

At her feet, the hatchling stirred, sending her a mental yawn the color of an early morning sky, light blue shot through with yellow.

"Hello to thee, too, my darling," Akki said aloud. "I'm

taking thee out to the garden before we have any accidents. I think Henkky will kill me if thee leaves fewmets on the rug."

She got out of the bed, stretched again, shucked out of her nightshirt and back into the same leathers she'd worn the day before. Glancing at the two party dresses hanging on a hook near the door, she shook her head. There was no reason to get into either of them, not until it was close to debate time. And hanging in the closet was the other set of leathers, just like the one she had on. No need messing them before she had to. She would take the hatchling to the garden, have a quick breakfast, then check out the basement lab.

The garden was bathed with the same yellow light as the hatchling's sending. Akki sat down in one of the chairs and watched while the little dragon leaped in and out of the pool, then did her business in a sandy spot behind the pool, almost hidden from sight. When the dragonling was finished, she walked over to Akki and sat down at her side, her neck scarcely long enough to allow her to lay her head on Akki's knees.

Soon Aurea would be twice that size, and then doubled again in another few months. In two years, she'd be ready to breed.

And dead soon after if the secret got out — as secrets always do. Dead at the hands of Austarians desperate for dragon hearing and dragons' hearts.

Aurea glanced up at Akki, her eyes small sparks of light.

"No danger," Akki said out loud, sending her bouncing yellow bubbles.

Not as long as I find a solution. But she kept that to herself. She meant to make the most of her time here before returning the dragonling to the nursery.

Time. It was what she feared the most. There was so little time. She put her head in her hands and was on the point of weeping. Things were hard enough, without Jakkin off playing games somewhere.

"Takk?"

Akki looked up. Senekka was holding out a tray on which sat a double takk pot, a single teapot, two cups, a lizard-egg omelet, and sweet toast.

"Tea, please. Thanks. I don't eat anything made from dragons. And you didn't have to . . ."

"I wanted to talk to you, anyway," said Senekka, in that low, throbbing voice, "and *they* won't be up for hours." Putting the tray down on the table, then pouring tea in one cup, takk in the other, she gave the tea to Akki, kept the takk for herself.

"Talk to me about what?"

"About the senator."

"Why me?" Akki said carefully, talking into the cup. "Why not ask him." She looked up.

"Ah." Senekka smiled and squatted down on her haunches so that she and Akki were about the same height.

Akki suddenly realized that she was a beautiful girl, her eyes so dark, they were almost black. There was a small black spot by the side of her lower lip, a blood score most likely, from Senekka's time in a nursery. It hadn't ruined her face but somehow enhanced it, making her look both vulnerable and heroic at the same time.

Senekka pursed her lips before speaking. "You know the senator. He's a politician. He'll tell you what he thinks you *want* to hear, not what you *need* to hear."

"Then ask Dr. Henkky."

"I don't dare." The voice throbbed even more.

"Why not?" Akki watched Senekka carefully and saw various answers warring across her face.

"She's afraid that if I make demands and she can't meet them, I'll leave. And then the senator will want her to do all the cooking and cleaning."

Akki laughed. It was such a silly answer, it deserved the laugh.

"She's a doctor." Now Senekka looked down at her cup.

It was a look Akki recognized. She'd seen it on Henkky's face only the day before. So she said plainly, "You *love* him."

Startled, Senekka stared at her, cheeks flushed. Now *she* began to laugh.

"What's so funny?"

"Not him," Senekka whispered. "Oh, God, not *him*."

For a moment, Akki couldn't think of a response. Then she whispered back, "You love *her*?" Such pairings were not unknown to her. There'd always been at least one bonded pair of women at Sarkkhan's Nursery ever since Akki could remember.

"I won't ever leave unless they send me away. But if the senator loses, he'll have no money in his bag. And they'll make me leave. Will the senator win? *Will* he?"

Akki was silent.

"*Will* he?" Senekka demanded.

"I don't know. But I'm sure he has money from else-where. You're worrying about the wrong thing. He's not in the senate for the money."

Senekka looked stunned. "For the power?"

Akki was silent for a moment. Then she said, "I think he enjoys it. Like a game . . ."

Senekka nodded, then taking her own cup and the takk pot away, she left Akki to finish her breakfast alone.

As Akki sat with the food, her mind was awhirl. She ended up nibbling a bit on the toast, took one bite of the egg, and then abruptly stood.

"*Come*," she sent to the hatchling. "*Aurea, come.*" But the dragonling was too busy eating more wort.

Akki worried that if the little dragon stayed much longer in the garden, there'd be no wort left. *A few days' supplies, no more.* She wondered if there was some kind of park nearby. When Rokk Major had still stood, dried wort was trucked in for the fighting dragons by the hundred-weight. Would it have come from farms in the outlying neighborhood, or large areas of parkland within the city it-self? She realized she had no idea.

But first she had to check the basement lab. Only after that would she think about getting the hatchling home. *It was stupid to have brought her here,* she scolded herself again. No matter what Henkky and Golden thought, setting up the lab and getting the hatchling home were much more im-portant than any silly debate.

She left Aurea in the garden and went down the hall,

opening doors one by one until she found stairs that led down.

The basement was far larger than she'd hoped, running the entire length of the house. There were four parts to it: a waiting room, an examination room, a hospice with four beds, and then the lab itself. In addition, to the right of the entrance was a small closed office the size of a huge closet. All three sections had side doors that opened out on to the street, which — Akki realized — must have meant a huge amount of earthmoving when the house had been built. Or when it had been refitted for Dr. Henkky.

She ignored the waiting room, with its pretty curtained windows and the profusion of books on the side tables. Though when she tried to imagine the Rokk women waiting there, she wondered how many of them could actually read. Most of the nursery bonders were not able to. In fact, the majority of bonders on Austar couldn't, though the masters were all literate.

The examining room had a steel sink and a well-worn steel table with a leather mat and metal stirrups. A small wooden chair sat next to a table on which pamphlets about women's diseases were prominently displayed. These had plenty of pictures. Again she wondered whether reading skills allowed the patients to get the full benefit of the information, or whether Dr. Henkky explained everything to her visitors and then used the drawings to emphasize what she'd just said.

But it was the lab to which Akki gave her full attention. She was pleased to see that it was expertly equipped with workbenches, a fume cupboard, a refrigerator, and four discrete storage units. There were flasks, funnels, pipettes, tubes, tongs, clamps, burners, and other equipment that she had no names for, much of it still in the original boxes. She was pleased as well when she spotted several microscopes, three boxed and one out on the wooden counter and already set up.

She guessed that everything she might need was on display, which was a relief. With the embargo, even if a few hospital ships got through, she might never get to replace anything that broke, so being careful of the equipment would have to be paramount as she did her lab work.

Lab work. It was a fine concept, but she didn't know where to start. And she couldn't very well ask Henkky. A secret between two of them was dangerous enough without bringing in a third person.

And of course the doctor would speak to the senator.

Then, God only knows how many people the senator would bring in on the secret. Soon, instead of a secret, it would be a conspiracy of the kind Golden so dearly loved.

Suddenly she realized how out of her depth she was. *I know how to doctor dragons. In a pinch I can nurse an injured man.* She'd had a few years of apprenticing, first to the old vet who worked for the nurseries around her father's place, and then coming to visit doctors in The Rokk, like Henkky. She'd drawn blood, understood a bit about DNA, and could read an X-ray. The vet called her a "bone wizard." If coached, she could interpret the printout of brain waves. But that was not nearly enough.

I'm smart, she told herself. *I can figure out new ways to heal from old knowledge if given a deadline.* She sighed. *Or enough time.*

But now, seeing the steel and glass lab, she finally had to admit to the truth of it: *The dragons of Austar are doomed, and our society with them, if it's only up to me to figure this out.*

Still, she couldn't just give up.

Quickly she opened every drawer, every door in the room, finding even more baffling items. Every piece of equipment that was put away was clean, much of it still in the original containers, seemingly unused. Whatever Henkky had outfitted the lab with, she hadn't found time or energy to try much of it yet. Akki spun around, trying to take it all in. On her second time around, she saw Henkky standing in the doorway, smiling.

"Find everything you need?"

Akki shrugged. "Actually, I'm not sure. There's so much here — and most of it untouched."

The doctor nodded. "As soon as Golden heard the rumor that the Federation might place an embargo on us, I decided I had to outfit a state-of-the-art lab."

"You mean stockpile?"

Henkky smiled. "You're looking at the original medical hoarder. I have my girls to worry about. I don't know what kind of accidents, diseases, even plagues, might arise in the future. So I've overbought."

"It looks like a medical store," Akki said.

Agreeing, Henkky added, "One of the pilots flew in this lot for me — well, for Golden, really. Their mothers were offworld friends." She opened several drawers randomly, fingering the contents, then turned to Akki. "I'm sure we'll find what you need."

"That's . . ." Akki hesitated. She put a hand on the one microscope that was out of its box. "That's the problem. I don't know what I need. Except . . . except maybe a tutor."

Folding her arms, Henkky asked, "What field?"

"Chemistry, I think. I need to understand dragon's blood."

"Interesting. And —"

Akki held up her hand. "And that's all I can tell you. Now."

"That's fine." Henkky looked directly into Akki's eyes. "You'll tell me the rest when you're ready. I wouldn't be much help, anyway. My chemistry courses were too long ago and I was never particularly brilliant in them. Besides, I know women, not dragons."

"I wasn't thinking that you'd —"

Henkky held up a finger. "I think I've got just the person for you. And he should be at the debate tonight. He had a stroke some time ago and can't handle things in the lab now. His hands shake too much."

"Can he still speak?"

Henkky laughed, a short snort through her nose, which reminded Akki of a dragon. "Endlessly. I think teaching you might be the saving of him. And now let's get you fitted for the debate." She turned and walked back into the hall.

Closing the lab door, she followed after Henkky. *That went well.* But a little voice in her head said: *Too easy.* It sounded remarkably like the hatchling's cry of *"Danger."* Probably the chemist wouldn't be at the debate, or too addled to teach her anything. *Or I may be like Henkky, not particularly brilliant at chemistry.*

However, one thing she did know. Now she had to go to the debate. Not for Golden, but for the dragons.

☾ 26 ☾

AKKI CHOSE the blue dress, which fit perfectly, possibly because Henkky had been tall as a child. It had short sleeves, a scoop neck, and a tiny pocket that shut with a bow. It was very pretty — for a rich twelve-year-old. *A good disguise.* No one would expect a seventeen-year-old bond girl to dress that way. The shoes were more sophisticated than she was used to, with a small heel. Having worn nothing but low shoes all her life, she wondered if she would last the evening so shod.

Golden and Henkky were even more dressed up. And Senekka was astonishingly beautiful in a dress the color of the little Beauty dragon: a sunny yellow, with a band of red around the waist.

They were all picked up by a senate car for the short ride to the hall. The driver was a small, dark, bald man with a gap in the middle of his smile. He came to the house and knocked on the door. Golden opened the door, his tie not yet knotted.

"Senator," the driver said, "everyone here?"

"Dikkon, as ever, you're on time."

"Senator, as ever, you're *not* on time." He flashed his gap-toothed smile.

Once they were seated in the car, Golden said, "With the embargo full on, one of the first things I'll do when re-elected —"

"*If* you are reelected," Henkky reminded him.

"You're supposed to be the one with the sunny disposition," he said sourly.

"Who told you that?"

"*I'm* the one with the sunny disposition, Senator," Dikkon called from the front.

Golden laughed. "You're the one who's supposed to be quiet and not listen in on conversations in the car."

"Who told you *that?*"

Sitting next to Akki, Senekka shook with silent laughter at the exchange, which made Akki bounce a bit.

"*Danger?*" The sending was gray, tremulous.

"*Don't be silly,*" Akki sent back. "*Nothing dangerous about a laugh.*" She enclosed the gray sending with a yellow border that slowly squeezed the gray into a single line that shot away like an arrow and was gone.

"If and when I'm reelected," Golden went on, oblivious to the laughter, the dragon's reaction, and Akki's response, "the first thing I shall do is to get rid of the senate cars. Goodness knows when we'll have the fuel to drive them again. It was all supplied by the Feders. I don't know why we don't walk. Protection, I suppose."

"Protection from what?" Akki was suddenly on alert.

Golden refused to answer.

"Senator, you get rid of the cars, you gotta do something for the drivers. We're voters now, too, you know," Dikkon said from the front seat.

Golden shook his head. "I know, I know. Voters and eavesdroppers the lot of you!"

Dikkon chuckled.

"Furthermore," Golden said to him, "all life is a series of compromises, and some have to compromise the most. I will have to walk and you, my friend —"

"I have to eat, Senator. I have to feed my family."

"He makes a strong point," Golden said, his finger waggling at Dikkon.

Henkky patted his hand. "You said 'one of the first' and then 'the first.' Which one is it to be?"

"Fewmets, woman!" he roared, which made the dragon go all quivery again. It took Akki a full minute to quiet her.

And why did I bring you? She knew she'd done it as much for her own comfort as the dragon's. She didn't want to have to worry about what the hatchling was doing to the house in her absence. Or the garden. And of course the little creature hated to have Akki out of sending range for very long.

Henkky smiled and patted Golden's hand again. "Just doing my job."

"I know, I know." He hung his head in mock contrition. "Which should I say?"

"One of," Henkky said.

"One of," Akki agreed.

"One of," Dikkon called from the front seat. "Makes me want to vote for you."

"One of," Senekka said, "because it gives you the ability to do it all at once or later."

"*She means I have latitude!* I like the way this girl thinks. If she weren't such a good cook, I'd make her an adviser."

"Over my dead body," Henkky said, and winked at Senekka. "Trust me, I need her more than you do."

Even in the shadowy inside of the car, even in Senekka's dark cheek, Akki could see she was blushing.

Golden raised his voice. "As for you, Dikkon, I'd hoped you were going to vote for me, anyway. Because of my happy disposition."

"And your good tips," Dikkon replied. He pulled the car over to the curb, then got out. He opened the door and when Golden got out said, "Take the car away and make me an adviser, Senator, and I'll always tell you the truth. Not like them, their hands always out for something." His chin jutted toward the crowd already gathered in front of the auditorium.

"Even if I don't want to hear the truth, Dikkon?" Golden gave him his broadest grin.

"Especially then," Dikkon said, closing the car door.

"You're on, my friend," Golden said to him. "Now, ladies . . ." He gathered them around him and steered them toward the building.

A buzz of well-dressed men and a few women in long skirts stood outside the hall. Several of them were smoking, hazy clouds curling above their heads. Akki wondered if they were smoking wort or the last of the offworld tobac.

A fat man came over to them. "Senator Golden, I presume?" His jowls quivered as he spoke.

"Senator MacMaster, without presumption," Golden replied, nodding at the man. "Are the other debaters here?"

"You're the last to arrive. But —" MacMaster struck his chest with the flat of his hand. "But first in our hearts." He laughed. "*If* you win." He laughed again, a low gulping sound. "Why so late?"

"Women, you know," Golden said, gesturing to Henkky and the girls. "Takes a long time to get them dressed."

"Only if you do it single-handedly." The fat man laughed so hard at his own joke, his jowls bounced. He walked them toward the door, a hand on Golden's elbow. Henkky was right behind them, nodding confidently at the smokers.

"Maybe the first thing Golden should do is change the way he speaks about women," Akki muttered.

Henkky turned and shook her head. "That's not what Golden *thinks*," she said. "Don't mistake him. It's only a game he plays with the other senators, who are, at heart, afraid of us women and our power." Then she and Golden disappeared into the crowd.

Boys and their games. Akki smiled ruefully. *But oh! How I wish Jakkin was here right now.*

The hatchling's response thrummed against her arm.

The hall was packed, and Senekka pushed people aside, pulling Akki after her. As Akki threaded her way through the crowd, the hatchling snuggled into her armpit, tail around her upper arm.

"Either thou has gained weight overnight, or this is an

awfully awkward way of carrying thee," Akki whispered to the little dragon. Pressing even closer, the hatchling thrummed some more, just from the sound of Akki's voice.

"Over here!" called Henkky, waving her arm. She was standing in the front row. An elderly gray-faced man stood by her, leaning on a carved wooden cane.

As Akki and Senekka waded through the people to get to Henkky, they were jostled and spun about. At one point, Akki slipped and Senekka grabbed her arm to help, which shook the hatchling loose till she dangled by just her tail. Akki gathered her up quickly, wrapping her arms around the terrified dragon. Gone was the happy thrumming. Now Aurea sent wave after wave of grayness. In fact, she was so terrified, she didn't even have the energy to send any color at all other than gray. Akki held her close, willing her to calm down.

"Argent, Senekka, this is my old friend Dr. George Smithers. Formerly of Tenebrum in the Federation. A chemist by training. A teacher by preference." She winked at Akki.

It was very noisy in the hall and Akki had to strain to hear. For a moment, she'd forgotten she was supposed to be Argent. Then she remembered and nodded, holding out her hand to the old man.

"Alas, girls, no longer either chemist or teacher," he said. His face was long, the chin dropping to his chest, as if it and the rest of his body had recently succumbed to gravity. Yet even old, even ill, his voice was strong, probably from years of lecturing to a class. He took Akki's hand.

"But surely your brain hasn't retired, sir," Akki said loudly, giving him her *pretty* smile.

Henkky's laughter rang out. "She's Golden's niece and goddaughter, the student I told you about. Argent. Silver to Golden's gold."

So now I'm both. Akki smiled inwardly. *That's a smart move on Henkky's part. None of us can make a mistake that way.*

"Ah," Dr. Smithers said, "the dragon's blood girl. Well, she has her uncle's gift of the silver tongue indeed."

Henkky put a hand on his shoulder as he let loose of Akki's hand, turning him slightly and speaking right into his ear, for he was, it seemed, somewhat deaf. "And this is Senekka, the girl I cannot do without."

Once again blushing, Senekka took the old man's hand. "Just the cook and house girl, sir."

"Chef. *And* my right hand," Henkky amended.

Just then the four men running for the senate seat ambled across the stage and sat down in four straight-backed chairs behind the debate table. Immediately, the buzz in the hall quieted and everyone quickly found a seat.

Akki shifted the dragon to her lap, stroking Aurea's scaly head till she settled down. Till they *both* settled down. Then Akki began to study the men.

Golden had come in first and sat on the far right. He looked totally relaxed, even leaning his elbows on the table and waving at friends. Next to him was a short man with thinning red hair, who seemed ill-at-ease being stared at by so many people. Next was a tall, narrow-bodied, bronze-colored man, his nose long and thin as well. He exercised his fingers while waiting for the debate to start. His fingers were long and thin, too. Akki wondered if his voice would be like that, a long string of a voice. The fourth man seemed pleasant enough, well tanned and smiling. His hair and eyebrows were so blond, they were almost white. There were patches of color on his cheeks, as if he'd painted them on, but when he folded his hands in his lap and closed his eyes for a moment, the patches faded, so Akki knew they were real.

A fifth man walked across the stage, taking his place behind a raised podium to the right of the table. He was the jowly fat man who'd whisked Golden out of the car. As he strode along, Akki was amazed that he practically danced, his movements giving the lie to the fact of his weight. He reminded her of Sssargon coming down to earth, all that poundage floating easily through the air.

"Dragons here?" The sending was full of caricatures of different-colored dragons, some walking, some flying, some settling down.

"Only thee," Akki sent back, focusing on the smallest of the dragons in her sending. *"Only thee."*

"Good evening," the fat man said to the crowd. "You all know me. Or if you don't, you soon will. I'm Master Mac-Master that was, though only plain Mac these days. But still a master . . . of ceremonies."

A polite laugh ran around the room, and the hatchling shivered with the sound of it.

"So, as I'm in charge here, the boys beside me have to follow my instructions or off they go."

Boys! Akki snorted, and so did the hatchling, though it came out more of a sneeze.

Jowls waggling, Mac continued. "We will hear from them in order of reverse seniority — that means from young to old to you illiterates out there."

There was a smattering of hisses from the audience, and one voice cried out, "The only thing you've read, Mac, are the instructions on cookie tins!" He received a round of light applause.

Henkky leaned over and, wrinkling her nose, said to Akki, "This is why I rarely attend these meetings." She petted the hatchling on the head, then sat back up and whispered something to Dr. Smithers, who coughed — or perhaps laughed — into a gray handkerchief.

Grinning, Mac held up his meaty hand for silence, and the room swiftly returned to normal. "At least I *can* read, Elric. So as my great-great-grandma would say, 'Shut yer cakehole.' And she had the fist to make it so." He formed a fist and shook it at the audience.

This time the applause was fierce.

Mac waited till the clapping died down, then said, "So Anders Sigel, there, goes first, being the baby of the group *and* the most nervous. Though God knows why, since he's run for the senate before." He pointed to the short man.

"Then Run-on Macdonald will speak. Those of you who have followed politics will remember that he was a senator in his youth." That was the thin man.

From the audience someone shouted, "And a long time ago that was!"

His comment was greeted by cheers.

Mac let them settle down again, before going on. "Not *that* long ago." He pointed to the white-blond man. "Then our newcomer to politics, Jay Dark." Dark's cheeks were once again patched with red. Akki wondered if Dark's name had recently ended in two *k*s, which would explain why he was a newcomer to the senate race.

Mac extended his entire arm this time. "And the last speaker will be our current senator, the once and future king, Senator Durrah Golden."

There was an appreciative laugh.

"After their opening remarks — of no more than ten minutes, as I must now remind you — the free-for-all will begin. Responses, rebuttals, recantings, refusals, regurgitations, rejections, remonstrations, retributions, and any other rewinds you would like."

"How about reformations?" someone called.

Giving a jowly smile, Mac said, "That, too, my friend. And ladies, those brave enough to be here, there will likely be cursing as well, I have no doubt of it." He waggled a finger at them. "So be prepared. There's two *f* words here to remember: We've got no *fainting* in politics but plenty of *fewmets*." He paused for the laugh he knew would come.

"But remember . . ." Mac pointed to a side window, where the sky was a dark blue slate on which nothing had been written. Yet. "The free-for-all runs only for an hour. Unless you want to freeze your cohoes in Dark-After. Or stay here and sleep on the floor. Me, I'll have a glass of the senate's chikkar after the debate and then get home and tucked in with my missus before the second moon is glimpsed by any of you still-not-persuaded voters."

He turned to the panel. "Sig, you're on. I have a wrist-watch, a souvenir of Old Earth, that lets me know the time. And if you go over, I'll signal like this." He put two of his huge fingers into his mouth and let out a piercing whistle.

Akki smiled. *There's no way that nervous man will go over his time.*

She was right.

Mac moved back behind the panel and changed places with Sig, who stood up almost reluctantly and walked to the podium dragging his feet. Once there, he put a hand on each side and held on so fiercely, his fingers went nearly white. When he began speaking, it was so quiet, Akki had to lean forward, as did Henkky, and *they* were sitting in the front row.

In his passionless way, Sig spoke about Austar IV, how it ran hot and cold, so hot the sands could burn you and so cold the moons could freeze you, but that just made the Austarians all the stronger. He said they had a chance to win back their place as a Protectorate, even a member of the Federation, if they just kept their heads down and worked hard. "As I mean to do as your senator if you elect me," he said. And that — it seemed — was the end of his speech.

There was a smattering of applause, mostly from the men in the front rows who could actually hear him. But when Akki turned around to glare at the people in the back, they were lolling in their chairs or whispering to their neighbors. A few were exchanging coins as if they'd laid bets on Sig's performance. She doubted they'd heard a word he said.

And then Sig walked back to the table, watching his feet as he went. He exchanged places with the thin man who, once standing, moved as if none of his parts were actually connected except, perhaps, by strings, like a puppet. Unlike Sig, he disdained putting his hands on the podium but stood quite still. When he spoke, his voice could easily reach the back rows, though it never seemed as if he was using any special effort.

"Well, at least we can hear *him*," Akki whispered.

"That was his one trick as a senator," Henkky whispered back. "He could be heard anywhere. Unfortunately."

"Why unfortunately?"

"He'd nothing much to say and said it a lot." Henkky leaned back against her seat, her hands clasped in her lap. "That's why they call him Run-on."

Akki stifled a giggle, then passed that tidbit on to Senekka, who laughed as well.

Henkky's assessment proved true. Run-on had nothing much to say and he spoke endlessly. It was all stuff every Austarian already knew — that Austar was the fourth planet of a seven-planet rim system in the Erato Galaxy. That it had once been a penal colony marked KK29 on the convict map system. That it was metal poor and covered by vast deserts, and that there were five major rivers.

At that point, the back rows exploded in a chant with the names of the rivers: *"Narrakka, Brokk-bend, Left Forkk, Rokk, and Kkarrrrrrr."* They rolled out the final *r,* and then the chant began again, continuing for well over a minute.

Run-on turned and gestured to Mac with his right hand. "Mr. Master of Ceremonies, I claim back a minute of my time because of that danged chant."

Mac nodded and waved him on, seemingly indifferent to the crowd's preferences.

Then Run-on spoke about the desert plants, the spikka trees, about burnwort and blisterweed.

At that, the back rows erupted again, with shouts of "Wort! Weed!" They mimed smoking and falling about with silent laughter.

Run-on continued speaking over them. "But what we are best known for," he said, his voice rising dramatically, "are our dragons." He raised his hand to make the point, though the dramatic gesture was undercut by the fact that his hand was shaking as if on the end of that invisible string.

This time the entire audience — with the exception of the front row — shouted, *"DRAGONS!"*

For some reason — Akki was never to understand how or why — this communicated to Aurea, who disentangled her tail from Akki's arm and pumped her little wings, effectively hovering above the front-row seats.

This of course led to a huge roar of laughter and then thunderous applause.

Frightened by the noise, the hatchling burped smoke and dove back into Akki's lap, burying her head there, and singeing the borrowed dress.

Run-on was hooted off the stage and he headed straight out the side door. He didn't return.

"Oh, Dr. Henkky, I am so sorry about the dress . . ." Akki began.

Henkky grinned at her. "I'm not. At least it shut him up. Maybe for good."

Wild applause broke out around the hall when it became clear that Run-on was not returning. Mac let it go on until it began to die down on its own. Only then did he stand and wave his hand. "Now, folks, let's let Jay Dark speak before Dark-After traps us all here for the night."

"That would be me," shouted Golden, "since I speak after Dark."

The laughter that followed made everyone calm down, and Dark walked over to the podium. Then he came around and stood in front of it.

"This should be interesting," Henkky said.

Akki thought so, too.

Dark waited until the silence stretched like a horizon line. And then, almost casually, he began to speak. His tone was soft, confiding, as if he were sitting knee-to-knee with a good friend, drinking takk and talking, but he could still be heard everywhere in the hall.

"Anders Sigel talks about hard work, and so he should. We have — boys, girls — much hard work ahead of us. And our other speaker, Run-on Macdonald, has drawn our attention to the deserts and rivers, the plants and animals of Austar. But only in passing did he mention the thing that makes our planet so special. The scum of the galaxies were sent here, to a KK planet, a jail cell the size of a world, and here we were left to rot. That's what the Feders did for us."

He stopped for a moment, to gather the listeners even closer to him. Akki felt herself leaning in, riveted. Dark was a storyteller, and something else. Something familiar. She had no idea what it was.

Dark said, "My great-great, seven times, great-grandmother was sent here for stealing food for her younger brothers and sisters. She never saw those little ones again. As an introduction to Austar, she was raped by three wardens one after another for a week, then thrown out of the house into the start of Dark-After."

Hardly anyone moved, though the story was one that almost everyone there could have told.

"A street-cleaner going home for the night found her and brought her to his hovel with him. Though she didn't know it for a month after, she was pregnant with twins. The boy died, never had a chance. But the girl lived and she was my great-great, six times, grandmother." He smiled. "Like the rest of the KKs, she worked hard and pulled herself out of the muck."

"What about the wardens?" shouted someone.

Dark looked at the audience, his hand shading his eyes so he could see better, since the light was on the stage, not on the listeners. Pointing a finger at the speaker, he replied, "Glad you asked, son. The wardens might have had more money and better houses than we KKers did — but they were just as stuck in the muck as we were."

"Enough history," someone called.

Dark laughed. "All history ends in the word *story*. So here's the end of this particularly hi-*story*. When we wardens and KKers started to make a noise together, seven generations after we were thrown into Austar, the ones who first flew us into this world cell flung us back again."

He looked around, saw that he had every eye on him, and said, "*Embargo!* That's what I'm talking about. Embargo is the Feders' way of showing us that they are still in control, still in charge."

"What are you going to do about it?" a man called from the back.

Akki turned to look. He was the same man who'd shouted out before. She wondered if he was a friend of Dark's, or just an interested voter.

Dark smiled. He reached behind his back and pulled a gun from under his shirt, where it had been stuck in his belt. He held it up. "Mac has his souvenir of Old Earth and I have mine."

There was a gasp from the front row.

"Don't worry, ladies," Dark said, smiling down at them, "there are no bullets in it. Yet."

A ripple of laughter ran along the row. Even Akki laughed.

Then Dark pulled on a chain around his neck, and out came a bond bag. "I am a man," Dark said. "No one chains me." His voice rose. "I am a man. No one brands me." His voice became almost apocalyptic. "I am a man. I fill my bag myself." He took a deep breath. "That's what we said before. And I say it now. Never fear — if they embargo us, *we* will embargo them."

And that's when Akki realized why Dark had seemed so familiar. Yes, the hair was now light, not black. Yes, his face was tanned, not pale. Yes, the mustache was gone; he was cleaned up, turned out, and charming. She began to tremble.

"Danger?" the hatchling sent. A gray rain of arrows fell into Akki's brain.

"Oh, yes," she whispered to the dragonling. "Danger indeed."

She didn't know what to do, except to act as if she had no idea who he was. So she stared up at Dark, pretending to be a young girl in the front row, Golden's goddaughter and niece, totally captivated by what he had to say. But really, with sweat running down her back, she was trying to recognize in his bland, tanned face the harsher, angry, taut face of Number One, the rebel leader Swarts, who'd given Jakkin and her the bag of explosives that had brought down Rokk Major Pit.

She shook her head. *Maybe* she was wrong. *Maybe* he was just someone who'd known the rebel creed, the words they were all made to recite at the beginning of each cell meeting. The words she'd learned when posing as a rebel. *Maybe . . .*

"Time!" Mac called, and Dark smiled at him, before walking slowly back to the table.

The crowd burst into thunderous applause. Several men whistled approvingly. Not to draw attention to herself, Akki applauded, too. But her mind was still racing. *Is he . . . isn't he?*

"Well, now we know which one is going to be our problem," Henkky said.

"Yes," Akki said. *More than you know.*

Should she tell Henkky? *Maybe.* Tell Golden? *Surely.*

But Golden was already standing, then striding to the podium, coming around as Dark had done. He held a sheaf of papers in his hand, which he slowly, methodically tore into pieces, before slamming the pieces down on the table's edge. "After Dark's passionate speech, no written statement will suffice," he said.

Henkky whispered to Akki, "I don't know what he just tore up. He never writes down his speeches."

Golden looked slowly around the room. "But a response is in order. And it is this: What happened to our many times great-grandparents is, indeed, history. But the story we must write now is our own, not theirs. If they were alive today, that's what they would tell us because they lived and died trying to leave us a better world than they had come from, trying to leave us a better world than they had come to know."

There was a smattering of applause and a man cried out, "What about the embargo?"

"Shut up!" someone else said.

Golden held up his hand. "No, no, we must never shut one another up. Asking questions is the only way to get to the answers. And the embargo is the most important question of our lives right now."

He looked down at Henkky and smiled. "I told my pairmate as we came here that if I'm elected, one of the first things I'd do is get rid of the senate cars. They are too expensive, and we need whatever fuel we still have for essential vehicles. It was the right answer, but the wrong question."

"What's the right question, then?" two men roared out together.

"The right question is what do we have to do to make fuel available to all of Austar," Golden said. "The right question is how do we make sure we are no longer beholden to the Federation — for fuel, for medicines, for scientific discoveries."

He stopped, drew a deep breath, and began again. "For, make no mistake, friends, we are still in bond as long as we think we have to work hard to please the Feders. We are still in bond as long as we think we are only a gathering of facts and figures about a planet. We are still in bond as long as we are fighting the old wars, righting the old wrongs between us with pistols or stingers, with machetes or knives. We must stand on our own. We must make a *new* history, not be bound by the old stories. Warden-kin *and* bonder-kin together. Men *and* women together. And, I suspect, dragons, as well."

How can he know that? Or is it just a wild guess? Akki began to shiver. *Was the secret out already? Did Henkky tell?*

Golden jabbed a finger at the audience. "*That* is what I will fight for, whether as your senator or just one of the voters of this great planet. We owe it to our past, we owe it to our present, and we sure as hell owe it to our future."

Henkky sprang to her feet clapping, as did the entire front row after her. And slowly but surely so did the entire hall. The cheering went on and on, but all Akki could think of was how soon she might get to Golden and warn him. *He has won the battle but he may have lost the war.*

⟡ 27 ⟡

THERE WAS such noise in the room that Mac declared the debate over and announced that they should go right to the party, where if they wanted to indulge in a free-for-all over glasses of chikkar, they could. And if they wanted to ask their questions there, they could. He screamed out the information.

The rush to the door was so frantic, Henkky signaled for Akki and Senekka to wait.

"You two can go home now if you'd like. It'll just be a crush and a drunken brawl. I have to stay and be the elegant pair-mate. Shake hands. Kiss cheeks. Sigh at the right places," she told them. "All this to make sure we can keep our hospices afloat."

"I need to talk to Golden," Akki said. "It's important."

"It can wait till we are all home. Or tomorrow."

"No!" she told her. "I have to speak to him *now!*"

Henkky looked at her with irritation. "I know you've come out of the mountains with a list of grievances, Akki. But tonight is not about *you*. It's Golden's night. There is a time and place —"

"If I don't get to him now, there will be no more time.

And maybe no place left, either." Akki turned away from Henkky, who shrugged dramatically at Senekka.

"I'll go with her," Senekka said quickly.

Shoulder to shoulder, the two girls made a dash for the door, catching the tail end of the crowd of men eager to get to the free drinks.

They found Golden surrounded by a double circle of men, and by ducking under a wall of arms, they made their way to him. He was expounding on the subject of the embargo to two walleyed men, clearly brothers, while the others in the circle listened closely. Akki touched his shoulder.

Looking around, Golden gave her a huge grin. "Gentlemen," he said expansively, "my niece, Aurea."

"Argent," she told him.

He shrugged. "Girls. Always changing their names. That's the third she's had this month! You men would do well to change your shirts as often."

A huge laugh ran round the circle.

One man, wearing a broad-brimmed hat, asked, "Why haven't we heard of this pretty little girl before?"

Golden put his arm around her protectively. "Because an old baggerie flame of my dead brother just decided to let me know. But I never quibble about these things. It would be useless, after all. See how much she looks like me."

Akki looked at him, unbelieving, and said, "I don't look *anything* like you, Uncle Golden."

He laughed. "Neither did my brother!"

The crowd loved it, roaring their approval, and she realized that whatever they thought she was to him didn't matter. He was telling them simply that she was under his protection.

I could be just as protected back in the lab, anonymous. But she reminded herself that in such a small society, that might not be entirely true. What Golden had done was to draw a line in the sand, but he'd done it in his typical way — with humor. Still, she was finding it hard to forgive him.

I should just leave him to stew.

The little dragon shook its wings out, then climbed onto her shoulder, leaving pinpoint holes in the bodice and sleeves of her dress. Akki was about to pull away from Golden's arm when another man stepped into the circle of men.

Dark.

For a moment his eyes caught hers, and she quickly looked down. *You're just an innocent little girl, Golden's niece,* she reminded herself. So she pitched her voice higher than usual. Throwing her arms around Golden, she said excitedly, "Oh, Uncle, you were so wonderful tonight." She worked hard at ignoring Dark so close by.

Golden noticed Dark at the same time and grinned broadly. "I don't see you with a glass of chikkar, friend," he said, "to toast to the first of our three debates." He turned a bit, Akki's arms still around him. "Someone bring Dark here a glass." He whispered into Akki's hair. "What's wrong?" He'd guessed.

The minute Dark turned to take the glass, Akki said urgently to Golden, "I have to talk to you. Now. There's danger."

The dragon sent shivers through her head, no longer gray but red-hot.

Golden laughed, then said in an expansive voice that broadcast around the circle, "Here? Surrounded by friends?"

He was careful not to repeat the word *danger*. "How can you be shy here?"

She replied in the same high-pitched voice, "I just am."

Dark insinuated himself into their intimate circle. "You won this day, Golden, and deserve to celebrate with your friends. And your pretty niece. No doubt I still have a chance to win the next debate now that I know where you stand. The next one, or possibly two. Who knows? You may even decide to step down once you hear from me again."

Laughing, Golden held up his glass toward Dark. "You have the true Austarian spirit."

"Why shouldn't I," Dark said. "I, at least, was born here."

Still smiling, Golden said, "You think because I was born offworld, I have less of a claim to Austar?" His tone was light but Akki could hear the iron underneath. "But for an early delivery, I would have been a native. I was brought here by my mother and father as an infant. I have lived here all my life."

"I do not protest your birth, Master Golden," said Dark, "though mine was an accident, too."

The crowd loved this thrust, applauding wildly — which spilled many a glass of chikkar.

"But I was born by accident into a bonder's family. Look at you — how long have you held on to your status?"

Golden's smile never wavered. He used it to draw them all in, even Dark. "Do not mistake my lifestyle for my policies. I was born neither bonder nor master but a new sort of Austarian. I made my money the old-fashioned way, by working for it. One dragon at a time. And as much as I liked making it, I have enjoyed spending it, too."

"Hear! Hear!" the men around him called out.

"He's funding the restoration of The Rokk out of his own pocket," said one man.

"Well," Golden said, a hand up in a kind of protest, "not *all* of it. I have some friends I've tapped."

"And tapped out!" Mac said, his bulk moving several men over as he entered the circle.

Laughing, Dark raised his hands. "I give up for now. I don't wish to argue here but will wait till the next debate."

"You did well for a first debate in a first run," Mac told him sincerely. "Standing in front of the podium — brilliant."

"Do not mistake my style for my substance," Dark said in the exact tone that Golden had used. This brought another smattering of applause. "And now I am leaving. It's getting late. I am extremely sensitive to Dark-After. And staying on the far side of the city. Oh, by the way, I can escort your niece home. Argent is it — this month?"

Akki's reaction was so immediate, so visceral, so violent, the hatchling lifted from her shoulder and fluttered for a moment before landing again.

Dark looked over and his mouth curved. On anyone else it would have been a smile.

Golden bowed slightly to him. "Silver to my gold, she tells me, though even last week she was Aurea. Young girls are so changeable. I think I will never understand them."

"Ah, Aurea, which means gold, named after you, I see."

Smiling, Golden said, "You're a very well educated man for —"

"For an ex-bonder."

"There's a car," Golden said, then laughed. "But of course, I am no longer using a senate car."

The men cheered.

"No, I want to stay with you, here," Akki said. The dragon hissed from her shoulder.

"It's not a long walk," Golden told her. "And Senekka will be with you."

Senekka, who had been quiet the whole time, nodded. "I will."

"And Henkky?" he asked, looking around.

"She's shaking hands and being charming," Akki whispered. Briefly she considered telling him then and there, exposing to all of them who Dark was. But that would mean revealing who she was as well: Sarkkhan's daughter, the one who — all inadvertently — blew up Rokk Major. And if Golden wanted to ease into it, prepare the way, she would ruin things. Blow them up again. And ruin Golden's senate bid. Hand it over to men like Dark. And then where would the dragons be?

And what if I'm wrong about Dark? she asked herself. *I could expose us all — and for nothing.* But she knew now that she wasn't wrong.

Just then, as if conjured up by her name, Dr. Henkky joined the circle, and Golden took his arm from around Akki and put it around Henkky's waist. "Done with the handshakes and charm, darling?" he asked.

She looked around the circle. "Only getting started. More chikkar, boys?"

They raised their glasses.

"See you in the morning, girls," Henkky said, and turning her back on them, she raised her glass to the men. "To that dragon of debaters. To Golden!"

"Golden! Golden! Golden!" they cheered.

The cheer muffled their movements as Dark, smiling broadly, led them out a side door into an alleyway. Though Akki tried to hold back, Senekka led her on.

"Come on," Senekka said, "they wanted us gone. *She* wanted us gone."

"We should have stayed," Akki whispered. "Dark is —"

Senekka misunderstood. "We have plenty of time till Dark-After. Even walking. Two hours at least."

"Come on, girls," Dark said, still smiling, and signaling them with his hand.

He was at the end of the alley. Suddenly he stopped, leaned forward, and checked the street both ways. When he turned back, he had the gun in his hand and was pointing it at them.

Senekka looked startled. Then she laughed. "I get it. It's a joke."

Akki gasped. "No joke."

Senekka stared at her. "He said it wasn't loaded. In the debate." She spoke louder so Dark could hear. "You said it wasn't loaded."

Akki was suddenly ice-cold and the hatchling on her shoulder shivered as well, tail curling and uncurling around her arm.

No longer smiling, Dark glared at them. "Sorry, girls," he said. "I lied."

☾ 28 ☾

SENEKKA TURNED to Akki. "He couldn't possibly shoot us. We've done nothing to him."

"Tell her, Number Four," Dark said.

"Number Four?" Senekka asked.

"I don't know what he's talking about. He thinks I'm someone I'm not." Akki was no longer cold. She was ice. And the dragon was sending her huge icicles bearing down on her like daggers, no longer gray but glaring white. The sendings all but drowned out Senekka's voice. And Dark's.

If she wanted to make out what the others were saying, she'd have to build up a wall in her mind, stone by stone, as she and Jakkin had learned to do in the caves of the trogs. Only that way could she shut out the hatchling and concentrate on what was happening around her. So she bent her mind to the wall.

Stone.

By.

Stone.

By.

Stone.

When at last she'd shut out the dragonling's insistent sendings, she realized that she'd completely missed whatever it was that Dark had said next.

"She can't be *that* horrible person," Senekka was saying. "She's Golden's niece. His goddaughter. From a dragon nursery. Not a rebel. Not a murderer. Not a ..." Her hands were wrangling together. "You have to let us go. We won't say a thing about the gun. We'll —"

Dark cut her off. "Oh, she's that person, all right. With the stink of worm still on her despite her pretty blue dress and new haircut. Trying to look younger than she is. And sillier. But what's bad for me is that she's alive, which I hadn't counted on. I didn't think anyone who knew me before Rokk Major blew up was still alive. Or on Austar IV." Backing down the alley, the gun still held on them, he signaled them to follow.

"We can jump him," Senekka whispered. "He can't shoot us both at the same time."

"He can if we stick together," Akki whispered back, still keeping up the wall in her head. "And if he's a good shot."

"Is he?"

"How should I know?"

"I knew you couldn't be that person he says you are."

"Never mind *that* person," Akki said. "We have to concentrate on Dark. I'll rush ahead and bump into him, send the dragon at his eyes, while you run back through the door and get help."

"Will it work?"

Akki had no idea. "It *has* to."

"Come on, come on, you two," Dark called.

"No, I'll do the bump . . . if he shoots me, what does it matter?"

Akki shook her head. "It matters. And since it's me he seems to be focusing on, I've got to be the one."

Before Senekka could argue further, Akki took off at a run toward Dark, screaming, "I'm alive and so is Jakkin, you piece of worm drool!" As she ran, she grabbed the hatchling off her shoulder, tearing the dress at the seam. Then she threw Aurea toward Dark. But she'd forgotten the carefully built wall, and the hatchling was puzzled when it couldn't reach her mind, spending precious seconds trying to break down the wall for instructions. Then the hatchling circled Dark's head, wings beating, making a piteous squeaking sound.

"Danger! Danger! Dive at him. Dive!" Akki shouted, at the same time hurling a blood-red sending through a small chink in the stone wall. Behind her, she could hear Senekka hammering on the door, which must have locked shut automatically when they went out.

"Dive!" Akki screamed again at the hatchling. "Danger!" She flooded a blood-red river through the enlarging chink.

The hatchling dove.

With his left hand, Dark tried to bat at the dragon, keeping it from getting to his eyes. The other gripped the pistol. He sighted along it, and squeezed the trigger twice in rapid succession.

Senekka screamed and the dragon — having gouged Dark's left temple badly — wheeled away.

Not knowing if they'd been hit, Akki continued her headlong rush toward Dark, hands like claws stretched toward his face. At the last minute, her right ankle twisted because of the heeled shoe and she fell headlong into his chest instead. He smashed the gun barrel down on the top of her head.

Blood rained into her eyes. *Scalp wounds are the worst.* She raised her hands to her face. *Or else it's a sending.* Then the pain began and she knew it was real.

The wall began to crumble entirely, and she fell onto Dark and into the dark.

~

AKKI WOKE to streams of cold running across her body. Black was all around her. At first she thought she was home in bed. Then she realized she was lying on some sort of mattress or pallet on a floor. The mattress was thin and lumpy. Turning over carefully, she spotted a ray of gray light through a chink.

In the wall? She quickly realized the wall in her head was down, though there were no frantic sendings coming through. The chink was not in her mind at all, but in a wooden shutter over some kind of window.

Window. Light. Cold. She tried to make sense of it.

Her head was sore. Not like a sore head after a night of drinking chikkar; that soreness usually began in the back of the throat and radiated into the temples. This soreness hurt from the outside in. She tried to put a hand to her head, and that's when she found that her hands were tied behind her.

She thought again: *Window. Light. Cold. Dark-After.*

As quickly, she said aloud, "Dark," though she wasn't sure what she meant by that.

But now she began to remember some of what had happened to her. Some — not all. She remembered the debate and the four men speaking. First the scared man and then the boring man and then the man who stood in front of the podium. *That man!* She remembered recognizing him. His name was Dark. She remembered the chikkar party and leaving early with Senekka and . . . and after that — after that, everything was blank.

Had someone kidnapped her? Was Senekka taken, too? And what about the hatchling?

She called out for Senekka, but there was no answer. She called again, louder, her voice croaking. Still nothing. Then she tried a sending, in case the hatchling was around. She'd barely formed a gray bit of an arrow, when she had to stop. Her head simply hurt too much. She wondered if she'd been concussed.

"Fewmets!" she said aloud. *Jakkin, where are you? I need you.* But thinking about him hurt, too. In a different way.

She closed her eyes, then as quickly opened them again. If she had a concussion, the last thing she should do was to fall asleep again. But she was so tired. So *very* tired. Her head hurt. Her hands were numb. Her memory was gone. She was alone. And it was Dark-After.

She slept.

WHEN SHE WOKE this time, light was streaming through the chink in the shutter. Her head still hurt, her bound hands were numb, and that numbness seemed to have moved up to her elbows. She had to pee, and she wondered why she was here, why she was alive.

She tried again to remember what had happened. She recalled the debate and after . . . a party. Yes, with chikkar. Had she drunk any? Was that what happened?

But chikkar couldn't explain her present situation. She looked down at her dress, a girl's blue party dress. For the first time, she saw the blood. All that blood. Her head hurting. Possible concussion. *Scalp wound,* she thought. *Someone has hit me on the head.*

And then she remembered — well, *remember* was not quite right. She had a flash of insight, of stumbling against someone in the dark. No — against one of the speakers at the debate. Against . . .

Then she had it. Or part of it. The man who called himself Dark, but she'd known as Number One. Also known as Swarts. A very dangerous man. Somehow she'd stumbled against him. He must have recognized her and grabbed her, brought her here, wherever *here* was. Brought her here alive but concussed. And tied.

But why?

Her head hurt from so much thinking, but she *had* to puzzle it out. She couldn't move her hands, but she *could* think.

But why? she asked herself again. And then she got it. Alive, she was a liability to him. Of course he could have just left her to die here — unburied, undiscovered, unmourned. Well, maybe not unmourned.

Please, not unmourned.

But that wasn't right. It would have been easier just to leave her in the alley. *The alley!* Now she remembered some more. Something about going out through the alley with Senekka. And the hatchling. And Dark.

And his gun!

Oh, God! He has a gun. That was important. But she didn't think she'd been shot. Not her. Maybe Senekka? Maybe the hatchling? It would explain why they weren't here.

But why am I?

She fell asleep again.

—

THE NEXT TIME she woke to dark, her mouth fuzzy, her mind muzzy.

Where am I? Why am I here?

Those same questions again. It took her nearly an hour to re-create her thinking of the time before. She worried that she'd lost some pieces, and she painstakingly went over and over the bits she could recall.

Surely, leaving me dead in the alley along with Senekka and the hatchling would have been safer for Dark than hauling me here. And he *had* to have hauled her. She certainly hadn't walked here by herself. *Wherever here is! He couldn't have chanced carrying me over his shoulder in the street.* So there must have been a car.

Which car?

The only one she knew of was the senate car.

And what about the driver? That nice man. Dikkon?

Her head, even awhirl with pain, was full of questions.

So why am I here?

She felt tired again, closed her eyes.

Why am I alive?

Trying to make it make sense hurt her head.

Why am I alive and here?

Though she tried to stay awake and follow the thread of that thought, she fell asleep.

Again.

~

THIS TIME when she woke, her head seemed clearer. Her arms were no longer bound behind her, but in front, tied at the wrist. Though she was still lying on the mattress, there was enough light to see that the mattress was thin. And gray. And filthy. She worried about the borrowed dress. The blood-soaked borrowed dress. The torn-at-the-shoulder blood-soaked borrowed dress. It would never recover and what would Henkky say about that? Then she scolded herself. Henkky wouldn't mind as long as she was returned safe.

The shutters on the window were now wide open. Akki sat up and turned her head. The world seemed to spin around. But the thought of lying down again was worse than the pain of being upright.

"Awake at last."

The first sound of the voice gave her hope. But even before she looked around and saw him, she recognized that voice. Dark was perched on a straight-backed chair. His voice was a low rumble. He had a black eye and a long wound — still aflame — that went from his scalp to below the blackened eye.

Did I do that? Akki wondered. And then she had another small flash of memory, of the hatchling flying at Dark's face, talons out. *"Thou fine fighter,"* she sent, even though the dragonling was nowhere around and sending made her head hurt.

Akki felt as if she'd been sick for days. Her mouth was foul. Her stomach was growling. She'd obviously wet herself while she slept. Oddly enough, those things didn't make her feel ashamed, just relieved.

Relieved! She laughed out loud at the pun.

Dark leaned forward. "What are you laughing at?" He sounded both puzzled and furious.

I can use that. He thinks I'm not frightened, that I'm laughing at him, and clearly he doesn't like it. She kept on laughing, tried to make it sound unforced. Hysteria lent a hand.

He stood up and walked toward her.

It's like training a dragon. She was careful not to show her fear. *This is the point where it's decided which one of us is to be master.*

He glared down at her, his mouth open, like a wound. "Where's your boyfriend, then?"

That was a question she wasn't expecting. How could he possibly have known about Jakkin? Suddenly she flashed on what she'd said as she'd run toward Dark. *I'm alive and so is Jakkin.* Had that been a fatal mistake? Or had it actually saved her life? She stopped laughing, considered it quickly. Clearly Dark thought she had information.

Information! It was a bargaining chip. The only one she had. Though she'd never gambled at the pits, she would have to gamble on this. She laughed again. *Some bargaining chip.* She'd *no* idea where Jakkin was.

She held up her bound hands. "Untie me and I'll tell you what I know. And get me a needle and thread and a wet cloth and I'll sew up your face. You wouldn't want it to become infected." Of course if she gave him any real information, he'd kill her. Actually, he was probably going to kill her, anyway, after he got the information he wanted. She was surprised at how calm she was. Must have been all that time in the mountains with the trogs. She'd faced death before. And anyway, she'd take *later* rather than now.

Later gives me a chance to escape.

It was the only chance she had.

"You can rot here awhile longer till you're ready to speak," Dark said. "And if you think I'll let you loose with a needle near my eyes, you're clearly still reeling from that head wound." He turned his back on her and walked out a door that was on the wall opposite the window. But in his eagerness to show her who was boss, he forgot to lock the shutters. He forgot to retie her hands behind her.

I can use *that,* she thought again.

＊

ONCE DARK'S FOOTSTEPS faded away down the unseen hall, she stood, kicked off the heeled sandals, and began to walk barefoot around the room, getting her legs going, moving away from the filthy, wet mattress. She lifted her arms over her head a dozen times, as they were all pins and needles, which helped a bit, though they began to burn as feeling returned.

Is there anything I can find to help me? She wasn't actually sure what she needed. *A knife, a hammer, a piece of long rope?* Clearly the rope around her wrist was too short, even if she could get it off.

She saw now that she was in a large attic room, about seven meters wide and ten meters long. The roof slanted down at the window end, the window being built into a dormer that was too high for her to look out of without standing on her tiptoes. *I should have kept the shoes on.*

Outside, the sun was now so bright, Akki had to blink a few times before she could actually see anything. When she could finally make out some buildings, she realized that she didn't recognize them. But clearly, she was on the outskirts of a city. There was some strange kind of arch to the buildings — odd-looking. They weren't at all like the houses in the center of The Rokk, which leaned toward one another. These all seemed to be leaning away. They were large buildings with few windows. Off to the left she could just make out part of a field. The room she was in seemed to be on the third floor, too high up for the rope around her wrists to help.

These buildings were city buildings, not village or farm buildings. Krakkow wasn't close enough for him to have driven there before Dark-After. Though even unconscious, *she* could have withstood the cold, *he* couldn't stay alive in the bone-chill, the car giving scant protection. *This must still be The Rokk.*

Knowledge is good, she told herself. *And the fact that I'm still here.* She sighed. *Golden will already be looking for me.* At least she *hoped* he was looking for her. Which he would be if this was just the next morning, if Senekka had been found in the alley, if the hatchling . . . But if Senekka had not gotten out of the alley, she'd be dead from the cold. And maybe not yet found. *Golden and Henkky might not even know I'm missing. Yet.*

Her stomach growled again. She had no idea how long it had been since she'd eaten last. More important than eating, though, was finding water.

By this point she'd paced around the entire room. There wasn't any sink. There was nothing in the room except the mattress, the chair, a single window, the shutters, and bare boards. The only way to get water was going to be through Dark.

Bare boards have nails. She was suddenly alive with hope. *I can use the nails.*

The first time around the room, she'd paced like a newly caught feral in a stall. This time she went around more slowly, until she'd gathered half a dozen nails, loosening them first with her fingertips and then pulling them out. She split off half of her left thumbnail in the process.

Something else that hurts. Then she realized: *Doesn't matter.*

Quickly she sorted through the six nails, chose the sharpest, hid the other five under the filthy mattress. Flopping down on a dry part of the mattress — as far away from the wet spot as possible, as close to the window for the light — she began picking at the rope around her wrists with the sixth nail.

It was slow work, especially with her wrists already rubbed sore. She tried not to cry, but the picking went infinitely slowly. And everything hurt so much: her wrists, her torn nail, her head. But if she cried, she wouldn't be able to see what she was doing. So she snuffled a couple of times, then went back to work.

Suddenly, she straightened up. *Even if I free my hands, I can't fight Dark. He's bigger and stronger — and he has that gun.*

"Don't be worm waste," she whispered to herself. "You have to do one thing at a time." She bent back over and stuck the sharp point of the nail into the rope, picking out another bit of the strand. The nail slipped, and scratched the back of her hand. In her current book of pain, it didn't even rate a mention.

But that small bit of unraveling was all she managed, for just then she heard footsteps coming up the stairs. Putting the nail in the little pocket of her dress, she lay down on her side, her back to the door, closed her eyes, pretended to sleep.

And actually slept.

—

SHE AWOKE and found herself half off the mattress. The shutters were closed, but a bit of light through the chink showed her that it was coming toward Dark-After. Again.

Her hands were still tied in front, her feet twisted in a thin blanket, hardly more than a worn piece of cloth. Dark must have come in while she slept this last time and placed it over her. She must have kicked it off in her sleep. However, she understood the message. He was determined to be master, doling out bits of comfort along with the bad stuff — the bound hands, the filthy mattress. *Carrot, stick,* she thought. *Stick, carrot.*

Of course, what he didn't know was how little she needed the blanket. And how much she needed water.

Standing, hands still bound in front, tied at the wrists, she began to walk carefully toward the window. Dark was surely sleeping now. In a soft bed with sheets and blankets. Having had a full meal. A hot bath. Possibly having gone out to look for her with Golden and the others. The next debates would be put off. Everyone would marvel at how ceaselessly Dark gave of himself. And, of course, how he blamed himself. Possibly he would tell them that an armed man had jumped them in the alley. He'd probably point to his blackened eye. Tell them how the man took the gun away from him — his useless, bulletless gun — knocking him out, stealing the girl. The live girl, not the dead one. Probably holding Golden's niece for ransom. Golden, a rich man like his name.

Oh, he's a sly piece of lizard waste, she told herself, sure she'd figured it out. Opening the shutters, she tried to open the window, but the latch was too high up. She'd have to carry over the chair, stand on it.

So she felt her way to the chair, found it, started to pick it up — which was the hardest thing she'd ever done, because she was now quite weak and getting disoriented. Suddenly, something that had been sitting on the chair began to slide toward her. She caught it before it crashed to the ground, but not before something spilled onto her dress.

Water!

She lowered the chair carefully, felt around the bowl. There were several fingers of water left. She gulped the water down, then wrung out the skirt of her dress into her mouth, not so easy to do with her wrists still bound. There wasn't enough water to ease her thirst completely, but it was certainly better than nothing. She put the bowl on the mattress and went back to the chair, lifting it carefully so that it didn't scrape on the floor.

She got it to the window. Putting the chair down carefully, she climbed up onto it, worried all the while that the chair was going to tip over. Feeling along the glass till she came to the latch, she gave it a twist. It seemed to be painted shut. She slammed the side of her fist against it and felt something give way. This time when she tried to twist the latch, it moved a bit. She rested, tried again. *Now* she was able to turn it.

She managed to crack the window open. The cold of Dark-After crept in. It sneaked along her hands and arms like a trickle of cold water. She closed the window again and put her hands on the glass. Leaning forward, she sent out a silent cry.

"*Danger,*" she sent.

"*Help,*" she sent.

The sendings were arrows, blood-colored and pus-colored and puke-colored. Gouts of blood. Puddles and lakes and rivers of death. They went straight out into the cold streets, banging against the darkened windows of the other houses in the arc of buildings.

Her sendings continued until she was emptied of all feeling. Then she closed the shutters, assured that she could open the window when she finally figured out how to use it to her advantage.

She walked back to the mattress and lay down, but this time she didn't sleep.

She was done with sleeping.

☾ 29 ☾

AKKI WORKED on the rope feverishly through Dark-After. Now her left hand was badly scratched in three places, though in the dark she couldn't really see the wounds. She hardly felt a thing. Pain was simply a constant, and another hurt just didn't register.

More important, two of the strands of rope had already frayed and parted, and she could feel that the ones beneath were beginning to come apart, as well. If she could free her hands, she'd get the chair and wait by the door. When Dark came in, she'd bring the chair down on his head as hard as she could, then race down the stairs.

Or as soon as it was light, she'd see if she could use the blanket as an extended rope, hammer one end to the windowsill, using her shoe as a hammer and all the nails she'd gathered, and go out the window.

Or she could try using the longest nail to pick the lock of the attic room door and get out before Dark was awake.

Or . . .

Her ideas of escape were now coming so fast, she began

to wonder if she had the strength to actually do any of the things she was considering. *Maybe I'm actually dying in the alleyway from a hematoma of the brain. Maybe none of this is real.*

Another strand and she was almost free. Of the rope, not the room.

As she worked, she strained to hear if anyone was on the stairs, but the house was silent.

Too silent.

What if he's left me here for good. No food. No water. If that was true, she had to work faster. Get out faster. Find her way back to Golden's house faster.

She was careless again, and this time the nail dug deep into her hand. She no longer minded. Pain, she reasoned, meant she was still alive.

A quick unraveling of the next strand and the hated rope literally fell apart. Rubbing her aching wrists, she raced to the chair, almost tripping over it in her haste. Her hands were now so stiff, she could scarcely close them around the wooden back.

The silence stretched on and on.

When she got to the door, she lowered the chair, then tried the door handle. Of course it was locked. Taking the nail from her pocket, she felt for the keyhole, stuck the nail in, jiggled it about.

Something fell out the other side, landing on the floor with a sharp *plunk!* It sounded louder than a dragon's roar.

The key. It had to have been the key.

And Dark has to have heard it!

Trembling, Akki went back to the chair, moved it closer

to the door, trying to remember which way the door opened. She'd only actually seen it open once. She needed to be on the side opposite where it swung open, so she could bring the chair down on Dark's head without the door getting in the way.

There was a *whoosh*ing noise but she couldn't figure out where it was coming from. Just in case, she lifted the chair, hoisting it above her head, heedless of her stiff hands. She tried to breathe shallowly so as not to drown out the noise with her own breath.

Suddenly she was bombarded by a sending, so strong, so red, so full of fire, it nearly brought her to her knees.

"Danger! Danger! Danger!"

Now she realized what that noise had been — the flapping of wings. She returned the call, sending a jumble of red ropes, red blood on bound hands, red keys.

"Where? Where? Where?" There was an aerial view of the city outlined in the same fiery red, the streets twisting like crimson rivers.

"I don't know," she whispered, sending a blank back. Then revising that, she sent a cooler picture of the scene outside her window, gray outlined in blue.

The dragon seemed puzzled, and the return sending was muzzy. *"Where . . . where . . . where . . . ?"* The sending was now less red and more . . . pink.

Thinking that she might do better at the window, Akki put the chair down carefully, then raced across the room. Flinging the shutters open, she stood on her tiptoes, sore hands against the glass.

"I am here," she sent, now able to focus the picture of the arc of buildings outside the window as well as send flashes of her hands, the glass, the waning cold. The outside was not all dark but a kind of soft gray, signaling that Dark-After was coming to an end. *"Here!"*

No sooner had she sent that then the door was thrown open, banging against the wall. Dark entered, then kicked the chair aside.

Akki turned, her excitement now devoured by real fear. Dark was wearing two sweaters and gloves, dressed for the cold, carrying a lantern in one hand, a gun in the other. His face was so angry, it had turned colors: red chasing gray.

"What are you doing, you little fewmet?" He lunged toward her.

In the lantern light, the wound that ran down from his eye was now an unhealthy red. *Probably infected,* she thought with satisfaction.

"Thinking of climbing through the window, girl? It's three floors down. And piercing-cold still. You're not dying till you tell me what I need to know."

She trembled, considered running, but there was nowhere to run. "Food," she said. "Water." Her voice was little more than a croak. And it was a real croak; she wasn't putting it on.

"First give me what you used to knock out the key."

To buy time for the dragon to find her, Akki reached into her pocket and gave him the nail. She let him tie her up again, this time sitting upright in the chair, with a new rope he'd brought with him. She even smiled tremulously at him, letting him think she'd been tamed.

When he was sure she couldn't move, couldn't slip out of her bonds, he announced he would get her food and water. "Work with me," he said, "don't fight me, and I'll take care of you." To show he meant it, he reached down and picked up the blanket, draped it over her shoulders, patted her head, carefully, to avoid the place that hurt.

She nodded, as if she were cowed, tamed, broken. She didn't care. The dragon had heard her. Would find her. Would bring others to her. She could play along with him now. She'd already won.

"*I am here,*" she sent again. "*I am here.*"

There was no reply.

Dark went out of the room, closing the door behind him. She heard the door lock.

Akki wept, tears running down her cheeks and into her mouth. She sucked the salt water in. It might be all the moisture she would get.

~

A FEW HOURS later, when it had begun to get warm again in the attic, Dark returned. This time he carried a bowl and a glass. Feeding her some kind of porridge with a spoon, he smiled as she ate greedily, held the glass of water to her lips so she could drink.

Akki resisted kicking him. The way he was standing, she could just reach his knees . . . or higher. But instead she carefully drank until the last of the water dribbled down her chin. After all, the dragon had found her. Surely she was soon to be saved.

Putting the bowl and glass aside, Dark leaned casually

against the window. His body was outlined by the rising sun, and for a moment it looked as if he were on fire. He stared at Akki for a long time without speaking. Finally, he said, "You see, I *can* be good to you. But you have to give me what I want."

She made her voice soft, almost pleading. "What *do* you want?"

"To know where your boyfriend is."

"Boyfriend?" She opened her eyes wide, tried to look innocent.

"You must think I'm as stupid as a flikka!" he roared, striding to the chair and looming over her. "The boy, that Jakkin, the young dragon master, the one you went with to Rokk Major. You shouted at me that he was alive, as well."

"I lied," she said, remembering at the moment she said it how he had used the same words in the alley before . . . before . . .

Dark nodded. What he meant by that, she didn't know, so she continued. "Jakkin died, out in the mountains. With his dragon. You must have heard the story." She kept her voice steady.

He glared at her. "I've heard many stories. *You* didn't survive in any of them."

With a sudden burst of inspiration, she said, "I was in jail." Then she took a deep breath. "And I almost *didn't* survive." It was a calculated risk lying like that. But she just needed him to believe for a little while longer, until the dragon came back.

He leaned over till they were eye-to-eye. She thought

about kicking out at him, knowing she could hurt him
badly, but at the last minute reality set in. Tied the way she
was, even if she injured him, she wouldn't be able to get
down the stairs, wouldn't escape his eventual retribution.

He snorted. "That's the best story yet, girl."

She became expansive, looked at him with wide-open
eyes. "Golden believes I've been rehabilitated. He's going
to use me in the campaign to talk about the rebellion, how
it even sucked in the children of masters. 'Not in the first
debate,' he said. But later. When everyone is in the palm of
his hand."

"Oh, I *want* to believe you," he told her, his face getting
a sly look. "But you see, I would have heard if you'd been
in jail. I have too many of my old boys and girls there still.
The ones who weren't shipped offplanet."

Akki had to think quickly. "Because Golden's my uncle
and godfather, I was kept out of the usual jails. Hidden and
put under house arrest. I swear that's true."

He laughed quietly, smoothly. Then he turned away.

She dared to hope. Sending out a few ribbon-slim tenta-
cles to the dragon, she waited for a reply. But the dragon
didn't answer, had been silent for far too long. *Why?* She
closed her eyes, tried to think.

Dark turned back and — without warning — hit her
with a closed fist under the chin so hard, her neck nearly
snapped.

"Tell me what I want to know or you don't get out of
here alive. And that's what *I* swear is true."

Akki tried to open her mouth and explain what she'd

meant, but she hadn't the breath. Instead she vomited up pain, pure pain, all over herself, and then onto the floor. Now she was ready to tell Dark the truth. Even ready to tell him all about Jakkin, if only the pain would go away. So she did the only thing she could do to stop the pain, the fear, the possibility of telling. She fell into the dark once again.

~

WHEN SHE WOKE at last, tied to the chair, it was light. She had no idea if she'd slept through a full day and night or had just gone unconscious for a bit. All she *did* know was that she was starving, and that the dragon was truly gone.

DRAGON'S HEART

☾ 30 ☾

THE NIGHT was growing cold as Jakkin was led out of the cave by the trogs. Two of them went before him, two behind. That was the bad news.

The good news — if there was any — seemed to be that the trogs assumed he could go outside in the cold, just as they could. In another few hours it would be Dark-After and they'd still be outside.

If nothing else, Jakkin mused behind his thought wall, *my being able to get around in Dark-After will convince them that all Austarians can live in the bone-chill.* So maybe the trogs wouldn't be eager to attack the nurseries or cities at night. Perhaps that was a small victory.

Still, right now even a small victory is enormous.

However, he had little time to enjoy that victory, for the trogs were already pushing him forward, along the deserted road, back the way he'd just come. After looking quickly both ways and seeing no telltale headlights, the forward two trogs raced across the paving.

Jakkin walked more slowly. *He* didn't need to check for

trucks. No one would be out this close to Dark-After. Loosening the stone in his thought wall again in case the trogs let fall a hint of where they were taking him, he listened carefully. *"Smooth bad, bonds bad,"* they were saying, and then *gabble, gabble, gabble.* One of the trogs behind Jakkin poked him hard in the back; Jakkin picked up the pace. *No need to anger them early.* He had a lot to figure out.

As they hurried to the other side of the road, Jakkin looked up and checked the stars. *North.* They were heading north. Toward the mountains, he presumed. He slowed his pace because he didn't dare let them take him there. Once in the trogs' caves, he might not get out again so easily.

Easily! He snorted, remembering the long underwater swim through the cave pool. Remembering the dragons dropping down the waterfall. Remembering the heartstopping moment when he and Akki waited to see if Auricle could figure out how to pump her wings and fly rather than be dashed on the rocks below. There'd been nothing *easy* about that escape.

"Auricle!" Without meaning to, he sent a long gray tentacle back toward the nursery, or where he thought the nursery might be. Something large, sharp, brutal, sliced the tentacle, chopped it into large pieces, diced it, and then casually shattered part of his thought wall as well.

"No send!" came the command from all four trogs, brutally loud in his head. At the same time, one of them gave him a shove from behind. He fell heavily and had to roll to escape their flailing legs. He hit his right shoulder hard. But harder still was the fact that they'd gotten into his head without any trouble. *I'll have to shield more carefully or I'll*

never . . . He waited to finish that thought — lying on the ground and getting his breath back — till he'd rebuilt the wall in his mind.

Stone by stone by stone. Two layers. Three. Until he was certain it couldn't be breached.

They yanked him to his feet, and then retied his hands in the front, to make it easier for him to move. Clearly they wanted him alive — for now.

TRUDGING NORTH in the sand, they went on for miles before suddenly turning eastward. Soon the road was simply a long gray memory behind them.

The trogs didn't issue another command, though, and Jakkin kept the wall high and solid inside his head, so nothing broke the awful silence. Strangely, even the usually loud and insistent insects were unaccountably still, as if the wall kept out the sound of their voices, too.

When they stopped at last for a quick rest, the trogs untied Jakkin so he could relieve himself, though embarrassingly enough, there was always one trog to check that he didn't run away.

As if there were somewhere to run!

A chuckle burst in his head, little green poppings. One of the trogs had gotten through the wall again. Jakkin was forced to rebuild it once more, adding extra stones. At the same time, he watched the skies, trying to spot his brood, or even a feral dragon. If only he could call for help from someone.

The twin moons were making their way across the blue-black sky, and now clouds had begun to obscure them. Even if a dragon did fly by, he might not see it, with all the clouds. At a guess, though, he'd say Heart's Blood's five were probably fast asleep back at the oasis, Sssargon no doubt commenting repeatedly about his dreams. He didn't dare count on them. Besides, the trogs knew how to handle dragons.

No. If I'm to get away, I have to do it on my own.

He sorted through his options. Even with his hands untied, he didn't dare fight the trogs. Not only were they amazingly strong, they outnumbered him four to one. And his shoulder was stiff from his fall.

He wondered briefly if he might be able to outrun them. Probably in the short term. They didn't look built for speed but for endurance. However, that meant in the end they'd run him down. Still, if their route took them anywhere near water — the river wasn't far from here — he *could* dive in.

I've never seen a trog who could swim. It was a long shot, but it might be the only shot he had.

Then he reminded himself that the longer he delayed the trogs, the more likely it was that the dragons would awake. Or nursery folk. Perhaps Golden might even fly by in his copter.

Yes, his first line of defense had to be delay.

Foot drag.

Twist an ankle.

Start a fight.

Fall down.

All of the above.

Because he had to do whatever it took to slow their headlong rush toward the caves. And maybe along the way, he could figure out how they'd found him and why they'd targeted him. And if they knew where Akki was.

He was suddenly afraid they might have caught Akki, as well. And if she'd been taken to the caves, he'd have to go there without a second thought.

But then, before he could spiral down into panic and despair, he began to think more clearly: Akki had left in a truck during daylight, heading for The Rokk. The trogs couldn't tackle either a truck or the city. If she saw them — and they were unmistakable — she'd have urged the driver to go even faster. No, there was no chance the trogs had gotten her. *He* was the only one in danger from them. Akki, at least, was safe in The Rokk. He could relax about her and concentrate on getting himself out of this mess.

One thing at a time, Jakkin.

Checking the thought wall again, he began to plan: a dive in the river, or fire from the brood. Or both. Fire *and* water. That's the way he'd break free.

He couldn't have been more wrong.

☾ 31 ☾

SINCE JAKKIN'S only plan was to delay the trogs, he figured the best way to do that would be to fake a fall. Not one in which he hurt himself, of course, but one convincing enough to slow them down.

His first, falling forward onto his bound hands, earned him a quick drag up to his feet and a punch in his side. His trip over the roots of a lone spikka tree, then twisting backward — a drag and another punch. Bumbling against two of the trogs, causing one of them to land hard on hands and knees — a drag and a great deal of shouting. Though what was shouted Jakkin couldn't have said.

What hurt most were not the draggings up or the punches, or even the mind-shouting. What hurt most was that nothing seemed to slow them at all.

It's time for more drastic measures.

As they trotted along, Jakkin occasionally stumbled, just to remind everyone of how weak he was. All the while, though, he kept looking for something that could be considered "drastic measures." Yet, for the longest while, no such opportunity presented itself. Jakkin grew increasingly worried. Stall and stumble as much as he might, the trogs kept moving forward at an alarming and increasing pace, and they were pushing and pulling him along with them.

Now the twin moons shone down like giant lanterns, the hills so highly illuminated, any cracks and crevices stood out as black wounds on a lighter skin. Jakkin and the trogs were moving so quickly, the tree where he'd slept a night or two ago was well behind them.

They'd just neared the top of a smallish rise when Jakkin suddenly — and without mentally warning the trogs — flung himself sideways onto the ground. Rolling back down the hill, his bound hands now above his head to guard his face, he banged against small pebbles and fist-sized rocks. He was bruised a bit but not too badly.

But because of the odd shadows, he hadn't noticed a rock that humped up like a hatchling's back on the left side of the trail. The rock was in the middle of a patch of high grass, so it had been hidden from casual inspection. As luck would have it, when he rolled past the rock, the back of his head thunked hard on it and not the grass.

Jakkin rolled on down the hill, gathering speed and losing consciousness at approximately the same rate. The trogs clattered down after him, calling to one another like demented dragonlings, pipping both anger and distress. By the time Jakkin reached the bottom, he was out cold, surrounded by the angry trogs.

He came to with a splitting headache and a strange feeling of motion. And then he realized that his hands and feet had been tied to a long pole fashioned from the limb of a spikka. Finding the tree, trimming the limb, and trussing him up must have taken a great deal of time.

Good, he thought grimly through the pain. He'd managed to slow them down at last.

Two trogs held up the front end of the pole, and two the back. They were carrying him between them, like a captured animal. The swaying of the pole could have been comforting, could even have rocked him to sleep, but instead the movement turned his stomach.

"Stop! Stop!" he cried aloud, afraid he was about to be sick.

The trogs paid no attention and kept on walking. Walking slowly, for sure — carrying him this way was awkward — but they were still on the move. Jakkin could see that they were now in a bit of a valley, the hills mounding up on either side of the rocky path.

Now the trogs stepped carefully but were more casual with the pole, letting it swing back and forth, back and forth.

Jakkin's appreciation for their slowness didn't help his stomach any. In fact, the more he swayed on the pole, the worse he felt. At last, he turned his head to the right side and — with neither warning nor apology — threw up on the stony ground. The spew hit the stones, rebounding backward, and sprayed over the legs and sandaled feet of the trog nearest his head.

In the midst of his agony, he almost laughed because the trog growled and dropped his hold on the stick while he tried to jump away from the spray. The other three growled back, and then they laughed uproariously, a strange kind of hooting sound. Then they set the pole down.

As soon as Jakkin touched the ground — solid, unmoving — he turned over onto his stomach and threw up again. And again. Then he scrabbled backward on his hands and knees, dragging the pole with him, to get as far away from the stinking mess as he could.

Once his stomach was completely empty and the spasms had passed, he had time to think. What if he had a concussion from hitting his head on the rock? Right after thinking that, he passed out again.

❦

WHEN HE came to, besides a splitting headache, besides the bumps and bruises, he felt fine. If you can be fine upsidedown and carried on a pole by four subhumans going up a hill. If you can forget that your mouth tastes like fewmets, that your stomach feels as if a dragon has rolled over it. Fine if you aren't scared that everything you love is about to be slaughtered.

At least the trogs were now huffing a bit and going slow. Jakkin wished he weighed as much as Kkarina, to slow them down even further.

"Set me on the ground," he said aloud. Then tearing down the top section of his thought wall, he sent them a fiery scene of the pole burning, which then set all four of them alight.

To his surprise, following a flurry of sendings to one another, they lowered him down.

"Walk now!" one trog sent to him, a meaty hand outstretched and pointing at Jakkin.

"Okay, Big Boss."

The others busied themselves untying Jakkin's hands and feet. At each touch, he got a flash of what they were thinking. It was a combination of anger, weariness, fear. But mostly anger. At him, at being away from their caves, and — surprisingly — at Big Boss.

Good to know. He carefully shielded the thought from the trogs.

Sitting up slowly, Jakkin wasted several minutes by rubbing his wrists and ankles, still surprised that the trogs had set him free. But he guessed they were tired of hauling him around on the pole and felt they could make better time if he walked on his own. They were probably pretty sure he couldn't escape. After all, he'd been limping and throwing up. He couldn't have much energy left.

Well, are they in for a big surprise!

After about five minutes of flexing his wrists and standing up slowly, he reached for the pole. His head had stopped aching.

Two of the trogs started toward him, but Big Boss stopped them. He picked up the pole and slammed it into Jakkin's hand.

"WALK NOW!"

The sending was loud enough to start Jakkin's head throbbing again. Automatically, he put a hand to his temples and winced. He hadn't planned to do that, wasn't faking, but the four trogs nodded at one another, clearly believing him weaker than he actually was. So, slowly, he took the pole and started walking, leaning heavily on it as if his legs could scarcely hold him.

"FASTER!" That was clearly Big Boss, who seemed to have only one volume. *Loud.*

Jakkin stopped, faced the trog leader, then said, "If you want me to go faster, you'll have to carry me again." It was too many words for Big Boss, but Jakkin's meaning was clear enough, because at the same time, he sent a gray and blue picture showing himself lying down next to the pole, ready to be trussed up again.

Big Boss nodded, grunted, turned his back on Jakkin, and walked away, two trogs in his wake. Jakkin and the fourth trog were meant to follow and they did.

They reached the end of the valley and turned.

Not north as Jakkin had supposed. Not toward the dark brooding shadows of the mountains and the caves where the trogs would be safe and he would remain a prisoner. But slowly they headed southeast toward the dunes.

And that, he realized with a sinking heart, would lead straight to the oasis. And after that — the nursery.

Had he underestimated them? Had they been planning to attack the nursery from the beginning, to get Auricle back themselves? *If so — why did they capture me?* He was afraid that the answer was that they'd seen the direction the copter had chosen and when they were ready — made a plan — they'd gone that way until they'd come upon his tracks. Only it had been his *new* track, toward The Rokk, that they had followed. And since he was without the dragon and hatchling when they found him, now they were backtracking to get to the place where he'd left the two. That track would lead them right to the nursery.

Leaning heavily on the pole, he limped after Big Boss and his followers, followed in turn by the final trog. As he walked, Jakkin began building the thought wall up again, stone by stone, till it was thick and sturdy and impenetrable. Only then did he try to figure out what everything really meant.

If they went directly to the nursery to attack it, he could call out for his friends. *We have numbers and firepower on our side. But only if the trogs don't attack during Dark-After.* In the cold he'd be on his own. He wondered if the trogs knew that. He turned around and checked the sky. The moons were almost down behind the mountains. Dark-After would begin any minute.

If they detoured through the oasis, he might be able to signal the dragons. But he'd have only a single chance before the trogs shut him up. He already knew how they controlled dragons with their minds. Did he want to put any of the brood in danger, just to save himself? That's how Heart's Blood had died. He couldn't allow such a thing to happen again.

He wondered if anyone would be on night duty in the incubarn. If any of the hens was nearing time to lay, one of the senior men would definitely be there. He hoped so. The boys simply couldn't hold this crew off. Slakk was presumably still too weak from the drakk attack. Errikkin would be a disaster. He'd be just as likely to help the trogs to get even with Jakkin for some imagined slight. L'Erikk — well, he would be a joke in more than one way. Jakkin hardly knew what to think about the other boys.

He wondered if he could reach a stinger in time, without a key to the cabinet. Maybe he could race to the bondhouse for a stinger. Could he figure out how to use one? Could he kill a man? Even a caveman? Would Auricle go peacefully back to the caves with the trogs? The number of questions simply overwhelmed him.

And then he realized that the trogs couldn't leave him alive. Alive, he'd lead his friends into the mountains, right to the caves where the trogs lived. *No. Not only am I expendable, they* have *to kill me.* The real question was whether they planned to kill him sooner — before they mounted their attack — or later, after he showed them where Auricle was kept. *Or will they march me back to the mountains to be sacrificed in some awful way?*

Silently, he hefted the pole. When he set it down on end again, he leaned heavily on it as if hardly able to move. *At least — at least now I have a weapon in hand.*

⟨ 32 ⟩

HIS THOUGHT WALL held and none of the trogs showed the slightest bit of interest in him, other than to push him on. He stumbled along as if he could barely move any faster. Clearly, he had them all fooled.

Big Boss, the tracker of the group, stopped every once in a while to point out the way to the others. The trogs listened to him, gabbling mind-to-mind, and there was hardly any argument. He seemed to have some kind of hold over them. Jakkin couldn't figure out what it was. Maybe he was just that much bigger or older or stronger or smarter. Maybe he'd been appointed the head of this group of four. Whatever that hold, Big Boss was definitely the one to worry about.

Jakkin tried to listen in on their mind conversations through a small chink he'd bored through his thought wall. He'd hoped to overhear something of their plans, but the only thing that leaked through was a kind of *gabble-gabble-gabble*. He could find out nothing tangible.

He began to panic. There was now little between the trogs and the nursery but sand and oasis and time. And not much time, at that. Glancing up at the sky, he saw that the twin moons were gone from the horizon. Dark-After was about to start.

Since there'd been little wind over the past few days, his tracks showed clearly. It wouldn't take much skill to follow the trail to the oasis, even in Dark-After. How naive he'd been.

"Fewmetty trogs," Jakkin muttered to himself, earning a smack on the head from the one behind him.

"Ow!" Jakkin turned without warning and whacked back at the trog, hitting him on the head with a closed fist, which surprised them both.

The trog made a sound like *whaaa* and Big Boss glared at him.

"No kriah!" The sending went directly to the crying trog, but Big Boss's anger leaked out so that Jakkin also caught some of it. It was like a sliver in the eye. Jakkin wondered what the full blast must have felt like and was glad he didn't know.

Poor trog! he thought sarcastically. *Hope it hurt like drakk's blood.* He remembered Slakk kneeling in the barn, burned by such blood, and the sudden burst of fear that had emanated from him in a kind of sending. He was suddenly sorry he hadn't visited Slakk before leaving and wondered if he'd ever see his friend again.

Then he shook himself mentally. *What worm drivel.* His left hand made a fist, the right held tight to the pole. *I have to be cold. I have to be tough. I have to be . . .*

He never got to finish that thought, because they'd

found the oasis from the back end, looking down on it from a dune. Jakkin was startled. The oasis — this soon? He was not used to coming upon it this way, and he was certainly not ready to be there. He took a deep breath, a gasp really. The stars gazed pitilessly on them all, outlining them in shadow.

Jakkin didn't move. He stood leaning against the pole, watching as Big Boss and the trogs slid down the sand hill on their bellies and into the water. They gulped noisily as they drank.

Big Boss looked up, suddenly realizing that all three of his companions were with him, which meant no one was guarding Jakkin. He began to give them a mental lashing. One of the trogs started to stand, ready to go back and take care of their prisoner.

Jakkin was parched as well, but he was furious, too. The trogs were trashing his most private memories simply by being in Heart's Blood's pool. And he stoked that fury to a white heat, all in seconds, then ran screaming down the dune, flailing with the pole.

At the pool's edge, he struck forward and back with the pole, hitting out as hard as he could. He connected first with the head of the standing trog, who fell sideways and immediately slipped under the water, wavelets lapping at his now submerged head. On the backswing, Jakkin connected with the trog next to Big Boss. It didn't drown him, but smashed his shoulder, and his right arm drooped as if the bone were broken, effectively putting him out of commission.

Big Boss turned and, still sitting in the water, grabbed at

the pole end and yanked it out of Jakkin's hands, though the action sent him sprawling backward and he lay for long seconds in the water.

At this point, Jakkin simply let him have the pole. Then showing speed none of them expected from him, he raced around the far side of the pool and ran through the patch of wort. Since it was night, and Dark-After, the leaves were closed tight and so none of the wort burned his legs.

He kept on running, and even though the cold of Dark-After was snaking across his body, he was sweating. He guessed that at least two of the trogs would soon be on his trail, but they'd have to stop to check his tracks in the dark.

Advantage, he thought grimly, *to me.*

As he ran, he gave a quick shout and a sending to the dragons. It was like a bright red and white fire fall. This was not the time to worry about the trogs hearing him. Of course they'd hear. But he needed to find the dragons — and fast. He needed their fire and their might.

They didn't answer.

He kept calling and sending as he ran. But all he met with was silence. Wherever the brood was, it wasn't here.

So now he kept quiet and used his energy for running. He broke into a loping, ground-eating run, and made it back to the weir in record time.

As he crossed the weir, he hoped that it would also buy him time, since the trogs wouldn't know which way he'd gone in the water. Though when they got this far, they would be able to smell the dragons in the barns. If he was lucky, they'd go to the stud barn first. That would slow them down. *If* he was lucky. The way things were going, Jakkin didn't plan to rely on luck.

Dripping, cold, he stayed in the weir until the last minute, then dashed across the yard to the incubarn and tried to open the door. It was locked from the inside, so he hammered on it.

After long moments, the door squalled as it was opened a crack.

I'm worm waste, he told himself. *I should have oiled that door when I first thought about it.* Slipping in, he turned, pulled the noisy door shut after him, and put the latch back on. The hall was unlit. There was a roaring fire in the hearth.

"Jakkin?" The voice was high, querulous, unsure. Light from the hearth behind him outlined a boy looking sleepy, disheveled, unbelieving, shuddering from his single moment near Dark-After. "But it's bone-chill out there. You're soaking wet. How can you —"

"Not now, Errikkin," Jakkin said. "Is there anyone here with you?"

Errikkin rubbed a fist in his eye, nodded.

"Who?" Jakkin pressed.

"Old Lik-and-Spittle."

"Where is he?"

"It's not his watch yet and you know how he —"

"Get . . . him . . . here now!" Jakkin said in a loud whisper. "We have major trouble!"

Errikkin's eyes got wide. "More drakks?"

"For God's sake." Jakkin couldn't believe this: of all the worst combinations to fight off trogs, Errikkin and Likkarn were it. He'd rather have fat Kkarina and mopey old Balakk. "Get him while I bar the door." He went to the nearest table and dragged it over to the door.

"He's on the —"

Shoving the table against the door, Jakkin raced back to the visitors' room to get the sofa.

"— sofa," Errikkin finished.

Likkarn was already sitting up. He looked alert for a man who'd just been awakened, though his face seemed to have fallen in on itself.

"We have visitors," Jakkin blurted out. "From the mountains. Coming to steal the breeding dragons." He didn't want to single out Auricle. It would take too much explanation. "And kill me. Because I know where they live."

"How many?" Likkarn stood, and grabbed a stinger from a small table. When he saw that, Jakkin's eyes went wide.

"We weren't sure we'd gotten all the drakks," Likkarn said. "And with two dragons near to laying . . ."

Jakkin nodded. He understood. Then he told Likkarn, "These are worse than drakks."

"Worse?"

"They're humans. Well, sort of."

"Ah . . ." Likkarn said, as if he understood.

And perhaps — Jakkin remembered that Likkarn had spoken about being in the mountains himself — *perhaps he does.*

"How many?" Likkarn asked again as they pushed the sofa against the door, the stinger close at hand on one of the sofa cushions.

"Two, maybe three. I —" Jakkin gulped. "I drowned

one. Was only trying to slow him down. Broke another's shoulder. Two definitely and one wounded." He said it baldly, trembling at the memory.

"Good boy," Likkarn said. "You only did what needed to be done. So we're three to two." His steady voice helped, and Jakkin stopped shaking.

"Don't be fooled. They're tough, and we're —"

Likkarn nodded. "Not so tough."

Errikkin cleared his throat. "But it's Dark-After."

"Not now, Errikkin," Jakkin and Likkarn said together, then looked at each other and laughed. For the first time in days, Jakkin felt a ray of hope.

Just then the front door shuddered. Somebody pounded on it. Pushed at it. Cursed. Or at least that gabble sounded like a curse. Jakkin's head suddenly hurt with a sending of bright orange fire.

The trogs had arrived.

Likkarn rubbed a knuckle in his good eye.

Trying to wake up? Or did he get some of that sending? Jakkin wondered.

Likkarn simply shook his head, then picked up the stinger. "Sorry — there's just one here," he said. "But I'm a good shot, so I'll keep hold of this."

"*Who's* out there?" Errikkin asked, his voice quivering. "Who could *possibly* be out there? It's Dark-After."

"So you've observed," Likkarn said coolly.

The door shuddered again, but the latch, supported by the table and sofa, held.

"*What's* out there?"

"Get your knife," Likkarn told Errikkin in a steadying kind of voice. "And there's a hammer by the door of Heart's Ease's stall. Bring it for Jakkin." He turned to Jakkin. "Stall needs work."

Errikkin was still staring at the door.

"*NOW!*" Likkarn shouted, and added, "You pulsating bit of worm slime."

Errikkin took off at a run.

That's when Likkarn looked hard at Jakkin, his good eye steely. "He just wants a strong master. Makes him feel strong himself. Coddle him, and he feels nothing but pity — and shame. Now, Jakkin, tell me everything I need to know."

For a moment, Jakkin considered lying. But lying served no purpose. They had to live through this in order to save the dragons. He'd swear Likkarn to secrecy afterward. Likkarn was good at keeping secrets. "The men out there are the great-greats of the earliest settlers who escaped from bond and made their own communities in the caves," he told Likkarn.

"I've met a couple," Likkarn said laconically. "Or rather I spied on them. Never got *that* close. Quiet sort of folk."

"They don't talk out loud much," Jakkin said. "Mind link. With each other. With the dragons."

Likkarn nodded as if he understood.

Just then Errikkin returned with the knife and hammer.

At the same moment, the trogs stopped trying the door and suddenly everything went horribly quiet.

After a bit, Errikkin asked, "What do you think they're doing now?"

"We'll find out soon enough," Likkarn told him.

The silence from outside stretched on and on.

Jakkin tried to imagine what the trogs might be getting up to. Tackling the stud barn? The bondhouse? Going back to the mountains to get reinforcements? *Whatever they're thinking, it won't be good for us.*

He felt a probe into his mind, and he hastily built up the wall again. But the probe told him one thing. The trogs hadn't left. Yet.

The sound of glass breaking made the three of them jump.

"The window!" Errikkin cried, saying what they already knew.

Probably used the pole.

Likkarn turned, stared at the window, grunted. "The shutters should hold for a while."

"But the cold," Errikkin whined.

"Give me the stinger," Jakkin said. "I can stand the cold. You two get back in with the dragons. Their bodies will help keep you warm."

"How?" Errikkin would simply not shut up. "How can you stand the cold?"

"Don't ask." Jakkin held out his hand for the extinguisher.

Without a single question of his own, Likkarn showed Jakkin how to use the stinger, his comments concise. "This setting to stun, this to kill. Here's the trigger. Sight along the barrel. Don't hesitate. Keep firing in a circular motion. Don't worry — you'll hit something that way."

Though Jakkin said nothing, his face gave him away.

"Kill!" Errikkin said. "You've got to kill them all, whoever they are. Listen to Likkarn. Don't hesitate!"

"Will the stun setting stop them?"

Likkarn puffed his lips out for a moment. "It can stun drakks and a small dragon. It can certainly drop a man in his tracks, scramble his brains for a while. But these fellows . . . I don't know. Errikkin is probably right." He jammed the stinger into the kill position.

The trogs were now pulling at the heavy wooden shutters. At each pull, frigid air flooded in. Errikkin's teeth were already chattering.

"Latch the door into the stall area and don't open it, even if you hear me beg, unless I say Heart's Blood's name," Jakkin told them. He held out a hand to Likkarn, who shook it. And then to Errikkin, who did not.

"Go!" Jakkin said as they heard the sound of the shutters being pulled off.

The two bolted toward the stall area, slamming the door behind them. Jakkin turned and went to the doorway of the visitors' room, readying the stinger. He stood in the darkened hall; that gave him a bit of cover. The window was partly lit by the hearth fire, which was vainly trying to beat back the cold. At least Jakkin knew he would be able to see to shoot.

A figure was half through the window, already picking its way past the broken glass.

Jakkin sighted along the stinger, pushed the setting back to stun, then pulled the trigger. The first shot missed but not by much, hitting the left-hand shutter and exploding it into pieces of wood. The shot startled the trog and for a couple of seconds he looked around, not sure what was happening.

He's probably never even heard of anything like a stinger. Jakkin kept firing in the circular motion that Likkarn suggested until he eventually hit the trog — once, twice, three times. It hardly slowed him up at all. He jumped down from the window and headed directly toward Jakkin.

Jakkin slammed the lever from stun to kill and again sprayed the room with the stinger, round and round, until finally the trog fell, his legs scissoring a half dozen times before he died. Shaking, Jakkin kept firing at the downed body until the stinger ran out of energy.

"Well, that didn't go the way I meant it to," Jakkin whispered. Yes, he'd stopped the smallest trog — much to the dismay of his stomach, which was threatening to heave up into his throat. But the stinger was now useless. And Big Boss and the wounded trog were still out there.

Somewhere.

☾ 33 ☽

JAKKIN RAN to the stall door. "One down, but the sting-er's empty," he shouted. He didn't mention that the trog was dead.

"Worm waste!" barked Likkarn. "Maybe it's just jammed. They do that sometimes." He pulled the door open. "Let me see it."

"No! No! No — he didn't say Heart's Blood!" Errikkin screamed, slamming the door shut.

Evidently the door shut on Likkarn's fingers, because he began to curse on and on, even after the door was opened slightly and then closed again as quickly.

"Heart's Blood!" Jakkin cried. "For God's sake, Errikkin, don't be a big fewmet. I'm all alone here."

The door was opened again. Errikkin was flapping his hands. "What's the good of a password if you don't use —"

"Give it here," Likkarn said, reaching out with his left hand. The right one he cradled against his body.

Jakkin was about to hand over the stinger when a noise behind him made him freeze. Glancing over his shoulder, he glimpsed a shadow dashing toward him. He turned, swung the stinger like a club. It connected with the arm of the already injured trog, who dropped to the floor screaming, a strange high-pitched cry of pain. This action threw Jakkin onto one leg.

Taking a deep breath, he tried to right himself, but before he was ready, something large leaped out of the darkness and hit him a body blow. He went down on all fours, struck by a sending so black and nasty, he nearly passed out from it.

Big Boss!

"Help!" Jakkin cried, his voice suddenly as weak as his body. "Heart's Blood!"

Behind the half-open door, Errikkin pushed aside Likkarn, who seemed momentarily stunned. Then he dashed out and launched himself at the trog's back. With his knife, he punched down, again and again and again, till the knife grew so slippery with blood, it slid out of his grip.

Big Boss reared and shook him off and Errikkin was slammed to the floor. He lay there, hardly breathing, something broken in his back.

"Worm drizzle!" Likkarn cursed, then raced toward the bloody trog before Big Boss could turn his attention back to Jakkin. Using his left hand — the right still pretty useless — Likkarn slung the hammer at the trog's head. It nearly missed, but hit him above the eye with a loud crack, then bounced off. Immediately the eye closed and blood sprayed from a deep cut above it.

Big Boss's sending ended with that blow and Jakkin was

able to grab the messy hammer. Heaving up to his knees in a single motion, he slammed the hammer into the trog's other eye.

Effectively blinded, Big Boss howled and reached out for Jakkin, but Jakkin had already slipped behind him. Picking up Errikkin's body, he scrambled over to Likkarn.

"Get him back inside, into one of the stalls, any hen without chicks will do. He needs the warmth."

"I know what he needs, but that big troll —"

"Leave him to me," Jakkin said. "I have things to settle with that one." He handed over Errikkin's body and wiped the fair hair away from his friend's face. "Hang on, bonder," he whispered. "Hang on."

Then Jakkin went back to the trogs, one sitting with his hands up to his ruined eyes, one lying down. He looked around, found both hammer and knife, and took another deep breath. Then, standing behind them — Big Boss first and the smaller trog after — he slit their throats. He felt no more than did the stewmen who killed dragons for their meat. Maybe even less, for unlike the dying dragons, the trogs made no sound or sending to trouble him.

Jakkin dropped both hammer and knife. They clattered noisily onto the floor. Then he began to wipe his hands compulsively on his leather pants over and over and over again as if he could wipe away what he'd just done.

After a minute of this, he shook himself mentally. *Stop thinking so much. Just do what needs doing. And then do the next.*

Swiping a forearm across his eyes, he forced himself to breathe slowly. In and out, in and out. He thought of Akki,

Heart's Blood, her brood. He must have let loose with a sending, because Auricle sent him back a tremulous landscape of grays and blues with something hunched and dark in the back.

"Danger?" she asked.

He smiled tentatively. *"Not anymore, not for me, nor thee."* He pictured the oasis, with dragons romping in the water.

By then he was finally calm, so he went over to the sofa still guarding the front door. Pushing it and the table out of the way, he flung open the door. A sliver of light was pushing up along the horizon. He walked outside. The tendrils of Dark-After's cold were already drifting away.

Soon it would be dawn and warm enough to bring Errikkin back into the bondhouse. There he'd be cleaned up, warmed up, and cared for in the hospice. There they could all eat and drink takk and rejoice at their close escape. Because it *had* been close. Now that it was over, he could admit that. He started to run his hands through his hair before realizing how sticky they were. Once again, he tried to rub away the blood on his leather pants. The pants were sticky, too, even clammy. He let his hands drop to his sides.

Jakkin had one more awful duty to perform. Dragging out the three trogs one at a time, he laid them out by the side of the barn. That way, they wouldn't disturb the hen dragons, and it would be easier to bury them.

In the rising light, the dead trogs no longer looked big or strong or threatening. They were somehow shrunken. Even rather sad. All of a sudden, Jakkin began to sob — for the dead trogs, for Errikkin. He took a big gulping breath, hearing Big Boss in his head: *Do not kriah.*

But I'm not a trog and I'm not ashamed to cry. He kept on sobbing, though now he did it silently. When he was done crying, he went back into the barn to check on his two wounded mates.

~

ERRIKKIN LAY in Likkarn's arms, each breath long and labored. Likkarn had taken off his own shirt and wrapped the boy in it. They were both snugged up against Heart's Ease, who looked strangely uncomfortable with them at her side, as if they were misshapen hatchlings. However, she was — as her name suggested — an easy dragon, with a mind as soft as her manner. She trusted old Likkarn, so she let them stay.

Jakkin sent her a cozy pink sand scene, with pink water from an oasis lapping at her pink feet, by way of thanks. She responded by stretching her neck around the two men, radiating even more heat.

"How is he?" Jakkin whispered.

Likkarn shook his head. "I think something's broken."

"Arm? Leg?"

"Back."

"That's bad." Slipping next to Likkarn, Jakkin put his arms around Errikkin's shoulders. He was ice-cold, even with the extra shirt and the dragon's warmth.

Jakkin pushed Errikkin's hair back from his broad forehead. "That was the bravest thing I ever saw anyone do," he whispered. "Errikkin, you're a hero."

For a moment, Errikkin roused. He tried to smile. His bland face suddenly took on real beauty. "I did it for you," he whispered back, his voice slow and cracking. "For . . . my . . . master." He pushed out each word as if they were boulders being rolled uphill.

"The best bonder ever," Jakkin said, trying to keep his tone light. "*My* best bonder ever."

Errikkin closed his eyes and sighed. "Your *only* bonder." Then he started shaking, tremors running up and down his body. It caused Heart's Ease to begin hackling.

To calm them both, Jakkin began humming two verses of the dragon lullaby, all the while stroking Errikkin's hair. It worked like a charm and soon both boy and worm quieted. But when Jakkin finished the second chorus, Errikkin suddenly gave three long shuddering breaths and was still, his mouth slightly open.

Sunlight touched the incubarn, splashing in through the broken window and shutters of the visitors' room. The stalls seemed eerily silent until Heart's Ease heaved herself to her feet and started rocking back and forth. She sent a picture of the boy covered in black.

Likkarn scooted away from her, still holding on to Errikkin, who never once stirred.

Jakkin looked down at his old friend. He noticed how quiet he was, how white.

The dragon continued her odd rocking, and now all the dragons in the incubarn were keening, a strange wailing pounding in Jakkin's head.

"Is he . . . is he gone?"

"Gone to the highest master of all," Likkarn said. It could have been meant as a joke, but his face was fiercely serious.

"He'll like that." Jakkin's voice cracked on the last word.

"Let's bring him home," Likkarn said. He got to his feet carefully, with an assist by Jakkin, Errikkin still in his arms.

Heart's Ease stopped rocking, but the keening by the other dragons continued until Jakkin opened the front door of the bondhouse, ushering in Likkarn, who was carrying Errikkin's body as easily as if he were a child.

☾ 34 ☾

"WHAT DO I say to them?" Likkarn asked.

"As little as possible."

Likkarn nodded.

"We can't hide the trogs, of course, but no one needs to know the rest."

"I agree."

The kitchen door opened and Kkarina stood there, hands on her ample hips. When she saw Errikkin's body, she started to wail.

Four nursery folk raced out of the dining hall to find out why Kkarina was carrying on — young Terakkina in the front, then redheaded Vonikka, Slakk looking white and drained, and at the last, old Balakk.

Jakkin couldn't hear anyone else nearby, especially with Kkarina moaning so loudly. "Where is everybody?" It was unusual for only four people to have been in the dining room for breakfast.

At that, oddly, Kkarina flung her apron over her head and began wailing even louder.

"Be quiet, woman!" warned Likkarn, before looking

down at the boy he was carrying. "We'll talk of that other later. Right now we have something more important to do."

But Slakk, as always, had to be first with bad news. "Jakkin, they're all off to The Rokk to help find Akki."

"What do you mean, *find* her? Is she gone?" Jakkin thought his voice no longer sounded like his own.

"Taken," groaned Kkarina. "Someone's gone and taken her!"

Jakkin had never felt so cold before. He could hardly think. *Have the trogs gotten Akki? Not in the city, surely? Dragged her from the truck? It doesn't make sense. Still . . .*

"We've got to go."

Likkarn glared at him. After a thoughtful moment, he said, "We've got three things to do first, and then I'll drive you there myself."

Distracted, Jakkin asked, *"What* three things?"

Peeling the apron from her face, Kkarina answered, "Why, we have to clean thee up, boy, and then feed thee up." She spoke to him as if he were a dragon. "And we have to bury this poor child." She put her palm against Errikkin's cold cheek.

"But —"

"There's many a nurseryman already gone to the city to look for Akki at Golden's call," Kkarina said, her voice suddenly calm, nothing remaining of the wail. "All of ours but the ones you see here. We needed some to keep the nursery going. What can you add that's not already being done?"

"I can hear her in here . . ." murmured Jakkin, touching his head. Then he stopped.

Likkarn nodded. "So can we all."

Heeding the implicit warning in what Likkarn said, Jakkin allowed himself to be led to the showers by Balakk, where the water first ran blood-red and then clear. But his mind remained bloody. Now he realized how bruised he was. He could see the purple and yellow of the older bruises on his wrists, and newer, blacker ones on his legs and arms. He supposed there were more along his back. Possibly some on his face. None of that mattered, of course. Finding Akki was the most important thing.

~

LATER, IN THE dining hall, Jakkin managed to gulp down a boiled lizard egg and two quick cups of tea, including one made of yellow dickory. Kkarina insisted it helped with bruises.

"It better," Jakkin muttered, "because it tastes too awful for just drinking."

They all finished eating in record time, serving themselves. Kkarina had been occupied with washing Errikkin's body on a long table in the bondhouse kitchen. Alone, she'd put the oil at the back of his hands and on his feet. Then she dressed him in clean clothes.

They assembled in the small cemetery, Jakkin, Balakk, and the two young women carrying the spikka-wood casket. It was heavier than Jakkin had expected and had no name etched into the top. There hadn't been time.

"Twice in a week," Kkarina said, wiping her eyes with her apron. "Bad things come in threes, I shouldn't wonder."

She means Akki. Jakkin shuddered before grabbing hold

of one of the two shovels. Balakk used the other, and they quickly dug a grave in the soft sandy soil under the weeping wilkkins.

As they lowered the casket, Vonikka started up the old hymn they'd sung for Arakk's burial:

> *Oh, God, who sends the double moons,*
> *Who spreads the singing sand . . .*

The others joined in a thin, ragged chorus, but not Jakkin. *Too fast, too fast.* He meant the burial had been pushed ahead too fast, knowing Errikkin would have hated the rush, would have wanted the entire nursery there. But Likkarn said they had no idea when the others would be back from the search for Akki, and — as Jakkin well knew — in a hot desert world, all bodies had to be buried as soon as possible.

He hardly listened to Likkarn speak of Errikkin's bravery, how in death he'd found himself. Jakkin couldn't concentrate on Likkarn's voice, the way it broke during its delivery, so unlike him. Already Jakkin's mind was turned to The Rokk.

We've spent too much time already. He grimaced. *I should have killed those pieces of worm waste sooner.*

~

ONLY JAKKIN and Likkarn rode in the truck, heading at breakneck speed toward The Rokk. Everyone else was needed to keep the nursery going.

"Besides, I'm the only one of that lot who can drive," said Likkarn as they barreled along the road.

Drive was too kind a word for what Likkarn was attempting. With his right arm bound up by Kkarina, he had to drive left-handed. The truck seemed to keep careening from one side of the road to the other. Luckily, no one was in the opposite lane most of the time, but even so, Jakkin held himself rigid as they went along.

However, on the approach to Krakkow the road began to fill up and Likkarn's erratic steering earned them blaring horns and many hand gestures that purported to show how big the fewmets were that they resembled.

Jakkin stopped himself from returning the hand signs and kept his right hand on the door handle, his left on the dashboard hold-bar. He was ready to grab the steerer if need be. It was not easy riding with Likkarn.

"What about those invaders?" Likkarn asked. It was the first he'd spoken of the attack. "Their bodies."

"I told Balakk they needed burying. Told him no coffins needed."

Likkarn houghed like a dragon. "What did he say to that?"

"Not much. Just that he wasn't considering it."

Likkarn houghed again.

"I told him they were odd-looking thieves," Jakkin added. "And that there was one more drowned in the oasis, out beyond the weir."

"Hah!" Likkarn said.

Jakkin didn't wonder at his response. Balakk had answered, "Out where you trained your young red?" which *had* surprised him. But Balakk said he knew about the oasis from Likkarn, who'd been told by Sarkkhan, who — Jakkin thought — presumably had learned about it from Akki.

Akki. It all came back to her.

"Hah!" Likkarn said again, but Jakkin ignored him.

All Jakkin wanted was to be in The Rokk looking for Akki.

As they careened along, he sent Akki colorful images, but there was no response. Nonetheless, he was sure that once in the big city, he would find her. He *had* to find her.

～

LEAVING KRAKKOW, Jakkin finally asked Likkarn, "What *really* has happened to Akki?" It was a question he'd been afraid to ask. Then needed to ask. But once they'd gotten started in the truck, Likkarn's driving had kept him from asking anything at all, lest the questions take any more of Likkarn's attention off the road. But after they had reached Krakkow, the questions just seemed to fall out of Jakkin's mouth. "Where is she? Is she all right? Has she been hurt?"

Likkarn turned his head and stared at Jakkin.

"The road!" Jakkin cried, pointing. "Watch the worm-eaten road!"

The truck had drifted dangerously into the oncoming lane, which was now filled with traffic. A horn blared. Then another.

Likkarn jerked the wheel and the truck swerved drunkenly back into its lane, shuddering with the effort. The old man seemed undisturbed by the wobbles. "Golden sent a driver and a big van, asking for help. Seems Akki went missing after an evening debate."

"A debate? What debate?" Jakkin asked, adding quickly, "Watch the road."

Another swing of the wheel, another shuddering of the truck. Jakkin decided not to ask any more questions, but just let Likkarn talk.

"Golden's running again for senator. He was on a panel debating with other candidates."

Jakkin knew little of politics and cared even less, especially after having been taken advantage of in The Rokk by the rebels a year earlier.

"Afterward, he and Dr. Henkky stayed to shake hands and have drinks with their followers. Akki and another girl, who works for Golden, left to go back to the house. Someone shot —"

"*Shot?* With a gun? Is it Akki?"

The truck did its lane-to-lane dance before Likkarn yanked it under control again.

"Shot the other girl. She's still in a hospice. He winged the hatchling."

Then, it wasn't trogs, after all. They know nothing about guns. Jakkin wasn't sure if this was good news or bad.

Likkarn said, "And then he kidnapped Akki."

"*Kidnapped!*" He'd heard of it before. Maybe kidnapped was better than just taken. Usually the kidnapper wanted money and then let the victim go once the money was paid. "How much does he want?" Not that he had any money, but Golden surely did.

"Golden thinks it's not for money but to make him pull

out of the race, though they hadn't been contacted last I heard."

"When . . ." Jakkin had to know. "When was that?"

"The night after the day she left."

That makes it the night I slept in the hollow of the tree. Why, oh why hadn't I just kept going. Or left earlier. Or . . .

Likkarn's hand on the wheel was so tight, the knuckles turned white. "Stomach. Sorry. Got to pull over for a minute," he said, and they jounced onto the grainy shoulder of the road, plowing down a line of small green plants that had hardly managed to poke their heads above the sand.

They both climbed out; Likkarn slid down over the sandy brow of the road, disappearing from sight to relieve himself. Jakkin remained by the truck, simply happy to be free of the crazy driving for a minute. But all the while his head whirled with worry about Akki. Who could have taken her? Was she being well treated? And he couldn't stop recalling what Kkarina had said: "Bad things come in threes, I shouldn't wonder."

As the old bonder struggled back over the brow, his feet slipped in the sand, and Jakkin offered him a hand.

"Thanks," Likkarn mumbled.

"No — thank *you*."

Likkarn looked puzzled. "Not for driving, surely. You'll have noticed that I'm not . . ."

They got back into the truck and Jakkin said, "At least you *can* drive. But my thanks is for helping me back at the incubarn without question, without argument . . ."

Likkarn put his head to one side as if considering something.

"I know you've never liked me," Jakkin continued, "but . . . but that's the second time you've saved me. And now we're off to save Akki together."

Likkarn's lips were set in a thin line. Then he said without preamble, "I didn't want to muck it up again, like I did with your father."

"You *knew* my father?" Jakkin was so astonished, for a moment he couldn't think of a response. All these years, Likkarn had known his father and had never said anything. Jakkin didn't know if he was furious or . . . excited.

"He was my . . ." Likkarn took a breath, his face suddenly gone white. "He was my brother." As if to stop any further conversation, he turned quickly to look behind them, checked the traffic, rammed the truck back onto the road.

"Your brother?" Jakkin repeated in disbelief. The truck was wobbling across lanes again. Horns were barking at them. Jakkin had to shout to make himself heard. "My father's brother?"

"Half-brother, actually." Likkarn eased off the pedal and brought the truck back into their lane, and everything seemed to settle down. "We were fifteen years apart. And when our mother died, and I was left to bring him up, I was . . . well, I wasn't very good at it. And I hated doing it. He was very charming, funny. I let him get away with things I shouldn't have, and then I got mad at him for getting away with them."

Charming? Funny? Jakkin tried to remember his father and could only remember him angry and unhappy.

Likkarn continued. "I wanted to raise dragons, which

he hated. So when I got taken on by Master Sarkkhan, instead of coming with me, he ran off and I didn't look for him. *Good riddance,* I thought."

"To your *brother?*"

Likkarn took quite some time before he answered. "Well, I said I wasn't good at it. He went to the city, failed at a couple of things there. Met your mother, who was the daughter of Master Ortran, a dragon master with a big nursery not far from The Rokk, and charmed her into marrying him."

My mother. Jakkin only remembered big eyes and a lot of sadness.

Likkarn went on. "They had you. Then — knowing nothing about dragons, only knowing that his big brother worked with them and his wife's father trained them — he tried to capture and raise a feral in order to impress us all. And . . ." Likkarn's hand was once again white-knuckled on the steering wheel.

"And it killed him."

"I believed for the longest time that *I* had killed him," Likkarn said. "At least your mother told me so."

Jakkin shook his head. "Any nurseryman knows better than to try to tame a feral by himself. She was wrong. *You* didn't kill him."

Likkarn's cheeks were suddenly flushed, and the old blood scores on his face looked like deep pits. There was something red and angry in his mind, too, and it trickled out to Jakkin.

Jakkin rocked back, remembering the last time he'd

been able to go into Likkarn's mind. *Maybe I can do it be-cause we're related by blood.*

"Your mother didn't like me, of course. Fewmets! *I* did-n't like me. I was smoking a lot of weed and wort then. She put herself in bond rather than ask her father for help. When she was dying — of a broken heart, I believed then and still do — she begged me to keep an eye on you because I was family. *Family!* I couldn't think of a worse person to have asked."

The truck wobbled again and a man leaned out of his van window to shout at Likkarn.

"To you, too!" Jakkin yelled as the van sped by.

Likkarn paid attention to neither the van driver nor Jakkin. It was clear that he was determined to finish the story he'd started so as never to have to refer to it again. "I decided to be hard on you because I wasn't hard enough on your father. And . . ." He leaned forward, glaring through the truck's front window as if something out there could save him from the last bits of his story. "And I nearly got you killed twice."

Jakkin unlocked his left hand from the dash bar and pat-ted Likkarn's forearm. It was like steel, corded and tight. "No, Likkarn, I almost got *you* killed twice. *You* were the one who saved me."

Likkarn's shoulders seemed to have relaxed a bit, but his hand on the wheel was still tense.

"But now we have to go and save Akki," Jakkin said softly.

Likkarn gave a quick sideways glance, then once more

stared out of the window. "They know the man who grabbed her. He was the driver of the car that took them all to the debate. Both car and driver are missing. Still, if we're lucky, by the time we get to The Rokk, she'll already have been found."

"If we were lucky, *Uncle* Likkarn, we'd never have landed in this mess."

Likkarn started to laugh.

"What's so funny?"

"Calling me *Uncle*."

"Sorry, I won't do it again." The old man's laughter was so unusual, Jakkin found himself joining in. *"Laughing, that's something families can share."* He clapped his hand on Likkarn's arm.

"That and tragedy." Likkarn's sending was barely audible, but undeniably there.

"You can . . ." Jakkin didn't dare say further.

"Sometimes," Likkarn said. "But only with Heart's Ease and, it seems, you."

"When did you first know?"

"Her first try at egg-laying. Things were going badly. The eggs weren't coming out. The doctor was at another farm. I was afraid of losing her, so I cut her open and pulled the eggs out by hand. The blood burned. I screamed. She screamed. And her voice was in my head, telling me what to do."

Jakkin nodded. "Akki and I sheltered in Heart's Blood's egg chamber to keep warm during Dark-After. And then we could hear dragons, too." He didn't say anything more, but supposed that Likkarn — *Uncle* Likkarn — could guess.

They rode the rest of the way in silence. Jakkin dozed, dreamed, woke drenched in sweat, and dozed again. He didn't remember what he dreamed, but clearly it was awful. And Likkarn stayed out of his head the whole way there.

☾ 35 ☾

IF JAKKIN had been nervous about Likkarn's driving on the great double-laned road, he should have been terrified by the old man's maneuvering through the small mazed streets of The Rokk. But Jakkin was paying little attention as to how they clipped the occasional sidewalk or scraped by the occasional pole. Instead he totally concentrated on sendings to Akki.

For him, every new turning was an opportunity, bumps and all.

He sent the same thing over and over, a bright red heart embroidered with burning wort. And her name, with the message, *"I am here. I am here. Where are you?"*

But there was nothing sent back. He didn't know what that meant. *Is she hurt? Too far away? Or . . .* No, he wouldn't think about that, though Kkarina's voice came back again, and now it really haunted him: "Bad things come in threes, I shouldn't wonder."

"We're getting close to Golden's house," said Likkarn, breaking through Jakkin's bleak thoughts. "It's somewhere around here."

"That's the best you can do — *somewhere?*"

"Well, at least I know we can't drive right to the door. I'll park, and we'll find it together. Number seventeen."

Jakkin stopped listening to Likkarn because there was suddenly a small, thin, weak sending threading into his head. It was a ragged strand, a burnt-orange color. *"Here."*

At first Jakkin's heart thudded in his chest. But then he realized: *It's not Akki.*

"Dragon!" he said aloud, which startled Likkarn into glancing at him so that the truck jumped onto the sidewalk, nosed a pole, and stopped.

Likkarn pulled up the brake as if the sidewalk had been his actual goal, then turned off the engine. "Where?"

Jakkin rolled down the window and looked up at the sky. It was a blank blue slate. He tried sending again, this time to the dragon. *"I am here. Where are you?"* It was a picture of the street lined in red and gold.

"Here. Here."

"Where's *here?*" Likkarn asked, startling Jakkin, who was going to have to get used to the old man's ability to listen in on some of his inner conversations.

The landscape sent back to them looked a lot like the oasis, and Jakkin cursed, thinking that couldn't be right. The oasis was miles and hours behind them. He turned to Likkarn. "Is there an oasis nearby? You know — water, trees, reeds."

"You mean like Sukker's Marsh? Don't be stupid, boy. This is a city. We're right by Golden's house. There." He pointed down a street that had small trees and large houses.

Jakkin stared at the houses. He'd only been to Golden's once before. It had been at night, for a party, a year and a lifetime ago. Did he recognize the house, or did he just want to?

"Are you sure about the oasis?" he asked Likkarn.

Before Likkarn could answer, a pulsing rainbow entered Jakkin's brain. *"Here, here, here."* Jakkin opened his door, leaped down, and with the sending still swirling in his head, he headed toward the source.

"Hey, worm waste!" Likkarn cried. "How do you know which house it is?"

Without slowing, Jakkin looked over his shoulder and shouted: "I know!" Within moments he found himself in front of number 17 and recognized it as Golden's front door. He was about to knock when the door opened.

There stood Jo-Janekk, clearly ready to walk out. His eyes widened. "Jakkin. Where have you been? How did you get here?"

Jakkin pointed over his shoulder where Likkarn was just steps behind. "Has she been found? Akki — has she been found?"

Jo-Janekk shook his head. "We've been up and down these fewmetty streets for the last two days, knocking on doors, climbing around attics, and there's nothing. *Nothing.* No sign of her."

"You're not giving up, are you?"

"No, not at all. She's one of us. We'll find her."

"Is Golden here?"

"No, he's out with the searchers. But Dr. Henkky is. I've just gotten bags of food from her to bring back to my crew."

He held up a large leather sack. "She's feeding everyone and taking care of Senekka."

Jakkin looked puzzled. "Who?"

"The girl who got shot," Jo-Janekk said. "She hasn't regained consciousness yet. A bullet evidently struck her in the head. Something about swelling in her brain." He nodded at Likkarn, who had just reached them. "Coming along?"

Likkarn shook his head. "I'll get something to eat and a takk for the road, then head back to the nursery. I should get there just before Dark-After. There are only three men and three women left, counting me. And Slakk is still not really well enough for heavy work yet."

"Hah!" Jo-Janekk laughed snidely. "Even well, he hardly works."

Likkarn laughed, too, as if sharing a private joke.

"He killed a drakk single-handedly," Jakkin reminded them.

They had the grace to look embarrassed.

"Wait a minute. Who's missing from the work detail? Not that little flake Errikkin."

Jakkin and Likkarn stared at one another, and Likkarn said, "I'll handle this." He turned back, put his hand on Jo-Janekk's shoulder, and said, "Let me tell you about an unlikely hero."

"I'm going to talk to Henkky," Jakkin said, "and then go out on the search." He wasn't about to tell Jo-Janekk that he was going on his own because he'd be using sendings and whatever dragons he could gather. But as he thought about dragons, doubt like an old friend crept in. How could there be any dragons here, in this small place?

"Here." The sending, like a golden thread, entered his mind again. And then he knew — it was the hatchling, of course. Akki had brought her along. Surely the hatchling could help. She could be his eyes and ears, flying above him as he tracked through the mazed streets of The Rokk.

"We'll be meeting back here in three hours, if no one has any news," Jo-Janekk said. He was looking sad and chastened, having heard about Errikkin from Likkarn. "I'll tell the others." Shaking his head, he went off.

As they entered Golden's house, Jakkin immediately remembered it, with its gaudy colors and fountain and pipes. He blushed and turned his head. Likkarn just chuckled.

"Everyone is exhausted," Dr. Henkky said, coming into the room. "Thanks for helping. We can use fresh blood." Certainly *she* seemed exhausted, her face almost as gray as the dress she was wearing. "Three-hour shifts, morning and afternoon, two-hour shifts at night, then back here to sleep through Dark-After. Two full days and nights with only four hours of sleep." She stopped when she recognized Likkarn. "Oh, it's you. Any news from your end?"

He shook his head.

"And nobody's found *anything?*" Jakkin asked.

She held out her hand. "And you are . . . ?"

"Jakkin. Akki's friend."

"Oh — oh, of course you are. No, Jakkin. Nothing. Not the gun, not the man — he was Golden's driver, you know. They haven't found Akki. And no ransom note, either. The wardens are baffled, and so are we." She took Jakkin by the hand. "You look like you could use a cup of takk. And you, Likkarn — something stronger?"

"Don't give him anything stronger. He's driving back."

She looked at Likkarn quizzically.

"We have to keep the nursery going. Dragons don't care for themselves. And if anything happens there that we can't handle, I'm the only one of the short crew who can drive. We've buried two boys this week Jakkin's age, and the nursery folk need me there."

Henkky raised an eyebrow, questioning. "Sickness?" Then she shook her head. "And you said you had no news. I could send a doctor back with you, though I have to stay here, of course."

"Nah, nah. One died from a fall from a tree, going after drakks, and one . . ."

Jakkin held his breath, wondering what Likkarn was going to say next. If he mentioned the trogs, things would start unraveling fast.

"And the other, when three thieves captured our boy here and forced him to lead them to our nursery. You know, the usual."

"Two boys dead hardly sounds *usual*," Henkky replied.

"Dragon nursery's not an easy place, ma'am."

Jakkin was afraid Likkarn was overplaying the country bumbler, but Dr. Henkky didn't seem to notice. She accepted Likkarn's explanation and showed them into a room with a fireplace. Jakkin remembered that room, with books spilling all over its carpets. This time there was a large table, where platters of food were ruled over by an elegant takk pot.

"Did they hurt you?" Henkky asked Jakkin.

"Who?"

Suddenly her face had a suspicious look. "The thieves."

Jakkin shrugged. "Some bruises."

"Show me."

He held up his hands. The bruises on his wrists were now yellowing.

"Hmmm," she said. "Tied?"

He nodded, turned, lifted his shirt.

"Those have purpled nicely," she said. "I can give you a salve."

"They don't hurt."

"Nevertheless."

He nodded. Anything to get outside, onto the street.

She poured him a cup of takk.

"I prefer tea, actually."

"Ah, just like Akki," she said, and poured sand-colored tea into a delicate cup. He took it from her gratefully.

"Is Akki's hatchling here?" He tried to keep his tone neutral.

"Out in the garden."

"Ah, a garden." That explained the oasis in the sending. "Can I . . . see her?"

She waved in the direction of another door down the hall. "Out there."

He drank the tea quickly, and said good-bye to Likkarn, who pressed a couple of coins on him.

"You never know when you might need them," the old trainer said before he gathered up several slices of meat and a traveling mug of takk and was gone.

~

JAKKIN FOUND his way into the garden, where he saw a yellow Beauty curled up in a garden chair. He shuddered because he couldn't stand the Beauties, artificially stunted as they were.

"*I am here,*" he sent. The Beauty ignored him, but behind her, close to a small pool, and all but disguised by the reeds and some high tufted grass, lay the hatchling. There was a bandage — somewhat the worse for wear — on her left wing.

Jakkin circled the edge of the pool and squatted down next to her. Raising her head, she stretched her neck its full length so that he could scratch under her chin. He obliged her and she began a light thrumming.

"Brave dragonling, how art thou now?" he asked, before sending the same in a yellow burst of sunlight.

Gingerly, she lifted the injured wing for his inspection. It trembled, and she shut it again very slowly.

With a sinking feeling, he realized that she wouldn't be flying for a while so she would be no help.

"I know. I know it hurts thee," he murmured. "And Akki? Where is she?" This time the sending was a portrait in cool blues.

The hatchling sat up awkwardly. Clearly the wing bothered her a lot. She wafted the good one, but the wounded wing barely fluttered. Her mind was in a turmoil. *"Bad man. Bad man."* In the middle of the sending was a whirlwind of gray and white, in the center of which stood a faceless man with a gun, the wind blowing his white-blond hair around like a halo. The gun went off soundlessly and a dragonling fell from the sky, landing at his feet.

"Bad man indeed," Jakkin sent back. Then he stroked her until she calmed and lay down again. To further help her, Jakkin began singing, *"Little flame mouth, cool your tongue . . ."* Soon her eyes closed and she thrummed herself to sleep.

Jakkin waited a few minutes, until he was sure the hatchling was deeply asleep, then went back inside to look for Henkky. He found her downstairs in what looked to be partly a lab and partly a hospice with four white-sheeted beds. She was bending over one bed and washing the face of a slim dark-haired girl, who lay quite still, a sheet pulled up to her shoulders.

"I don't mean to bother you," Jakkin whispered, "or her."

"She's beyond bothering right now," Henkky said. "But she does seem a bit more alert. She squeezed my hand this morning."

"Is that a good sign, then?" Jakkin remembered how Errikkin had roused to speak one or two sentences before he died.

"Possibly," Henkky said. "Possibly not. Only time will tell."

"Will she be able to say who shot her and took Akki?"

"Usually brain injury patients can't remember anything that happened right before they were hurt. But we're pretty sure it was a man called Dikkon, who was Golden's driver." She sighed. "I always thought he was such a nice man, too."

Jakkin wondered how to phrase the next question. Then decided to plunge right in. "Do you know a man with whitish-gold hair who carries a gun?" He shrugged. "It's a worm-blasted description, but it's all I have."

She surprised him. "Of course. That's Dark. One of the candidates running against Golden. In fact, he was injured trying to save the girls and the hatchling. He ended up with quite a bruised face and a massive headache."

Jakkin tried to fit her description of Dark with the hatchling's "bad man." He supposed that to dragons most humans looked the same, especially if they couldn't do sendings. "Can I speak to him?"

"He's off with one of the groups looking for Akki. Even bruised, even with a headache, he's been working tirelessly trying to find her. He worked with Golden to organize the searchers and has been out every day. Maybe when his group returns for food you can speak with him." She paused, put her head to one side. "He often goes home instead of eating with the others. Most of the searchers are from the nurseries and I think they tire him with their incessant talk of dragons." She put a hand to her mouth. "Oh, I'm sorry, Jakkin. I don't mean *you*."

"No insult taken," he said. "Can you lend me a map and show me where your house is on it?"

"Of course. Follow me." She straightened out the girl's

bed with a quick pat. Leading him upstairs, she took him back to the room with all the books. There was a pile of maps on one of the shelves. She took one, opened it, and with a pen, made a circle on a street in the middle of the map. "This is Golden's house." Then she looked up kindly. "I'm sorry, Jakkin — can you read, then? I know a lot of the nursery folk can't."

He nodded. "Enough."

"Right," she said. "Oh!" Her hand went to her mouth. "I remember now." She smiled. "I lent you a book once."

He stared sheepishly at his feet. "I'm afraid I didn't get through it all." When he looked up, a small smile was playing around her mouth. "I'm also trying to find where five big dragons have gotten to. Heart's Blood's brood. They were with me, but after the thieves . . . Well, I think they may have come ahead here. They knew that's where I was heading."

"How could they possibly know that?" Henkky asked, puzzled.

"Well, they were following me and I was heading in this direction. Until the thieves got me, that is, and . . . forced me to go back to the nursery."

Henkky appeared confused. "Golden has been up every day in the senate's copter looking for signs of Akki. What could the dragons see that he couldn't?"

Jakkin fretted about how to answer her. Should he say that dragons had better sight day and night than a human? Or that dragons and Akki could speak together mind-to-mind? He decided it was safer to say nothing. Let Henkky think he was being sentimental about the dragons. It didn't matter, so long as she answered his question.

Finally, Henkky shook her head. "No, I haven't seen five big dragons around here. We don't get ferals, certainly not in the city's central area. Not enough food for them. And usually any tame dragons are installed below the pits. Those have all been moved to the outskirts of the city since Rokk Major was blown. Oh!" She put her hand over her mouth again. "I seem to keep stepping on my tongue with you, Jakkin."

He wasn't surprised that she knew of his involvement in the explosion. After all, she and Golden had been together for some time. He turned his hands palms up. "Don't worry."

"Well, what I mean to say is that big dragons are hard to keep — feed and water — in the city center except at a pit. There are four small pits now. So your dragons may be off on the northeastern outskirts of town, where I wouldn't get to see them." She pointed to several circles on the map. "There, to the left, that's the warehouse district. It's set off from the city and there're plenty of fields where dragons could graze." She made a red circle around seven squares at the northwestern end of the city. "Dark and his group have already searched those warehouses quite thoroughly."

Jakkin nodded.

"And here . . ." Another circle, between the warehouse and the pits. "These were once a group of farms. Lots of weed and wort grow around there now. They're 'volunteer' plants that grow up without cultivation. Sometimes, I'm told, feral dragons can be found there."

"How far away to these places on foot?" he asked.

"Half an hour if you go at a good clip, closer to an hour if you stroll. Though there's at least that much time between the warehouse district and the pits. A large triangle, you see." She outlined it with her finger.

He did see. He understood he'd have to make some choices very soon.

"Was Akki wearing her gold hair band?" Jakkin asked.

Henkky looked startled. It wasn't a question she'd been expecting. "No, she was in an old blue dress of mine. And some heeled shoes."

Jakkin took a deep breath. "Then could I have it, for a kind of luck charm?"

"Oh. Of course." She went away for a few minutes, then came back holding something. "This it?"

He bit his lip, then took the gold band and wrapped it around his wrist. A piece of Akki.

"Now, be careful," Henkky said. Jakkin forced himself to listen again. "If you're late getting back, find a pub. They put people up during Dark-After." She felt in the pocket of her skirt. "Here are five coins. That should cover it."

"Likkarn already —"

She ignored him. "I'll wrap up some food and give you a sling to carry it in. And a thermos of tea."

He nodded, eager to be on his way.

Mistaking his silence as anxiety, she tried to reassure him. "We'll find her, Jakkin." It sounded rehearsed, like something she'd been repeating for days to strangers and no longer quite believed herself.

Jakkin took her right hand and spoke with great passion. "She's not dead, Dr. Henkky. I'd know it, here." He touched himself on the chest with his left hand, over his heart.

At that, Henkky burst into tears. "Please, *please* find her. It's killing Golden. He blames himself for bringing her here, for trusting the driver. He almost lost her last year when the two of you went missing. It changed him. Golden doesn't show his agony to anyone but me. Sarkkhan was his closest friend. Akki's his goddaughter. We *have* to find her or I'll lose him, too." She wiped a hand across her eyes. "The last words I spoke to her were sharp. I don't know why. I would take them back if I could. Please, Jakkin, find her."

"I will," Jakkin promised. "Oh, I will." And for that moment he believed it himself.

ʕ 36 ʕ

THE MAP was easy enough to read, and Jakkin walked briskly along The Rokk streets, casting a loud sending every block in all four directions. A simple, declarative sending, a red map and arrow showing where he was standing. *"I'm here, Akki. I'm here."*

He didn't let himself hope too much. The Rokk was a big place. The larger houses within the center must have already been searched. Akki might have been moved somewhere else in the last two days. *Or buried.* His hands and shoulder still felt the heaviness of Errikkin's coffin, aching with the memory.

No, I can't think like that.

He passed a group of men and women — obviously searchers with food sacks on their backs. They were just knocking on the door of a sand-brick house. He could tell they were nursery folk, for they were in bonder leathers and sandals, but he didn't recognize any of them. He nodded at them and they returned his greeting.

"Sarkkhan's," he called out, flat of his hand to his chest.

"Master Drakkan's," replied one man, about forty years old, hair the color of smoking burnwort. He made a circle with his forefinger, pointing to the three men and one woman with him, then his hand went to his own chest.

"Anything yet?"

The man shook his head. "Nothing. We've done this whole area once and are back again, in case we've missed something." He came over and shook out a map that was just like the one Jakkin had. As he pointed out where they'd already searched, the door to the sand-brick house opened slowly and the group walked in. The redhead shrugged, then, folding his map, ran back to join them.

Jakkin took a moment to send to Akki again, listening carefully to the silence. He brought the gold hair band to his lips. Then he opened his own map, tracing with his finger where he was, how far he'd come. He was about halfway between the warehouse district and the small dragon pits now. Checking the sky, he saw that he still had a few hours till dark, and then another few till Dark-After.

According to Henkky, the man called Dark and his searchers had already been all over the warehouse area. Still, it looked to be a perfect place for stashing a victim. He should have asked Henkky more about that search. He should have asked the man from Drakkan's. He should have waited to talk to Dark. If they had already been over the warehouses, maybe he shouldn't waste his time there.

However, he reasoned, if he went directly to the pits, he might be able to find out where his dragons were, even if he didn't find them there. Trainers were great gossips. Once he found the brood, he could use them as his eyes and ears. Together, they could find Akki.

He had to make a decision now; Akki's life could depend upon it. For a long moment he couldn't move, trying to decide. He thought about taking out one of the coins and flipping it. Heads, he'd go to the pits; tails, he'd head to the warehouses. Anything to keep from having to make the decision himself. He was so afraid of being wrong.

But he'd already decided. He'd go to the pits. If the owners and trainers couldn't tell him anything, surely the dragons could. And with a dragon or two by his side, he'd be ready to face down the kidnapper, gun or no gun.

So, he'd head toward the pits. That would give him two advantages — the dragons, and Dark-After. With those advantages, he could then tackle the warehouse district and the rest of The Rokk if needed.

~

JAKKIN ALTERNATELY trotted and fast-walked the rest of the way, always sending to Akki at each new block. *Just in case,* he reminded himself, *just in case.* He only stopped once, for a quick sip from the thermos of tea.

It was a straight shot to the first of the pits. He saw that it was smaller even than the Krakkow minor pit, though it looked like a miniature of the lost Rokk Major, being a round two-story building, with stalls underground, or so he supposed. There was a light illuminating the central bubble of the fighting pit, but even as he watched, that light went out. They were already shutting things down for Dark-

After. Trainers and dragons alike would get a long sleep and rise early.

He began to hear a massive twittering in his head. All the dragons were sending back and forth, as oblivious to the humans' thoughts as the humans were to theirs. Most of the trainers would sleep next to their worms, for warmth as well as for safety, without knowing or caring that the worms could talk back and forth without making a sound.

For the first time, Jakkin wondered if giving everybody the ability to speak to dragons was actually a good idea, after all. Everyone on Austar could be a trainer, then. No one could earn his way to becoming a dragon master. And they'd *never* shut up!

Then he shook his head, laughing at himself. It still would take skill and care to teach a dragon to fight well in a pit, and the dragons could become true equal partners, even choosing their own trainers. *Of course, there will always be dragons like Sssargon — self-involved, oblivious. And sweet nonfighters like Sssasha. And dragons like the triplets, who — well, who knows what they really think or feel.*

He reminded himself that a Heart's Blood came along maybe once in a lifetime. Not everyone could have handled her. He'd been a good trainer, the right one for her, but without her spirit and love, he knew he would never have had such great success in the pit.

The twitterings grew louder. Fearing he would miss the brood's call when it came, he sent a huge black storm to the dragons, blanketing them with dark, driving rain for the moment. As the storm subsided and the dragons began to send again, he listened carefully for any voices he recognized. But these dragons were all strangers.

The second and third pits were the same: already darkened and shutting down for the night. He'd have to make a show of staying over at the fourth pit, then try to sneak away during Dark-After. He'd go out an unwatched door or window. That way he'd have the streets of The Rokk to himself and maybe — just maybe — he'd be able to rouse Akki.

~

HE REACHED the fourth and smallest pit just as the moons began their chase across the sky. He couldn't imagine the pit housing more than a dozen dragons. In fact, all four pits together were only half the size Rokk Major had been. Because of the embargo, and no more rocketship bettors visiting the planet, there was no need for a huge pit. At least, not right now.

Suddenly a familiar sending threaded into his brain, like a theme, a phrase. A rainbow of reds. Just as suddenly, he realized he couldn't be sure who it was. He'd need to check on each dragon in their stalls. But at least it was a lead, the first one he'd had so far.

Ducking through a small, unlocked door — obviously for trainers, not dragons — he found himself in the lower part of the pit, filled with a line of wooden stalls, the rest of the building rising high above him into a whitewashed dome.

With great and sudden force, the musky smell of dragons and the hundreds of bundles of wort hit him, wrapping around him like an old and comfortable blanket. He could hear the sound of at least a dozen dragons chewing mindlessly, and the casual talk of the trainers trading tips on how to back a winner or gossiping about dragons and trainers from other pits.

It was all so familiar, he almost forgot why he was there. *Almost.*

"*Sssargon?*" he sent, with a tentative landscape, the oasis in blues and tans. "*Sssasha?*"

"*Hmmmmm.*" It was only a contented thrum, but definitely one of them. The return sending added the wort patch to the side of the pool.

"*Akki is in danger.*" The sending was an outline of Akki, bright red, laced with blood.

The word *danger* must have leaked, because all at once, dragons throughout the area stood, their heads suddenly rising above the open stalling. They began to stomp and hough through their noses, some even trailing smoke and alarming their trainers, who obviously thought they'd gotten the worms all settled for the night.

Jakkin could sense something else, not sendings exactly, but as if a couple of bright lights that had been illuminated were now sputtering, dimming. It took him a moment to realize that he was hearing a few of the trainers. Possibly they'd gotten the gift from old blood scores or their close association with dragons. Or maybe, like Likkarn, they'd had their hands in a hen's egg chamber, helping in a difficult birth. And then he remembered the stewmen as they executed the culled dragons and old fighters past their prime, and how the men had linked with the dying dragons. *Maybe,* he thought, *maybe only some Austarians will ever be able to link with the dragons, whatever we do. Like some people have red hair or long bones or the ability to sing or . . .* But here his imagination failed him.

He thought, agonizingly, *Akki would know.*

A quick lightning strike of a sending burst into his brain, then was gone, back to a low hum again. This time he knew who it was.

"Where are you, Sssargon?" As Jakkin walked by the stalls, he kept sending, trying to pierce Sssargon's food-daze. He'd gotten past the first half dozen stalls and still hadn't found the big worm. Soon it would be too dark to see anything in the underground area.

"Sssargon here," the dragon sent. *"Sssargon eatsss. Sssargon getsss Akki."* That wonderfully familiar self-satisfied voice.

"Keep sending," Jakkin whispered, honing in on Sssargon's babble despite the competition from the other dragons for room in his head.

"Sssargon standsss. Sssargon . . ."

The corridor took a turn downward and Jakkin followed it around to a new tier of stalls, down in a sub-basement. One dragon's head was above the wooden wall, not quite standing yet. Sssargon never did things precipitously. He was just lumbering to his feet, like a growing mountain, and commenting on everything he did.

"Sssargon risesss. Sssargon liftsss head. Sssargon . . ."

"Got you!" Jakkin said aloud.

A trainer was standing alongside Sssargon's stall, trying to convince him to settle down. He was a dark man, with as much hair on his arms as on his head, and a dark mustache, as well. His face was scarred with blood scores. Flexing his arms — which made the muscles look as big and menacing as a trog's — the man jutted out his jaw at Jakkin. "Got who?" he asked.

Jakkin probed his mind but it was empty. Not a stray thought in it. *So, not everyone who has blood scores or works with dragons can hear them.*

"Got who?" repeated the hairy trainer. He took a step toward Jakkin, his manner menacing.

Jakkin refused to back away. After all, hadn't he just killed four trogs with a stick, a stinger, a hammer, and a knife?

The trainer took another step forward.

"You've got *my* dragon," Jakkin said, pointing to Sssargon, who looked at them both lazily.

"Are you calling me a thief, a dragon whacker? Are you? Are you?" The trainer strode over to the stall door, effectively blocking Jakkin from coming in.

"I don't know where you found him," Jakkin said, "but I can prove he's mine."

A crowd started to gather, just a black mass in the darkened corridor. But they were muttering about a fight and clearly hoping for one.

"Simmer down. Simmer down." That was the master of the pit, who'd been alerted by the noise that there was trouble brewing. He carried a light. Unlike the trainer, he was a small man and his nose twitched constantly. Shoving through the crowd, he said brightly, "Now what is this?"

The trainer at the stall door pulled his shoulders back, which made him look even bigger and fiercer. He thrust his thumb at Jakkin. "This outrider's calling me a thief."

"Nah, nah," a trainer cried from the safety of the crowd. "He said you *found* that worm, not stole 'im."

Someone else added, "It's the only way Garrekk can afford a dragon. Of course he stole it."

A laugh ran around the crowd, now bigger again by half as the trainers from the upper tier swelled their ranks.

Nose twitching, the master lifted a hand for silence and the trainers obliged. "Now, Garrekk, you tell me first. Buy it, steal it, or find it?"

"Found it. What do you think I am?"

"A dolt!"

Garrekk looked around the crowd, trying to find the speaker, and when he couldn't he raised his fist in the general direction of the voice.

"Where did you *find* this dragon, Garrekk?" the master asked, voice steady, as if they were having an ordinary conversation.

"Out in the wort fields, of course. Eating up a storm. Easy to take."

"That sounds like Sssargon." Jakkin smiled.

"See," the original trainer shouted. "No feral, then. Garrekk could never take a feral. Not him."

"He's still mine. Been feeding him up ever since," Garrekk said. "Possession being ninety percent of the law." He put his hands on either side of the doorway, blocking anyone from coming in.

The master turned to Jakkin. "Can you prove it's yours? That ten percent will outweigh Garrekk's possession. By the law. Everything by the law. Is the dragon registered? Have you papers? Is it tagged?"

"I didn't bring any proof with me," Jakkin admitted. "I thought he was still back at the nursery."

An outraged cry came from the crowd, and suddenly there was a shift toward Garrekk.

"But I can show you," Jakkin said, "that this worm only listens to me."

A laugh ran through the crowd.

"Go on," someone called.

The master of the pit raised his hand once more, and the crowd grew silent again.

Garrekk sneered. "This sack of waste? Listen to anybody? He doesn't do anything but eat." He laughed. "Oh, and sleep. Not even the prod gets him going. His looks made me think he might be a fighter. But I'm beginning to doubt it."

Jakkin ground his teeth. No one had ever put a prod to *his* dragons. He'd been willing to simply reason with the man. Before. *Now* he wanted blood. He'd take the dragon and take Garrekk's fewmetty prod as well.

"Time to find Akki, thou great worm. This man will give thee naught but another prod. But Akki will give thee love." This time the oasis sending included Akki, her hand out, smiling.

"And wort? Sssargon likesss wort."

What an impossible beast. Jakkin was careful not to send that to Sssargon. Instead he laughed. *"And wort."*

The master of the pit nodded. "Stand aside, Garrekk. Let the man try."

"Man?" Garrekk laughed. "That's nothing but a stall boy." But he moved aside. In the pit, the master's word was final.

Jakkin could feel his fists closing and unclosing. But keeping Akki in the forefront of his mind, he stepped into the stall. *"When I raise my hand, Sssargon, thee must do a hind foot rise."*

"Sssargon risesss . . ."

"No!" Jakkin said aloud. Then he sent, *"Not till I raise my hand!"*

Sssargon quivered. He'd never heard that tone from Jakkin before.

"Not a stall boy, then?" Garrekk sneered. "Works in the kitchen, does it? Out in the garden? Look at his ickle sling. Did mumsie pack you dinner? And the gold bracelet. Such a tootle." He turned to the master. "Why are we wasting time on this piece of fewmet?"

The master thrust out his chin defiantly. It brought him not an inch higher, but when he spoke, all the authority of the pit was in his voice. "Because I said so, Garrekk. There's been a challenge to ownership. I cannot let that go by without testing it legally." Then he turned to Jakkin. "And now, boy, we must have proof or I'm turning you out. You'll have to duff down in another pit for Dark-After, though, or Garrekk here will have your ears."

Jakkin nodded. He hoped Sssargon was alert enough, willing enough. *"For Akki,"* he sent to the dragon, *"when I raise my hand."*

There was a sudden strange light in Sssargon's eyes that Jakkin had never seen before, except when a dragon was about to hackle.

"When I raise my hand," he said quickly to the master, to Garrekk, to the other trainers, "the worm will do a hind foot rise, as I have taught him."

"Hah!" said Garrekk. "That one's unteachable. God knows I've tried. Even the prod don't work."

"Then watch," Jakkin said, sending, *"Now, Sssargon, now! Now, thou mighty worm."* And he raised his hand.

For a long moment nothing happened, except Garrekk chuckled. "Garden boy," he whispered.

"Up! Up!" Jakkin pleaded in a sending.

Sssargon looked at him, then sent back, *"Sssargon risesss. Sssargon goesss up. Sssargon . . ."* And Sssargon went up slowly, majestically in a hind foot rise.

There was a smattering of applause from the crowd, which grew into a huge crescendo. Jakkin turned around, grinning at the astonished Garrekk.

Even the master of the pit was moved to applaud.

"Well done, well done. He's yours," said the master, then glanced around a bit nervously. "My word!"

In every stall the dragons were rising onto their hind legs.

"Down all," Jakkin sent quickly, in as sharp a tone as he could manage, catching them all before too much damage was done. Even Sssargon settled down.

Jakkin began to laugh. "Look at them all mimicking my worm," he said, hoping that would amuse everyone.

There were smiles, laughter, even a couple of elbows into ribs.

Only Garrekk was not amused. "That was a trick. You saw the dragon beginning to hackle. You guessed it signaled a hind foot rise. You can't possibly do it again."

Without stopping, Jakkin turned back to Sssargon with his hand up. "Rise now, my great dragon," he said, and at the same time sent, *"Again, and after we will be out of here into the air where there is much wort. And Akki."*

"Wort for Sssargon. Akki for thee," Sssargon sent back, with a great rosy rainbow, then stood up on his back feet for a second time.

"You can stay the night in my pit for free," said the master. "And fight that dragon here any time you wish."

"I won't stay tonight, Pit Master. I can't trust your Garrekk," Jakkin told him, "even if I take his prod."

The master smiled. "I think we'll leave him with something."

Jakkin nodded, then making up a lie on the spot, he said, "Besides, I have friends in the first pit."

"Master Ortran's pit?"

"Yes," he said. He was sure he'd heard that name before. But where?

"All right, but best hurry. Dark-After is about to start." The master gave him a handshake.

"We'll go immediately." He grabbed Sssargon by the ear and led him out of the stall.

A tall, painfully thin trainer showed him to the dragon's

door, pointing in the right direction. He could hear the rest of the trainers back in the stalls poking fun at Garrekk, calling him a thief, and a bad one at that. One said, "Did you see how that *garden* boy ear-hooked the dragon? He knows his worms, he does."

Then the door was shut behind them and Jakkin and the dragon were out in the growing cold.

☾ 37 ☾

JAKKIN LED Sssargon by the ear until they were well past the pits so no one could see them. He wanted to get the big worm up in the air, first to find the rest of the brood, and then to fly over the area and have him call for Akki. If Akki was anywhere in The Rokk — and aware — one of them would surely hear her.

They walked on the far side of the street, through wort plants that were high enough to hide them should someone be looking out of a window. Though normally everyone slept through Dark-After, Jakkin figured it was safer to be out where he and Sssargon wouldn't be seen from an un-shuttered window.

It was slow going and Sssargon kept stopping to graze on the tenderest of the plants. While he ate, his mind be-came just a low buzz. His tail swung lazily back and forth, and Jakkin had to be careful to stay away from it. One blow of that mighty tail, even by accident, and he could be out for hours. He didn't know if Akki had hours left.

A huge silence surrounded them. That surprised Jakkin,

who'd expected more sound from a city, even during Dark-After. But the field was on the backside of the small pits, where there were no windows, or at least none lit, and of course nothing was on the road. He could have been anywhere out in the country.

While they were on this side of The Rokk, Jakkin decided to recheck the warehouse area. A hunch, really. He couldn't get the hatchling's sending about the white-haired "bad man" out of his mind. Going to the warehouses might be a mistake, but he couldn't go into houses during Dark-After, anyway, so with the four hours of cold, the warehouses seemed the best area to explore.

Henkky had said it would be a half-hour brisk walk from the pits. But if he had to haul Sssargon the whole way, it was going to take twice that. The dragon was still eating wort, a dark mountain moving across a dark field. He wondered if Sssargon was ever going to be full. And if he became really full, would he be able to fly. Most dragons required hours to sleep off a big meal. But Sssargon had to fly.

Sssargon was his only hope of finding the other dragons. Jakkin needed all the eyes and ears he could get.

Now it was fully Dark-After, the bowl of sky lit only by the flickering stars. He'd have but four hours, stumbling about in the dark, to search the warehouses. So he planted himself in front of Sssargon, put his hands on either side of that long, scaly face, and gazed deep into the dragon's eyes.

"Thee must find thy sisters," he sent, making that a command, not a request. He pictured Sssasha and the triplets, individually, and then as a group in rainbow colors. *"Bring them to me still in the dark at the place of great houses."*

He sent a picture of the map, with a red circle around the warehouse district, hoping this would make sense to Sssargon, to all of them.

"Dark?" Sssargon was evidently able to chew and send at the same time, just not able to think.

"Before the sun comes up," Jakkin said, sending Sssargon a picture of the sun rising over a pinkish landscape, which included The Rokk.

Then he rubbed his palm down Sssargon's nose. *"There is danger. I need thy help."* The scales were cold under his fingers. *"Fly, mighty worm. Find Sssasha and the triplets. Then we find Akki. Together."* He stepped back and flung his right arm up, pointing to the sky. *"Go, go, go."*

It took Sssargon a moment to chew the last of the wort he'd snagged with his long tongue, another moment to digest what Jakkin had asked of him.

"Akki is in danger!" Jakkin sent, wondering how long it would be before Sssargon finally got it. Just when he was beginning to wish he'd taken Garrekk's prod after all, the dragon made a startling noise, something like a takk pot beginning to boil.

"YYYYYYYYessssssss!" Pumping his mighty wings, he leaped rather heavily into the air, his tail a rudder. *"Sssargon goesss. Sssargon fliesss."* The mountain met the sky as he sailed low and sluggishly over the wort fields before turning north.

Jakkin could only hope Sssargon knew where he was going. Hoped Sssargon knew where he could find his sisters. If the dragon found another wort field before then, Jakkin would have no backup at all.

"Fair wind!" Jakkin sent, along with the picture of the big dragon sailing across the stars.

There was nothing more he could do now but get to the warehouses himself, and as quickly as possible. He could tell by the intensity of the cold river running across the back of his neck, it was past time for him to move along. He'd already wasted half an hour of Dark-After getting this far with Sssargon.

Now he started to run briskly along the walkway, but he was already exhausted by the long day, the battle with the trogs, his days of captivity. By the end of the second long block, he had to slow down, then stop.

He suddenly remembered he hadn't eaten since the cup of tea at Dr. Henkky's house. He took out the thermos and had several sips of the sweet hot tea and ate one of the hard-boiled lizard eggs in the sling. There was a cake there, as well, and he scarfed it down, followed by some more sweetened tea. Except for wort plants in the field across the street, there was little to see, especially in the dark. This was a wasteland, where someday — he supposed — more houses would be built.

He began running again, with a new burst of energy. At the end of each block, he sent his message to Akki.

Nothing but silence greeted him.

～

AT THE END of a fifth block, he came upon a broken-down farmhouse within acres of unkempt land. Even with the starlight, he could barely make out the ruins of the house.

Still, he took the time to walk its perimeter, calling to Akki in long sendings, full of golds shot through with fireworks. *Just in case.*

The roof of the house had caved in, as had two of the walls. There was an old barn behind it that he hadn't seen at first. Sections of the barn's roof had also fallen down, though one part bulged out oddly. He legged over a collapsed stone wall, nearly twisting his ankle in the dark.

Steady, steady. The last thing he needed to do was to get hurt before he could find Akki. Without thinking, he rubbed his wrists, and the pain reminded him that he had Henkky's salve in the sling. *Later,* he promised himself.

Working by feel, he managed to lift one end of the bulging roof and found a steel door underneath.

Truck — or car!

He was surprised. Had the old farmer — or his heirs — left such a valuable object in the broken wreckage of the barn? That seemed unlikely. Living on a metal-poor planet meant that everyone knew how to recycle old metal appliances. A truck or car, even if it no longer worked, would be worth a fortune in parts. *Especially now, with the Feder embargo.*

Jakkin felt along the lines of the vehicle. It's back was too low-slung for a truck, of that much he was certain. *Still, it might be useful.* He'd never driven one before. *But how hard can that be?* He couldn't possibly drive any worse than old Likkarn. He smiled. *Uncle* Likkarn. Besides, he had two working hands, unlike Likkarn, who'd driven them to The Rokk with one. *And there won't be any traffic during*

Dark-After! A car would get him to the warehouses faster than walking. He found a handle, pulled, and the door opened.

Something tumbled out at his feet.

The smell was awful.

He bent and touched a hand.

"Oh, Akki! Akki!" Jakkin cried aloud, tears blurring his eyes. Turning the body over, he realized with relief his mistake.

"It's a man!" he whispered. He knew that dead bodies smelled after a day, stank after a few, and then the smell dissipated. This one still stank. That told Jakkin the man hadn't been dead all that long. He forced himself to feel the man's head. It seemed to be moving, till he realized there were bugs, *maggoties,* he thought they were called. He shook his hands frantically to get them off his fingers. Then he stopped. *No hair. The man has no hair. He's completely bald.*

Not the bad man of the hatchling's sending, then. *But who?*

He stepped away, thought a minute, had it. The low-slung car. The newly dead man. The old barn. *This must be the driver of the senate car. The one who everyone thinks kidnapped Akki.*

In a whisper, he said, "But if he's dead and been stashed here . . ."

For a moment he wondered if the driver had actually killed Akki, then himself. Her body might be inside the car as well, might have been there all along, dead alongside her kidnapper. Climbing into the car, he went from the front to the back, feeling his way along. Terrified, stomach ready to heave out its contents.

But there was no other body in the car. And no gun, either.

Jakkin's mind was awhirl with questions. *If there is no weapon, how did the man die? Who stashed him in the old barn? And who now has the gun?*

Then an even more troubling thought hit him. *Why has no one searched this place before?*

He wondered if he should race back to tell Golden what he'd found, but then shook his head. *I* can't *go get help — not in Dark-After, anyway.* He'd end up giving away the secret of the dragons for nothing. He was sure he knew who the killer was, the kidnapper. It had to be the white-haired "bad man" that the hatchling saw. The man who was so helpful, who searched the warehouse area himself. Who said he'd been attacked by the driver. The dead driver. Who'd probably said he searched this building and found nothing. Not once, but several times. On his lunch hours away from the rest.

"I have to get to the warehouses *now!*" Jakkin told himself. It was the only place that it made sense to search. Close enough to this old barn and the hidden car for someone to stash it and get back to the live victim.

The live victim! Akki *had* to still be alive.

The dead man would wait.

I can do the search in the cold, which no one else can do, Jakkin thought. And even if he didn't find Akki there, he'd go back in the early morning to report what he'd discovered here, in the barn. Let Golden and his crew know who to look for then. Jakkin and the dragons would find Akki all on their own, in their own way.

He sat in the front seat, hands on the wheel, thinking again that it would be faster to drive the rest of the way. But finally he had to admit to himself that he had no idea how to start the car. None.

I'll actually go faster by foot. And I'll be less obvious. The last thing he wanted to do was to alert the kidnapper by driving through Dark-After, in case he was in one of the warehouses himself.

Getting out on the far side of the car so as not to stumble over the body, he headed back to the road. His heart was thudding in his chest, his palms sweating despite the cold. He felt — no, he *knew* — that Akki was somewhere near. He only hoped she was still alive. The dead man was no comfort, no comfort at all.

He called for her, a blood-red spear of a sending piercing the air. *"Akki!"*

He walked on, waiting for an answer. *"Akki!"*

He sent cascades of red hearts. *"Akki!"*

And still there was no sending in return.

~

AT LAST he came to the first of the three-story warehouses, laid out not in a straight line, but in a kind of large rainbow, a crescent, so that part of the first of the seven block-long stone buildings could look across to the last. He supposed they were out here on the road to make it easy for trucks to load and unload, and easy access to the pits and the city without getting in the way of the houses.

He tried to think like a kidnapper. *This is where I'd take my victim. As far from the center of the city as possible.*

Especially at night, in Dark-After, the crescent of warehouses seemed really far from the city, though during the day, without an embargo, and with a full complement of pits going, it might be quite a beehive of activity.

So, he thought, *I've stashed my kidnap victim here, kept her quiet, told everyone I've searched it thoroughly. When I'm done with her . . .* It was an ugly thought, but he'd done a lot of ugly things in the last few days, so he found it easy to put himself in the kidnapper's head.

I could put her body in a car I'd already stashed for the purpose nearby. Drive them both out on my lunch break into the wort fields. "Or better — right before Dark-After, when no one is on the roads," he whispered. *Leave the gun, with a single bullet left in it, in the passenger seat.*

And then discover it with a group of searchers from the nursery!

He shuddered at the thought, but figured it was probably pretty close to what the fair-haired man planned. Jakkin hated him, whoever he was.

Taking a deep breath to steady himself, he tiptoed around the back of the first building. A long, rickety, outside staircase led from the ground to the flat roof. For such large buildings, there were few windows, mostly near the top, and all in the front.

This was the drill, then: He'd circle the perimeter of

each warehouse and check every door to see if any opened. And if he couldn't get in, he'd have to cross the roofs as well. The warehouses were very wide buildings. Akki might not hear his sending from one side to the other. *Especially if she's stuck somewhere in the middle* . . . Well, he'd have to get closer, either on the inside or from the roof.

He kept sending as he went around the first building. There were no lights on anywhere, no sounds. The doors were all securely locked. No one sent back even a single syllable or picture.

He'd have to go across the roof, then.

Climbing the stairs, he was glad that it was still Dark-After and that the twin moons were firmly tucked behind the mountains. Even with the starlight, he couldn't actually see the ground. Not that he was scared of heights exactly, but . . .

As he crisscrossed the roof, he began sending again; as before, he heard nothing in return. Nothing. Nothing from Akki or a dragon. Or a drakk or a lizard, for that matter. The cold ran across his arms, down his sides. It was the deepest part of Dark-After. The silence was so great that he began to shiver, and not from the cold.

Looking up to the sky, he whispered, "Sssargon, where are you?" because now, on top of his other fears, he worried that it had been a mistake to let the dragon go off on his own.

Taking a quick sip of tea, he peeled and ate the second egg, washed it down with more tea, then went on.

The second, third, fourth, and fifth buildings brought the same results.

"Nothing!" he said, thinking that maybe he should walk around them all again, in case Akki had just been sleeping. But he had to tackle the rest of the buildings first. Though even without getting a response from her, he was convinced she was here somewhere. The dead man had convinced him. The hatchling's sending about the "bad man" convinced him.

When he went to drink some more tea, he noted that there was less than half a thermos left. *If Akki is here, she might need some.* He noticed he'd used the word *if*.

Have I given up on her? Had the dead man shaken him that much? Should he have waited till dawn and searched the farmhouse barn more thoroughly?

Now the light was beginning to go gray, which meant there was about a half hour of Dark-After left. He'd taken too much time with Sssargon, with the dead man and the car. Calling himself an idiot, worm waste, he raced around the next building so fast he almost threw up with the effort. In fact, he'd had to stand behind the sixth building, bent over, till the spasm of nausea went away. *Wasting time. Akki's time.*

Also, his knees were beginning to get weak, which meant that when he climbed the stairs, he put himself into danger and maybe Akki, too. Desperate, depressed, about to throw himself down on the stony ground and weep, he came around the building to check its front. The *floop-floop* of large wings overhead made him look up.

"Danger. Here." The sending was full of pinks and reds, but decreasing as the dragon flew away, toward the north. Jakkin could just about see its outline in the graying light. He thought he recognized that sending.

"*Sssasha?*" He sent a trail of red footprints running after her.

She turned, flapped back to him, settled down where he stood, by the front of the sixth building. Then she lowered her neck till her head was close to his.

Putting his hand on her head, he whispered and sent at the same time, "Akki's in danger." He felt tears welling up in his eyes.

Sssasha's head jerked up. "*Akki here. Danger here.*"

"Where?" he said out loud. Then silently, in a sending, trembling as he sent it. "*Where?*"

She looked up, stretching her neck as if pointing at the seventh building, but said nothing.

"*Where?*"

She made a peculiar growling sound low in her throat, and looked around again.

"*Where?*"

She stomped her foot and swatted him with her tail. He was so exhausted, he tumbled over onto his hands and knees. She nudged him with her nose. "*Up. Up. Here.*" There were shards of glass, cascades of foaming water, gouts of blood in her sending.

After all the time he'd been looking for Akki, he now hardly dared to believe. His disbelief must have communicated to Sssasha even without a sending.

"*Here!*"

"Okay, I believe you, but where? *Where?*"

The picture Sssasha sent him was from inside one of the buildings, of a pair of hands on glass, the scene from the point of view of someone looking out. He saw the gray sky as Dark-After was ending, the arch of the warehouses.

Dragons have little imagination. Their sendings consist of things sent to them, or nature they've observed. Sssasha couldn't have seen that view from the inside of the building. Only from the outside. *Someone* had to have sent that to her first — the picture of the hands on the glass looking out.

"When?"

Dragons have two times: now and not-now. *Now* could mean anytime in the understandable present, an hour, even a day. The scene Sssasha sent had been set as Dark-After waned.

"Now," Sssasha sent.

"Akki!" He breathed her name. *"Alive."*

Carefully, he stood and walked around the front of the seventh building. It was the only one where that picture could have originated. Looking up, he saw that the few windows were shuttered, except for one.

Except for one.

That window was on the third floor. *"Akki,"* he sent.

Even though there was no response, he was sure she was there. Sssasha had heard her.

Dragons can't lie. They can pull pranks, heavy-footed, tail-swatting pranks. They look at the world differently than human beings do. But they are incapable of telling a direct lie. And even if they could, Sssasha wouldn't lie about this. He was sure of it.

The window was not shuttered. The view . . . the view was definitive. He turned to look behind him where, in the graying light, he could see the exact scene that Sssasha had sent him, except he was three floors below.

Who else can it be up there but Akki? And then he had a secondary, horrifying thought. *Is she alone?*

Getting up to the third floor silently would be hard. The doors on all the other warehouses had been locked. He doubted any would be open on this building, especially if Akki was being kept here. *And what if the kidnapper is still inside, waiting?*

He considered how Akki had sent to Sssasha and minutes later had been silent. It could mean one of three things. She might have been moved. She could be injured or asleep.

Or dead.

I won't think about that, he told himself sternly. And then — not for the first time — cursed himself for being too slow. Well, he couldn't afford to be slow any longer.

Turning quickly, he went around to the back of the warehouse, the dragon following him.

"Do? Do?" Sssasha sent, with a series of popping yellow balloons. *"Do?"*

"Hush," he whispered. "And I will tell you what we are going to do." He sent it to her, his sending all in cool blues. Yes, he had a plan. It was dangerous. Foolish even. But it was all he had.

☽ 38 ☾

JAKKIN CLIMBED the outside staircase on the seventh building as quietly as he could. The horizon was starting to suffuse with light. It would make his plan easier because he could now see what he was doing. And harder because anyone else could see him.

Sssasha flew overhead, keeping an eye on anything or anyone who might be stirring. Where Sssargon and the triplets were, Jakkin didn't know. He could only hope they were heading his way.

As frightening as climbing the outside stairs in the dark had been, it was even worse going up as the sky lightened. Suddenly he could see how far up he'd come, how far down he could fall. After one awful look, he kept his eyes resolutely on the next step. And the next. And the next one after that.

He got to the top of the stairs before it was fully light, walked around the outer edge of the roof toward the front, convinced it would be quieter than making a beeline across the center. As he went, he sent messages to Akki over and over. The silence was worrying.

When he reached the front of the building, he knelt down, lay fully on his stomach and, looking carefully over the side, located the unshuttered window. Then he crawled across the roof on his belly to the place where he figured the window stood.

Sssasha, flying over the nearest wort fields, sent him a message. *"Too far. Too far."*

Evidently he'd missed the window by a bit. He leaned over again and checked. Yes, he'd overshot his mark. Crawling backward on his stomach a few centimeters at a time, he checked again, while Sssasha sent him a whirlwind of golden flowers, like small suns.

They both understood that the only way for his plan to work was for him to be precisely over the window. But the next bit was going to be even trickier.

Sssasha flew back and landed lightly on the roof beside him. That is, the landing was light. Light — but not silent. *After all, she* is *a dragon!* That was worrying enough. But he also worried that the flat roof couldn't hold her body weight and that she might crash through.

They waited, Jakkin biting his lower lip. But though the roof creaked, it held. Whoever had made that roof knew the danger dragons posed and had considered that when the warehouses had been built.

Sighing with relief, Jakkin shrugged out of the sling and then his shirt. He knotted them together into a rope, making a noose at one end. At the same time, he sent to Sssasha, *"Thou art a mighty worm."*

She gave him a toothy, lipless grin. *"Thou art a mighty*

worm, too!" Not a lie, because it wasn't meant to be believed. Just her idea of a joke.

Grinning back at her, he slipped the noose end of the rope around his waist. The other end Sssasha drew toward herself, using her extended nails — the unum, secundum, and tricept. She set the rope end under her right front foot. Then she lay down close to the edge of the roof and tucked the foot with the rope end under her. The rising sun backlit her dusty scales. Her tongue lolled out of her mouth.

"Do not let it go till I tell thee to." He sent the picture of what he was about to do.

"Or splat!" It was her favorite bit of foolishness. The sending was full of popping bubbles.

"Splat indeed, thou lovely queen of dragons. Art thou ready?"

She snapped her tongue into her mouth. Her tail twitched. *"Ready."*

Checking one last time over the side of the building, Jakkin sat up, then dangled his feet over the edge. He brought his wrist — with Akki's hair band wrapped around it — to his lips. Turning onto his stomach again, he wiggled down till he was hanging by his arms. He was still a good foot or so above the top of the unshuttered window.

He hoped the makeshift rope would hold. He hoped the dragon would hold. He hoped his stomach would hold. And his luck.

Then he let go.

Dangling at the end of the cobbled-together rope, Jakkin was now even with the window, but unfortunately the rope had twisted him about before he'd time to look in. Kicking his legs, he managed to swing around again, then grab on to the upper part of the window and pull himself to it. Peering into the dark room, he could just make out a mattress with a blanket at one end. It could have been there for years, or been put there for a prisoner. For Akki.

Akki! For a minute he thought he heard something, a sigh perhaps. But that was all.

Pulling himself closer, he stared further into the room. Something to the right side of the window caught his eye. A leg — no, two legs — someone sitting in a chair. He tapped lightly on the window. The legs stirred.

"Akki!"

"Danger . . . Go away . . . Find . . ."

The sending was weak, but he recognized it at once. Hauling himself up a bit on the rope, he then kicked away from the building, and when he swung back, his feet went through the window and he landed amid broken glass on the floor.

He'd cut his left hand a little. It hurt, but not too much. More important — he was in.

"Let go, let go!" he sent to Sssasha, and the rope immediately went slack. Shedding the rope, he turned to Akki. She was tied to a chair; her strange blue dress was torn at the shoulders and under the arms, and smelled awful.

Nevertheless he put his arms around her. "I'm here. And I've brought you the gold band for your hair . . . Why, what have you done to it?"

She looked up at him. "Oh, Jakkin, I cut it. With shears.

Please don't ask why. Just get me out of this." She was trembling.

He knelt behind her and worked at the knots with equally trembling fingers. In minutes he'd untied her and pulled her to her feet. She just barely managed to stand.

"Now, isn't that sweet," said an icy voice from across the room.

Jakkin swung around. In the open door stood a man with white-gold hair, looking exactly like the bad man in the hatchling's sending. He was holding a gun.

"Behind me," Jakkin sent to Akki.

"He has a gun."

"I see it."

Taking a step toward the man, Jakkin still held Akki behind him. "It's over," he said. At the same time, he sent to Sssasha, *"Danger. Now."*

"It certainly is." Dark laughed. "For you."

That laugh! Jakkin suddenly remembered that laugh. "But you're . . ."

"I certainly am."

Dark came toward them slowly. He pushed the mattress aside with one foot, never looking away from them. "She wouldn't tell me where you were, but that doesn't matter now, does it? All that pain, little girl, and for nothing. Now I have both of you, anyway. The only two people who can possibly identify me with the group that blew up Rokk Major. With you gone, I can safely run for senator, and I have the ability to win. Golden will be grieving too hard to go on. After senator — who knows."

"The group?" Jakkin asked. Anything to stall. "What do you mean 'the *group* that blew up . . .'"

Dark laughed. "Oh come, young dragon master, you didn't really think that the one little bag of explosives you carried could have brought down the pit all on its own, did you?"

Jakkin sighed. Yes, he'd carried that burden of guilt. Akki, too. But he wouldn't say it aloud. Instead, he sent, *"Sssasha! Now!"* But Sssasha was unaccountably silent.

"Come away from that window," Dark said. "It's daylight, and cars might come by any minute. I wouldn't want them to see you. Or what is about to happen to you. Don't worry. It won't hurt for long. I have enough bullets to put you both out of your misery. No need to prolong it. And then in a week or two, when we search this building again, there you'll be, in each other's arms. Victims of the kidnapper, who has died. But you, young man, will die a hero."

They moved as he told them, Akki still behind Jakkin.

"What do we . . . ?" Akki began.

"I have a plan," Jakkin sent back, thinking that the plan needed Sssasha, who'd suddenly gone quiet. He strained to hear if she was still on the roof, but could detect nothing.

To stall for time till the dragon could come and help them, he said, "I found him, you know. The driver. If I can find him, others can, too. They'll figure it out. It won't work. He'll have been dead longer than us."

Dark laughed. "Only if they find you today or tomorrow. But a couple of weeks from now . . . you'll all look the same."

"Then — let *her* go. You'll still have me. She won't be able to tell anyone as long as I —"

"Do you think I'm stupid?"

Jakkin snorted. "I think if you shoot us in the day with the windows open, you're more than stupid."

"I was just getting to that," Dark said, going to the window, where he closed one shutter, still keeping an eye all the while on Jakkin and Akki. He started to close the second, when a sound made him stop. He glanced out quickly. A trio of dragons were just hovering outside, their wings thrown open in a stall.

"What's —" he said, and then it was too late.

"Drop!" Jakkin sent to Akki, turning to her and pulling her to the floor. *"Danger now! Fire, fire, fire!"* he sent.

The triplets didn't hesitate. They let go with three great streams of fire that combined into a single pulse. The fire caught Dark in the middle of his chest, and in seconds he was fully engulfed in flames. His scream was horrifying, high-pitched, though through it all he shot his gun out the window at the three dragons.

Jakkin knew that the bullets would bounce harmlessly off their scales unless hitting the vulnerable neck. The triplets would have shuttered their eyes even before the first shot. It would take stingers — a lot of stingers — to bring a trio of yearling dragons down.

The triplets roared back at Dark, which stopped their fire for a minute. Then they combined the three streams of flame once again.

The burning man remained upright for a moment

longer, then fell silently, and lay on the floor, blackened and still.

"We can't just let him burn," Akki cried.

"We already have," Jakkin told her. Standing, he lifted her up to him, trying to shield her from the sight, but she started to pull away.

"Akki . . . I didn't mean . . ." That's when he realized she wasn't angry with him but had simply passed out. So he picked her up in his arms, horrified how light she'd become — practically skin and bones. Then, carrying her, he went as quickly as he could through the open door.

Walking down the three flights of stairs with Akki in his arms was an agony. Not that she was heavy, but all the adrenaline Jakkin had used to keep going had suddenly dropped away. Several times his knees threatened to buckle, but he would not let her go.

Once outside, he set her down carefully in the field across the road. When he turned and glanced behind at the building they'd just escaped from, the top floor of the warehouse was red with flames.

Jakkin thought about how Dark's last moments must have been horrible, agonizing, but he couldn't find it in himself to care. The trogs who'd mistreated *him* had done so because he'd taken something from them. *I might call it liberation, but they thought it was stealing.* Yet Dark . . . Dark killed the driver, shot the girl Senekka. He had tortured and starved Akki. And for what? Just to get Akki to tell where he was. *Dark deserved everything he got.*

Jakkin sat down next to Akki and took her hand in his.

He wished now that he still had the sling with the tea and the last lizard egg. It would be a long way back to Golden's house. Akki could use the nourishment.

Just as he was getting ready to pick her up again, he heard the sound of something overhead.

Dragons? But it was too loud for that.

Looking up, he saw a copter above him. He jumped to his feet and waved his hands wildly. "Here!" he cried, then sent Akki a picture of a soft bed and food.

Lifting her up, he felt her stir.

"Jakkin," she whispered.

"I'm here."

~

JAKKIN DIDN'T leave Akki's side except when Henkky shooed him out so she could wash Akki and put her into a nightgown. When he went back into the hospice room, standing at her bedside, Akki was sleeping, with a tube running into her right arm.

"What's that?" he asked, terrified.

Henkky smiled, put a hand on his shoulder. "Something to get fluids into her quickly. She's had a rough time."

"Will she . . . is she . . . ?"

"She'll be fine, except for bad dreams. I expect you know something about those yourself."

Senekka was sitting up in the bed next to Akki's. She was very pale, but Henkky said she would make a full recovery. "Is she some kind of hero?" Senekka asked.

He nodded.

"I knew it!" Senekka said. "I just wish I could remember why."

"When she wakes up, maybe she can tell you," he said.

"You'll want to see the hatchling now," Henkky told him.

"But Akki?"

Henkky looked at him. "She'll sleep for some time. There's a sedative in that fluid as well."

~

THE HATCHLING had already caught some of the sendings between Jakkin and Akki when they were first brought back to the hospice by Golden. He'd landed the copter right outside the door of his house, on the paving between the spindly spikka trees, where cars weren't allowed to go.

"Nor copters, either," Henkky had reminded him.

"What's the use of being a senator if you can't claim privilege every once in a while?" he'd said.

Jakkin found the hatchling in the garden. She was lying down, eyes closed, chewing on a sprig of wort. When she heard him come in, her eyes went wide.

"Danger?" she sent.

He squatted down beside her. "Not anymore," he said, sending it at the same time. Then he scratched beneath her chin till she began to thrum.

~

THEY ALL ate dinner that evening at Akki's bedside — eggs, salad, a berry pie and a berry liqueur for dessert. Jakkin refused the last. What he had to say was too important to say tipsy.

Likkarn was there, having been fetched by copter. Jakkin had insisted on it. The other nursery folk had stopped by and were told the story of the rescue, then were driven back home to the nursery.

The driver Dikkon was returned to his home in a casket. There was to be a major funeral in a few days. Golden planned to speak at it. Insisted on it, actually. There was to be a widow's pension, larger than Dikkon's salary. Golden was planning to fund it himself.

Senekka was now settled in her own bedroom, much improved. So it was just the five of them at dinner: Jakkin and Akki, Likkarn, Golden and Henkky.

As she sat up in the hospice bed, eyes like bruises, Akki said she felt better. "I'm not tied up and starving, so it's a major improvement."

"Tomorrow I'm going to try you on tea and dry toast," Henkky said.

Golden cleared his throat. "Jakkin, why did you want us all here?"

Jakkin was holding Akki's hand carefully, the one with the torn thumbnail. He'd already discussed with her what he wanted to say. Taking time to look at each of them in turn, he said, "We need your advice."

Henkky leaned forward. "Is it about this dragon problem, the one you alluded to before . . . before . . ."

Akki nodded.

"It's a dragon problem, but a people problem, too," Jakkin said. "We thought it would be simple, but it's not."

Akki put her other hand on top of his. "Just tell it from the beginning, Jakkin."

So he did, going back to the time they'd sheltered in Heart's Blood's egg chamber for warmth, then had emerged in the morning utterly changed. "We could stay out in Dark-After, we could talk to dragons mind-to-mind. And to each other that way as well."

"I have a bit of that, too," Likkarn said.

Henkky and Golden just looked astonished.

Henkky said, "Mind speech?"

"That's rubbish," Golden said.

"Not at all." Likkarn's voice was calm.

Jakkin continued. "In the mountains Akki and I were captured by the very same trogs who came after me just days ago." He spoke quickly about what he'd endured while being captured by them, and how he and Likkarn and Errikkin had killed all four.

Raising his bandaged arm, Likkarn added, "One of them gave me this in the battle."

Jakkin laughed, remembering that the wound had come from Errikkin closing Likkarn's fingers in the door, but he didn't contradict the old man.

"What you need to know is that the trogs also know the secret. They must have discovered it generations ago. They slaughter their hen dragons after the hens give birth, in order to place their own babies in the egg chamber. And they have all but given up speech in favor of sendings."

Akki sat up a bit more in the bed. "I came here to use Dr. Henkky's lab to try to make a vaccine using tissue or blood from a dragon's egg chamber so everyone can have these same gifts. The change has to have happened chemically not magically, and we should be able to reproduce it in the laboratory."

Nodding, Henkky said, "I agree."

"That's not all," Jakkin said. "When my friend Slakk killed a drakk in the incubarn last week, he had a moment when his hand was in her egg chamber and I could hear him," Jakkin said. "Just a moment."

"Drakk blood . . ." Akki's eyes got wide. "Maybe . . ."

Golden threw up his hands. "All right, everyone — I believe you. Akki, you can work here. Or we can build you a lab at the nursery. Or . . ."

Interrupting them, Jakkin said, "But as I watched the warehouse burn, I suddenly wondered what could have happened if Dark had had the ability to talk to dragons, to force them to blaze away at anyone he didn't like. Look what I did — and I'm not a bad man."

They were all silent for a moment, then suddenly began to talk all at once, assuring him he was actually a hero, telling him that motive made things right.

Jakkin held up his hand to stop them. "I'm not worried about *me* being bad. But who judges motive? Which one of us can make that decision for others? I've been thinking that maybe Akki shouldn't work on such a vaccine now, if men like Dark — who want to rule the planet — could harness it to their own ends."

This time the silence lasted longer. Henkky opened her mouth several times, shutting it without speaking. Likkarn chewed on his lower lip.

Finally, Golden smiled and spread his hands out, palms

down. He seemed to be looking at his nails as he spoke. "Jakkin, if we waited on progress until the planet was filled with only good people, we'd never move forward at all. Human beings are a funny combination of good and bad. We work to make the good ones better, to weed out the bad ones. Sometimes we miss. We certainly missed Dark. He killed Dikkon, who was a good, honorable man. He almost killed Senekka and he tortured Akki."

Golden looked up now, talking directly to Jakkin. "He would have killed you, too. But he didn't because you had something he never had. You have beings who love you unconditionally. Who count on you. Who stand up for you. Who know your soul because it is entirely open to them. *He* only had a gun and a black heart."

Likkarn laughed. "A *really* black heart now."

"*Uncle* Likkarn!" Jakkin said.

And suddenly there were other things to talk about, explain, marvel at — like family history.

Henkky finally interrupted. "Now, now. You're tiring my patient. Outside, the three of you. And take the dishes into the kitchen."

~

LATER, WHEN the rest were all asleep, Jakkin walked outside. It was several hours till Dark-After, but he had five more of his "beings" to see. He walked quickly, purposefully, to the blackened and empty warehouse. It took a little time, but time was a resource he now had in plenty. Once there, he waded out into the wort field.

"*I am here,*" he sent, "*I am here.*"

And suddenly, as he'd hoped, he was surrounded by his dragons.

Sssargon was lying down, munching on fresh plucked wort leaves. "*Sssargon getsss sister. Sssargon good. Sssargon eatsss. Sssargon fliesss.*"

"*Sssargon is a hero,*" Jakkin sent, picturing a great red dragon in a hind foot rise.

"*No danger.*" Sssasha's sending accompanied a picture of a long golden rope curling beneath a dragon's foot.

"*Thou art a hero, too,*" he told her, and in his sending, the dragon pulled on a rope, and a boy and girl caught in it are pulled to her heart.

The twittering, indecipherable sounds of the triplets were full of fire.

"*Oh, thou great trinity of heroes,*" Jakkin sent to them. "*Thee burned up the enemy.*" He didn't try to warn them about ever doing it again. He understood now that they'd only done it to rescue him. And Akki. They weren't ferals, after all.

"*A few more days here,*" he sent, "*then we go home.*"

"*Home!*" they sent back.

He petted them until they thrummed their pleasure. Then he walked slowly back to Golden's house, the cold of Dark-After spilling across his shoulders like a river in full spate. He slept the rest of Dark-After in the chair next to Akki's bed, just in case she should need him in the darkest part of the night, or even in the full light of the new day.

AUSTAR IV is the fourth planet of a seven-planet rim system in the Erato Galaxy. Once a penal colony, marked KK29 on the convict map system, it is a semiarid metal-poor world with two moons.

A Federation embargo was imposed in the mid 2500s, after disgruntled bond-slaves, understandably angry at their continuing low place in Austarian society, began to foment a revolution. This revolution ended in a series of violent confrontations. The worst of these was the bombing of Rokk Major, the greatest of the dragon gaming pits on the planet. Thirty-seven people were killed outright; twenty-three died later of their wounds. Hundreds of other people, both Austarians and offworlders, were seriously injured.

After a year of further conflict, Austar's senate voted to free the bonders, but by then the embargo was in place for a term of not more than fifty years or until the planet was considered safe again. The embargo kept all official ships from landing, which meant that Austar IV was then without sanctioned metal replacement parts or technical assistance for that period of time, except for the visit by a Federation hospital ship every two years. However, it is known that occasional pirate ships slipped through the embargo lines. (See the holo of *The Golden Deceiver,* one of several such star-class ships, and read its log.)

Another pirate vessel, *Golden's Hope,* managed to report back to the Federation that during the ten years following the start of the embargo, a vaccine was developed by a young researcher, Akkhina Stewart. That vaccine was created from the blood of an indigenous flying lizard, the omnivorous drakk. (See the holo of the vaccine's recombinant DNA structure, in the medical section.) That vaccine was life-altering for the inhabitants of Austar, enabling most of them to live outdoors in the below frigid cold of the period of Dark-After for the first time. Once given, the vaccine proved to last a lifetime, and anyone who has had the vaccine has passed its protection on to his or her children. Offworlders who have recently settled on the planet do not seem to be able to tolerate the vaccine, nor do inhabitants whose ancestors came from the following planets: Mars Colony, Vulcana, the Harris Habitats, and the Centurion Belt.

There have also been rumors that some of the people given the vaccine could thereafter "talk" to the planet's creatures, but it's believed that this is just planetary folklore. (See "Fairy Ointment, Briggs, English, Earth" in the folklore section.)

The Federation concluded the embargo after ten years and offered the planet Protectorate status again, which the senate — under President Durrah Golden — refused. Still, the planet of Austar IV has remained a primary R&R stop for long-haul starships and rocket guards from around the galaxies. Under Federation law, no short-term offworlder is allowed the vaccine.

— excerpt from *The Encyclopedia Galaxia,*
thirty-fourth edition, vol. i: Aaabarker–Austar